ONE BAD
THING

ONE BAD
THING

BILL EIDSON

FORGE®

A TOM DOHERTY ASSOCIATES BOOK
NEW YORK

ONE BAD THING

Copyright © 2000 by Bill Eidson

This book is printed on acid-free paper.

Edited by David G. Hartwell

A Forge Book
Published by Tom Doherty Associates, LLC
175 Fifth Avenue
New York, NY 10010

www.tor.com

Forge® is a registered trademark of Tom Doherty Associates, LLC.

ISBN 0-312-87646-7

First Edition: September 2000

Printed in the Untied States of America

0 9 8 7 6 5 4 3 2 1

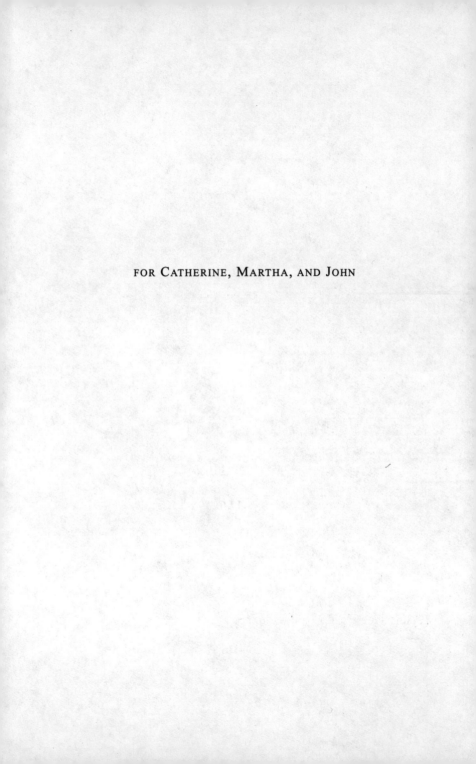

FOR CATHERINE, MARTHA, AND JOHN

ACKNOWLEDGMENTS

I would like to thank Frank Robinson, Richard Parks, David Hartwell, Jim Minz, Jennifer Marcus, Heather Drucker, Kate Mattes, Nancy Childs, Richard Rabinowitz, and Sibylle Barrasso for their help with my career and as well as this story.

In addition, I'd like to acknowledge the help of Chuck Geller for details about the diamond business. Thanks also to Peter Paul Biro of Biro Fine Art Restoration for his advice on detecting art forgeries. Any mistakes are mine, not his.

As always, special thanks to Donna and Nick for everything.

ONE BAD
THING

CHAPTER 1

MCKENNA REALIZED LATER THAT CAIN HAD BEEN TOO ANXIOUS TO SAIL away. What McKenna had taken for a look forward to the sea had actually been Cain's frightened look over his shoulder.

Cain, with his shaggy hair and crooked, engaging smile, had plans for McKenna. And although his plans had fallen through in a fairly spectacular way, in the most important regard of all, Cain had succeeded.

As McKenna began to shiver, he told himself that it had all started in heat, in bright sunshine. That out of such a beginning, he should have done better. That he should have found a way to step aside it all.

That he had no one to blame but himself.

McKenna was deflating the dinghy on the dock when Cain arrived holding the little index card between his thumb and forefinger. It was a warm, painfully brilliant morning in early May. The sunlight bounced up under McKenna's sunglasses, the water impossibly blue through the polarized lenses. Tortola, in the British Virgin Islands. Around McKenna, people hustled, moving their boats up to the fuel dock, loading water and food. The winter charters were over, and boats were flocking back to the U.S. mainland.

Kneeling there on the Zodiac, McKenna looked up, getting a sense of the young man. The sun was at his back, casting his face into shadow. McKenna put his hand up to block the light and saw the flash of white teeth. Young guy, early to mid-twenties. Cutoff jeans, boat shoes, tee shirt. Longish sun-bleached hair, a few day's growth of beard. Duffel bag over his shoulder.

"She's beautiful," the man said, looking over at the *Wanderer*. "Have you read Sterling Hayden or did you come up with the name yourself?"

"I'd like to think both." McKenna stood.

"Guess we better lock down the booze then," the young man said with a smile. American, like McKenna.

The young man put out his hand. "Tom Cain. Most people just call me Cain." He handed McKenna the index card. "If you haven't signed anyone aboard yet, I could help you take her to Boston."

McKenna held the card, turning it over as if reading it for the first time. He felt at a momentary loss and then said, "Why do you want to go?"

"It's what I've been doing, the past two years. Came here from Southampton on a trimaran, and now it's time for the skipper and his family to spend some quality time, cruising around the islands themselves. And it's time for me to go home, face the real world. Got three transatlantics under my belt. Finish this leg, I'll have my fourth."

"Got to be honest," McKenna said. "That's more than me. I'm on my way back for the first time."

"You're here," Cain said with a grin. "You must know what you're doing." He nodded toward the boat "All provisioned?"

"Lot of the staples I already had set for two. I'd have to stock up on more fresh food."

"So you're ready to leave?"

"Just about."

The young man had shifted and the sun was full on his face. He was a good fifteen years younger than McKenna, about the same height as McKenna's six-two, but very fit.

Cain said, "Lost your crew, huh?"

McKenna looked at him sharply. But there was no trace of sarcasm, no inference. His blue eyes were friendly. McKenna knew some marinas were like Peyton Place on the water, where everyone talked about everyone's business. But he would like to believe that here on Tortola everyone was too transient.

McKenna said, "Something like that." He hesitated, and then tried it on for size. "My wife decided not to sail across. She flew home."

Cain nodded. He took in the *Wanderer* more closely, and McKenna envisioned seeing her through a stranger's eyes. Far from new, but gleaming. Forty feet long, navy blue fiberglass hull, weathered teak decks. Sloop-rigged. Steering vane mounted on the stern. A small traditional cockpit and transom. Good for shrugging off following seas. Clearly a heavy-weather boat.

"Full keel and attached rudder?" Cain asked.

McKenna nodded. "*Wanderer*'s a strong lady." Unable to hide his pride in her, no matter the damage she had caused to his marriage. His life.

Cain looked at the new aluminum mast. "You do the upgrades yourself?"

"Mostly."

Cain shifted gears. "I'm not too shabby as a cook—as long as taste isn't your top priority."

"Three transatlantics, you say?"

"That's right. And I'm headed to Boston, too. This will be perfect for me."

"That's where you're from?"

He shook his head. "Connecticut. Went to school in Boston, and my fiancée still lives there."

"What school?"

Cain smiled sheepishly. "Harvard. I haven't exactly made the best use of my degree, but I'm enjoying myself." He gestured to the index card. "Is the tomorrow morning departure for real?"

"Sure is. Any problem with that?"

"It'd be perfect for me. I want to see my girl."

"How much stuff have you got?"

Cain hefted his bag. "This is it."

"I intend to clear customs." McKenna looked at Cain carefully.

The young man shrugged. "Sure. My passport's in order and I'm a U.S. citizen. They have to let me in."

He took his passport from his back pocket and showed it to McKenna. "You're welcome to look through my gear."

McKenna looked at Cain frankly. He reminded McKenna of R. J. without actually looking like him in any way. R. J. was thin with a shock of white-blond hair always falling in his eyes. If Cain was uncomfortable under McKenna's scrutiny, he didn't show it.

No, this guy wasn't another R. J., McKenna decided. Whereas R. J. projected an entirely undeserved sense of superiority, Cain looked strong, capable. He radiated energy.

Normally, McKenna was a man who checked references, did things by the book. But since Caroline left last week, there was a lassitude inside, a weariness mixed with free-floating anger that made it hard for him to concentrate or take on anything extra.

Almost as bad as the time after Samantha.

Caroline had posted the index card on the bulletin board inside the marina's store. Her last bit of attention to their marriage.

"So what do you say?" Cain asked. "I could use some good news here."

McKenna hesitated. Neither he nor the boat were truly prepared for a single-handed voyage.

It would be pathetic to lose the boat, he thought. *To drown.*

McKenna handed the passport back to Cain. "We've got a lot to do before morning."

Cain looked relieved, even though he hadn't appeared anxious before. "You want me to stow this dinghy, Skipper?"

"Call me Rob," McKenna put out his hand. "And welcome aboard."

CHAPTER 2

THE NEXT MORNING, MCKENNA METHODICALLY REVIEWED THE *WANderer* from bow to stern, with his little tape recorder in hand. As he had done since his working days, he dictated clipped but detailed notes about what needed doing.

Afterward, he would use a yellow pad to organize the tasks necessary to complete before embarking on the seventeen-hundred-nautical-mile voyage to Boston.

Once they had set sail, he intended to make it in one shot. No plans to stop in Bermuda. He'd take advantage of the Gulf Stream and cruise off the Eastern seaboard. Maybe stop in Baltimore or New York, but most likely do the entire distance. There would be no picking up an extra impeller, clevis pins, shackles, or O-rings. No spare tools. No stopovers to buy vegetables, fruit, or meat. It was either take it now—or do without it for about three weeks.

But beyond that, McKenna was trying to relax into having a stranger on board. Unfair as it was, he couldn't help but see Cain as the embodiment of McKenna's life without Caroline.

McKenna sighed. Caroline's going seemed to have ripped away the blinders he had carefully placed. There was a dull ache in the middle of his chest; he often found himself absently rubbing the spot. That was Sam and Caroline.

The past few nights, he had dreamed about Sam when she was a toddler. Even though she was seventeen when R. J. Mitchell took her to that party.

Last night, McKenna again felt Sam's warmth in the crook of his arm. She was probably no more than three. Red hair, freckles. An easy, giggling laugh. God, he loved holding her. Her hair tickled his face as he read her *The Velveteen Rabbit*. It was one of her favorite stories, and as he read, she settled down into him, solemn and drowsy. Her thumb in her mouth. They were in the first apartment in Belmont, and when Rob looked up, Caroline was standing beside the sofa.

She was so beautiful, too. Mid-twenties, her black hair still long. His green-eyed, golden-skinned wife. But she wouldn't look at him. Just at Sam. She reached her hand out. "Come on, Sammy Girl. Let's go."

Truth was, McKenna was mad at Caroline but didn't want to admit it. He didn't want to upset Sam.

"Come on, Sammy Girl," Caroline repeated.

"How can you do that?" McKenna said.

Caroline shook her head. She wouldn't talk about it. Which wasn't like her.

McKenna hadn't wanted to move, didn't want to shift for a moment in that chair. Knowing the second he did, Sam would get up, the warmth would be gone.

That both of them would be gone.

But each night, much as he tried to stay frozen in place, McKenna would move, and once again he was alone.

To his credit, Cain quickly got past the bumping-into-each-other stage. Without being obsequious, he would circle round to McKenna's checklist and then tackle projects himself.

Around noon, McKenna took out the remaining bread and lunch meat, and made hefty sandwiches for both of them. Then they sat in the cockpit and McKenna went through the provisions list, tallying the extra food necessary to sustain two people instead of one. He said, "Now's the time to put in special requests."

Cain reached for the list, reviewed it quickly, then said, "Suits me. Just double the coffee ration. I live on the stuff."

McKenna waved him toward the dock. "Get as much as you want. The store where you got the postcard has just about everything we need, food and parts. I've got an account with them."

"Got it."

Cain started up the dock.

McKenna glanced at his checklist. With Cain, he was doing better than he expected at this point. Still he was feeling the slightest of misgivings about not taking the time to check Cain's credentials.

He looked at the next item on his list and sighed. Changing the oil. Should have assigned that one to his new mate.

McKenna was tightening the water-pump belt when Cain returned, wheeling a dock cart filled with groceries and a small cardboard box of turnbuckles and shackles.

McKenna climbed out of the engine compartment, then sat wiping his hands on a rag. "Just stack that all on the dock. I'll put it away. How about you take a look at the rigging? I tuned it a couple of days back, but I wouldn't mind a second opinion."

"You bet." Cain climbed onto the coach roof, first sighting the mast, and then walking around to each of the stays, pulling on them to test the tension.

McKenna ducked down below, washed his hands, and began to put away the food. He worked in silence, his face emotionless until he heard Cain call, "This seems to be catching a bit."

McKenna smiled briefly to himself and then went up on deck.

"What's that?"

Cain tugged at the jib halyard.

"Let's see." McKenna went forward and pulled the line back and forth. Indeed, there was a faint, but noticeable catch, as if the line was beginning to wedge inside the block. A task that wasn't on the list.

McKenna said, "He who finds it . . ."

"Goes aloft," Cain said. "Point me in the direction of the bosun's chair." McKenna sent him below, and a few minutes later, Cain came up with the canvas chair, wearing the tool belt and pouch. McKenna opened one of the storage lockers in the cockpit and rustled through the spare parts to come up with a halyard block. "I picked this one up used in Southampton, but it's clean and solid. Should do the trick. When you're done, I'm afraid I'll need to send you back to the store for a couple of spares."

"No problem." Cain snapped the spinnaker halyard onto the bosun's chair ring, and McKenna wrapped the free end of the halyard around the winch, inserted the handle, and began cranking the younger man up the mast. McKenna said, "Better you than me. I hate climbing that damn stick."

"That's what I'm here for, Skipper. I'll give you a yell when I'm done."

McKenna cleated the line and went back below to continue stowing the food. A small touch of relief was still with him. Cain had passed McKenna's little test. That jamming halyard had been on his mind, if not on his list.

Maybe this wouldn't be so bad after all.

The next morning, McKenna and Cain motored over to the customs office in Tortola and docked. The customs agent was a jolly faced black man in an immaculate uniform. His friendliness faded just slightly when he heard Cain had just joined McKenna as a pickup crew. "I'll have to take a look at your boat, mon." He handed back their passports. "These seem in order."

They followed him out onto the dock.

He stood back and regarded the *Wanderer*, his hands on his hips. "Strong lady, huh? I try to be quick, but it's gonna take some time."

"Is this really necessary?" McKenna asked.

"If I say so, mon," the agent said, flashing his white teeth.

He stepped on board.

"Sorry about the hassle," Cain said quietly to McKenna. "Boat bums who've just signed on don't look good in the eyes of customs. But there's nothing to find, so we'll be all right."

It took the agent almost an hour to come to the same conclusion. In doing so, he went through virtually every bit of storage and personal space, taking out boat hardware, clothes, food, spare parts, the tool chest, looking through both of their duffel bags, in their shoes, into the bilge, in every corner of the engine compartment. The agent even looked in the empty waste-holding tank, flashing his light around, before he was satisfied.

"Who's going to clean this up?" McKenna said.

The agent smiled. "Put your crew to work." He stepped off the dock and gestured to the line of waiting boats. "Got some more to check now. Take a mooring there, you want to straighten her up." He threw them their lines and waved them away, looking friendly enough for a tourism poster.

CHAPTER 3

AFTER SORTING THE BOAT OUT FOR ANOTHER HOUR, MCKENNA MOPPED the sweat from his forehead. The sun was beating down directly; almost noon.

Abruptly, he pulled off his tee shirt and kicked off his boat shoes. He stood up on the cabin roof and made a long, flat dive, his toes just touching the lifelines.

He plunged through the surface, driving down through the clear green water to find the layer of cold below. Below him was a mass of coral, interspersed with patches of sand: a soft wash of green, red, and yellow to his unprotected eyes. McKenna stayed down as long as he could, ignoring the pressure in his lungs until his body took charge. Then he kicked off the bottom and flew to the silver shimmering above.

When he broke through the surface, there was Cain, standing with his hand on the shroud. Cain's smile was curiously tight. "I thought you were in a hurry to leave."

"No," McKenna said. He flipped over onto his back, sucking down great lungfuls of air. "But it's time anyhow."

* * *

The two of them sat in the cockpit as the sun fell, turning the water red and gold. The wind was blowing at a steady fifteen knots right over the beam, and the *Wanderer* slipped over the swells at an easy seven.

McKenna looked at Cain. The younger man was leaning back against the bulkhead. He looked quietly pleased. Smug almost. But all he said was, "She's a sweet sailor."

"That she is." McKenna looked at the compass and then back at the steering vane. It made steady, small changes, keeping the boat on course better than he could have himself.

"Got a name for it?" Cain asked.

McKenna smiled. "Mortimer."

Cain grinned. "Faithful, dull, and consistent. Just what you want out of a self-steering vane. Seeing as Mortimer's doing such a good job . . . what've you got for a toast?"

McKenna hesitated just slightly.

Cain laughed. "Don't worry. I'm not a lush."

McKenna stood and stretched. "I've got some scotch."

Cain's smile had a bit of a twist to it. Like he was going to say something, then thought better of it. McKenna hesitated on the way down below. Cain had been nothing but helpful so far, and yet McKenna felt strange around him—stodgy. As if the young man was secretly amused by him.

McKenna got the fifth of scotch and brought it up. He used the ice pick on the remaining block of ice, dropped the chips into two glasses, then handed one up to Cain.

To his surprise, Cain was sketching something in a small pad. He smiled at McKenna and showed him what he was working on. He had captured the *Wanderer*. She was backing away from a dock piling, and a figure at the mast had the mainsail half raised; a bearded figure was at the wheel. The boat looked powerful, well built, beautiful. To McKenna, the little sketch suggested release from land, adventure.

"Just a starting point," Cain said. "I dig into it, she'll come to life."

"You've already done that," McKenna said, impressed.

Cain flipped the pad closed and put it in his front pocket. He raised the glass. "May the wind be at our backs, the sun in our faces, and our women waiting for us on the dock." He downed the whiskey.

McKenna sipped his own.

McKenna put them on four-hour watches and took the first himself. The night air was cool enough for him to wear khakis and a pile jacket. The *Wanderer* surged along as the wind shifted to come across the stern quarter and freshened to just under twenty knots. He disengaged Mortimer and took the wheel. It was an exhilarating ride, with the knot-meter showing over eight knots at times.

McKenna considered a sail change, replacing the jenny with the working jib, but decided against it. The partial moon gave him some visibility, and he'd just as soon give Cain a solid rest.

Their roller-furling jenny had blown out when he and Caroline were crossing over to the U.K. The bearings froze on the roller furler itself. Now he was back to doing it the old-fashioned way. Raising and lowering one sail at a time. Part of the refit in Southampton. It had been cheaper to buy a set of salvaged sails sooner than replacing the roller-furling system and buying a new sail.

But the real damages to their finances—and Caroline's confidence in the voyage, the way McKenna saw it—had been the knockdown on the way over. About two-thirds of the way across. A rolling, squally day. Short, angry waves, dark sky. Gusts up to forty-five. Caroline had wanted him to simply run before the wind on bare poles. But he thought that was overreacting. He came to life under those circumstances. He could forget about Sam and concentrate on the task at hand.

Then a quick succession of sixty-knot gusts put them over: green water was rushing into the cabin and both of them were hanging on to their safety lines. There was a cracking noise from the mast, and when at last the *Wanderer* righted, there was a noticeable fracture in the mast, about six feet up.

From then on, they had limped along with a reefed main and small working jib until docking in Southampton, where the shipyard owner confirmed what McKenna already had feared. The mast was irreparable: they had to replace the entire thing.

Money and trust. The knockdown had signaled the end of both.

Caroline said they were living beyond their means. That the voyage was just an escape that they couldn't afford, either emotionally or financially. That, for him, it was just an escape from her and Sam.

He had told himself that she was taking out her grief on him. That she was baiting him to make him react. Make him fight back at her. Say what she thought needed saying. That he saw it as her fault. That he would have kept Sam away from that boy.

From R. J.

R. J. Mitchell.

He was ever present in McKenna's head. Even more so now that McKenna was heading home.

Home. Just where was that supposed to be now?

They had sold the house not long after they bought the boat. Had to.

Pretty old place in Newburyport, about an hour's drive north of Boston. Their home had been a small federal-style house poised right on the edge of the Merrimack River, across from Carr Island. Oaks on the lawn, a well-worn care about the place. Sam's little catboat moored right beside the Boston Whaler. McKenna hadn't realized then just how happy they had been. Just the three of them, until R. J. showed up at the door.

That shock of blond hair, the pale blue eyes. Showing up at McKenna's door about a month before it happened, before that party.

About a month, shit.

Six weeks.

Six weeks noted, cataloged, and firmly implanted on McKenna's brain. Nasty little loop of film.

"Hey, Mr. McKenna," the kid had said, as if they already knew each other. "Sam ready?"

Good-looking kid on first impression. Slim, strong looking. No tattoos, no nose rings. Black Volkswagen Jetta behind him in the driveway. Father was a Volkswagen dealer; McKenna knew him slightly.

The boy was clean. Dressed in faded jeans, polo shirt.

With Sam's seventeenth birthday behind her, R. J. wasn't the first boy to show up on her doorstep. The first with a car, yes. The first to take her out on a "date" instead of a bike ride to the beach, perhaps. Certainly the first to kiss her the second she was in the car, making her blush and virtually duck down in front of McKenna as the boy turned from her to back out of the driveway and speed away.

McKenna had called out to Caroline, "I hate him."

Caroline had laughed from the kitchen, then come to the doorway to join him. "Knew you would. Sam and I ran into him at the grocery store. Handsome boy."

"Sammy Girl's a little traitor," McKenna said.

"You're right," Caroline said. "Growing up on us. Ungrateful for all you've done for her."

McKenna had found himself growing increasingly churlish as the first weeks passed and Sam talked about nothing but R. J. This surprised no one more than himself. He had always taught Sam to think for herself, to take risks, to have confidence in her own judgement. He thought he knew how to keep his distance so she could do just that.

As an only child, Sam had always been comfortable around both parents and good at playing by herself. She was popular enough at school and always had several good friends. Some of them boys. She had blossomed past the early teenage coltishness, tall, long legged. With high cheekbones and her mother's green eyes. Otherwise, she was very different, with fair, lightly freckled skin and red hair. A happy, exuberant little girl who had turned into a lovely, kindhearted teenager.

On her way to being a beautiful woman.

But her reaction, her affection for R. J., was something McKenna hadn't seen before. She couldn't help but touch R. J. when he was there, her hand on his back, pushing the hair out of his eyes, getting things for him.

She probably told her friends she loved him.

Hell, she probably *did* love him.

About two weeks in, McKenna realized that his daughter was most likely sleeping with R. J.

"What do you think?" he had asked Caroline later.

"Possible," she said. "Probable. I've talked with her before, I'll talk to her again."

"And say what?"

Caroline had touched McKenna's cheek. "About how to be careful, sweetie."

"Ah, damn it," he'd said. "How about how Daddy'll hurt the boy?"

"No, dear."

Sam was seventeen, Caroline reminded him. Next year, she would be off at college and almost entirely beyond their control.

I know, he said. I know, I know.

He knew that time passed, that things changed. She couldn't be his baby forever. She couldn't even be his sixteen-year-old, who the year before had been still happy to do an overnight bike-hike in New Hampshire with her parents. Climbing up and down the hills on her new road bike, leaving her father and mother behind during the first thirty miles. Then practically in tears at the end of forty, when they stopped early because her legs had cramped up. She had lain on a picnic table as her parents, her buddies, massaged her legs and teased her unmercifully.

She had been half laughing, half crying. "What a dope," she moaned. "I was *sooo* much faster than old Mom and Dad . . ."

No, McKenna had loved his daughter. He wanted her to find the right guy. For her to love and be loved.

The problem was R. J. himself.

He had reminded McKenna of his own father, Bobby McKenna. Sixty-six and presumably still a kid. Took off when Rob was five. Since then, McKenna hadn't seen his own father more than a half-dozen times in his entire life. The last time had been a few years back. Silver-haired Bobby. With money, and charm, and a wife about two years younger than Caroline. Bobby, who had spread his arms wide and said, "Look at you, it worked out fine. Best thing I could've done for you, hitting the road. I just wasn't right for a kid."

No, McKenna felt he knew, R. J. down to his bones.

"What do you expect?" Caroline had said one night. Sam had left earlier and the two of them were sitting at the kitchen table drinking coffee. Getting used to the empty sound of the house. "You think she's going to find the right guy the first time out? Did we find each other that fast?"

"Just about."

It was true. He and Caroline had been married in their early twenties. Caroline was pregnant with Sam. But in those days, during those six weeks or the seventeen years before them, McKenna never had dreamed of being without his wife. That they would ever consider their marriage a mistake.

McKenna found R. J.'s arrogance intolerable. The way he affected indifference; or worse, truly felt it.

And then there was the money. He always had cash. In the early weeks, he showered Sam with presents. With small pieces of jewelry, with a portable CD player, with clothes.

"Where does he get all the cash?" McKenna had asked Sam one night. They were in the kitchen, and R. J. was due to pick her up in a few minutes. "What does he do for work?"

"His dad's place," she said, shrugging. "I guess."

"You guess? You put the summer in waitressing at the Galley; you know how hard it is to earn spending money. How's he doing it?"

Her face turned stony. "Different people do things differently."

"What's that mean? Does he do drugs?"

"I said he works for his dad!"

"You've seen that?"

"What's with you?" The color on her face had risen. "Why don't you like him?"

Caroline had stepped into the kitchen. "Rob, can I see you?"

McKenna had bit his lip. He had nothing. No evidence. *Overprotective father*, he told himself.

Caroline said the same in the hallway off the kitchen.

That night, McKenna had tossed and turned, unable to sleep until Sam returned home. It was already approaching two in the morning.

Caroline had rubbed his back. "Ease off, honey. We don't want Romeo and Juliet on our hands. Sam will drop him or he'll fade away soon enough. She's beginning to get fed up with him, I think. Leaving her stranded at the mall last Tuesday made a big impression. Besides, he's not *that* bad. I've seen worse."

Caroline had been a high school teacher for fifteen years. McKenna trusted her judgment.

But he still didn't trust R. J.

"He's careless with her," McKenna said.

Careless with her feelings. Four weeks in, he'd break off dates at the last minute if something better came up with his friends. One day, McKenna had picked up the phone and it was R. J. He was on his car phone: "Hey, Mr. McKenna, tell Sammy's something's up. I won't be able to see her tonight, tell her I'll make it up to her."

"What's the problem?" McKenna had asked, and the boy had yelled that he couldn't hear, that he had to hang up.

But McKenna could hear just fine, and he thought he heard laughter in the car. It sounded like R. J. was grinning when he said it—as if he didn't care at all if his girlfriend's father realized he was lying.

Tears had sprung into Sam's eyes when McKenna passed along the message. For that, McKenna wanted to put his hands on the boy himself.

Instead, McKenna just asked, "You sure he's worth it?"

"I don't know. His parents are screwy, and he's had his problems. But I think we're going to be all right."

McKenna wanted to step in right there. Say that things probably wouldn't be all right, shouldn't be all right . . . because the boy wasn't trustworthy. Wasn't worth his daughter's love; certainly not her first love.

But Caroline had stepped in. "We hope it works out for you, if that's what you want," she'd said. And she warned McKenna away with her eyes. Over that night's coffee in their kitchen, she said, "C'mon, Rob. She won't put up with this forever. Give it time."

But time, it turned out, was at a great premium.

Their last evening together, McKenna had argued with Sam. The three of them were midway through dinner when R. J.'s car horn sounded. Sam jumped right up. "Gotta go."

"Ask him in to sit with us," McKenna'd said. "You can finish your meal."

"Uh-uh," Sam said. "He says you make him feel uncomfortable. I'll just go out to him."

"Where are you going tonight?" Caroline asked.

"Movies."

"To see what?"

"Don't know." She shrugged. "Whatever's playing at the mall."

McKenna didn't buy it and he said so.

"Oh, come on, Daddy!"

"Rob!" Caroline snapped. "Let her go."

"I don't trust that guy," McKenna said. It was almost a whisper, and it was painful. As his daughter went out the door, he said, "You're smarter than he is—act it!"

She slammed the door.

Sifting through the chaff later, talking to the police, reading the reports, and then the dry news articles over the next few days, McKenna learned what had happened to his daughter.

Two nineteen-year-old skinheads had crashed the beachhouse party where R. J. and Sam had gone instead of the movies. And it turned out that although R. J. was not doing drugs himself, he was selling them.

McKenna never found out if Sam knew about the drugs or not.

Apparently the previous weekend R. J. had stiffed the two skinheads, Billy Bragg and Jeremiah Donovan, on a gram of coke. Cut in into a third with baby powder. At the party, they announced they were going to work it out of him. They were pumped on amphetamines and still wearing weight-lifting belts from their afternoon workout.

Reportedly, no one tried to stand up to the two, except Sam.

She got between them and R. J.

She tried to talk sense, tried to calm them down.

R. J. not only let her, he had apparently kept his hands on her shoulders and shouted at the two skinheads to drop it, that he'd make it up to them.

Then Billy Bragg hit her.

The autopsy said that her jaw had been shattered from the first blow alone. The cause of death was the damage to the back of her head. Apparently Bragg had flung her to the side in his attempt to get to R. J. She tripped over him and hit her head on the raised stone fire-place. They said she died instantly.

One of Sam's friends had started screaming that Sam was bleed-ing. That she was no longer breathing. Billy and Jeremiah stopped to investigate and R. J. ran.

The DA had started out with a homicide charge against the two skinheads, but downgraded it to manslaughter after Billy confessed.

R. J. had testified, his voice shaking somewhat. He denied the drug sale empathetically, and his parents were there with an attorney to represent him. There was talk of charging R. J. with drug trafficking. But as the DA explained apologetically to McKenna, when the police had searched R. J.'s house within an hour after Sam's death, they had found no narcotic substances. Instead, they found R. J.'s mother and father sitting with him in their living room. R. J.'s room bore the marks of a hurried but efficient cleaning, as did the upstairs bath-room. R. J.'s father insisted that none of them would answer any questions until after their attorney arrived.

So there had been no real evidence to hold R. J. Just the outraged hearsay of the two skinheads.

When all was said and done, Billy Bragg got five years, Donovan got three, with eligibility for parole in one. Sentenced to MCI/Con-cord.

R. J. walked.

Rob and Caroline McKenna left the courthouse bearing the weight of a life sentence in the location of their choosing.

Hours later, McKenna awoke on his hands and knees.

One moment, he had been asleep in his bunk, the next he was on the cabin sole.

Cain's watch.

McKenna's head cleared almost instantly. Outside the wind shrieked through the rigging, and the *Wanderer* groaned as she was knocked all the way down on her side.

McKenna's heart tripped rapidly in his chest, but he kept moving, pulling himself to his feet.

"Get up here, Rob," Cain called.

Slowly, the *Wanderer* came back up and headed into the wind.

The jenny was snapping and popping, sounding like a machine gun. Much more of that and it would rip itself to shreds.

"We've got to get that sail down," Cain called down. "That gust was over fifty. Who could've figured on this just one day out of the BVI?"

McKenna pulled on a pair of shorts, went forward and grabbed the working jib, and hustled it up into the cockpit. The seas were running about fifteen feet, the tops being whipped off. The boat was stalled, in irons. She began to drift back slowly. Cain spun the wheel to head the stern toward the wind. Luckily, a breaking wave pushed the bow over and the jenny snapped full. The *Wanderer* began to make way again. McKenna let out both the jenny and the main and the *Wanderer* limped along with both sails luffing heavily.

"Start the engine," McKenna said.

Cain turned the key, and the diesel rumbled to life. He kept the boat idling along at just over two knots while McKenna used the jiffy reefing to shorten the mainsail from the cockpit.

"I'll get that jenny down," Cain said.

"I've got it," McKenna said.

"C'mon, Skipper. You don't even have a harness on yet."

McKenna hesitated then realized Cain was right. He took the wheel. He began shivering; he'd come on deck without his foul-weather gear and the temperature had dropped noticeably.

Cain snapped his own lifeline onto the cabin rail and quickly headed up the leeward side, then he stepped up to the mast to release the jib halyard.

McKenna edged the throttle ahead to help steady them against the waves. He headed the boat into the wind slightly and released the jenny sheet altogether. The big sail began to beat against itself again.

Cain untied the jenny halyard.

But nothing happened.

"C'mon," McKenna said under his breath.

The younger man swore and then looked up.

McKenna saw the halyard hang limp—no tension on it. And the big jenny had not shifted at all.

"*Damn* it!" McKenna said. Just what changing the block was supposed to have prevented. The jenny was stuck.

He looked at the wind indicator. On average, the wind had leveled off to just over thirty knots.

He set Mortimer, ducked below quickly for foul-weather gear and a harness. Back on deck, he snapped on a safety line and hurried up to the mast.

Cain saw him and wordlessly ducked past the beating sail, then he braced himself against the pulpit and tried to tug the sail down at the luff. McKenna worked the halyard end, using quick rolling flips, trying to center the line on the pulley.

But the sail didn't budge.

Cain looked at McKenna. "The block must've jammed."

The used block. The one McKenna had picked up in Southampton.

Cain looked aloft. He had to shout to be heard over the beating sail. "I'll get the bosun's chair."

McKenna opened his mouth and shut it. Another gust almost knocked them down again. It would be hell to be aloft in this kind of weather. But nothing compared to losing the mast.

"I'll go up," McKenna said.

"Forget it," Cain said. He crawled down into the cabin and turned on the spreader lights, so that the deck was suddenly illuminated. He came back a few minutes later with the bosun's chair, the tool belt, and pouch.

McKenna reached for the bosun's chair, but Cain pulled it away.

"I said I'll do it." Cain unsnapped his safety line.

"This isn't a democracy around here, Cain. Give it to me."

A wave crashed over the bow, sweeping the feet out from under both of them, knocking the boat over. McKenna grasped Cain by the arm, and held on to the mast. The younger man scrambled to gain purchase on the deck. His head swung round and McKenna could see the young man was frightened, but not panicked. McKenna closed his eyes and pulled with all his strength, conscious that if he let go, the younger man was no longer wearing his safety line.

The rush of water eased and the *Wanderer* came back up.

Cain scrambled up to the mast. "Thank God you're strong as an ape." He jerked his head up. "Look, Skipper, you've got what, fifteen, twenty pounds on me? And how many years? C'mon, I rock climb for a hobby. Help me up here."

McKenna hesitated, then looked up at the pitching mast and said, "All right." He wrapped two loops of the spinnaker halyard around the winch and began cranking.

Slowly Cain began to rise up the mast. He clung to it tightly, trying to keep from being thrown free. Once, he did anyhow, and flew out into the jenny itself. As the boat rolled back into a trough, he swung hard at the mast, but got his legs out front and deflected it with his feet.

Nevertheless, McKenna could feel the vibration in the mast when Cain hit. In the illumination of the spreader lights, the younger man looked dazed and McKenna saw blood on his face.

McKenna called, "You all right?"

"Just peachy. Now get me higher."

McKenna kept cranking until Cain got an arm around the spreader, the flat horizontal piece that kept the shrouds away from the mast.

"Hold it here a second." Cain's face was above the spreader light now. He rested his upper body against the spreader, his head down.

McKenna said, "How're you doing?"

Cain looked down at him and then held on tight as the *Wanderer* was knocked over again. As she came up, Cain yelled, "I'm having a hell of a great time. Wish you were here."

McKenna grinned. "You ready?"

Cain nodded. "Haul away."

McKenna cranked him up to the next spreader, and finally, all the way to the top of the mast. Cain was at face level with the head of the reefed mainsail now, so he lashed a line around his waist and the mast to keep himself in place. "The halyard's jammed at the block," he shouted. "I'm going to take off the quick-release shackle on the jenny so you can haul it down. Then I'll put the new block on."

McKenna cleated the spinnaker halyard to keep Cain aloft, and then hustled over to the bow to pull down the jenny. The sail fought him, snapping and flinging jib sheets with enough force to draw blood if he let them connect. But he managed to collapse the sail without injury, then he threw open the bow hatch and stuffed the sail in. The deck was suddenly much quieter.

"Watch it!" Cain cried.

Something hit the deck just beside McKenna, and he turned to see a black block bounce once, roll down toward the scuppers, and then tumble out into the sea.

"Sorry," Cain yelled. "That was the old piece of shit!"

McKenna stood back and watched Cain attach the new block. It took three times as long as it would've under normal conditions. Cain had to keep an arm for himself on the mast, and one for the boat.

But he did it. He hauled up the bitter end of the halyard, fed it through the block and then McKenna let him down. Cain handed him both ends of the line.

Cain's face was covered with sweat and seawater, his legs and arms were trembling. His knuckles were bleeding, and a steady stream of red trickled down his cheek from a cut on his right temple.

"You all right?" McKenna said.

"Couldn't be better."

"Was it the block?" McKenna said.

"Yeah. Wheel inside cracked and split in half. Whole thing was blown out, jammed the halyard. The new one I put on is a stainless-steel Harken. It's not going anywhere."

Cain looked like he was going to say something else but he didn't.

"Take the wheel while I put on the working jib," McKenna said. "Then I'll finish your watch and you can go below and get some sleep. You did a hell of a job."

Cain nodded abruptly. "Thanks."

"It's the least I can do."

Cain didn't argue with him.

Why should he? thought McKenna. He felt flushed and angry with himself.

Cheap used block. Part of the Southampton refit. It looked perfect when he bought it. But it could've cost them the mast. Hell, it could have cost them the boat and their lives. One of Caroline's objections proved legitimate once again.

That they simply couldn't afford McKenna's escape to the sea.

CHAPTER 4

"YOU'RE GOING TO DROP ME," MARIEL SAID. "TOY WITH ME, MAKE ME breakfast, and then go running back to your husband. It hurts, even though I'm not into women." Mariel was Rob and Caroline's former neighbor and Caroline's best friend. Mariel toweled her wet hair vigorously, then pushed it back. They were on the back deck of her house in Newburyport, overlooking the Merrimack River.

"You'd be the one, cutie." Caroline put down a tray laden with the bagels and strawberries she had bought on the way back from her walk that morning.

"Hah." Mariel spread butter on a bagel. "See what I mean? Toying with me."

Caroline had been awake since five. Still not able to sleep right. Outside, the sun beat off the river. Caroline shaded her eyes as she looked out at her former house, which was poised right on the river's edge. She saw a child's toy tractor out front. Caroline tried for a light tone. "Can't believe you've *never* had the new neighbors over."

"Tsssh," Mariel said. "They're nice enough, but they're no Rob and Caroline McKenna."

Caroline smiled back at her friend.

How different they looked: Mariel was blue-eyed, blonde, fair skinned, and appeared elegant until her essential toughness surfaced.

Caroline, with her Italian mother and Pennsylvania-Dutch father, had high cheekbones, rich black hair, green eyes, and skin that tanned rather than burned. Because of her natural athleticism, Caroline was more often called "striking" than beautiful. She always felt like a tomboy next to Mariel.

An exhausted tomboy at the moment. She said, "I won't be here long. Soon as I get my own place."

Mariel waved that away. She took a second to admire her red nails. "You know I love your company."

"Hah. You love your privacy, too," Caroline said, just as Mariel's lover, Elliott, joined them.

"Ladies," he said. "Don't mind me." He knelt beside the table and poured a good half of the pot of coffee into his travel mug. "Gotta run."

Elliot was a wiry black man, tallish, in his mid-forties. He wore jeans, running shoes, and a white cotton shirt. His close-cropped hair was just beginning to gray at the temples. He said, "I don't really care for these stale doughnuts, but I'll take a couple just to be polite." He scooped up two bagels.

"Good of you, sweetheart," Mariel said. "See you tonight?"

"Hope so," he said. "Depends on where middle-aged lust takes me."

Caroline raised her eyebrows.

"Not his," Mariel said, wrinkling her nose. "My client's husband."

She was an attorney; he was an investigator. Divorce work was a staple for both of them.

"My middle-aged lust takes me to you," Elliot said.

"It better," Mariel said.

Elliot kissed Mariel and then touched Caroline on the shoulder before he took off.

"Nice guy," Caroline said.

"Nice as he can be, considering what he does every day." Mariel smiled after him as he moved lightly down the long stairway to the brick patio below.

"Of course, the same could be said of me." She turned her attention back to Caroline. "For now, let's forget that I bust marriages apart as a livelihood."

She raised her juice glass to the river, which led out to the Atlantic. "I don't want to hear any more about squalls, boat repairs, and being short on cash, and all the silly arguments around the same. Tell me the real reason why you're here, and he's out there."

"I've been a bitch," Caroline said. "That's part of it."

"Oh, bull. I mean, you put me on a cramped little boat with some guy, any guy, I'd be doing a number on him the first day we lost sight of land. But that's not you."

"Different ways of handling it."

"Sam?"

Caroline nodded. Unable to say her daughter's name right then for fear she would cry. She could still see Mariel at the funeral, her pretty face twisted with grief almost as intense as her own. Sam had called Mariel Aunty M. ever since she first saw *The Wizard of Oz* when she was eight. Caroline said, "After Sam, everything's been different."

Mariel lifted her palms. "Of course."

"Me, I got scared. Tried to control every damn thing. Hold on to what we had. Scared I was going to lose him, that more tragedy was right around the corner."

"Believe me, divorce is a tragedy."

Caroline nodded, thinking.

Mariel waited.

Caroline poured herself some coffee and warmed her hands with the cup. She said, "It's brought out different stuff in us. Rob's always been there for me, for her. She was a mistake, you know. Couple of idiots, me and Rob. Got me pregnant when I was twenty, he was twenty-one. Pretty much scotched his dream of taking me sailing around the world. He was going to finish school, become an architect. Sail the world before we had our babies.

"Then we had Sam. Rob dropped out of school and wound up in real estate. Sketches of sailboats up on the wall, and we bought that little catboat just before you moved here, remember? Sam must have been seven." Caroline smiled, sadly. "Rob taught her how to swim, and then took her sailing. We bought the Cape Dory when she was nine, got a berth at the marina. I'd go with them on the weekend trips, but they were such buddies, the two of them. Any evening or spare hour or two on the weekend. She'd be sitting beside him, her head barely over the cockpit coaming. Little baseball cap. If he ever wished for a son, I never heard it. She just delighted him."

"That's the Rob I know," Mariel said quietly. "You saw firsthand what I went through after Van left me. Trust me, divorce and death aren't that far apart. And it took me quite a while to find Elliot. There are a lot of kooks and wounded birds out there. Rob's a good man."

"I know that," Caroline said. "I just don't know that I can live with him anymore. Follow what he's doing."

"Which is?"

"Now, for him, life equals just moving, being a nomad on that damn boat. Soon as we get to port, he's looking at his charts, seeing where else we can go. No pleasure in it. Just in escape."

"Loss of a child, escape is a pretty common reaction, don't you think?"

Caroline shook her head slightly. "Rob's always had the capacity . . . he's always had a hard edge. Not something he ever directed toward me or Sam. But it's there. Came from his Uncle, I suppose. Tough, good guy, his Uncle Sean. Very strong protective streak. Once he beat up a drug dealer, this connected guy who tried to get Rob to pick up some dope off his trawler. This was when Rob was fifteen; Uncle Sean was almost fifty. Afterward Uncle Sean came back to Rob and said, 'That's one for free. Now I'm gonna teach you how to take care of yourself.' And he spent months after that with Rob every day, teaching him how to fight. Teaching him how 'to take care of you and your own.' "

"Nothing wrong with that."

Caroline shook her head. "No. Not as long as you succeed in keeping your family safe. But if you fail?"

Mariel leaned forward and spread jam on her bagel. "Shades of his dad, right? I got Rob to talk to me about him once. He was over putting the shutters on for me, and I'd been whining about my divorce for so long, I made him tell me something that went wrong in his life. Back then, you guys looked so perfect from where I was sitting."

Caroline looked bemused. "He told you about his dark secret, his irresponsible joke of father? Good old Bobby? I knew you and Rob were getting too close to leave alone—what else were you doing?"

Mariel smiled prettily.

"Rob got in touch with Bobby a couple years back, you know," Caroline said.

"See, I didn't know that," Mariel said. "You're still the one."

"Mmmnn . . . well that's debatable, isn't it?" Caroline still remembered how Rob looked when he came home. How it made him sick to see how much he and his father looked alike.

Caroline had only seen pictures of Rob's mother. A good-looking dark-haired woman with a cheerful, open face. She died when Rob was ten. She was working as a waitress after her husband ran out on them and was killed in an accident trying to get away from a drunk who followed her home.

Within the week, his Uncle Sean quit the merchant marine, setting his career aside to come home to take care of his nephew. Worked on the loading docks first, got on to a fishing boat in Gloucester, and eventually bought a boat of his own. Rob worked right alongside of him.

Caroline said, "I guess Uncle Sean was a great guy, but he wasn't an easy guy. Rob always had the sense his uncle was watching him, making sure his father's side didn't emerge. Now, the way Rob sees it, he's done worse than his dad ever did. He let Sam get killed. He didn't stop her. He didn't trust R. J. from the start. He—" Caroline's voice caught, but she put her hand out when Mariel started to move beside her. "He set aside his misgivings about R. J. . . . because of me. I said that we couldn't keep Sam in a cocoon."

Caroline's voice was shaky now, but she remained dry-eyed. "Ease up," I said. "That even if R. J. did have a bit of that smartass pampered-boy attitude, it was time for Sam to figure these things out for herself."

"It was reasonable—"

"I know that. God, I've told myself a million times that I could only make the decisions with what I knew at the time. That doesn't change it that I was wrong. So *goddamn* wrong."

"And he's blaming you?"

Caroline shook her head. "I ask, he denies it. Looks me in the eye and says it's not so. Holds me. But then he's back up at that helm. Separating himself from me. I don't know that I believe him. I think he must on some level. Must."

"Or you do, and you want him to confirm it."

"Shut up," Caroline said, smiling slightly. "Doctor Mariel."

Mariel smiled sweetly. "Part of the service."

Caroline gestured to include the house, the town. ". . . this daily life, people. It was the way R. J. skated that did it for Rob."

"His own dad bails on him," Mariel said. "And then a kid like his dad winds up getting his daughter killed. Tough to just accept as part of life's grand design."

"Rob almost didn't. The day after the verdict, I saw Rob going to his car. He didn't have a gun, he didn't have any sort of knife or anything. But I knew the way he was moving, the way he had been silent for the whole day that it was possible."

"You're sure?"

"Yes. He was going to that boy's house. He was going to put his hands on that boy if he could. And I think there's a good chance he would've killed him if he did."

"What stopped him?"

"Me. I begged him. I begged him to stay for me. That I couldn't lose him, too. That if he did this, he would be put in jail, and I would be alone. That we somehow had to move on, stay alive."

Caroline hesitated, and then said, "I woke up the next morning, about three o'clock. He was in the kitchen. I could hear him talking quietly. Using that little tape recorder of his. There were charts, boating books on one side of the table—our financial records on the other. He was outlining the qualities he wanted in a sailboat—a cruiser that could take us around the world. His face was gray, and it was like watching a dead person going through the motions of life. But he said that it was time we took our voyage. That he figured out we could afford it—just. That we would have to sell the house and the business."

Caroline's voice shook. "It was the worst time to sell the business: we'd bought the Four Winds apartment complex just about that time."

"I remember."

"Well, we'd overextended ourselves to buy it. Put in just about everything we had. And you know how much work the place needed before we could begin to rent the units out . . . but Rob just didn't have it in him to oversee the job. What was the point, he said, and I agreed.

"He said we should sell the Four Winds as is and take the loss. We could cash out all the mutual funds, including the one we had set aside for Sam's education. With that, we could get a boat and go for at least a year, maybe two. That alone, we'd keep Sam alive in our hearts. That we'd find a way to live again ourselves."

"Sound's like he was trying."

"He was. But somewhere along the way, he stopped. He's just moving like a shark through water, looking for the oxygen to keep alive, no more."

"And that's where the fights come in?"

Caroline nodded. "Me poking and prodding. Trying to make him fight for me. Blame me, if he has to. But come back to life. Even this . . ." She shook her head, then looked away.

"What?"

"It's so childish, I'm embarrassed to put words to it."

Mariel did come over then and put her arm around Caroline. "You expected him to call? To fly home the day after you left and make it all right?"

"Yes." Caroline's eyes were no longer dry and she rubbed at her cheeks. "Yes, I guess I did."

"That's not crazy," Mariel said. "That's you still loving him. And he might still show up, honey. Maybe not as fast as you hoped. It might take the whole voyage back for him to figure what he's losing. That Sam's gone, but you're not. It might just take the whole voyage."

CHAPTER 5

THE NEXT TIME, MCKENNA WAS AWAKE. HE WAS BELOW AT THE NAV station jotting a few brief comments into the log: *Good speed, clear skies. Six knots or better most of the day.*

The *Wanderer* hit something.

There was a sickening thud in the starboard bow quarter, and then something scraped and then punched the outside of the boat, making the hull flex right before McKenna's eyes.

"Shit!" he heard Cain yell.

McKenna struggled to his feet. Whatever it was hit again. As he steadied himself, there was a muffled metallic sound. The *Wanderer* seemed hooked by the stern, her forward momentum stalled. The headsail began to pull the bow down and the stern lifted.

McKenna climbed into the cockpit to see Cain leaning over the stern, apparently oblivious to the fact that the *Wanderer* was rounding to leeward and heading toward a flying jibe. His small sketch pad lay open on the cushion beside him, the pages fluttering in the breeze.

McKenna released the jenny sheet, clearing as much of the line as he could, so the big sail could stream before the boat instead of fill. The mainsail boom began to rise, ready to jibe over . . . and with another jarring clunk under the stern, the *Wanderer* surged free.

Cain spun the wheel, heading the boat up, and then both of them immediately turned back to look in the wake. Cain said, "Goddamn it, there it is."

McKenna shaded his eyes. It was a log, about the size of a small telephone pole. Most likely driftwood from a cargo ship.

"How's the helm?"

Cain sawed the wheel back and forth quickly. The *Wanderer* headed up and down. "She's responding fine. Rudder must be okay."

McKenna hurried back down into the cabin and to the bow. He tore up the floorboards—there was just a little water, nothing unusual. He shoved aside Cain's bedding and pulled up the cover over the waste tank. There were about six inches on each side of the plastic holding tank where he would have access to the inside of the bow. Too dark to see, but he couldn't hear the splash of water. He hurried back to the main cabin for a flashlight.

Cain set Mortimer and joined McKenna. "How're we doing?"

"Go back up," McKenna said, curtly. "There may be more where that came from."

"Let me help you." Cain started for the bow.

McKenna shoved past him. "Damn it, do what I told you." McKenna crawled back on top of the bunk and flashed the light down the waste tank hatch. He looked all around the big plastic tank.

He gave his first sigh of relief. No water to starboard. None to port, or at the apex of the bow. He looked straight down at the edges of the tank.

There was something there, a tight bundle of cloth. It gave him a moment's pause, but then he passed it off as unimportant.

He moved back to the main cabin and pulled up the rest of the floorboards.

Fine. Not even enough water to activate the pump. He pulled out his own bedding, and he looked at the hull over the water tanks on the starboard side.

From the cabinway, Cain said, "How's it look, Skipper?"

"So far so good. What do you see ahead?"

Cain said, "We're fine here."

"Well, I think we got lucky. Very, very lucky."

"I was watching, but I missed it."

"You sure your head wasn't down over that sketch pad?"

Cain was silent for a moment.

McKenna looked up at him.

"Listen," McKenna said. "I know it gets boring, and your sketching helps pass the time. But when you're on lookout, that's just what you've got to be doing. You know that."

"Absolutely," Cain said. "And I was."

McKenna didn't believe him, but he told himself to let it go, that Cain should've learned his lesson even if he wasn't willing to own up to it. McKenna pulled the pins on the cabinway stairs and flashed his light to the starboard and port of the engine.

Nothing still.

He felt the tension in his back began to ease.

He climbed up into the cockpit and Cain said, "Frigging ships dump that kind of hazard. Should be a way to sue them. We could've been screwed here."

McKenna's temper flared. "That's why we keep watches."

Cain waved that away. "Be cool. We're all right."

McKenna opened the engine hatch and looked down on the compartment from the top.

Maybe Cain was right.

Then McKenna thought about the way the *Wanderer* had lurched and lifted at the last moment. That soft metallic ring. The clunking sound.

He spun the wheel back and forth himself. It felt fine.

Then he reached over and pulled the gearshift to neutral. The driveshaft rotated for less than a full turn, and then stopped abruptly. There was a small click against the hull. A slow trickle of water came in from the stuffing box around the drive shaft. Nothing the pump couldn't keep up with, but greater than normal leakage.

"Damn it," McKenna said.

"What?" Cain said.

"I think the shaft's bent. Or the prop. Or both. I won't know until I take a look. Drop the sails while I get ready."

McKenna went below and put on a bathing suit. When he came back, he grabbed the mask and fins from the cockpit locker. He took a line, cleated the bitter end, and put a loop around his wrist.

He put his hand over the face mask and stepped over the side. The water was still cold, and he wished for a wetsuit. He blew water from the snorkel, took a deep breath, and then flipped upside down to make his way to the rudder. It was unnerving, being under the boat. It rose and fell above him like a small whale. He felt aware of the oppressive weight above and naked to whatever was below. Sharks sometimes followed boats.

McKenna groaned aloud. He could see that the shaft was bent so badly that the twisted blade of the prop was pressed against the hull.

The end of the floating log must have nailed the prop squarely.

McKenna kicked away from the boat and surfaced. He swam the length of the boat and saw where the bottom paint had been scraped by the log, but there didn't seem to be any other real damage. After going up for air, he jackknifed back down to the rudder to look for cracks around the driveshaft.

None, thank God.

"I could use some good news here," Cain said as McKenna climbed up the swim ladder.

McKenna told him.

Cain looked at him incredulously, as if it were his fault. "So no engine?"

"We can run it in neutral to charge the batteries, keep the power and refrigeration. But no propulsion."

"Damn it," Cain said. Both of them looked at the wind gauge. A steady fifteen knots.

McKenna said, "We just hope this keeps up."

CHAPTER 6

OF COURSE, IT DIDN'T.

Later, McKenna would think how differently things might have worked out if the wind hadn't died.

But the day after the collision, McKenna awoke to a dead calm.

The sea was a mirror reflecting a white, hazy sky. The *Wanderer* sat like a toy boat, the only movement was the purposeless bang of the slatting sails.

McKenna put them both to work, making small repairs. Keeping them busy. Along the way, McKenna took the time to really look and listen to his new mate.

And to realize that he was a liar.

"Take a sight?" McKenna offered Cain the sextant.

They were closing the second day with virtually no wind. Sweltering heat. The sun was low on the clear horizon. Already stars were faintly visible in the blue sky.

Cain shook his head, irritably. "You've got the GPS. We know where we are."

"Match it," McKenna said. Not sure why he was pushing. "See how close you can get. Then we'll get back to the trim."

Cain shook his head. "I don't need that antique to tell me we're a day north of the Bahamas, two east from the Florida coast. *If* we were moving. But right now, we're nowhere. *Fucking* nowhere."

It dawned on McKenna that Cain didn't know how to use it. McKenna was somewhat surprised, but not entirely. Many good sailors never learned how to use a sextant.

Cain slopped on more oil with the paint brush.

McKenna almost said something when he saw it splash up against the cabin, but let it go. The heat was shortening his own temper.

He'd taken a series of sightings with his sextant: the sun, the moon, and two faintly visible stars, Diphda and Denab. He decided to shut up and just take the last one, Capella. The sextant was a beautiful piece, made of brass. It normally felt good in his hands, but as he raised it to his eye, it felt slippery in the sweat of his palms. He made the sighting and immediately made note of the time.

Caroline had given him the sextant for his thirtieth birthday, her way of saying that the voyage was still ahead of them, even if the big boat and time to do it was just a dream for the future.

As the sun settled behind the horizon, McKenna laid the instrument into its case, and looked back at Cain. "I know this calm is getting on both our nerves—"

"Look," Cain said. "The other boats I've sailed on have had all the electronics they needed. You've got a GPS, why screw around with that antique?"

"Batteries die," McKenna said. He gestured to the sextant. "It's a skill worth having. I'll teach you if you want."

"Teach your coolie some tricks?"

"What?" He stared at the young man. Not for the first time in the past few days, McKenna thought about that little bundle near the holding tank.

Why hadn't Cain just put it at the bottom of his lazarette? And it clearly hadn't been there when the customs agent was searching the boat: he would have insisted it be opened.

McKenna said, "You think I'm working you too hard?"

Cain looked as if he was going to answer him, but then just waved his hand dismissively. "Drop it."

McKenna's own temper flared. The arrogance of this kid was coming out now. And while he was reasonably competent, his level of experience didn't match his supposed credentials. McKenna thought of Cain looking back at the wake while the *Wanderer* was hooked on that log, ready to jibe.

McKenna said, "Tell me about those other boats. Tell me about those three transatlantics."

Cain paused. His eyes met McKenna's and then the younger man's face hardened.

Cain said, "I've got a better idea." He stood slowly.

McKenna hesitated.

Without a word, Cain took the few steps toward McKenna and retrieved the sextant from the box. He held it up to his eye, sighting toward the moon. In a lazy drawl, he said, "Ah, you're right. I should've looked through this before. By my calculations . . . we've gone too far to turn back." He looked directly at McKenna and opened his hands. "Ooops."

The sextant banged against the hull, and then sank instantly, the brass winking briefly underwater before it was gone.

"You son of a bitch!" McKenna stepped forward with his fists balled.

"New game plan, Skipper." Cain stepped into McKenna slightly.

McKenna refused to budge.

Cain got right up against his face, still wearing that smile. "This is the situation." Cain put his hand against McKenna's chest and lightly shoved him. "You're in charge of the boat. I'm in charge of *me*."

McKenna shoved him back.

The blood rushed to Cain's face. "We get started this far out, it's going to be a disaster for one of us. Maybe both."

McKenna forced himself to hold back. Rage, fresh on tap, was right there. He could feel it in his arms and chest, feel the blood singing through his veins.

"Oh, Skipper," Cain said, backing away. He laughed, put his hands out. "We can do this, but you know what a broken arm, or a concussion, or even a bad cut getting infected will mean out here. Look, you need a hand changing a sail, taking a watch, I'm your guy. But do your own scut work."

"What's your real name?" McKenna said. In his mind's eye, he could see the little bundle. He almost said, *And what have you brought on my boat?*

But he didn't.

"Doesn't matter," Cain said. "You just think of me as a passenger. And keep out of my way."

Mercifully, the wind came up again early the next day. For the remainder of the week, they kept on the move. Sometimes the wind held at a steady ten knots, sometimes a squall would gust it up to the mid-thirties. Either way, they continued on in a new sort of routine.

McKenna would give his orders, and Cain, by and large, would obey them. He would even turn to some of the routine maintenance if the mood seemed to strike him.

But mostly, he lay in his bunk and sketched. Or lay back against the bulkhead under the dodger. Many of these little sketches were of the subjects around them, the flying fish that landed on deck one morning, McKenna's hands on the wheel. But other times he purposefully would work up a portrait of McKenna which he then might briefly reveal before letting it flutter astern. These little pieces of artwork were genuinely painful for McKenna: far from mere caricatures, they were amazingly well-executed pieces that somehow managed to both reveal and mock McKenna's anger and self-restraint.

It infuriated McKenna to share this last sail, most likely his last voyage on the *Wanderer*, with this kid.

In his sleep, McKenna dreamed about R. J. sitting at the kitchen table, that white blond hair hanging in his eyes. Smirking at God knows what. The way his eyes twinkled slightly whenever Sam walked into the room. The delight in tweaking McKenna himself, as much as happiness at seeing Sam.

At least that's the way McKenna dreamed it.

Caroline at the door, telling him it was all right. "Let her make her mistakes," Caroline said, as their daughter got into the car. "You can't control everything."

It ate McKenna that most likely Cain had sucked him into some smuggling scam. As master of the boat, McKenna was responsible for what happened on it.

McKenna wasn't too worried about customs. He and Cain made it through the BVI check, and going into Boston could be handled with a phone call. But the Coast Guard was another matter. They were charged with finding drug smugglers on the high seas and private sailboats were a prime target.

It all came down to what was in that bag.

Heroin? Cocaine? A gun? Or perhaps nothing but dirty under-wear?

Mentally, McKenna quietly went round and round the topic. He could tell Cain was watching him, especially when he went near the cabin in the bow.

McKenna wanted to know.

But he also wanted to finish the voyage without escalating the sit-uation into a fight with Cain. McKenna thought about what his Uncle Sean would've done. His leather-hard uncle, with his thin, sunburned face, bright blue eyes, and his unshakable sense of right and wrong. Probably would've walked directly into Cain's cabin and opened the bundle. Fought Cain, if necessary.

"Tackle your problems straight on, Robby," was one of Uncle Sean's truisms. "Before they tackle you."

McKenna loved his uncle, but the man's humorless, often simplis-tic view of the world didn't allow for shades of gray.

McKenna's head told him he may well not win against Cain. And even if he did what would he do with him? Tie him up, spoon-feed him—basically keep him a hostage until they reached port?

It wasn't lost on McKenna that he had begun to associate Tom Cain with R. J. Mitchell. He was afraid of what he would do if he found out Cain was running drugs. He could feel what it would be like, could imagine the synapses firing. A push becoming a shove. One blow turning to another, and then, in the confined space, in the heat, in his own rage . . . a knife, the winch handle . . .

God knows, humans could be so fragile. One punch and a shove, and Sam was dead.

Objectively, McKenna knew it was one of the luckiest moments of his life that Caroline had been there to stop him when he started off for R. J.'s house.

Objectively.

Just as now, his head told him where his own temper might lead him if he and Cain really got down to it.

McKenna resolved finally to let the little bundle alone. Act like it wasn't there. Make port in Charleston to repair the shaft and tell Cain to get off his boat.

It seemed the safest course.

CHAPTER 7

THEY WERE LESS THAN HALF A DAY AWAY FROM CHARLESTON WHEN McKenna saw the Coast Guard cutter bearing down on them.

He raised the binoculars to his eyes.

It was about a mile away.

Cain came out of the cabin and said, "What's up?"

McKenna just stared at him.

Cain saw the cutter and his face went carefully blank.

That's all McKenna needed to see.

"Looks like we're going to be boarded," McKenna said.

Cain's eyes flickered at him and about the boat. He looked up at the mast and back at the fast-approaching cutter.

McKenna got it then. He said, "You son of a bitch."

"What's your problem?" Cain said.

McKenna stepped around him and headed below.

Cain continued to stare at the cutter for a moment longer, and then yelled after McKenna, "What are you doing?"

McKenna ignored him. He went directly into Cain's little cabin, shut the door just as Cain jumped down the main stairwell. McKenna threw the bolt.

Cain hit the door. "Open it, McKenna!"

McKenna knelt down and quickly pulled back the panel to gain access to the through-hull valves for the head. He reached above them, feeling around until he found the little bundle. He pulled it out.

Cain hit the door again. Most likely with his shoulder this time. The door held.

McKenna opened the bag, his hands shaking. It was hot in the little cabin and the sweat was just pouring off him. He reached inside the bag. He felt plastic, something smooth and hard. He pulled it out. An aspirin bottle. A big "extra-value" size.

"Rob!" Cain's voice eased. "Hey, Rob, what's this about?"

McKenna fiddled with the cap for a second and then got it open. He snatched the cotton out and rattled the pills. He held the open mouth of the bottle up to the sunlight streaming in from the porthole. Something sparkled. Just a quick flash and it was gone.

Cain voice was a harsh whisper now. "You stupid bastard, you don't know what you're getting into!"

Abruptly, McKenna dumped the aspirin bottle upside down on Cain's blue sleeping bag.

And then the sunlight streaming in from the porthole refracted around the small cabin.

Diamonds.

Diamonds. More than a big handful. All of them cut, polished stones.

"Jesus," McKenna said. They were breathtaking.

McKenna certainly wasn't an expert on diamonds. And with Cain trying to break through the door, and the Coast Guard about a quarter mile away, McKenna was hardly in a position to even hazard a guess as to their value. But the rage Cain was displaying—

"You son of a bitch, open the *fucking* door . . ."

—was enough for McKenna to form some quick assumptions.

One, that these pretty stones were real.

Two, they were easily worth at least a small fortune and maybe much more.

And, three, they were most likely stolen.

* * *

McKenna turned and flicked aside the bolt.

Cain tried to push his way in. But McKenna surprised the younger man by grabbing his shirt to pull him off balance, and then immediately shoved him back across the cabin. Cain bounced back immediately—and then stopped when McKenna turned to scoop the stones into his right hand.

McKenna said, "Don't jostle me, now. I spill these, you'll never get them back before we're boarded."

Cain hesitated. He looked out the porthole toward the cutter. He rubbed his mouth. Clearly he was thinking fast, assessing his situation. "Look, just give them to me. I've made it through worse spots."

McKenna looked closely at the aspirin bottle. There was the residue of tape on it. "The top of the spreader?" McKenna said. "You taped these up there and damaged the block so you'd have an excuse later to go back up the mast once we were past customs. We could've lost the boat."

"*Fuck* the boat." Cain shook his head in frustration. "You could buy fifty of your precious boats with what's in there."

Cain raked his hair back and tried to continue in a conciliatory tone. "Look, I didn't know the block would fail so soon," he said. "Who expected that kind of wind one day out of the BVI?"

"Anybody. Anybody who really knew what they were doing." McKenna opened the porthole inside the head. It was on the opposite side of the oncoming cutter. He should be able to throw the diamonds overboard without the Coast Guard crew seeing him. "If you've got some bill of sale you want to show me on these, then we'll keep them and I'll let you explain to them why you didn't notify customs. Otherwise . . ."

Cain was incredulous. "You think you're going to dump them?"

"What do you suggest?"

"That's a fortune, you asshole," Cain snapped. "There's five million worth of diamonds right there." Cain visibly tried to regain himself. "Look," he said, "We *really* don't have time for this. Look at your hand. Look at those diamonds. With those, you've got a future. Without them, the best you can expect is to go home and get your divorce. Lose your boat. Far as I can tell, it's about all you care about. With these, you can go anywhere, do anything you want."

McKenna couldn't help himself. Some of the diamonds in his hand were as big as his thumbnail.

Just then they heard the sound of a megaphone over the roar of the cutter's engines. "Sailing vessel, *Wanderer*. Sailing vessel, *Wanderer*. Please furl your sails and prepare to be boarded."

McKenna sighed and dumped the diamonds back into the bottle.

Cain pleaded. "Do this one bad thing and you've got a life. But if you go up on that deck and be a Boy Scout, they'll impound the boat, and by the time I'm done, *you'll* be the one sitting in prison. Your prints are all over that bottle and those stones. I guarantee you, I've already wiped mine."

McKenna felt a jolt, but then let it go. "So I dump them."

The amplified voice came across the water again. "Skipper of the *Wanderer*. This is the Coast Guard. Please come on deck immediately."

McKenna gestured to the boat outside. "They're here, they're coming on board." He reached out the window with the bottle.

"Use your head," Cain hissed. "For Christ's sake, use your brains! You'll be a rich man."

McKenna stopped.

It was clear to McKenna that he had just one option. He couldn't really throw the diamonds overboard. They must belong to someone. He couldn't just throw five million dollars away.

He just couldn't.

What he had to do was simple: go up to the cockpit, and call the Coast Guard over. Point the finger. Let the pros hustle Cain onto their boat in chains. Maybe even suffer the indignity of being hauled away in chains himself. Cain *was* a wonderful liar.

Either way, the Coast Guard would tow in the *Wanderer*. Put her into drydock as evidence, and McKenna would have to scramble to prove his own innocence, go through all the bureaucracy and the lies that Cain would throw out. Lawyers, time, money.

"Ah, for God's sake," McKenna breathed. This could go far beyond inconvenience. This could mean months, maybe years of trouble.

"Don't be stupid," Cain whispered, looking over his shoulder.

"You have a chance, this is a once-in-a-lifetime deal. Right in front of you. How often is this going to come along, you—"

"Shut up," McKenna brushed past him, heading toward the companionway.

Cain said in a hoarse whisper. "You can go anywhere you want, any kind of boat. All the women you want. You've got this kind of money, you can have anything. Think!"

Can I have Sam back? McKenna asked himself.

But he hesitated at the foot of the companionway. McKenna knew the way he was brought up, his Uncle Sean. He knew how he and Caroline had brought up Samantha.

And what had any of it gotten McKenna?

The thought rushed through his head, capering and whispering like a living thing. Whispered in his father's voice. "What'd it ever get you, Rob? Doing the right thing? For Christ's sake, tear something off for yourself."

Those diamonds.

Those bright bits of fire. They could bring happiness to *some* people.

To McKenna, they couldn't offer that, but they could possibly offer the means to continue sailing. Suspended animation at best; purgatory at worst. But at least he could get off this course that he was now on—that of a divorced man, living in some condo he could barely afford. Working some job, most likely buying and selling real estate. Trying to connect with people and act like he cared about the things they cared about. Back on land, where you could work, and love, and hold on to your child, and she could still be gone with one misjudgement, one mistake.

Those diamonds. They could give him a chance to keep breathing.

The megaphoned voice spoke again; definitely suspicious now.

"What're you going to do?" Cain said. "Tell me how you're going to play it. Give me that, at least."

McKenna looked back at Cain before stepping out into the sunlight.

What has doing the right thing ever done for me?

He wet his lips.

"*Skipper of the* Wanderer . . ."

McKenna turned to Cain. "I'll stall them. You close off the through-hull valve for the waste hose from the head. Grab a screwdriver and unscrew the clamp. That aspirin bottle will fit in the hose. Jam it back on the fitting, and leave some water in the toilet bowl. Nobody's going to want to put their hand down there."

Cain looked at him closely and laughed, shortly. "Goddamn. Sixty-forty. I get the sixty."

"Fifty-fifty," McKenna said. "Take it or they take you." His voice was flat.

Cain took it.

McKenna went up on deck. *It's that easy*, he thought.

He felt scared, alert, and crackling with energy.

Alive.

The captain of the cutter stood far above him on the bridge of the vessel. He had close-cropped short hair and a neat black mustache. He looked about forty-years-old.

He put the mike to his face and the amplified voice said, "We catch you napping, Skipper?"

McKenna cupped his hands to yell over the cutter's engines. "Need to sleep sometime."

"Where are you out of, Skipper?"

McKenna told him the BVI.

With the wind was blowing just under twenty knots, the seas were running just high enough that the two boats rose and fell so that at times McKenna was almost level with the captain; at others the big cutter seemed a mile above.

The officer nodded to a crew of three and a junior officer who were standing by the lower railing. They were all wearing bright orange vests and were armed.

"Prepare to be boarded," the captain said. "Furl your sails and motor alongside."

McKenna yelled. "I've got a problem with the engine." He told him about the damaged prop.

"All right," the captain said. "We'll take you in tow."

He turned and spoke to the helmsman. The cutter surged ahead.

The *Wanderer* lifted and fell in the wash, spilling wind for a moment.

"I'm going to need you up here," McKenna said to Cain. "They'll wonder why my crew didn't help out."

"I'll be there," Cain called back quietly. "Just botch it when you sail up to them. Make them reposition themselves."

McKenna nodded. It was actually easy enough to do. The cutter was a bit high on the wind anyhow. When he saw the crewman on the stern ready to throw back a towline, McKenna headed the boat up just a little too soon. The sails shivered, and the forward motion quickly stalled. He ran forward as if to catch the line. The seaman shook his head, but threw the line anyhow. It fell short by a few feet.

McKenna raised his hands as if frustrated, and then hurried back to the stern. By then the *Wanderer* was in irons, and it took him a few minutes to get her backed down, and get her head over enough so that he could make way again. This time, the cutter moved just directly before him. "I've got to do it this time," McKenna said.

Cain appeared at the bottom of the stairway.

He had a fifth of scotch in his hand. "Listen to me," he whispered. "I'm taking a couple hits off this and you do the same. We're a couple of lushes. They already don't like us, so we give them a reason— we're drunks. You got it?"

McKenna bent down. He knocked back a mouthful of the whiskey. Some of it dribbled on his shirt, but he didn't suppose that would hurt. He coughed, and said, "You put the diamonds where I told you?"

"Don't worry where I put them," Cain snapped. "You just be kind've drunk and act like it's hard work for you not to be a belligerent SOB."

Cain went on deck.

McKenna sailed the boat closer to the cutter. A part of him recognized Cain's acting skills. He wasn't overdoing the drunk bit. Not stumbling around. Instead, he walked a little more slowly, handing himself along the safety lines more carefully than one would expect of an experienced sailor.

McKenna saw the seaman on the stern of the cutter look over his shoulder and say something to the junior officer behind him.

Again, McKenna brought the *Wanderer* up under the cutter's stern and headed up into the wind. Cain reached out for the towline and the seaman cast it to him. Cain passed the line through the bow chocks and almost lost it before regaining it to cleat the line.

He covered his head against the heavily luffing jenny and started back.

McKenna yelled at him to get the jenny *down*, goddamn it.

Now there were several seamen on the stern and they were shaking their heads and laughing among themselves.

Cain kept his back to the seaman. Suddenly he made a face, his tongue out, eyes rolling . . . exaggerating the drunk bit for McKenna's benefit.

McKenna wanted to laugh. He had to turn his face away.

Maybe it was just the combination of whiskey and adrenaline. Maybe it was because he was doing something he would never have considered before—something that was totally alien to who he was—and finding that he had some talent for it.

God save him, there was something fun about it all.

By the time they got the sails down and the junior officer and the three burly seamen were on board, McKenna had lost his sense of humor. The cutter towed them along at a steady five knots, fast for a tow. The *Wanderer* rose and fell in the cutter's wake, the bowline bar tight.

It made clear in a way that nothing else had that he was in someone else's control; that freedom could just as easily end as start from here.

"Captain," the officer said. "Have you been drinking?"

McKenna said, sullenly. "Long ways from drunk." He let his voice slur.

"That so?" said the young officer. He had a friendly smile and light blue eyes that watched McKenna carefully. "I like to give people a choice. Be straight with me from the beginning and avoid a lot of hassle. Or go for the works. I don't care either way, but the first would be easier on you and your boat in the long run. If you or your crew member have something on board—maybe a little weed, some coke, heroin, you tell me now and we'll work it out."

McKenna snorted. He gestured at Cain. "Goddamn mate, if he had anything like that I'd kill him. If he had anything like that, he wouldn't be hitting my scotch."

"Uh-huh," the officer said. He raised his voice to the seaman. "Let's take a look, gentlemen."

They went to work.

"Go through the basic systems, guys. Let's see if everything's working." The officer winked at McKenna. "We'll even see what's jammed that prop of yours."

The seamen made the customs search at the BVI look like an Easter-egg hunt. The cutter stopped the tow while one of the men pulled on a wetsuit and went over the side to look at the prop. Another went through every drawer, every bag, every inch of storage space. And the third went through the systems. He was a wiry young man with dark hair and grease stains embedded in his hands. He spent a good forty minutes on the engine, carefully probing inside the water cooler, closing and then pulling off through-valve fittings. McKenna's heart started pounding.

Then he moved to the galley. The officer watched McKenna carefully as the seaman started the propane oven. Apparently looking for a telltale reaction.

McKenna stared back at him.

"Check it anyhow," the officer said.

The wiry man sighed, knelt down, and looked throughout the stove. From there, he went to the sink, checking the drain, the drain hose, all the connections under the sink.

Then he went to the head.

McKenna felt his face growing tight and he almost stood up, trying to distract the man. But he felt a tap on his foot. When he looked over, Cain was apparently watching the sailors curiously. But he made a small, horizontal gesture with his right hand. Just a flicker, but McKenna felt relief surge through him.

Cain had hidden the diamonds someplace else.

After a half hour, the wiry man came back to his officer and said, "Anything else, sir?"

The officer looked first and McKenna and then Cain. "Do I?"

"Can we move on?" McKenna said. He didn't have to fake the tiredness in his voice. The tension was draining him, particularly now that the shot of scotch had faded to leave nothing but a nasty taste in his mouth, and a sinking awareness of what he'd done.

The wiry seaman began to wash his hands in the galley. He hit the soap-bottle nozzle a couple of times and turned the fresh water on high.

McKenna looked over, suddenly resenting that the man was using their drinking water instead of the seawater foot pump. "You think you can do that on your own boat?" he said, irritably.

The junior officer cocked his head at the wiry seaman. "Check the water tanks, Stevens."

The seaman smiled. "Yes, sir."

Cain rolled his eyes and stood. The seaman pulled aside the bedding and unscrewed the big cap to the starboard water tank. He used a flashlight to look inside, and then held a small mirror like a dentist might use to look through the half full tank. He had McKenna move, and he did the same thing on the port tank.

He made a face. "Sorry, Lieutenant. I'm not seeing anything."

The young officer shrugged. He stepped closer to McKenna. "So maybe me and the captain were wrong." Those blue eyes searching, somehow seeing the guilt in McKenna.

Or at least that's what McKenna imagined. His heart was beating rapidly and he almost said something. Tried to take it back, explain.

But he didn't.

The officer at last shrugged. "Maybe you're just a couple of drunks. Better get into port, Skipper. Get that prop fixed."

McKenna nodded.

The officer snapped his fingers and the other seamen joined him, then climbed back into their Zodiac. They clambered on board the cutter and the wiry seaman came back to the stern to give the towline enough slack so Cain could uncleat the *Wanderer*.

They were free.

CHAPTER 8

McKENNA AND CAIN STAYED IN THE COCKPIT, SIPPING THE WHISKEY together quietly as the cutter faded from sight. McKenna felt as if he were outside himself, watching the bearded, dark-haired man pass the bottle back and forth with the younger man.

People from McKenna's past assaulted him from each side. His former employees at the agency; his customers. People who had always regarded him as honest.

His family.

Uncle Sean was thin-lipped. Rigid with disapproval. Caroline was stunned, but trying to understand.

Sam was in tears.

"Daddy, you're stealing?" she said. "You're lying?"

It wasn't the way he'd raised her or been raised himself.

But possibly it was what he was born to be. McKenna felt his father looking at him, felt a certain smug reaction from the man. That time out in L.A. His father had invited him over to sit by the pool. Have drinks before they headed out to dinner. McKenna had told himself to be civil, if just for his own sake, to listen and understand who his father was.

And he had done that, but been appalled to listen to the man, and hear how he swept a lifetime of McKenna's core loneliness aside, how he ascribed his own flight and McKenna's mother's death as "bad luck, worse timing." Leaving the responsibility of raising Rob to Uncle Sean was a ". . . hard decision I had to make for the good of everyone."

McKenna had intended to be civil throughout dinner. Just get to know the man. But instead he'd told him what he had wanted to say for years. In a low, harsh voice, he told his father that he was a selfish arrogant bastard, and that he'd done more damage than he knew. "How did you think we were going to eat if Mom wasn't out that night?"

Bobby McKenna had listened wearily. And when Rob was done, he had leaned forward and said, "Time will come, Rob, even if it hasn't yet. When you just gotta take care of yourself. You'll see then." His father had knocked his drink back, gestured to his third wife doing her laps in the pool. "Maybe Lisa and I better go out on our own tonight. You always were a pious little shit. But I got faith in you yet."

Like father like son. McKenna knew beyond a shadow of doubt that his father would've been proud of him for scamming the Coast Guard. Would've been laughing that Rob's time had come.

And it doesn't matter.

McKenna felt bad. But he'd felt worse before.

Much worse.

"Huh," he said aloud. He reached out for the bottle, and Cain, his new best friend, handed it to him.

Later, McKenna asked. "So where did you put the diamonds?" Cain raised the whiskey bottle to himself. "My experience and your luck—together we make an unbeatable team."

"Meaning?"

"Meaning I knew they'd go for the head, the hoses, all that shit. It's the way they think. I almost blew it, though, and you saved our ass."

"I did?" McKenna cocked his head.

Cain mimicked McKenna, "Can't you do that on your own boat?"

McKenna remembered. That's what he'd said to the wiry guy, the one who was wasting the fresh water.

Cain said, "I hid the diamonds in the soap bottle. The one that sailor almost opened so he could wash his goddamn hands."

After about an hour, McKenna set Mortimer back on, and the two of them went below. Not having a watch on deck bothered McKenna somewhat, but the whiskey had softened his judgement.

He opened the soap bottle and peered in. The diamonds weren't visible. All he could see was the milky white of the soap. But the weight of the bottle was heavier, and the soap level higher. Something no one else would notice.

"Leave it there," Cain said. "Like most things, simple is best. Even in smuggling."

"You're a pro?"

Cain nodded. "Planes, trains, cars, boats. Hell, I've done bike tours through Europe with shit stuffed down the seat tube."

"Drugs?" McKenna's voice was harsh.

What have I done? What the hell have I done?

"No. Well, just once. Sophomore year, broke my cherry spring break. Went down to Colombia. Brought back some coke. Scared the hell out of myself and didn't like the method of transport."

"Which was?"

Cain smiled sheepishly. "Condom up my ass, in my colon."

McKenna lifted his eyebrows.

Cain laughed. "Don't worry, you're traveling in better company now. Way back then I figured out drugs were too messy and the people too whacked."

"So now diamonds?"

"Among other things."

"You're just a courier?"

Cain shook his head. "Not anymore. These are mine."

"How'd you pay for them?"

"You don't need to know that," Cain said. "It was payment for services rendered. They made out just fine, believe me."

"And *they* are?"

Cain didn't bother to answer that. Instead, he said, "We get to

Boston, I'll fence the stuff. You let me get rid of it, and we both get away clean."

McKenna said, "Sure."

Cain looked at him carefully. "And for that, I'm going charge you. I'm going to take back a percentage for handling it. Work my way back to the sixty-forty I said before."

"I said fifty-fifty," McKenna snapped.

"You had me in a spot back then, and I said what I had to say."

McKenna shook his head, stubbornly.

Cain said, "You go to pawn shops with this shit, not only will you get royally screwed on the price—you'll get caught. You let me take this to the people I know, you'll come out with about two million bucks, maybe more. Not bad for an hour's work."

McKenna hesitated. He could see that Cain was making sense. The diamonds without the contacts were useless.

But that's not what made him pause.

What made him pause was Cain himself. His manner. He wasn't as angry as he should be. He was putting it on somewhat, but in truth, he seemed too relaxed for a man who'd supposedly lost two million dollars over the course of the past few hours.

"Fine," McKenna said abruptly.

Because it really didn't matter. Fifty-fifty, sixty-forty, ninety-ten. The percentage points were all bull.

"It's fair," Cain said. "You see what I'm saying? They were my diamonds in the first place, and I'm going to take care of securing the cash. All you've got to do is get us to Boston and then sit back and take a hefty cut."

"All right," McKenna said. "Sixty-forty."

The way he saw it, at best, Cain would try to take off with the diamonds once they got on land. At worst, Cain intended to kill him and slip his body over the side of the boat before they even made it to Boston.

That night, McKenna took the first watch. And when it was Cain's turn, McKenna lay awake for almost two hours, his hand resting near the razor-sharp buck knife that he always kept on his hip. The knife that he now had tucked between the cushion and the wall of the hull the blade locked open, the handle within easy reach.

Finally, he began to nod and his eyelids grew heavy. Just as he fell off, he told himself that it was a skill he could learn. A skill he *must* learn, as necessary as listening for a change in the wind, as necessary as listening for an undue strain in the rigging or the hull itself.

In his new life, he needed to listen even while he slept. Listen for quietly approaching footsteps, for the pause before the attack—for the in-drawn breath before someone tried to plunge *their* razor-sharp knife into his heart.

CHAPTER 9

McKenna dreamed about Melanie Walsh.

She didn't come to him right away, though.

First came nightmarish scenes on the boat. He was on his knees in the bilge, searching for leaks that were springing up from bow to stern. Some that trickled, some that geysered a foot into the air. He pressed cloth, and wadded paper, and blocks of wood against the holes. Each of his patches simply floated away. He couldn't understand why he thought such clumsy attempts would work. An amplified voice demanded his attention the entire time, but the words were unintelligible.

Then he settled down. And that's when Melanie made her way into his thoughts.

Those few minutes in her apartment.

It was four years back. She had been about twenty-eight at the time. His best salesperson. Short black hair, elfin features. Lively green eyes. Very attractive, very smart. He had liked her enormously.

In his waking hours, McKenna thought of that day occasionally. And wondered if she'd even remember it.

He believed she would. Most of the time, that's what he believed.

They were on their way back from seeing a customer and she

asked him if they could stop by her apartment. She'd forgotten her appointment book that morning.

"Come in and I'll make you a sandwich," she said. "I'm starved myself, and we're not going to have time for lunch otherwise."

He had hesitated slightly. The basic caution of a married man. But then he'd gone in. She'd rented the sunny top floor above a candle shop in Market Square. He had told himself she was an employee and a friend, that surely he could go have lunch with her.

Yet, standing there in her apartment, seeing her photos, he'd realized how little he really knew about her. She was an avid traveler, and her photos reflected scenes from all over the world. Black-and-white studies, most of them. A young Hispanic boy sweeping through a semi-circle on his Rollerblades, his arms out wide. His grin cocky, yet shy. A white-haired woman scowling with mock ferocity at a pugnacious little girl who was surely her granddaughter. Moody scenics. Boston with a deep bank of fog swallowing the Longfellow Bridge and half of the city. The Hancock Building, reflecting sunlight above the clouds, slicing through the fog like a shining blade.

"These are great," he said.

"Better than my cooking," Melanie said, giving him a ham sandwich.

He took a bite and a blob of mayonnaise and mustard promptly fell onto his tie. He looked down in dismay.

"Oh, Jesus." She hurried back to the kitchen for a cloth, and while she was soaking it in a stream of hot water, he saw her shoulders start to move.

She tried to hide her grin when she turned around.

"What?" he asked.

"Nothing." She dabbed at his tie, smearing the mayonnaise even further. She bit at her lower lip, the laughter bubbling up inside her, and he put a hand on her shoulder. Suddenly he was aware of her proximity, the scent of her. He said, "This is your humor all the way, isn't it?"

"Oh, yeah," she said, looking up. Those green eyes under dark black lashes. She didn't move away.

He felt himself growing aroused.

She said, "Pratfalls. Mud all over you, pies in the face." She flipped the damp cloth over and made another attack on the tie. Water dripped down onto his pants, and that just did her in.

She backed away, laughing. "I'm sorry," she said. "You're a mess now. I'm afraid you've got to take all your clothes off while I wash them. Just like in the movies."

She looked at him directly for no more than a heartbeat.

Her smile subsided. He felt suddenly that it could happen. He could reach out, put his palm to the nape of her neck, and pull her close. He felt, he *knew*, she would come to him. Even though he truly loved Caroline, even though he'd never wanted to lose her, the temptation was there—not just to make love with Melanie, but to stay with her through the day, to sleep with her, to whisper and laugh with her in the night.

But he did nothing.

As the moment lengthened, she smiled brightly and said, "I think I've got another tie for you. Left by an old flame who knows better than to show his face around here."

She went into her bedroom and came out a moment later. He went into the bathroom, and changed his tie. They stood at her breakfast nook and ate their sandwiches, and were on the road again within twenty minutes.

Not long after that, she'd quit the agency to give it a shot as a full-time photographer. McKenna had thrown what work he could her way, several estates where topflight photos would help attract the right buyers. But she'd quickly moved beyond that stage. McKenna and Caroline had attended Melanie's first gallery opening, at the Firehouse Center, about a year after she'd quit the agency.

The last time he'd seen Melanie had been at Sam's funeral. As Melanie hugged him briefly, his thoughts had drifted to their particular road not taken. In that instant, he had wished he had. Not for her, not for him. But just so the road would have been different, because maybe somehow it would have pulled Sam along, too.

In the year since his daughter's death, he had thought a lot about that opportunity and other turns he had missed.

And he was thinking about them again when he awoke in the *Wanderer* with the knife in his hand.

There were other ways to live his life.

McKenna told Cain he had decided against making port in Charleston to fix the prop.

Surprisingly, Cain made no objection.

McKenna thought about that afterward, sitting up on deck while Mortimer sailed the boat. It wasn't the safest decision—under normal conditions it would've been smarter to have use of the engine as the shipping lanes converged.

But these weren't normal circumstances.

Two days later McKenna awoke to see that the barometer was dropping. They were at least a day's sail from the mouth of Long Island Sound—if there had been wind.

McKenna went on deck and stretched, looking at the red morning sky. The seas were rolling, but oily looking. The sails slatted back and forth, useless. McKenna felt a vague uneasiness and the breath of excitement. He looked down at his arms and saw the gooseflesh on them. Gooseflesh at eighty degrees.

Cain was asleep on the cushions.

McKenna nudged him with his knee. "You're supposed to be on watch."

Cain groaned, and sat up. He rubbed his face, making his growing beard rasp. "For what?"

"Can't you feel it?" McKenna went below and switched the radio on to listen to the weather service. The warning was delivered with flat urgency: *"Gale-force winds predicted. A small-craft advisory in effect for coastal waters off of Long Island Sound, Buzzards Bay, and the islands . . ."*

He went back on deck and said to Cain, "Now we'll see if we really screwed up, not getting this prop fixed. We've got gale-force winds coming in, and there's no way we can make for shore now, with no wind and the twisted shaft."

Cain looked out at the water uneasily. "What's the plan?"

McKenna shrugged. "We get ready for a ride."

They brought the main down to the third reef and changed the jenny for a small storm jib. Off to the south, McKenna could see a line of squalls coming up along the coast. He took the wheel as the wind began to build. Within twenty minutes, the temperature dropped ten degrees. Cain went below and carefully stowed the gear. He made a point of showing McKenna how he put the bottle of soap in a small backpack.

"Worse comes to worst," Cain said. He nodded to the life raft.

"We're not going to let it come to that," said McKenna. "You're going to have to follow my orders, clear?"

Cain looked out at the building seas. "You da boss."

Within twenty minutes, the steep crests no longer seemed to have any relation to one another. The wind whipped the tops off the waves. McKenna ran the *Wanderer* ahead of the storm out to sea, sliding down the face of one wave to the next. The *Wanderer* would surf, spinning the knot-meter up to twelve knots. McKenna rolled his shoulders and kept loose. He felt in tune with the boat, and relatively warm and dry inside his foul-weather gear. He sent Cain below to get some rest.

As the *Wanderer* rushed down each face, McKenna would head up before the bow buried into the next wave; she would rise and cut solidly through the top then start her slide again.

McKenna found himself grinning. Although he was glad Caroline was safely ashore, he also wished she could be along to share this ride.

The *Wanderer* continued for another hour with the wind blowing at about forty knots, when suddenly a gust up to sixty overpowered her, and she swung round into the wind.

The sails thundered.

McKenna backwinded the jib and got the sloop to back down. Soon they were surfing along again. But it was clearly time to get the sails down.

"Get up here," McKenna yelled to Cain.

Then an express train came through.

That's what it felt like, anyway.

McKenna heard it before he saw it. He turned to find a great green wall rising up behind him. The *Wanderer* began to race down the trough, but the wave was coming even faster. It was curling over the stern itself, higher than anything he'd seen all day; higher than he had ever seen, period.

McKenna whipped his head around and yelled to Cain, "Hold on!"

And then the sea was upon them. The wave swept over McKenna pinning him against the wheel. Cain's back had been to the waves; he was just sliding the last washboard to close off the cabin when solid green water filled the cockpit.

And Cain tried to climb out of the way of it.

"Stay down," McKenna yelled.

But it was too late. The *Wanderer* wallowed briefly in the trough, and then the next wave crashed over the stern, catching Cain as he was half way up the cabin roof. He spun and tumbled into the lee scuppers and the wave carried him along. McKenna was again plastered to the helm, the weight of the water holding him fast. The *Wanderer* staggered, weighted by the water up to McKenna's knees. Her sails filled and she began to heel sharply. McKenna spun the wheel round. She took another wave broadside before her bow came round into the wind.

Cain got to his feet.

McKenna saw that he hadn't snapped the lifeline onto his harness yet.

And McKenna, God help him, saw—and registered—that the backpack wasn't on the younger man, nor his life vest. Presumably both were down in the cabin.

Cain started for the mast to haul down the main when he stumbled. The next wave carried him under the stanchion lines.

He was half overboard.

He cried out to McKenna for help.

McKenna saw what this meant and was thrust into a decision he thought he would never even consider.

But he could.

He saw it in the young man's eyes, what he feared. What he certainly would have done had their roles been reversed.

"McKenna!" Cain screamed. "Please!"

In a millisecond, McKenna saw how Caroline would be lost to him forever; how he'd be lost to himself. Games with the Coast Guard notwithstanding, this was a different league.

As the pressure of water eased, McKenna wrenched himself away from the wheel and crawled up to Cain. He grabbed the young man by his harness and hauled him back onto the deck.

Cain rolled onto his knees and vomited seawater. McKenna hurried back to the wheel. He shouted to Cain, "Get your line on and get those sails down. We'll ride this out under bare poles."

Cain wiped his mouth with the back of his hand, and said, hoarsely, "I thought you were going to let me go. Let me drown."

"Yeah," McKenna said. "So did I."

CHAPTER 10

LANGDON TRIED OUT HIS NEW PHONE. BULKY THING, BIGGER THAN THE average cell phone. Direct-to-satellite thing, well worth the small fortune he'd paid. Could call anywhere, any time, without the roaming nonsense. Perfect for life on board his chartered cabin cruiser.

His sister's voice came through moments later.

"Good vacation?" she asked.

"Another brilliant day just about over."

This was his third day in the Virgin Islands, nice enough.

Ronnie said, "Playing boats while I'm dying back here. *Dying*, damn it, Ian."

"Yes, dear." He looked at the gear laid out on the bunk: Short wetsuit, tank, fins, mask. Knife in a leg sheath. Gun with silencer in double sealed plastic bags.

Ronnie was playing the histrionic; they both knew it. But she meant it, too. Part of her was dying; she'd hit forty a month back. He still had another year to go himself.

And now this. The whole thing had been a great loss of face for her. Very embarrassing. Ian felt her fury almost as his own, but he was good at hiding that sort of thing.

He looked out the porthole with his binoculars. Soon the light would be gone and he'd put on the scuba gear and swim out to the big trimaran. He'd been checking it out over the past few days, and he was determined to make his move that night.

The bloody man was never alone.

But at least his boat would be a help: multihulls offered such convenient hiding places underneath them. Big swim ladder on the main hull. Langdon could even clip onto one of the forward trampolines if he didn't want to soak in the water all that time, catching a chill.

He figured he would have to take some time under there, be sure the family was asleep before he crept in to wake them.

He frowned. He didn't really like the plan though. If even one of them got by him for a moment, they could raise such a ruckus. Besides, he wasn't into carnage for the sake of carnage.

"Why haven't you done it yet?" Ronnie said.

Ian saw movement and raised the binocs back up.

Well, well. The wife and kiddies were climbing into the dinghy. Vincent himself, was standing there, holding a drink. Waving them off.

They appeared to be heading into town for some dinner. Dressed up enough for a bit of dancing.

"Ian?" Ronnie said impatiently.

"Good things come to those who wait, sweets," he said.

So much for the wife and kiddies, all the gear, and the long wait for them to fall asleep.

Apparently, Vincent was going to be alone tonight.

Langdon rowed the boat smoothly, not attempting to appear as anything but another boater wending his way among the other moorings toward shore. The surface of the water was mirrored and soft, contrasting nicely with the tight, fierce feeling that Langdon had deep inside.

He always felt that way at this stage.

Langdon had run the dinghy around about twenty minutes ago under the outboard, so that the engine would be warm if he needed to take off quickly later. Even so, the little boat wouldn't be a rocket if he really needed to get away fast. But Langdon didn't really think that would be an issue.

"Lucky, lucky boy," Ronnie had said before they hung up. "You know it's always easier for the man. You're getting distinguished, I'm turning into a hag."

"I'll never grow tired of looking at you," Langdon said. A familiar exchange of words, but he still meant them. She still took his breath away, after all these years together.

As for himself, Ian Langdon knew he was no more than reasonably handsome. And even that was only on first impression, rather than in the details. In detail, his nose was a bit too large, his jaw long, eyes a pale blue. Skin burned now from the Virgin Island sun. Born in Connecticut, but he and Ronnie had been in the U.K. so long that London was home.

He knew how to project an image. He could be the mailman, the business executive, anything in between. Generally, he found a mild, unremarkable manner got him through the day most effectively.

He was an easy man to forget, when he wanted it that way.

Langdon bent to the oars, and took a brief look over his shoulder.

The trimaran was a fast-looking red thing. *Velocity*. Big gold *V* on the stern, same as the trademark for Vincent's Sporting Shops. Chain of more than a dozen throughout the U.K. Plenty big enough boat for Vincent, his wife, and two kids.

Of course, the kiddies weren't actually kiddies, anyhow. Young teens: a sullen-looking boy of about fourteen and a beautiful black-haired teenage girl about sixteen. The girl had made a friend of another pretty young thing touring around with her family on a big chartered Swan.

Even from his view from the various beaches and the distance of the moorings, Langdon had been able to read that the boy was totally enamored of his sister's new friend, a golden-haired little goddess who acted like she didn't know he was watching her every move.

Langdon had watched them get into one of those little buses with the fringe top, the two girls yammering while the boy tried to work his way into the conversation. Vincent's wife was along as chaperone.

Hours, Langdon thought. Hours and hours they should be gone.

Vincent's wife was a tall, stringy piece of leather. Once pretty, Langdon could tell. Vincent seemed to dote on her as if she were still a great beauty.

Ah, well.

Vincent himself was a going-to-stout bull. Langdon had watched him follow the family around yesterday. Black hair, cheerful face, indulgent. Flushed with his own success, it appeared. Very much the rugby star he had been years ago, even if his body had turned soft.

Langdon shipped his oars and drifted. He could wait. He was a patient man. But the trimaran seemed quiet. Vincent hadn't been on deck for almost an hour, and when he had, he had been sucking down a couple of drinks, probably to celebrate a night of peace and quiet with the wife and kiddies away.

Most likely napping below.

A hundred feet away from *Velocity*, Langdon took a moment to wrap a bit of cloth around each of the oars where they met the locks, to muffle the noise. He began rowing toward the trimaran again.

Langdon drifted up to the trimaran and dipped the oar blade so that the dinghy eased alongside the stern of *Velocity* . . . and then he stepped onto the stern swim ladder and quietly wrapped the painter around the rail. He was ready with a story about a frozen dinghy engine, if necessary, but there was no movement from Vincent in the boat. Langdon took the athletic bag from the floor of the dinghy and draped the strap casually over his shoulder.

He moved slowly forward on rubber-soled shoes. *Wouldn't do to scuff the deck*, he thought, amusing himself. *Always want to be known as a good guest.*

The trimaran cockpit was huge. Littered with vacation stuff: snorkeling gear, towels draped about the stanchion lines, bathing suits hanging up to dry. Still, under the clutter, it was easy to see the big money invested in the boat. The Harken winches and two big chrome wheels, the bank of weatherproof electronics. At least half a million U.S. dollars invested in the big red toy, maybe as much as double that.

Which was interesting because Langdon had Maddy back in the office do a little research on Vincent. The shops weren't doing that well lately. Growing pains. So Vincent *could* be in on it; he might be trying to raise cash.

Or it could be much simpler.

Either way, Langdon was certain he could get to the truth.

He stepped down into the main cabin, making no effort now to be quiet.

Vincent was on the settee, sleeping. He rolled over and said, "What?" He was wearing just a pair of shorts. His back and chest were covered with a mat of black hair.

"Caught you snoozing," Langdon said, cheerfully.

On the table, there was a cocktail glass full of melting ice cubes; Langdon could smell the scotch.

Vincent was confused. "What," he said again, a little anger and fear in his voice this time. He started to sit up. "Who the hell are you?"

Langdon moved quickly, shoving Vincent back. He took the gun out of the bag and put it in the man's face. It had to be frightening, especially with the long silencer on it.

Vincent reacted accordingly: his face blanched. "What's this?"

Langdon took a good look at him. "Ah, not keeping yourself in shape are you?" Langdon said. He gestured to Vincent's heavy chest, the sagging muscles in his thick arms. The big white belly. Langdon slapped his own stomach, hard as a washboard. "Diet and exercise. You should know that, you own sporting-goods stores, for God's sake."

"Who are you?" Vincent yelled. "Get out of here!"

"Certainly," Langdon said, lifting his gun to Vincent's face. "I've got a question for you first. Were you simply transport or are you in on it?"

Vincent looked genuinely confused. "What?"

Langdon repeated the question.

"What the bloody hell are you asking?" Vincent yelled. "If you want money, take my wallet and go."

Langdon casually reached over and yanked away Vincent's pillow. It made the big man flinch when Langdon reached over, but when he saw the pillow, he started to say, "What the—"

But then Langdon shot him in the right knee.

Naturally, Vincent wanted to scream over that, so Langdon put the pillow over the man's face so he could do just that. Unfortunately, Vincent began to make a bit of headway with his arms, beating at Langdon, and trying to lever himself up. Langdon reached over and fired first one shot, and then another, *psst, psst*. One for the right arm, one for the left.

Vincent screamed long, and he screamed loud, but the pillow was over his face, and by the time he was out breath, shock was surely on its way.

Langdon took the pillow off Vincent's face and said softly. "That's enough for now. I know you want to talk to me. Did you simply give him transport, or is there more to it than that?"

He saw the desperation in Vincent's eyes. "Who? Give who transport?" It took the fat man several attempts to get this out. His breath rushed in and out, and he struggled, trying to raise himself without the use of his arms.

Langdon put his hand on Vincent's chest and pushed him back down gently.

Langdon said, "You tell me. Blond fellow. American." Langdon reached into his coat pocket with his left hand and showed Vincent the photo. "Who is that?"

Vincent tried to rub the tears out of his eyes, but his arms couldn't move well enough. Langdon pulled out a handkerchief and quickly daubed the man's eyes. "Now look."

Vincent did, and then fell back. "The mate," he said. "Tom."

Langdon felt relieved. Up until that moment, he couldn't be sure that Vincent was the right one. "All right," he said, crisply. "Now we're getting somewhere. This man sailed away from Southampton on your boat about two weeks ago. My . . . associate . . . is *insane* that it's taken me so long to find this out, and she's complaining mightily. If only this Tom had the good grace to take an airplane he would've been easier to track, but, of course, he knew that."

Tears streamed down the side of Vincent's face. He was breathing in short gasps, sounding like one of those pregnant woman practicing for natural childbirth. He looked truly confused. As well he might,

Langdon thought, sympathetically. Sound asleep one minute, now this.

Langdon said, "What's Tom's full name?"

Vincent's eyes blinked rapidly.

"Come on," Langdon said, abruptly. "I'll get on the radio for an ambulance before I leave, so don't drag it out."

"Cain," Vincent said, gasping. "Bloody Christ. Tom Cain. I needed a crew, he signed up. That's all I know."

"You're sure?" Langdon watched him carefully. "Be honest now. You've got a wife and two kiddies and I can go to work on them any time."

Vincent's face screwed up, and Langdon saw real fear and grief. Vincent cried, "Oh, God. Oh, God."

"Look," Langdon said. "I know you're hurt, but think carefully and tell me the truth. You're telling me Cain picked you at random to sail away with? I think you were in it with him from the go."

"In with what? I don't know who you are. . . . Look, my partner was supposed to come . . . he couldn't. I needed a crew member. I put up a notice . . . Cain just showed up . . ."

"Ssssh." Langdon laid the gun barrel on Vincent's lips. "All right, I believe you."

And he did.

Langdon had butchered the captain who had brought Cain over from the U.S. Cut him, then burned him alive at the dock—right in his boat on the London docks. Captain Barrett. Tough old bastard who *was* involved; he was waiting to bring this Cain back to the U.S. with what he'd stolen.

What he had stolen from Langdon and his sister, Ronnie.

Langdon daubed at the sweat on Vincent's forehead with the handkerchief. "Now tell me where you let Cain off."

Vincent's voice was weak now. "Tortola."

"When?"

"Week ago . . . ten days."

"I see. And he went where?"

"Don't know."

Langdon aimed the gun between Vincent's eyes.

Vincent rallied himself: "Telling you the truth. He said he'd find another boat. That he was heading back home."

"Where in the U.S.?"

"Don't know."

Langdon saw that the man was trying, and so he simply waited.

Vincent said, "My daughter . . . he told her big tales about Boston and Harvard."

"Kept your eye on him, did you?" Langdon grinned. "Now what boat did he hook up with? Who's taking him back to Boston?"

"Don't know . . . he just got off at the dock . . . walked away."

Langdon stared at the fat man. His face was sheet white.

"You must believe me," Vincent said.

"Oh, I do," Langdon said, sighing. He stood straight. "I feel bad about all this." He gestured with his gun to the wounds, all the blood. "And I want to promise you that your wife and children are out of it—I don't have any questions for them."

"Thank you," the fat man said. More tears in his eyes, real gratitude.

Langdon was pleased he could at least give him that, under the circumstances.

Then the poor fool started making noises about Langdon calling the ambulance.

Langdon made a regretful face. "If I'd thought to bring a mask, maybe . . ."

Vincent said, "You said you would. You said . . ."

"Really, now," Langdon said, giving Vincent a friendly squeeze on the shoulder. "Just because I believed you, doesn't mean you should have believed *me*."

He moved the bloody pillow over Vincent's face, pressed the gun down, and pulled the trigger twice.

CHAPTER 11

MCKENNA'S WATCH WAS DRAWING TO A CLOSE AS THEY DRIFTED between Block Island and the Rhode Island coast. He knew that's where they were only because the GPS and chart said so—with the fog so thick he couldn't see farther than a boat-length away.

He was standing at the top of the companionway, sipping a cup of coffee, listening to the weather report. Fog, more fog, and then fog predicted.

A horn made its mourning sound somewhere in the distance. It was hard to tell from which direction in the deep blanket of cotton.

Limbo.

The sailor in McKenna was impatient. The boom swinging back and forth with the ocean swells; the sails providing zero speed.

The husband in him was impatient, too.

Even with the divorce in front of him, McKenna found he wanted to see Caroline. Talk with her. Wondered if she wanted the same of him. Ever since he had kept Cain from going overboard, McKenna had been mulling it over. How losing Caroline forever was what had motivated him to save Cain.

Maybe it doesn't have to end this way, he thought. The idea was fresh, appealing, and damned obvious, when he thought about it. But it hadn't been obvious before. Not until he made that choice with Cain.

It was time to say good-bye to Sam.

Tears welled in his eyes. He felt a traitor to his daughter. But he also knew he was right.

McKenna sighed, feeling at least the potential for peace. Maybe Caroline wouldn't agree. Maybe it was too late for her.

But McKenna abruptly decided that he would do his part. Send Cain and his diamonds away. Go to Caroline. McKenna wanted to be the man he had always been.

McKenna suddenly found himself on his back, the pain intense and momentarily paralyzing where he had landed on the thick fiberglass lip that protected the cabin from cockpit wash. The smell and heat of the coffee was all over him.

Cain had snatched both feet right out from under him.

Even as he struggled to roll over, Cain dragged him down. Dragged him down the stairs by his shirt and belt.

"C'mon up," Cain said, cheerfully.

And McKenna tried to do just that, to stand and fight. But Cain hit him on the head with something remarkably hard. Something McKenna recognized in a brief synapse as his wrench from the tool chest, the big rusty mother that was heavy and hard and had all the potential to crush his head like an eggshell.

That's all he knew for a time.

Small bits of consciousness came to him over the next several hours. McKenna found his perception was very selective and that he could form no judgements about what he was seeing.

Cain was standing above him in the cockpit. The cell phone in one hand, the portable GPS in the other. "I don't want to hear the details," he was saying. "Tell him to get out here fast and bring what I told you."

Later, McKenna woke to feel himself being moved roughly. Cain had him over his shoulder and was cursing as he shoved him through the small forward-cabin doorway. Cain flung him onto the small vee bunk.

"Your cabin," McKenna said, stupidly.

"Yours now," Cain said, holding McKenna up carefully and then hitting him with his balled fist.

Nothing after that for hours.

McKenna kept his head down the next time he awoke. He lay there and tried to assess how badly he was hurt. Keeping his breathing easy and steady, he quietly moved his hands, his legs and found he was tied up. He looked out through the open cabin door. Cain's duffel bag was packed and sitting on the galley counter. Cain was in the main cabin, opening first one hatch, then the other. He then went on to open the portholes.

Twice, McKenna saw him check his watch.

The radio crackled. "Tommy, come in."

Cain snatched up the radio mike. He held the GPS in his other hand, and simply read the coordinates. McKenna had sensed he was being discreet, knowing that anyone could be listening in. Cain said, "You should be able to see me on radar now. I'll do three blasts on the horn every two minutes. Forty-foot sloop."

He disappeared, and McKenna heard the horn sound three times.

McKenna swung his legs off the vee berth and sat up. He had a brief moment of double vision, and he felt sick to his stomach. Must have at least a mild concussion, he figured. He looked down at his belt. The little case was there, but Cain had apparently taken his knife. McKenna got down onto the cabin sole and crawled into the galley. It was hard to do, hands and feet bound like that. But he made it to the little silverware drawer and took one of the steak knives. He hauled himself back into the forward cabin bunk and was just pulling his legs up as Cain came back down the stairway.

McKenna's heart and head were pounding. He had to work to control his breathing so he could feign unconsciousness. The boat was spinning in his head as if he were drunk. Another wave of nausea swept over him.

Cain came into the cabin, and prodded McKenna in the chest. McKenna made a face, but nothing else. Cain prodded him again, and he took the opportunity to groan out loud and roll over so he was facing the hull wall.

Cain went back on deck.

McKenna could hear the low mutter of an approaching motorboat. He heard a voice, but he couldn't understand what was being said.

The *Wanderer* shuddered as the other boat came up alongside hard.

"Oops," Cain said, with a laugh. "Gleason, you scratched the man's paint."

Again there was a response, but it was too low for McKenna to decipher. He began to cut the rope between his legs. It sliced through easily. He sat up and put the knife handle between his knees and began to cut the rope between his wrists. The blade quickly slipped down, and he found the best thing to do was kneel, with the point of the knife digging into the cushion. He ran the rope up and down, the sweat just rolling off him.

There were footsteps overhead as Cain apparently tied the power-boat alongside the *Wanderer*. The boat rocked slightly as someone else stepped on board.

"What a frigging mess," the other guy said. He had a deep, wheezing voice.

"It'll work out," Cain said. "We clean up right here, and we'll be in good shape."

"Tell Barrett we're in good shape," the man snapped. "I done a lot of business with him."

"Yeah, he never made you rich."

"So he never made me dead before. You fucked him over, left him sitting at the dock."

"Oh, were you there? Didn't see you. Thought it was just me trying to get away from that nut."

"How come you couldn't keep it clean, just do the agreement?"

"What do you think? You forced your way in on this, and we were just going to eat your cut? We got *years* in on this."

McKenna kept working the knife against the rope, and abruptly, it parted.

Cain spoke again. "Gleason, look. We can talk about this later. Did you bring the sledgehammer?"

"Yeah, I got it," the man's voice said.

The two men came down the stairway into the main cabin. McKenna rolled back onto his side, facing away from them.

McKenna heard them moving closer.

"Who's this?" Gleason's wheezing voice filling the little cabin.

"The owner. Meet Rob McKenna, skipper of the *Wanderer*."

"Should've gotten rid of him a long time ago."

"What, and sail all the way here by myself? No, we're dumping him with the boat. We already hit a log on the way here; if anyone ever finds this barge and dives on her, they'll see the damaged prop, they'll see the hole we're going to put in the bow. They keep looking, they'll find a big piece of rotten meat in the cabin. But I don't figure anyone's going to find this thing, we've got almost a hundred feet below us. We get her down before this fog lifts, and I guarantee you there hasn't been any communication of this boat since the Coast Guard stopped us."

"Coast Guard?" the other man sounded worried.

"They got nothing. My passport stood up fine, and our boy here got greedy, thought he was going to get half the pie. Covered for me."

That brought a wheezing laugh from the other man. "Where you heard that before?"

"Yeah, you're laughing," Cain said. "C'mon, let's get off this scow. Hit him again, make sure he's out all the way. Then untie him while I take a couple of shots with the sledgehammer on his waterline. Make a hole about as big as a plate. Big as if we rammed a telephone pole."

"How about the rocks? Lemme see them."

"Don't worry about that. They're in my bag."

"I worry. Show me."

"Jesus," Cain said, his voice harsh with impatience.

But the two of them moved away, and after a moment, McKenna heard the water running in the sink. Cain said, "See. Here's a couple. The rest are in there, and let's leave them 'til we get to shore."

"Yeah, all right. I gotta get back, too. Before Jimmy starts looking for me."

McKenna heard the two of them move back behind him. Cain said, "Maybe it's not so bad you're in on this. I've never gone this far, you know? So you do him."

McKenna felt something heavy land against his leg and the cushion. It was all he could do not to recoil, certain it was the wrench, the one that had put him down in the first place.

Cain said, "Use this on him, make sure he's out. Just don't mess his head up so much it's obvious what killed him. He needs to be breathing when the boat goes down, so there's water in his lungs."

Gleason made his wheezing laugh again. "Glad you think I'm beginning to earn my keep. Everybody's gotta have a talent, and I got mine."

McKenna heard Cain walk away, climb up the stairs to the cockpit of the *Wanderer*.

Later, McKenna would wonder how he had known what to do.

When the man picked up the wrench, McKenna rolled over with the knife cocked back in his arm. The fat man grunted, surprised and tried to step back. But he stumbled, and then McKenna had him by the back of the collar.

He plunged the steak knife into Gleason's chest, and then his throat. Then back again into his chest, one, two, three times. Searching for the man's heart and making a mess of it. The man had time to scream; he had time to call out to Cain for help.

Blood splattered over McKenna.

But at last, he was done. The knife blade had broken off inside the fat man, somewhere in the area of his heart.

His gun dropped onto the cabin sole.

Gleason slid down the cabin wall, eyes wide open, a froth of blood dribbling down his chin.

McKenna felt, rather than saw, movement at the cockpit. It was Cain.

Cain looking in at him from the top of the stairwell.

Their eyes locked briefly, and then Cain jumped into the boat. He threw the sledgehammer underhand, and McKenna jumped back. The hammer splintered the door. McKenna fumbled for the knife, but, of course, it was just a handle. And Cain wasn't going for him anyhow. Instead, he grabbed the duffel bag out of the galley, spun around, and headed back up.

McKenna got it then.

Cain was simply going to run. Get onto the powerboat and take off with the diamonds. Leave McKenna with the mess.

McKenna picked up the gun and walked deliberately up the stairwell. He was still dizzy, but he knew what he was doing.

That was something he thought about later, too. That he couldn't even tell himself he didn't know his head, know his heart. Or that he mistook Cain for R. J.

Certainly he had thoughts like that.

The parallels were obvious, had been all along. Both of them, smug young punks, escaping responsibility. Doing their worst and expecting to just run away and leave others to deal with the consequences.

Cain was trying to start the boat, a center-console sportfishing boat, about eighteen-feet long. The outboard motor was chugging over fairly fast, but wasn't catching. Part of McKenna was so clear, so distant, that he realized Cain had snatched out the choke: something the outboard certainly didn't need as warmed up as it would've been after Gleason's search for them in the fog.

But Cain was desperate, and he was talking even as the motor cranked, "C'mon, Rob, we can work this out. We go back to the plan, fifty-fifty. We can work this out!" He tossed the duffel bag up into the cockpit of the *Wanderer*. "Take them. Take them all!"

McKenna raised the gun.

The young man was practically crying. McKenna saw R. J. for a second then, and it was satisfying to have that bastard in front of him. But it was Cain before him when McKenna pulled the trigger for the first time. It was Cain before him when McKenna kept on pulling the trigger until there were no more bullets.

McKenna knew who he was killing.

* * *

Seconds, maybe minutes, passed.

McKenna looked down at himself. He was covered in blood. Cain was dead; one of the rounds had gone in just under his right eye.

McKenna's knee's buckled and he fell back against the cabin roof. And then stood up quickly. He had left a bloody handprint on the white fiberglass. He could smell the blood. And he abruptly realized that whatever he couldn't clean up, he must throw away.

Throw away and explain to anyone who asked why it was no longer there.

Caroline.

He had to hide this from her. And everyone else.

Hide that he had lost forever the chance to be the man he had once been.

CHAPTER 12

A FOGHORN SOUNDED.

A different one this time. McKenna froze.

It sounded again. Closer.

A boat coming his way.

McKenna stood in the cockpit sucking down great gusts of the moist air. If they found him this way, with Cain's body out in the open, so be it.

Then the foghorn sounded again.

Much closer.

He looked through the deep mist, suddenly realizing changes to his moral code might be moot, that sitting there dead in the water without an engine, he and the *Wanderer* might be crushed under an oncoming freighter or fishing trawler.

The idea seemed vaguely amusing.

A ferry passed him by. The Block Island Ferry. That's what he assumed it was. He could barely see the shape of it. Less than a hundred feet away, a massive shape of darkness in all the white that passed him by. Immediately afterward, a steep little wall of water rolled under the *Wanderer*'s keel, making her bang hard against the powerboat.

McKenna rubbed his face and felt the stickiness.

He looked down at himself and gave a short, scared laugh. Thank God for the fog. If he could barely see the ferry, they could barely see him. Barely see the two boats tied together in the middle of the fog, a man on the deck saturated with the blood of two men.

Got lucky.

Second time he'd thought that today.

McKenna put on gloves and hoisted Gleason over to the powerboat.

The gloves gave McKenna some comfort. He could tell himself he was protecting himself from leaving fingerprints.

But, in truth, not having to touch the dead man directly was the real benefit. Because lugging the big man was horrible. Everything about it: hauling his bulk, his smells, his fat up the stairwell, across the cockpit, and dumping him down into the powerboat.

McKenna climbed down to the cockpit of the powerboat and tried to make himself think about what to do. For reference, he had only movies, novels, and his imagination.

He knew the police had incredible means of detection. Hair, fibers, DNA. With the mess below decks on the *Wanderer*, he couldn't imagine being able to get past that. Unless they never found the bodies at all. They must never connect with him, period. Never have his name come up with them.

Okay.

So the bodies had to go. First, McKenna went through Cain's pockets and found a wallet. He stuffed it in his own, to go through later.

He found the anchor for the powerboat in the bow and came back, gently lowered the anchor onto Cain's chest, and swung the chain tightly around his neck, his arms, and then his legs. Doing this made Cain's body move, giving it a strange animation. McKenna checked for Cain's pulse twice before awkwardly tying off the chain.

Doing all this, McKenna tried to keep from looking into Cain's face.

When he was done, he hauled Cain up to the cockpit rail and held him poised there. Thinking maybe he could still back out, knowing that he couldn't. Wishing that he had let Cain go over the side the time before. None of this would have happened if he had.

Better still, if he'd let the Coast Guard haul Cain away.

Done the right thing, that is.

McKenna shoved Cain overboard.

McKenna looked through the fat man's wallet. Theodore Gleason. Friends probably called him Ted or Teddy. Address in Revere, Massachusetts. McKenna went through the boat. It was a piece of junk, little more than a big lake boat. A single-layer fiberglass hull. Internal flotation from two cross-hull benches, held in place with flimsy looking brackets. Still, the boat had a huge Johnson outboard, plus a ten-horse auxiliary, a fairly new fish finder, GPS, even radar. Gleason either took his fishing seriously, or the boat was used for jaunts like this fairly often.

Underneath the console, McKenna found a registration for a boat trailer. So most likely Cain had called him in Massachusetts, and Gleason had towed his boat down to Rhode Island to come out and meet them in the fog. Newport or Point Jude.

McKenna braced himself in the rear well, then hauled the ten-horse auxiliary outboard off the stern bracket. He stood over Gleason, breathing harshly, and then abruptly knelt down and wrapped a line tightly around his chest and back. McKenna snugged the line up right under the big man's arms, and then tied the other end to the ten-horse.

He tossed the outboard over the side and let its weight against the line help him lift and shove Gleason overboard. The outboard took the fat man down, a white shape that McKenna could see drifting down into the darkness below.

McKenna was overcome by a terrible shivering as the body disappeared. He looked at the powerboat, covered with the blood of the two men.

McKenna found the sledgehammer and smashed the brackets of the two flotation tanks, freeing them. He put them on the deck of the *Wanderer*. He then bashed a hole in the floor of the powerboat, near the big outboard. It wasn't easy, the first few blows of the hammer bounced off the hard fiberglass. But he kept at it, and before long water began to gush into the open wound.

McKenna hurriedly jumped over to the *Wanderer* and put the swim ladder down. He got back into the powerboat, found a mop handle so he could jam the wheel straight, and then he cracked the throttle just slightly.

He shoved the choke in and turned the ignition key.

The engine growled, and he immediately jumped overboard. The powerboat wallowed forward, already heavy with water.

McKenna swam fast for the *Wanderer*.

And she took off.

The sails filled with a faint breeze; the wake began to bubble.

McKenna cried out, the stupidity of it all. The wind had been flat for hours, and in his haste, he hadn't even considered that the sails were still up, Mortimer still engaged.

He swam with all his strength.

Still she teased him. Her sails filled once again, but he kept after her, and finally the wind died.

He climbed on board, knelt in the cockpit, so exhausted he couldn't even stand. He stayed that way for several minutes, trembling, taking in huge gasping breaths.

Finally, he got to his feet.

A patch of blue sky peaked out seemingly not too far from the masthead. McKenna looked back and the fog was clearing so fast, he could still see the powerboat. Apparently, his jury rigged autopilot of a mop had come free and the boat had circled around. Her stern was completely down now, the outboard pulling her down farther.

McKenna watched until she slipped below the surface entirely.

His teeth began to chatter, and he clung to the wheel of his own boat, his own past, and tried not to think about what he had just done.

CHAPTER 13

IT WAS A WEEKDAY. TUESDAY, MCKENNA WAS FAIRLY SURE. THERE WERE only a few pleasure boats out, and the fishermen on the two trawlers McKenna could see were almost certainly too busy to take a close look at the cleaning habits of a yachtsman.

At least that's what McKenna hoped. He had already smashed open the fiberglass flotation tanks, ripped out the styrofoam, and sunk the shells over the side. After getting a few miles away from where the powerboat had sunk, he threw the pink styrofoam chunks overboard as well. They floated on the surface, a common enough sight in those waters.

As the sun began to burn off the fog, he took the bucket with the line attached from a cockpit locker, dropped it over the side, and hauled up his first pail of cleansing water.

And then he went to work.

He dumped bucket after bucket onto the bloodstains down below, and listened as the bilge pump began to spew water out the side. He scrubbed with soap and a hard brush, and then came back into the cockpit to do the same. He washed down the entire deck. After the first wave of cleaning was finished, he stripped off his blood stained clothes, wrapped them in the dinghy anchor, and threw it all overboard.

Dressed in a clean pair of shorts and a tee shirt, he felt more normal. Even though he was still logy from the blow on the head, he didn't feel as confused as before. He went about rinsing the boat below with fresh water, and then came up on the deck, which was largely dry now, and went about polishing all the handrails and rubbing down the mast, and any other surface where Cain may have left fingerprints. McKenna had been "turning to" on boats all his life, and he found relief in the mindlessness of the tasks. After putting in an hour and a half on the deck, he took out the wood polish, and went back below. After an hour of steady work, the wood gleamed in a way it hadn't for months. He washed and scrubbed the bilges with soap and fresh water, and then ran the pump with the clean water until he felt sure the coppery smell of blood was finally out of the close cabin.

Then he went back on deck and leaned over the rail and washed the sides of the boat as best he could, struck by an image that the bloody water flowing out of the scuppers and through the bilge pump may have stained the *Wanderer* for anyone to see at a mere glance.

McKenna removed the drain plates and washed them on both sides, then he plunged a soap covered wad of cloth down each drain valve as far as he could reach—and he still knew that wasn't enough if he were ever truly investigated.

McKenna found himself considering sinking the *Wanderer*. Maybe rigging an explosion.

It made him feel crazy, and he thought maybe the concussion was still affecting him.

And it made him taste just how different he had become.

Thinking of destroying the boat he loved.

What next?

McKenna came across Cain's duffel bag. Immediately, he began looking for something to weigh it down, anxious to get it off his boat. He decided upon the big wrench and just as he was slipping it into the bag, he saw Cain's passport—and the soap bottle.

McKenna gave a short little laugh.

Just an exhalation, as much a gasp as anything.

He'd almost thrown the diamonds overboard.

He swallowed carefully. Maybe he still should. He certainly hadn't killed Cain and Gleason for the diamonds. Hadn't done any of what he'd done in the past few hours for the money.

McKenna sorted through his limited supply of pots and pans until he found the colander. He opened the bottle and squirted about half the soap into the colander, and then ran cold water over the milky goop. Moments later, he was looking at a dazzling yield of precious stones, spinning and glittering under the rush of the water.

Rich, he thought. *I'm rich.*

He gave the short little laugh again. Laughing alone in the cabin. *I'm a rich killer.*

What a difference a day makes.

Around two, McKenna made himself a pot of coffee and opened a can of soup. He ate a package of crackers waiting for the soup to get hot, and then sat down with the small pot in front of him at the nav station and drank it down. He was ravenous. Some of the shaking in his hands subsided when he was full, and even after a couple of cups of hot coffee, he felt sleepy and drained.

He went back on deck and saw the fog had entirely burned off. As far as he could remember from the conversation he overheard between Cain and Gleason, Cain well may have been running from someone, but it seemed as if he'd been successful at getting away. So McKenna couldn't see how anyone would find his way to him.

McKenna closed his eyes, feeling the sun. Maybe he was all right. He was so exhausted at the moment, he felt like he could fall asleep right there on deck. In the sunshine.

He told himself he was safe.

CHAPTER 14

LANGDON DAWDLED AT THE BACK OF THE STORE UNTIL THE ONLY OTHER customer left, and the young woman was alone.

This was one of the few grocery stores on Tortola within walking distance of the main docks and marina. The store carried just about everything: basic foodstuffs with an emphasis on the nonperishable. Canned goods, freeze-dried vegetables. Rows and rows of marine parts: lines, chain, cleats, turnbuckles, fishing gear, outboard motors, charts, a wall of electronics equipment.

The girl—early twenties or younger—had a young child behind the counter. About two years old, maybe a little more. Whining, of course.

Langdon had good eyes, a requirement of the job. And he picked up that the girl wore no wedding ring. She was friendly with the last customer, but seemed tired. When she stepped around the counter to rearrange a display, he saw that her figure was good, not great. Little leather anklet, boat shoes, khaki shorts, and well-washed blue shirt. Honey blond hair in a single loose braid. Face looking rather pale behind her tan.

"Help you?" she called to him.

Langdon took her for an exhausted single parent and planned accordingly. He strolled up to the counter and picked up a copy of the local newspaper. "Good God," he said. On the cover was a picture of Vincent's crying wife and children, highlighted in the harsh white of a flash. Behind them, two grim-faced black men carried a stretcher laden with a body bag.

"Awful, isn't it?" The girl stood beside him, looking at the paper.

She was an American.

He sighed. "People come here on vacation to get away from this sort of thing."

"Tell me about it," the girl said, and rolled her eyes. "I'm from New York."

He smiled. "Well, awful as this is, you've still picked a better place to raise your child."

"Hmmn," she said. But he saw her looking at his hand quickly, also noticing the lack of ring, perhaps. She glanced at him appraisingly, and he smiled in a fatherly way. Better for what he was after.

"Well . . ." she said. "How can I help you?"

He put the picture of Cain on the counter. "I'm a private detective."

She looked at him in surprise. "You're kidding?"

"Not at all." He took out an I.D. that identified him as Stephen Cross, private detective. He'd chosen to locate Cross in Boston simply because Cain had bragged to Vincent's daughter about his supposed Harvard days. Langdon had his secretary, Madeline, ship the I.D. to him airborne. In truth, Stephen Cross was a child who had died six years ago of entirely natural causes. Little Stephen had a social security number, so Ronnie and Ian kept him alive in both a fictitious and financial sense.

Langdon said, "I told a young lady I'd look for her husband. Ex-husband. Deadbeat dad."

"Oh, I'm familiar with the term," the young woman said. She stepped behind the counter and leaned over the photo. Immediately, she gave a bitter little laugh.

"What?"

"Oh, yeah. This must be your guy."

Langdon felt a quick stir of excitement. "Why's that?"

" 'Cause I thought he was cute." She bent down, kissed her son's blond head, and said in that kind of lisp parents use when playing with their children, "I'm attracted to rascals. Right, honey?"

Attwacted. Wascals. Wight.

Langdon kept an indulgent smile on his face. It wasn't too hard, really. The girl was cute, so was the kid.

"That would sound like our friend," Langdon said. "I understand he's a charmer."

"Aren't they all," the girl sighed. She looked at the photo. "But he's not dangerous, is he?"

"Only if you're married to him," Langdon said. Then he threw in, just for salt, ". . . he's known to use his hands if he doesn't get his way."

"Prick," she said. "But that shouldn't be a problem, the boat he's going over on."

"Really? And why's that?"

She made a face and didn't answer.

That made him want to grab her and force things along a little, but he knew better. She was working at it.

"I can't remember their names. Captain is a nice guy, early forties. Quiet. Wife's a doll. Though I figured they were having some problems, that they weren't getting along. That's why she put up the little notice, looking for a crew. Yeah, she flew back to the States herself."

"Now who would this be?"

The girl closed her eyes, thought, and then shrugged her shoulders. "Sorry."

"You said there was a piece of paper? A notice?"

"Right." The girl walked around the counter and led him over to a bulletin board that was near the men's room. It was covered with fliers and little postcards. Dinghies for sale, used outboards, lots of windsurfers. Offers from people wanting to crew and boats offering crew positions. She looked over these carefully, and then shook her head. "It's not here. These are newer, anyhow. That boat's been gone a few weeks by now."

She turned to him and raised her palms up. "Wish I could help."

Just then, another customer came in. A young black man looking for a jam cleat for his sailboat. Langdon drifted away while she helped him. He made a point of keeping his back to the black man. No sense creating a witness in case it became necessary to get ugly in a few minutes.

He hoped it wouldn't come to that. He rather liked the young mother and her little boy and it would be a shame to have to hurt them. Besides, he had an idea when he saw the black man charge his purchase to his account. The girl wrote out a receipt.

After the black man left, Langdon came back to the counter. "It looks like you keep names and boats." Langdon pointed to the metal receipt box. "Perhaps you'll remember them if you see their name."

She made a face. "I don't know. I'd have to check with the owner about giving away names like that . . ."

Oh, you don't want to do that, he thought.

Langdon considered offering her cash. He certainly didn't mind the expense, but already she was looking a bit wary. She held herself well. The type to be offended by a direct bribe. Probably came from some money herself. But he had the feeling she was on her own. Maybe things weren't so good with mommy and daddy since the little bastard was born.

Langdon said, "I understand your concern. It's just that I promised this young lady. You see, it was easy for me to find him when he was in the U.S. Just a few calls, some clever work with the CDs, and I found him. But once he started traveling the world on boats, it's gotten a bit more difficult, but not impossible. She has one about your son's age and . . ."

"I'd *like* to help," the girl said. She tousled her son's hair. "I appreciate what you're doing. . . . I wish someone would do the same for me. If Billy had come through with *any* of what he should. . . ."

She shook her head, abruptly.

"Full of excuses, is he?"

"I'm sure. Wherever he is."

"Maybe he's sailing away with this guy," Langdon held up Cain's picture.

"In spirit, you bet. No, he's back wherever his parents have stashed him. They say they haven't seen him in years, that he just took off.

More likely they've got him working for one of their subsidiaries someplace, but I can't find him."

Langdon raised his eyebrows. "Want me to make some calls when I get to the States? If he's in the country, and if his parents are well-off and visible, I can virtually guarantee I can find my way to him. From there, it's up to your lawyer."

The girl looked at Langdon, thoughtfully. "You'd do that?"

"For a small fee, after you've made your settlement. But I do need to take care of my current client."

"Huh." The girl said, "Watch my little rascal, will you?"

She left him alone with the boy. Langdon reached over and stroked the kid's head. Blond hair as soft as a puppy's. The kid looked at him solemnly and then gave him a shy smile. Langdon smiled back but resisted the urge to turn his *r*'s into *w*'s.

Kids and dogs.

Langdon had noticed that in the movies they were supposed to have a sixth sense about who was good and who was the monster.

In his experience, they were as clueless as everyone else.

The girl came back with a box of receipts and went through the past month's stack. She slowed down about three weeks in, and then said, "Okay, yeah. That's it."

She turned three receipts over so he could read them. "The *Wanderer*. That's the boat. Rob and Caroline McKenna. Then here's the receipt where the guy you're looking for came in and signed his name to the *Wanderer*'s account. I told him that I'd let him take the stuff down, but that Mr. McKenna had to come in and settle the bill himself."

Langdon looked closely at the signature.

Tom Cain.

Langdon said, "The McKennas . . . do you know where they're from?"

"Let's see. They arrived almost a month before this . . ." The girl worked her way farther back, and said, "Here we go. Their first receipt. No home address, but we hardly ever get that. The boat is probably their home."

Langdon sighed. Still, he had names. Rob and Caroline McKenna. And he knew Cain had talked with Vincent's daughter about Boston.

The girl pointed to a small notation at the top of the first receipt. "The *Wanderer* is registered out of Boston. If it was Delaware, they could've been from anywhere—you know, for taxes."

Langdon didn't know, but he nodded as if he did.

"But Boston," she said, "Boston means most likely they live somewhere around there."

"That would make sense," Langdon said. "That's where my boy went to school, where he met my client. You've given me a very good lead." He smiled his fatherly smile.

"Glad to help."

"Now give me the vital stats on your young man," he said. Better to leave her happily working in collusion with him rather than wondering later if she'd given too much to a smooth talker.

He took the guy's name, description, parent's address, and the sad facts of her circumstances. Her "good family" looks were a bit of a sham. . . . she was actually a working-class girl from Newark who made it to Yale on scholarship, and then blew it all her junior year when she met and fell in love with one Billy DePriest.

Young Billy's family owned several plastic-extrusion factories, and he convinced her of the romance of chucking it all and sailing the world on his father's yacht before getting married. They stepped aboard in New York, and for a few weeks, it was pretty much as wonderful has he had promised. She was troubled when he admitted while drunk that he was on the verge of being kicked out of school for plagiarism. Three months later they landed in Tortola. She told him that not only had she missed her period, but she was feeling sick. The day after that, he stepped onto the dock and out of her life while she was in the head throwing up. A professional crew picked the boat up a week later while she was out looking for work. They left her few possessions in a new sail bag on the dock.

"I don't know what young men are thinking these days," Langdon said, shaking his head.

"C'mon, you're not that old," she said, meeting his eyes.

My, you do have an unhealthy taste in men, he thought. He said,

"I'll call you from the States as soon as I know something." Langdon squeezed her hand. For a moment, he considered her wish, and considered actually doing something about it. Chase the young man down and kick him around a bit. Break him, scare him down to his very marrow. Convince young Billy that if he didn't keep sending checks, Langdon would come back. Langdon had done things like this before: acts of goodwill simply to enjoy the power to give as well as take.

The girl—Laura, her name was—said somewhat awkwardly, "Thank you. I can tell you're the type of man who honors his commitments."

"I am at that," he said, dipping his head in farewell. As he stepped out into the hot sunlight, he looked down at his folded newspaper, at the crying wife of the late Vincent.

Langdon thought about his commitment to Ronnie, and he chuckled to himself. First things first. For now, he had to repay Tom Cain for what he'd done to Ronnie. Tom Cain, last seen with Rob McKenna, of the *Wanderer*, Boston.

Acts of goodwill would have to wait until later.

CHAPTER 15

"So do I snore?" Mariel asked. "Leave my stockings around? Steal your boyfriends? Tell me, I'll be a better roommate."

Caroline drew back the curtains. "Look—the spire."

Mariel said, "If you like churches, I suppose that's a selling point."

The two of them looked out as the late afternoon light bathed the Unitarian church and the Market Square skyline in gold. They were on the third floor of an old federal off State Street in Newburyport. The ceiling was low but the floors were beautifully finished wide planks, the walls freshly painted.

Mariel said, "Honestly, I don't see why you're moving this fast. Why don't you wait until he gets here?"

"You've saved my life," Caroline said. "Took me in, found me a job. But you and Elliot need your privacy."

"I made some introductions," Mariel said. "You got the job. And as for me and Elliot, we'll close the bedroom door if that's what's bothering you."

Caroline laughed. "You do that, there'll be nothing to keep me."

Caroline had just taken over managing a small women's clothing store downtown while one of Mariel's former clients took off to live with her new husband down in Philadelphia. Mariel's network of successful divorced woman was significant, yet a club Caroline wasn't at all sure she wanted to join.

Caroline was operating on feelings a lot lately. And, on one level, this place felt right. The owner, Sophia Benchley, was talking about selling the place but was willing to rent out the top floor on a monthly basis.

"Well, if you do take this place, hold out for a price," Mariel said. "I made her a fortune when her husband left her for some chickie. She can afford to be easy on you."

Caroline looked out the window again. Sophia was pruning her rose bushes. She was forty-nine, divorced for five years now. Still aerobic-class thin, her black-and-gray hair stylishly cut.

"You think she can hold on a decision for a while? I should wait . . . talk with Rob."

Caroline felt a bittersweet dismay seep into her, saying those last three words. Words that she'd said so many times over the past seventeen years.

The words of a married woman, a woman with a partner. Why hadn't she heard from him yet? He was at least several days past what she would've expected—she consciously avoided the word "overdue." She was an experienced enough sailor herself to know how easily a few extra days could creep into a voyage.

And yet, there had been some nasty weather along the coast of New York. The tension was rising in her. *What if I've already seen the last of him?*

Then there was another kind of tension altogether. One that made her feel weak, and furious, and out of touch with herself. What if he had put into Boston or someplace else and just hadn't bothered to call? What if he was simply resuming his life without her?

She ran her finger along the windowpane. It was spotless. The whole house was like that, polished and cleaned with obsessive perfection. She looked at Sophia down there, clipping at those hedges. In no hurry. Maybe doing what she loved. But maybe just keeping herself busy before sitting down alone to dinner.

Caroline had given Sophia her maiden name, Caroline Parker, when they met downstairs.

God, Caroline wished she could talk with Rob about this.

About them.

"What are you going to do?" Mariel asked.

"I'm sick of waiting," Caroline said.

"What is it you *want* to do?"

Caroline considered. "Run back into my husband's arms and forgive each other unconditionally. Leave him, so I won't be reminded of Sam every moment I'm with him."

"And since you can't do both?"

Caroline breathed deep. "Wait. Wait until I can talk with Rob and see if we have a chance together again."

Mariel said, gently. "And if that's not what he wants?"

Caroline felt like crying, but she didn't. She gestured to Sophia down below. "Plant my own roses, I guess."

CHAPTER 16

McKENNA SAILED INTO BOSTON HARBOR. HE CALLED THE MARINA AT Rowe's Wharf for assistance, saying his engine was dead.

My crewmate, too, he thought.

Two days had passed since he had dumped the bodies. He had avoided the Cape Cod Canal and taken the long way around, tacking past Martha's Vineyard and continuing on around Chatham, then past Provincetown. In all his years of sailing the New England coast, he had never taken that outside route.

But he didn't want to place himself on any records anywhere near the sunken boat, and hiring a tow through the canal would have done that.

So now it was almost four weeks since he had set sail from Tortola. Hardly a speed record for the trip.

But it takes time to kill a couple of guys and raise a fortune.

That's the way he found himself thinking. Black humor emerging about it all. Going past the Vineyard, he thought about the philandering president who vacationed there; he apparently never told the truth if a lie seemed like a better idea. McKenna thought of the young senator, the drowning woman. How these two men not only moved on, but thrived for years in the public eye. How they apparently told themselves something each night before they slept. Something that made it all right.

When McKenna closed his eyes, even for a moment, he would be back there plunging that knife into the fat man, feeling the blade break off . . . and yet . . . and yet other than that, Mrs. Lincoln . . . McKenna felt he was the same person as ever. He was still Rob McKenna. Not a perfect man, certainly. Always too controlling, perhaps too rigid about what he saw as right and wrong. Cold-molded by his Uncle Sean to never be the kind of man Rob's father had been.

McKenna had always tried to be fair. Responsible. Honest.

Not violent. Not greedy. Certainly not the type to kill a man for money.

Yet, while that's not exactly what happened, it had turned out much the same way. They were dead. He had the diamonds.

And the voyage was over.

The dockboy came out on a small gray workboat to tow the *Wanderer* in. McKenna tossed him a bowline and the boy looped the rope around the T-shaped post. The kid was probably about seventeen, short dark hair, eyes eager for the boat. He said, "Where you in from, Skipper?"

McKenna told him Tortola.

The kid looked back at the *Wanderer*, taking in the heavy-weather sails; the self-steering vane. "By yourself?"

McKenna hesitated just slightly. "No. My mate's asleep."

"That's going to be a surprise for him," the kids said. "Wake up, and the trip is over. Man, I'd like to take a voyage like that some day."

Minutes later, they eased the *Wanderer* into a slip, and McKenna stepped off the boat. His bare feet felt soft and uncertain, back in the real world. McKenna tied up the boat and walked up the pier.

The kid said, "I'm off this shift now. You need anything before I go?"

"Thanks, no." McKenna realized he didn't have any cash on him to give a tip. But the kid didn't seem to mind.

McKenna walked up the ramp until he was on solid land. He walked along the waterfront toward the aquarium.

A few minutes later, when he saw the kid get into an old van and take off, McKenna figured he had caught his first break. Now there should be no one at the marina to ever notice that his sleeping mate never awoke.

The city smells assaulted McKenna as he sat in the aquarium plaza. There was a street vendor nearby and from his cart drifted the scent of popcorn, hotdogs, sausages, and coffee. Under that, the pervasive smell of car exhaust. And then there was the noise. Cars: engines muttering, brakes squealing, the honking horns. The seagulls swooping and diving. And people talking, yelling to each other. God, so many people. People walking, driving, slipping by on skateboards. Music from open car windows. Things for sale, signs, billboards.

He had felt this sense other first days in port—this assault on the senses, this cultural déjà vu.

But those feelings were pale compared to what he felt now.

It was him.

He was the one who was different.

He kept looking at each of them passing, wondering if any of them would stop. Whether the college girl in the loose shorts and Hard Rock Café tee shirt would see it in him. Whether the little kid pushing his own carriage would stop and stare. Whether the derelict on the bench would realize that there was a killer standing in front of him.

McKenna stood watching the people go by for perhaps fifteen minutes. Not really knowing what else to do.

Abruptly, McKenna turned on his heel, walked down the dock, then he got back in his boat and quickly packed his duffel bag. Clothes, toiletries, shoes . . . and, watching himself the entire time, he threw the soap bottle into his bag.

Then he went out into the world.

* * *

He stopped at the Boston Harbor Hotel and went in the lobby. More people. Bustling, clean. He could smell himself, feel the salt on his skin. In the mirror behind the registration desk, he caught sight of the beard, the sunburn.

For a moment, he thought he saw blood on his shirt. But it was just rust. A bit of rust on his white short-sleeved shirt.

"Can I help you, sir?" The clerk looked a bit nervous.

McKenna said yes. That he was back from a long sailing trip, and wanted a room for the night. Amazingly, his voice sounded the same as ever. Calm, friendly.

Whatever, the clerk's face relaxed, and he went through the rates. McKenna didn't let anything show on his face, and indeed, didn't feel much when the clerk said it would be four hundred dollars for the night.

It wasn't that McKenna was feeling rich. Simply that he had gone through a lot, and if any of this made him feel better, he wanted it.

The bellhop carried McKenna's bag to the elevator, chattering the whole way. He'd overheard McKenna's conversation with the clerk and said he wanted to do what McKenna had done, sail the world.

Every boy's dream, McKenna thought.

This time he was ready with the tip.

When McKenna awoke, hours had passed. He looked out the big window at the harbor. He could just see the mast of the *Wanderer*.

He hated the boat suddenly. Hated what she represented.

After unpacking his bag, he took the toilet kit into the bathroom and took a hot shower. He soaped and scrubbed, let the water blast off him. He shaved carefully, taking the beard off. After wiping away the steamed mirror, he observed himself carefully.

He hadn't seen himself without a beard in a couple of years. His face looked younger than he had remembered. His cheeks were sunburned, but the skin underneath was sallow. It would have been comic, but his eyes made him look too tired and wary for that. He looked down at himself. He had lost a good deal of weight on the voyage, maybe ten pounds or more. The stress of living with a man you thought might kill you, he assumed. *Ought to write it up and make another fortune*, he thought.

McKenna went back into the bedroom and tossed his kit into the duffel bag. He pulled on a pair of jeans and a shirt. Everything smelled of salt.

He saw the bottle of soap, and, feeling guilty, took it out. Felt the weight of it in his hand. Wanting suddenly to see those stones, to wash them clean like he had on the boat, make them sparkle. See if that gave him at least a reason for why he was feeling the way he was.

But he didn't. He put the bottle down on the dresser and turned to face the telephone.

He should call Caroline.

She told him to start with Mariel. Back before she had left him alone on the boat, she said she would go to Mariel first.

McKenna didn't want to see Caroline there. He loved Mariel, she was one of his best friends, too. He didn't want to find out she was Caroline's lawyer, that together they were against him.

More to the point, he was frightened as to what Caroline could see in him. Other than his momentary flirtation with Melanie Walsh, McKenna had never cheated on Caroline. But he could imagine it would feel like this if he had. Unsure that he could meet her eyes.

McKenna sat down, hesitated, then picked up the phone and called information for the local customs service office. He took a deep breath, and punched in the numbers. A few minutes later he was talking to a customs officer, and he said cheerfully that he was just checking in, that he and his mate had arrived from Tortola.

The woman on the phone was pleasant, asked him for the name of his boat, and their passport numbers. McKenna read them both off quickly. He figured he would shred Cain's passport before leaving the room the next morning. "Good voyage?" the woman asked.

"Wonderful," he said.

"Welcome back."

He thanked her.

And that was that.

* * *

McKenna took Mariel's phone number from his wallet, and punched in the numbers.

"Mariel's house," Caroline said.

"It's me," he said.

He heard the sharp intake of her breath.

Then a short laugh, and he was fairly sure he heard a catch in her voice when she said, "Welcome back, sailor."

He felt a sting in his eyes. The urge to simply tell her what had happened was suddenly so real as to be almost overpowering.

Instead, he ended up giving a longer and more detailed lie than he gave the customs service officer. About an easy sail with a young man named Tom Cain, who took off as soon as they reached Boston.

"Why'd you take so long?"

He told her about the prop.

"Rob! Why didn't you get that fixed? You went all that way without an engine?"

"That's right."

"Why? That doesn't make sense."

"It's been done before, Caroline," he said, sharply.

He couldn't stop himself. He couldn't stand reiterating the lie, and it certainly wasn't fair to embroil her in the real mess.

Fair or safe.

Oh, the voyage was great, except I stole some diamonds and killed two men. And, oh yes, I dumped their bodies. Sank one with an anchor and lashed the other to an outboard motor. So what have you and Mariel been doing?

Her voice immediately cooled.

"Well," she said. "Let's get together. Where are you now? Mariel's waving at me telling me I can take her car."

"Not tonight," McKenna said.

"What?"

McKenna was rubbing his forehead. Pressing strongly between his thumb and forefingers. Wanting her, but thinking that if it was hard on the telephone, what would it be like trying to meet her eyes? And God, he was just so tired now, the whole thing.

"Tomorrow," he said. "Maybe breakfast. I'm just beat right now."

"I've seen you tired before."

"No," he said. "Tomorrow."

There was silence.

Then she said, simply. "Fine. Where are you?"

He told her the name of the hotel, and again felt the reproach of her silence. In their years together, they had only stayed in such an expensive hotel as a romantic getaway for the two of them. He could imagine her seeing this as minor slap; a sign that he was on his own now and willing to burn through their remaining cash.

"Don't worry about the money," he said.

"Oh? You know something I don't?"

She said it lightly, but it fell flat.

He shook his head, sitting alone there in his hotel room. Wanting her, wanting to tell her . . . but not seeing how it was possible. "Tomorrow," he said. "Meet me here?"

"I'd better," she said. "Otherwise, I expect your limo driver would just blow the horn, wake all Mariel's neighbors."

He laughed, and, constrained as it was, it still felt good.

"I missed you," he said.

"Me, too, Rob."

He waited until she hung up, and then put the receiver down gently.

CHAPTER 17

As he took his seat in the small turboprop in San Juan for the connecting flight to Boston, Langdon recognized someone.

It gave him a jolt. Hispanic kid, probably about twenty-five years old, but looked younger. Walking down the narrow little aisle with his bag. Dressed neatly, making like a pre-med student rather than the punk Langdon knew him to be.

The kid looked at Langdon curiously, and then his face blanched under his coffee-colored skin.

That made Langdon feel a bit better. Langdon had a good memory for faces and remembered him from a few years back when he met with Jimmy Dobyns. Remembered him, because it had been frankly amazing to see a Hispanic kid working for a Boston-Irish hood like Jimmy Dobyns.

Now, Langdon sighed. So much for a quiet entrance into Boston.

After the plane took off, Langdon stood up and stretched. He looked directly at the kid.

The kid was already on a cell phone; pilot hadn't even announced they could use them yet. Langdon walked back to the kid and saw him shrink into his seat, apparently afraid Langdon was going to hurt him ten thousand feet up.

Langdon smiled. Sometimes it was good to have a reputation that preceded you. Langdon swung into the empty seat beside the kid. "What's your name again?" Langdon said.

The kid tried to tough it out. "What the hell do you want?"

Langdon repeated his question. Finally, the boy said, "Luis."

The boy flinched as Langdon tapped the cell phone with his forefinger, and said, "Well, Luis, you tell Jimmy I'd like to see him."

A punk was waiting for Langdon and Luis as they walked out of the terminal at Logan Airport in Boston. The punk was big, had a blond buzz cut, a stocky frame, and shiny pink face. He wore a green Celtics jacket.

Langdon thought he looked like a six-foot walking thumb.

"Grab my bag, will you?" Langdon said to Luis.

"Limey bastard can get his own bag," the Thumb said.

"It's okay, Buddy." Luis took Langdon's bag.

Buddy looked disdainfully at the kid, and said, "Car's over here," and turned on his heel.

Langdon smiled as he saw the black Cadillac.

"Just the car I expected," Langdon said. He got in the front seat and let the boy sit in the back.

Buddy gave him a look of undistilled dislike, but said nothing. He drove the car through the airport fast, and got onto the Southeast Expressway. He took the exit for South Boston.

Langdon kept silent. Dobyns's people weren't always as enlightened as he was. Langdon considered giving them a few minutes of conversation. Let him hear his neutral accent from his childhood in Connecticut. Let him know that London was his workplace, not his original home.

But, then, why bother?

It was Jimmy Dobyns who mattered. And him only if it turned out he knew more than Langdon thought he did.

Buddy parked in front of a small, gray-shingled clubhouse near Castle Point. Boston Harbor shimmered in the late afternoon sunlight. A pier ran alongside the clubhouse, and at the end of it, Langdon could see Dobyns sitting at a picnic table. A tall black man sat on the railing and he and Dobyns appeared to be talking.

The kid stayed in the car. Langdon got out and started toward the pier. Two men stepped out of the clubhouse and drifted in front of Langdon. Buddy came up from behind and said, "Raise your arms."

The two men in front were both good sized. One was rawboned with a long jaw, flat black eyes. The other was hefty, sunburned. Buddy said, "They're gonna check you out. You got any weapons, you tell us now." They frisked him carefully.

"Just my hands," Langdon said, winking. "Dangerous weapons, you know."

"James Bond," Buddy said. "Even got the English accent. Goes over real big here in Southie."

Langdon let them take his pocketknife, and then handed them his bag and they went through it roughly. They wouldn't find anything but fresh laundry, and the picture of Cain. Langdon watched their reaction when they saw the photo:

Nothing.

Buddy took Langdon by the upper arm and tried to hustle him along the pier. When they reached Jimmy, Langdon said, "And so pleased to see you again, Mister Dobyns." He held out the arm Buddy was grasping.

Dobyns said, "Hey, Buddy. I said to pick him up at the airport, not carry him here."

The black man chuckled.

The look of dislike Buddy directed at the black man made the one he'd given Langdon in the car an expression of lasting friendship. But he let go of Langdon's arm and the black man just smiled lazily at Langdon, and said, "Bet he scared you, didn't he?"

"Shove it, Jerome," Buddy said, then turned away.

Langdon didn't bother to answer the black man. He wasn't there to chat with the help.

Dobyns waved Langdon to have a seat across from him at the picnic table. Jerome shifted his position so he was sitting on the railing near the end of the bench between Dobyns and Langdon.

Langdon didn't like the way the picnic bench encumbered his legs, but he didn't see much choice. He sat down.

Dobyns ripped open a grocery-sized brown paper bag. "Got ham and cheese or chicken salad. Pretzels, beer, coke. You want, I'll even have one of the boys run out and get you some fish and chips. Comes in waxed paper, not newspaper. Hope you can stand it."

He reached in the bag and took out a greasy bag, then he tossed it to the black man. "Here you go, Jerome."

The black guy caught the bag, looked inside it, and said, "Looky, looky."

Dobyns jerked his thumb at the black man. "Jerome here says he's gotta have fried chicken every day. I know he does it just to bust balls. Any day now he's gonna start ordering collard greens."

Dobyns was a medium-sized bald man with a hard little potbelly, and powerful-looking arms. His face was deeply lined and tanned, but he still had an open, cheerful look to him. He gestured to the bag. "So what do you want?"

"The chicken sandwich will be fine," Langdon said, opening the wrapping. "White bread. Nice and pasty the way we English like it."

Dobyns raised his eyebrows. "Connecticut, way I heard it."

Langdon smiled. "You researched me? How flattering."

Dobyns gestured to the three men waiting at the end of the pier. "These guys don't know shit. But that boy you flew in with, Luis? The things he can do with a computer and a telephone, just amazing."

"And what did he find?"

Jimmy Dobyns grinned, showing a cheap set of false teeth. "Besides the rumors you like to fuck your sister?"

Jerome laughed quietly. "Shit," he said, and then laughed some more.

Langdon hesitated just slightly, and then took a bite out of his sandwich and chewed it carefully before answering. In one sense, he was used to this sort of comment—had heard it since he was a teenager. He and Veronica—Ronnie, to him—were closer than most brothers and sisters. They did, in fact, have what she called, "a physical relationship."

Finally, Langdon said, "First of all, she's my stepsister, not my sister. And we chose long ago not to look at each other in those terms."

"Oh, well then . . ." Dobyns grinned. "Just a matter of point of view, huh?"

Without heat, Langdon said, "Secondly, if I chose to take exception to that comment, you'd be dead before those three got the toothpicks out of their mouths."

Jerome continued to eat, but now he looked frankly at Langdon.

Dobyns said, "I'll put my money on Jerome. Besides which, you want something this afternoon or do you just wanna piss on each other's shoes?"

Dobyns grinned through a mouthful of his own food. Charming sight.

Langdon said, "This place is secure?"

Dobyns waved that away. "Don't worry, I pay my bills. The FBI and company are off me for a while, not due back on surveillance another coupla weeks."

"You're that sure?"

"Talk," Dobyns said.

Langdon said evenly, "If your research is so good, then you know that Veronica and I have earned a place in life where we don't really care about the opinions of others."

Dobyns shrugged. "I'm just rattling your cage for fun. I really don't care. You know what a flexible guy I am. Shit, got a black guy working for me here in Southie. You could be fucking your doggie, and that'd be less of an insult around here."

Langdon smiled thinly.

"Screw that doggie," Jerome said, before ripping off a piece of chicken with his teeth.

Dobyns said, "You art dealers are always a strange bunch. But I hear there's money in those pretty pictures."

"Some suspect that you've known for quite some time."

Dobyns looked skyward as if for help. "Sure, people have been laying that Rosalyn Museum thing on me, what? Four years now?"

"Waiting for the statute of limitations to run out? Only a couple more years to go."

Dobyns shrugged. "That'd be nice if I had them. I could use a hundred million as much as the next guy."

"Three hundred million I heard."

"Whatever. Nothing to me, I don't have them."

"You know, Veronica and I would be the best broker you could possibly find. We know how to dispose of the . . . pieces."

Dobyns shrugged. "I know lots of people, too. I know lots of people who know other people who'd give their left nut for a frigging Rembrandt or a Degas."

Dobyns pronounced Degas as "Degass."

Dobyns grinned to show Langdon he was just playing with him.

"Anyhow," Dobyns said. "Doesn't matter. I honest to God don't have them." Dobyns leaned forward. "That don't mean to say I won't cut the balls off whoever does. Steal three hundred million of art in my territory and don't cut me in? Makes me look like an asshole."

Dobyns reached over with hard forefinger and jabbed Langdon on the chest. "So what brings you to town, and what've you got for me?"

"Personnel problem," Langdon said, with a shrug. "Runaway mule."

"With what?"

"Oriental vase." Langdon spun some detail for a few minutes about this rare, delicate, and totally fictitious vase.

"What's it worth?" Dobyns snapped.

Langdon made a deprecating gesture. "Fifty thousand U.S. dollars, perhaps. But it's very bad for business to have a product go awry while in transit."

"Yeah, you've got to stamp that kind of shit out."

Dobyns looked bored.

Good. That's just the way Langdon wanted him. Last thing he needed was to have Dobyns trying to "recover" the jewels himself.

Dobyns said, "So what can I do for the money I'm going to make you pay anyhow?"

Langdon showed Dobyns the picture of Cain. "Keep an eye out for this man," Langdon said. "Put me on him as soon as he's sighted. I could probably use your help with disposal afterward."

Dobyns waved his hand and Buddy came up quickly. Dobyns

handed him the picture of Cain. "Run down to the corner and have a picture made of this, make a couple dozen copies."

After Buddy left, Dobyns said to Langdon, "Seeing as we're exchanging baby pictures, why don't you take a look at mine?"

He reached into the lunch bag and took out a manila envelope. Inside were several eight-by-ten black-and-white photos, which he spread on the table.

They were graphic, harsh, and clearly the work of a police crime-scene photographer. However, the cops who were captured on the fringes of these scenes were bobbies.

First there was a wide shot of a burned-out motor sailer. A closer look inside the charred cabin of the same boat. A body. Then a close-up of the head and shoulders of the dead man.

He was badly burned, but even so, it was clear that his throat had been cut.

Langdon took another bite out of his sandwich.

"I give up," he said, after swallowing. "Somebody I'm supposed to know?"

"Name's Barrett. Local skipper around here. Not one of my guys, exactly, but we've used him for a few things. Chartered this boat down in Rhode Island and took off for a transatlantic cruise. Nobody knows why. Now I got his widow showing up bawling all the time looking for handouts."

Langdon waited.

Dobyns said, "Got to ask myself what's this crotchety old Irish bastard from my neighborhood doing all the way over in London? You know something about that?"

"It's a small country, but not that small." Langdon felt bad about his work on Barrett. In Langdon's haste, he had let Cain see him in the marina parking lot, and he had fled in his small van. Langdon had given chase, but he'd lost him. That had left Langdon only Barrett to work on, and other than the name of the rental-car company Cain was using, he didn't provide much. Rather, the guy passed out before Langdon got anywhere near the information he needed. In frustration, Langdon had cut his throat and set the boat on fire.

Sloppy, but then, Langdon had been embarrassed for poor Ronnie.

Cain did make such a fool out of her.

Still, he told himself he had found his way to Southampton by way of Barrett, and from there to the Vincents, so it wasn't all a waste. Just more time-consuming than he preferred.

Dobyns shrugged his shoulders. He didn't seem to be too concerned about the dead skipper. "All right, I'm not telling you we're gonna put a full court press on for this Tom Cain of yours. But if we run across him, we'll get in touch. Whyn't you stay at the Four Seasons? That'll be a nice spot for a poof like you, and I'll be able reach you."

"Thank you. One other housekeeping thing . . . Could I purchase a handgun? With a silencer preferably?"

Dobyns snorted. " 'Housekeeping.' Yeah, I'll sell you one. Even give you credit if you haven't got the cash on you. Wire me the money tomorrow. Cost you fifteen grand."

Langdon raised his eyebrows. "Excuse me?"

"That's for the gun, the holster, the silencer, and for the chance to walk around my town and use them. Now, if my people find this Tom Cain, and help you with disposal, it'll be another twenty-five."

Langdon shook his head, ruefully. "Expenses are beginning to outstrip my income on this job."

Dobyns chuckled. "Tell me about it." He jerked his thumb at the the three men at the end of the pier. "You know how much it takes to keep those boys in beer and groceries? Plus what I'm now shelling out for poor Mrs. Barrett."

"Plus a little something for yourself."

"Always a little something for me," Dobyns said. "Always."

Langdon checked into the Four Seasons Hotel on Boylston Street and went up to his room. Not bad. Not bad at all. He dropped the handgun onto the bed—a nice enough Smith and Wesson auto with a short barrel. Blue steel, freshly oiled, registration number neatly filed off. Langdon looked out over the Boston Gardens while placing his call. It was just about noon. "It's me," he said when Madeline picked up the phone.

"Good afternoon, sir," she said. She quickly passed on his messages. Nothing urgent. "Put me through to her," he said, abruptly.

"Certainly, Mister Langdon."

He smiled. Eight years with them, and Madeline had never once tried to call him by his first name. He liked that.

Ronnie picked up the phone.

"Where are you, sweets?" she said.

"Where I'm supposed to be."

"Wish I was there. Gloomy and gray here."

"That's London, dear."

"So was the local representative waiting like you expected?"

"Of course."

"Learn anything?"

"The same as before. Denied and left enough tidbits to make me want to jump. Good chance he was never involved and just bragging. Hard not to laugh at him, considering."

"What else?"

"Knew about us. Guess the word of our romance is out."

"Gee." She laughed.

That throaty laugh.

She never was a giggler.

He was ten, she was eleven when he moved into her home just outside Hartford.

His father was a mid-level executive at an insurance company. He took custody of his son after his wife took off from the suburbs to pursue what became a long and moderately successful career as an actress in New York.

Ian's mother was the most beautiful woman he had ever seen—up until he met Ronnie—but her attention to him ran to extremes: she either fussed or ignored him entirely. He was certain her leaving had more to do with him than his father.

Ian's father was already engaged to Ronnie's mother by the time he introduced Ian. Charlotte was a pale and pretty woman from a once wealthy family whose stockbroker husband had dropped dead of an aneurism at age thirty-five. Ian's father had fallen for her while overseeing the settlement of her husband's surprisingly small estate.

Perhaps Ian's dad was looking for someone more dependent than his first wife. Someone weaker, someone who needed him. If so, he found her in Charlotte. But that first day, as Ian stood there, sullen and speechless, he simply took in that his father had somehow found another beautiful woman. To himself, he vowed to not forget his real mother.

"Well," Charlotte said, looking him over. She gave his father a small smile, as if to say she would be good about it all. And then she called her daughter downstairs. She had to call Ronnie repeatedly to get her to come down, yet she didn't seemed to be embarrassed or even notice that the girl wasn't obeying her.

Finally, Ronnie came downstairs.

Ian could still look back and remember that moment. Still taste the feeling; it was something he still felt whenever she walked in the room. That almost palpable feeling of shock, and pleasure, and trepidation as she came off the stairway. "Oh my," she said, standing in the doorway. "It's my new bro."

She was as tall as he was, slim, dark-eyed.

With her year's seniority, she radiated all that was older, sophisticated, if he'd known the word.

His father said, "Ian, this is your sister." He stepped over to touch her under the chin, trying to be friendly.

She jerked her head away.

Charlotte didn't even blink. She said to Ian, "Ronnie is a very talented, smart girl."

"So I've seen him," Ronnie said. "Can I go back up now?"

Charlotte continued. "She tends to go her own way. Very artistic. Give her some time."

"He's not saying anything, Mom," Ronnie said. "Can't you find someone to help you with your pharmaceuticals who has a son who can talk?"

"Ronnie!" That finally got a reaction from Charlotte.

"Oh, sorry," Ronnie said, with a wink to Ian.

That confused him, but he found himself saying to Charlotte while his eyes remained on Ronnie, "Don't worry. My dad's works for an insurance company. Paying for drugs is no problem."

Charlotte went rigid, and Ian's father said his name angrily and shook him by the shoulder. But as far as Ian was concerned, they weren't even in the room. He saw Ronnie look at him, really look at him, and she smiled ever so slightly.

"Just keep away from my room," she said. "Or I'll be forced to hurt you."

Ronnie barely offered him a word for the first month.

She told him later that she took his silent acceptance for stupidity. It made her angry the way he wanted to follow her, to be with her. She said he trailed her home like a dog from school. He knew she was right, but he couldn't seem to stop himself.

Already she was aware of her looks.

At that age, boys jockeyed around her, showing their attention by trying to tease her. She seemed truly impervious, sailing through the day on her own course.

But Ian lived with her. He saw the way she groomed herself. He saw her looking in the mirror.

And one day on the way home, he realized she had been slowing down in front of the jewelers, just a bit, each day that week. The lipstick case, he saw. Flat, solid silver. Stocked with a range of lipsticks and rouge. A mirror inside.

The price tag was over three hundred dollars.

She looked at him and said, "I want that."

"Wait around the corner," he told her.

He walked in and started a pleasant line of chatter with the woman behind the counter. Ian—who barely said a word to anyone all day—found he could be charming. He handed the woman his watch and asked her for a new crystal. When she turned to make the exchange, he stole the silver case and put it under his shirt.

Afterward, he walked out and gave it to his stepsister, saying, "For you, sweets." Feeling more bold for using the endearment than for the theft.

She invited him into her room afterward, and he watched her apply the lipstick. Then she kissed him. They laughed, looking at each other in the mirror. "We're going to do things," she said. She kissed him again, and again, smudging him in red. "Lots and lots of things."

When he was twelve, he shoved Billy Simon off the sidewalk and stomped his wrist against the curb, breaking it. All for grabbing Ronnie's hair at recess. That night, she let Ian put his hand under her shirt and touch her nipples. She told him how her own father had done that, and more, for as long as she could remember. That her mother knew and did nothing.

"But you," she said. "You take care of me. I want you to do this. Just you."

They were making love by the time he was thirteen. They learned to conceal what they were doing, which wasn't too hard with the way his father traveled. If Charlotte was aware of it—and Ian believed she was—she kept it to herself.

In school, it was another thing. Not that anyone *knew* a damn thing, but they suspected. When he was a freshman and she was a sophomore, the two of them began to endure some comments. The next year, when he began to shoot up in size soon after his fifteenth birthday, he set about doing something about it. On three separate occasions, Ian took on what were supposedly the toughest guys in the school. He didn't know all that much about fighting then. He simply waded into each battle certain that these were the guys who had the best chance with Ronnie.

In each case, through determination and viciousness alone, he stumbled away, bloody but victorious. The other kids learned to keep their mouths shut. Not that their opinions actually mattered all that much: Ian certainly didn't need anyone other than Ronnie, and for her part, she didn't seem to need the friendship of anyone but him.

What she needed was more violence.

* * *

One night, just months before his seventeenth birthday, Ronnie dangled the keys to her mother's car in front of him and said, "Want to come?"

She was dressed in a tight black skirt and a loose sweater, and when he got in beside her, he found she had left a crowbar and pair of gloves on the floor.

He said, "What's this for?"

"You'll figure it out."

They drove to a roadside-motel bar about an hour and a half away, just outside New Haven. She leaned over, kissed him, and whispered, "Wait here," before walking into the bar.

She came out an hour later with a man who looked much like her father, whose picture was still displayed on the dining-room china cabinet.

The two of them went into one of the motel rooms.

Ian waited for fifteen minutes, and then followed them in, with the crowbar in his gloved hands. She'd left the door unlocked.

The man was bigger than Ian was, but Ronnie tripped him up as he lunged out of the bed. Ian crushed his skull with one blow, but Ronnie wanted him to hit the man some more.

That first time was messy, horrific, and very, very exciting: they screwed on the floor afterwards.

Ronnie took gloves from her purse and went through the man's wallet. She took the cash and said to leave the credit cards alone. Together, they wiped the place down. Ronnie went out to the car and came back with a change of clothes for the both of them that she had put in the trunk. They went south on the highway and tossed the crowbar and clothes into a river before doubling back to head home.

After that, she said that what they had done made them special. That they were in touch with passions and drives fundamental to the human animal; passions and drives that other people were afraid to acknowledge.

She saw herself as an artist. She saw them living all over the world. Her paintings and sketches, which previously had been little more than basic art-class fare began to evolve into violent abstract pieces of work that juxtaposed horror and sexuality. She talked about the fear of death as a motivating force behind the need to create. . . . and said that if you could control death, you controlled your art.

Ian was smart, but not that way. He knew how lucky they had been to get away with murder the first time. And though he had enjoyed it, he didn't see himself as a serial killer, beating and killing for the sake of it alone.

And he could see that despite Ronnie's artistic aspirations, she liked the things money could buy. Good clothes. She wanted a new BMW for the two of them, and she was outraged that Ian's dad wouldn't come up with the cash. Already, Ian began to think about how they might afford the kind of life she needed.

Ian kept looking at his dad. Going off to that insurance company every day. It panicked him, inside. Knowing that unless he figured something out, he was headed toward something similar some day.

He knew that wouldn't work. That she'd never put up with it.

That she'd leave him.

They were both accepted and went to college at the New York Visual Arts School. Ronnie began sleeping with one of her professors, a talented and abrasive man named Abrahams. First she told Ian that she was just working Abrahams for grades and connections, that Ian was still the only one who really mattered.

It was sheer agony for him. For a terrible three-month period, he would see her for only a few minutes a day, when she would stop in at their apartment for a change of clothes. Sitting on the edge of their bed, pulling on a fresh pair of jeans. Her saying that maybe it was time for him to move on, too. Him saying that was impossible, the things they'd done together.

She would recognize the threat and slip into the covers now and then to appease him.

But still he remained miserable.

He contacted his mother. Hadn't heard from her in years, but there he was in New York. He went to see her in a play and then called her the next day. She agreed to meet for coffee.

She was still gorgeous. Not someone's mother. Impossible to believe she was his. Golden hair, deep blue eyes. His mother, getting glances from the men in the restaurant.

She looked at his wool jacket, his plain face, and said, "Aren't you the picture of your father."

She talked about her career with her eyes trained just over his shoulder. He realized he bored her.

Ian wanted to tell her that he had killed a man. That he had the love and passion of a beautiful woman.

But, of course, these were things you didn't share with your mother. And perhaps it was no longer true about Ronnie, anyhow.

Instead, he blurted, "Why'd you do it?"

She had looked at him then. And sighed. She held her hands up to reveal her face, her hair, and then reached out toward the window, to take in New York. Quietly, she said, "I didn't care for what I had become and certainly not where I was going. I made myself what I am now. It's up to you, too."

She touched the back of his hand quickly and left.

He began to think he might have to kill Ronnie's professor soon.

Luckily for Ian, Abrahams made the mistake of giving Ronnie the truth when she asked for an assessment of her work. "I suggest you study art history," he said. "Look into being a curator or dealer, perhaps. Far as I can tell, you've got the passion, some learned skills, but I don't really see the talent. I see you more as an appreciator, not a creator."

Although Abraham's judgement turned out to be entirely accurate, Ian was delighted to fulfill Ronnie's request by throwing the man off his apartment balcony. Ian left behind a carefully forged suicide note on the man's kitchen counter and walked home whistling.

Ronnie began painting furiously. She was determined to prove Abrahams wrong. Ian began to work on his craft as well. It was appalling how quickly the rent came due; how the things Ronnie wanted vaporized their monthly allowance from his father.

So Ian went to school with specific goals in mind. He wanted to acquire at least a veneer of sophistication. He learned what a well-read man should read and either waded through the material or read the Cliff Notes. He did take those art history courses and pulled Ronnie along with him. He studied accounting and finance, thinking the entire time about how to beat the system rather than work within it. He found the library had a fair amount of general information about money laundering and tax evasion, but he knew he needed practical experience.

And he learned how to fight.

He started his martial arts training; something he would continue for a lifetime. But in that year and a half, he quickly worked his way up to a brown belt. He approached his lessons with a cool and clinical passion. Unlike the other students, he not only saw these studies as part of his long-term career growth, but as something to help him through his part-time job—mugging people.

Unlike most muggers, poor against poor, he made the most of his conservative, preppie looks, traveling in the better neighborhoods. Worked his way into topflight hotels and pushed his way into the guest rooms. He was most pleased with himself when he overcame bigger or stronger men. But sometimes he picked up older women just to take them home and rip off their jewelry. Usually they were so relieved he wasn't going to rape them, they just handed the stuff over.

Disposing of the pieces brought him some trade with the local fences, which was, of course, very educational.

Unfortunately, none of it was enough for his and Ronnie's long-term needs.

So after Professor Abrahams's words were confirmed in the marketplace—and in Ronnie's own eyes—Ian took steps to launch what he saw as their real career.

He had been keeping his eye on several Hasidic Jews in the jewelry district who walked purposely through the crowd with their briefcases handcuffed to their wrists and bodyguards in tow. When Ian told Ronnie what he had in mind, she was willing—excited even—to help.

The very concept of taking action helped her out of her terrible depression, which alone was its own reward for Ian.

Together they scoped out the parking garage where one young

jeweler parked his car. There were no video cameras and the jeweler normally parked on next to the top floor where the traffic was light, presumably to get a space near the elevator. The morning of the robbery, they stole a van and parked it next to a small Mercedes sedan in the garage. Ian stuck a knife into the left rear tire of the Mercedes. When the jeweler and his bodyguard arrived moments later, Ronnie stood by the Mercedes looking helpless.

The bodyguard, a stocky blond-haired man with a small mustache, was too wary to actually help with the tire; he even tucked his coat behind the gun on his belt. But she got her hand on his wrist and that gave Ian all the time he needed.

He slipped around the van with a little .22 automatic and put the bodyguard down first, and the jeweler as he tried to run away. Then Ian and Ronnie hauled both bodies into the back of the van. Ian placed the jeweler's wrist on a small chopping block and swung the hatchet. They tossed the bloodied briefcase into a duffel bag, Ian changed his clothes, and together, the brother and sister walked down the stairs to the street.

They moved to London. Ian sold the diamonds using a connection made through one of his New York contacts, and then he and Ronnie found their new apartment in London.

"Flat," as they called it there.

Those diamonds brought in just under four hundred thousand U.S. dollars and set the pace for their life's work. Buying, stealing, couriering, and making very good money on stolen jewels, and eventually, virtually any kind of artwork.

Ronnie had become a dealer, as Professor Abrahams had once predicted.

Time passed.

It caused Ronnie intense pain at times to see others move ahead as artists. And, indeed, she crushed more than one promising career out of spite. But, by and large, she and Ian built their reputation as discriminating dealers who could get just about anything. For evidence of her success, Ronnie had only to look at the beautiful townhouse that Langdon and Langdon, Ltd. moved into in their tenth year.

Their legitimate business was lucrative enough and provided a ready means to explain their income. But their real business was executed for a few trusted customers for whom they would "actively pursue" virtually any collection—from initial burglary through delivery, and, sometimes, subsequent security.

They went home to Connecticut just once, and that was after Ronnie's mother ate a bottle of pills, soon after her sixtieth birthday. Ronnie surprised Ian and herself by being absolutely distraught.

At the funeral, Ian had touched his father's shoulder. Sorry for the man, but secretly despising him. The white, shaken look.

Poor old guy. Always getting left behind.

Ian Langdon never went back to see him again.

On the phone, Langdon said, "Our local rep wants a fee. Goodwill sort of thing."

"How much?"

"Fifteen now, twenty-five if he delivers."

She whistled. "Oh, hey, he's tough." Her voice was brittle. She was trying to keep it light, but he could feel the tension in her.

"So he thinks," Langdon said.

"Anything else?"

"Uh-huh. Seems the captain who met with the accident was one of his. But he didn't know what the man was doing there."

"Is Dobyns looking at us?"

Langdon closed his eyes and waited. *Using the man's name, for Christ's sakes.*

She got it in a second and gave what passed for an apology from her. "I'm distracted," she said. "We've got a visitor here."

"Who?"

"Saudi," she said. "Staying in London until the problem is resolved."

Langdon rubbed his forehead.

Ronnie continued: "Sits across from Madeline in the waiting room. Ugly little man with a lot of hair who politely comes in and asks the status. Nine o'clock, two o'clock, and then as I'm walking out the door. Got Madeline scared to death."

"Not as much as she is of you," Langdon said.

Ronnie went on. "The little man wants me to understand that our customer doesn't give a rat's ass about the individual pieces themselves, but, 'The acquisition of the entire collection is what is most important.' "

"Ronnie," he said warningly.

She was silent for a moment. Another form of apology.

Langdon broke the silence. "Actual threats yet?"

"It's implied," Ronnie said. "And the customer himself is due here next week. Six days, Ian." Her voice shook. "Six days or the little man says they will 'take steps.' "

Langdon sighed. By his last count, he had killed sixteen men. The man in the motel being the first and Vincent being the last. The one thing Ian knew was that anyone could be killed.

Including him and Ronnie.

So while he was quite willing to take on individuals, weed them out like so much crabgrass, he stayed away from the organized types. The Saudi Arabian amir was another fellow who could make him and Ronnie dead if he put his mind to it.

Langdon said, "Tell the little man there's been progress. I got a good lead before I left the island."

"Who?"

He didn't answer.

She said, "You give the name to the local hotshot?"

"Of course not," he snapped.

"Don't be angry with me," she said. "I just feel so stupid."

"We'll get past this," he said.

"It's all my fault," she moaned.

She had told him of the opportunity that her young lover, Cain, had proposed. He was one of their new mules, and he had proved very effective in the past year. He had said there was an incredible situation he had stumbled into—a contact had identified the stolen Rosalyn Museum art through a personal connection. This friend was in a position to steal the art, and Cain could deliver it—but he needed a buyer.

Ronnie had kept calm and said, simply, "That's what I was put on earth for, sweetie. You get the collection to me, I'll get the money."

And then she went and told Ian.

Ian was stunned. Jealous beyond words. Through his own careful orchestration, over the years they'd amassed a modest fortune of just over four million dollars.

Now this kid was talking about waltzing in with the greatest collection of stolen art in the world.

But as stunned as he was, Ian instantly realized there were millions to be made, and Ronnie to win or lose.

Ian had harbored every intention of throwing Cain off a balcony, so to speak, once Ronnie was through with him. But would she ever tire of the man who made her wealthy beyond her own high expectations?

Ian simply congratulated his sister on bringing them the opportunity, but said to be careful, that he didn't trust Cain.

Ronnie said, "Back off. Tom deals with me and me alone."

"Did he ask for that?" Ian asked sharply.

"No. I'm demanding it. Now don't screw this up for us. He wants to be paid in diamonds. He's freaked enough about transporting the paintings, he doesn't want to have to smuggle cash back, too."

Cain had come through. First with tightly cropped photos and paint chips, which their expert, Geoffrey, judged as genuine. Then Cain delivered the Govaert Flinck *Landscape with a Pillar*; Geoffrey inspected it carefully and also declared it authentic.

Ronnie had kissed Cain wildly, and then looked over her shoulder at Ian as if to say, "See?"

Langdon handed Cain the first installment, just over a hundred thousand worth of diamonds—paid for with their own money.

Cain quickly walked them over to the florescent light table and looked at them carefully through a loupe.

Ronnie said, "All VVS all of D to F color, Tommy. One to three carats."

"They're genuine," Langdon said. "Just make sure the paintings continue to be."

Cain looked up from the lamp. "Hey, no games here."

"Ian's delighted," Ronnie interrupted crisply, moving between the two of them.

Soon after Cain left, Ian dispatched a very discreet private detective to follow him and to get a photographic record of wherever he went. From his detective, Langdon not only collected painful pictures of Cain and Ronnie, but he also found out about Cain's method of transport: a forty-two-foot motor sailer, docked in London, apparently handled by a skipper and Cain alone.

Ronnie brokered the deal with Amir Abaas, a Saudi they had worked for once before.

After delivery of the Flinck, the amir forwarded five million dollars worth of diamonds, entrusted to Ronnie for Cain's payment. In truth, she had negotiated a fifteen-million-dollar deal with the amir. The five was up front, but the remaining ten million was strictly for her and Ian, and it was payable only on final delivery of the complete collection.

Abaas wasn't into art; he was into power. Possessing the world's greatest stolen collection of art would meet that need.

Ian was thwarted every step of the way. He said that he would oversee the delivery to the U.K. personally, but Cain refused. He would not divulge where the collection was coming from.

Ian insisted that they receive the pieces at a small safe house in London, rather than allow Cain to make a direct delivery to Saudi Arabia. He didn't want to be cut out of the equation. Ronnie agreed, and she assured him that he would be there the night of the delivery, to oversee Geoffrey's appraisal personally.

But a good ten days earlier than Ronnie had told Ian to expect Cain, her lover arrived—at their townhouse—in a small paneled truck. Ronnie was waiting for him with Geoffrey, and together they lugged four shrink-wrapped wooden boxes into the labratory housed in their basement. Ronnie stood enthralled as Geoffrey opened the first box and began laying the pieces against the wall under the light.

Cain stopped him. "Turn around," he said to Ronnie. "Close your eyes."

And she did.

He set Vermeer's *The Gathering* on an easel, and then turned her around. By all accounts, this was the most valuable piece in the collection.

"Oh, my God," Ronnie cried. "Tommy!"

Tears streaked down Ronnie's face, which Cain kissed away.

Geoffrey went to work immediately on the Vermeer. But he told her up front, that it was his impression that the piece was authentic.

"I was just beside myself," she said later to Ian. "Tommy seemed to really care about me. Is that so impossible to believe? He didn't know all the things I've done. And you frightened him so. He said you would never let him leave with his share, that you would have killed him. That he and I had to do this between just the two of us because we trusted each other."

To make her feel better, Ian had told Ronnie the truth: he *had* been planning on killing Cain and keeping the five million as well. "So you see, he figured us both out and played us against each other."

Ronnie said, "He was just so eager. Saying how he'd couriered stones for so long, and now these were his. He couldn't wait to be rich. I fell for it completely."

That night, she and Cain left Geoffrey to study the remaining pieces:there were five Degas, a Manet, and a Chinese bronze beaker from the Shang dynasty.

And three Rembrandts.

Ronnie and Cain made love with his five-million-dollars worth of glittering diamonds on the night table.

Afterward, Tom Cain quickly began to dress. She said she wanted him to stay, but he insisted he had to hurry.

Ronnie teased him, then grew irritated.

Nevertheless, he continued to dress. He scooped all the diamonds into a large aspirin bottle and told her he had to go.

"What is this?" she said. She took his arm. "Let's celebrate."

"I don't feel like it."

And that's when she told him that she insisted. "You've got to at least stay until Geoffrey's finished."

"No," he said. "I don't."

"I'm calling Ian," she said, turning to pick up the phone.

He hit her from behind. A solid, excruciating blow to her lower back. And then he spun her around and shoved her down onto the bed. With his right hand, he hit her three measured blows, a forehand, backhand, and then forehand. She had laid there, stunned. And then he leaned forward to whisper in her ear, "At home, I've got a woman who's young, who's pretty, and so talented, she makes you look like the hag you really are. It's so good that I'm rich, because I never want to work this hard, screwing something like you again."

And then he'd knocked her out cold. From the bruises on her neck, it looked as if he had tried to strangle her, but either lost his nerve for cold-blooded murder, or simply botched it, thinking she was dead.

Down in the cellar, Geoffrey reviewed several of the Degas charcoal sketches. As luck would have it, after finding them authentic, he decided to jump ahead to the last box and examine two pieces he had once admired years ago on a trip to Boston: Rembrandt's *Storm on the Ocean* and *Gentleman and a Lady.*

Even though he was somewhat lulled by the authenticity of the other works, Geoffrey felt his smile of anticipation fade.

Something was off.

It was too bright. *Storm on the Ocean* was too bright. Not by much, but it was off.

That's what he could tell at a glance, but more than that, he found himself cataloging small, barely defined bits of stylistic differences.

Something was wrong. "Shit," he said. "Shit, shit, shit."

He carefully took the piece into the small x-ray room, laid it under the tube. He left the room, and put on his lead apron before setting the exposure and illumination. He flipped the switch.

He did the same for *Gentleman and a Lady.*

A half hour later, he emerged from the processing room and laid the still-wet film up against a wall-mounted illuminator. He peered closely, feeling frozen inside.

There were two paintings. Two painting on each canvas, that is. The Rembrandts were painted over some other piece of work, presumably to provide the Rembrandts with appropriately aged frames and canvas.

They were fakes.

Geoffrey wasted more valuable time reexamining some of the pieces he had already reviewed. The Degas pieces were pencil and water colors, charcoals. An ink with white and rose washes. He was certain they weren't forgeries.

The Vermeer was authentic, he was sure of it. And the Flinck had been, too. He knew that one had already been delivered to the final customer, and he had a pretty good idea who that was.

It was a matter of just a few minutes before he screwed up the courage to disturb Ronnie Langdon. He knocked on her door repeatedly, and received no answer. He decided in the end it was best to go to Madeline's office and find Ian's cell-phone number.

So it was Ian who rushed across town to find his sister passed out on the bed, the ugly bruises on her throat. He held her, whispering urgently in her ear that she had to live, had to come back to him.

She burst into ragged sobs when she found Ian above her.

"He hit me," she said. "You've got to get him, Ian. Promise me you'll get him."

Now, alone in his room at the Four Seasons, Ian listened to Ronnie say, "I can't go on feeling like this."

"I understand," he said, softly. "Our friend will pay horribly. But business first. We recover what he took. We find the two pieces and complete our delivery—and accept our payment."

She sighed. "It's not that simple for me . . ."

"Not on the phone," he said quickly.

There was silence, broken only by the faint sound of her crying. The humiliation was just eating her alive. Though he felt impatient on some levels, he truly sympathized. "We'll take care of them," he offered. "Both of them."

She said, "I can just imagine them laughing. Tommy and his girl laughing at me."

"I'm sure they're not," he said.

But, in truth, he assumed they very well might be.

Ronnie said, "You'll send for me when you've got them?"

"Can't promise that. Trust me to do the necessary, sweets."

"Oh, Ian," she said. "I know you will. Every day seems so bleak and old here."

"That's London."

"No. It's me now."

"Nonsense. You'll be fine once this business is behind you. I'll see to it."

She sighed. "Thank God for you. Thank God for you and me."

Langdon chuckled. That sounded more like his Ronnie.

CHAPTER 18

SHE ALMOST DIDN'T RECOGNIZE HIM WHEN HE GOT OFF THE ELEVATOR. Or rather she did, but it was from a time before. Maybe ten years ago. His beard was gone. He looked sunburned, much thinner, and very tired.

What's wrong? she wanted to ask.

But for a moment, she didn't speak. Everything she could think of saying felt brittle, forced. That stunned her, not knowing how to talk to her husband.

"Hey," he said, and for an awful second she thought he was just going to shake her hand. But he put his arms around her, and she let him pull her close. She closed her eyes, but her body betrayed her and she crossed her arms across her chest. Looking for that little bit of self-protection.

He kissed her cheek and let her go.

"Welcome back, sailor," she said.

"Thanks." He nodded toward the restaurant. "They tell me this is fine."

"Sure."

They walked side by side, the awkwardness growing each second. She felt as if they were on the down side of a first date.

How can that be? she thought, almost desperate. *I've been married to this man for nineteen years.*

"You look good," she said. "Getting ready for the dating scene already?"

She meant it to be funny, but it didn't come across that way. He frowned at her.

The waitress joined them immediately and they ordered breakfast: oatmeal and fruit salad for both of them. Sesame bagel for him; raisin for her. She looked at his hand, saw he was no longer wearing his wedding band. Neither was she, but that didn't make it any better.

She sipped her coffee. "Tell me about the voyage."

He shrugged. "Just like I told you last night. Uneventful other than hitting that pole. Screwed up the prop."

"Why didn't you get it fixed?"

He waved that away. Not exactly irritable, but . . . evasive.

"No, really," she said, curious now. "It's not like you. Captain Spit-and-Polish . . ."

"It wasn't necessary."

He didn't look at her.

She cocked her head to the side. "Rob? What is it?"

He met her eyes then. "Caroline, you've lost the right of wifely interrogation."

He said it with a faint smile, but still he had surprised her.

She gave a short laugh. "Okay . . ."

Luckily, the waitress arrived with their food right then, and they ate quietly.

The normalcy of eating together eased the tension. The passing of the milk, the automatic splitting of the bagels so that each of them shared the two varieties, his pouring coffee for both of them until the small pot was empty.

They'd done this thousands of times before, Caroline figured. For an English teacher, she was good with numbers. Three hundred and sixty-five days a year together, maybe three fifty to account for travel days away. Even that was generous, Rob's business never took him out of town that much. Three hundred and fifty multiplied by nineteen years, was what?

Too confusing.

Twenty times three hundred and fifty was seven thousand. Subtract three fifty, and it was six thousand six hundred and fifty.

Six thousand six hundred and fifty breakfasts and dinners together. Of course that wasn't really accurate, she thought. All those mornings one of them was in a hurry for a meeting. Plenty of times they were all rushing out, grabbing their own bagels and coffee along the way.

But still. The number was certainly good for the times they had slept together. Turned the sheets down, kissed each other good night. Talked under the covers about Sam, about repairs on the house, about which of their two cars would make it another year.

And, of course, making love God knows how many times. Until Sam's death, Rob had always held onto his sense of wonder that he had Caroline, and together they had made their little girl. He brought that happiness into his and Caroline's bed, that happiness entangled with fear that it would all go away. What with his mother dying and, before that, his father deserting them . . .

Caroline had done what she could to assuage the fear, but she had also reveled in his intensity, the way he had just consumed her.

And now his worst fears were coming true.

She looked at Rob, his closed face, his distance.

She imagined that this is what it would feel like if he were having an affair.

The thought jolted her. *Was he? Could he?*

But then their eyes connected. And though there was something he didn't want her to see, she felt that he missed her.

She reached out and took his hand.

He hesitated, and then his shoulders eased. He enfolded her hand in both of his.

She asked, "What is it, Rob?"

He shook his head.

"Has something happened?" She tried for a light tone, but she had to know. "Meet some cute girl in another port?"

He looked surprised

She smiled and sat back. She could feel her face flush.

He grinned, losing another few years with that. "Met her this morning, by the elevator," he said. "Took her out to breakfast."

Relief surged through her. She didn't even realize she'd been holding her breath. "So what's the problem?"

"I'm not sure if she wants to see me again."

"Hmmm." Caroline looked out the restaurant window to the elevators. Then back to him. "You wouldn't believe what she wants."

There were other people on the elevator, an older couple.

So Caroline and Rob tried not to look at each other. And when he was fiddling with the plastic key outside his room, getting the card upside down first, and then backward, she laughed. "You *are* out of practice," she said.

"And you better be," he said as he finally got the door open. "You've been on land a lot longer than me."

"Count on it, sailor." She walked into the room, taking in the ocean view. She drew the curtains all the way back, letting the light flood in. "I think we're high enough up that nobody can peek."

He took her by the hand and led her to the mirror. "Let me look at you," he said.

Rob got behind her and she leaned back, feeling his hardness already.

He reached around to her and unbuttoned her blouse. In the mirror, he revealed her slowly, until at last the blouse lay on the floor. He simply looked at her for a few minutes, lightly touching her belly, her arms. Cupping the fullness of her through her brassiere, before unhooking that, too.

Her nipples stiffened, her chest flushed. He explored her as if she were his first lover.

He slid her zipper down slowly, and then he pushed her jeans over her hips. "There's my girl." His voice was hoarse.

She looked at herself, naked now, just stepping away from her clothes. Seeing herself the way he saw her, or at least made her *feel* as if he saw her. She knew that she wasn't twenty-five years old any longer. Thirty-eight in fact, forty an increasingly possible-sounding number. Hips slightly wider than those days, her small breasts some-what heavier.

But she shivered with excitement. In the mirror, she could see how good she looked to him.

"My turn," she said. She was a lot less gentle. Practically ripped his shirt off. Liking what she saw: the sun-darkened skin, his lean-ness.

She pulled his jeans down then laughed, pleased with how ready he was.

He pushed her down on the bed, both of them too eager to wait.

It felt so damn good, screwing her husband, in the middle of the morning twenty stories up. Knowing his body so well, but feeling more than their month of separation, feeling something different in his urgency entirely. She didn't know what it was, but it excited her.

She pulled his head up from her neck. Wanted to look him in the eyes as they did it. Something they hadn't done in the past year, not since Sam.

She wanted to look inside him while they made love.

As soon as she did that, she felt something change. He stayed with her. She saw his passion, maybe even his love. But she saw some-thing else—doubt, fear, something . . . and then he grimaced, and she felt that he had lost it.

"Sorry," he said.

"Don't be." She pulled him close. "I'm sorry I pushed you."

He shook his head. And she felt him stop. He'd lost it completely. He withdrew and rolled over onto his side.

She tried to tease him. "I told you that you're out of practice."

He lay there, his arm over his eyes, blocking out the harsh sun-light.

This hadn't happened more than a few times in their marriage, and those times it was because of stress, overwork.

"Hey," she said. "It's been a while for us. Lot of emotions going on here. Don't worry about it."

But he just nodded. "Sorry," he said again.

And then rolled to his feet.

"Where are you going?"

"Time to get dressed. I've got to check out."

"Tell me you're kidding." Caroline crossed her arms over her breasts. Feeling shy, as if it wasn't right to be naked in front of this man. "And do what?"

"I'll take the boat back up to Newburyport today," he said. "I'll stay on her until we get things sorted out."

Caroline felt stunned. It hurt, knowing how close she had come earlier to telling him about the apartment. Sophia Benchley's top floor. Telling him that she had lined up a place where they could both start over.

Instead, she said, "So you'll just take the boat up yourself?"

"Yeah, I'll single-hand it," Rob said. "That's what I do these days."

She got up and dressed without a word. When she left, he was packing his duffel bag.

CHAPTER 19

IT WASN'T EASY LEAVING BOSTON HARBOR. THE KID WAS HELPFUL enough, towed him out a ways. McKenna raised a light jenny and began to tack against a fickle westerly wind for the next four hours before he made enough distance to settle into a close reach along the coast.

That was all right, he told himself. It was good to have something to do. He was churning through lots of emotions.

The ironic aspects weren't lost on him. Killed two men one day, surprised by a limp dick a few days later. Which one bothered him most?

It actually made him laugh out loud sometimes. Sitting there at the wheel, raking his hands back through his hair. Not knowing who he was anymore.

That morning when he'd looked into Caroline's eyes, he'd deflated like a leaky tire. Even worse, he couldn't behave like an adult afterward. Just hold her, enjoy being together. Try again in a few minutes. He was just so shocked and overwhelmed by the dichotomy that she still loved him—but he could no longer be honest with her.

Jesus Christ.

The two men, he still saw them when he closed his eyes. And the horror of it was there, the blood.

But there was something else, too. That rage within himself, reserved supposedly for R. J., that rage had been appeased somewhat. Standing on the deck emptying that gun.

McKenna told himself Cain had intended to leave him to drown in the forward cabin. That Cain had once run drugs. That he had the enormous ingratitude to ignore that McKenna had saved his life.

Well, screw him.

At that moment, as the wind beginning to freshen, McKenna decided that if he could only get his head together, there was a chance he might get past this. Maybe he *could* handle it.

Maybe he'd even chase R. J. down, he thought. But he knew that was just bluster. Shooting Cain had lanced that rage.

All McKenna really wanted now was a way to look his wife in the eye.

Just before midnight, McKenna sailed up the Merrimack River into Newburyport. He picked out the buoys with his flashlight, a long police model filled with D-cells. Luckily, the wind put him on a steady broad reach, the water bubbling quietly under his lee rail. The tide was low and McKenna was glad he'd made this approach hundreds of times before. The Joppa Flats to his port side were covered by no more than two feet of water.

Up ahead, he could see Swan Perkins under the gas dock light. Swan was the manager of the marina. He clapped slowly enough so that McKenna wouldn't let it go to his head. "Let's see if you can hit the dock, Rob."

"Swan."

McKenna put the helm over and spun the *Wanderer* around into the wind. Swan took his bowline, and McKenna jumped onto the dock to secure the stern. He got back on board immediately to drop the sails.

"So, a transatlantic behind you," Swan said. "Guess you're going to be an even bigger pain in the ass from now on."

"That's the plan," McKenna said.

As kids, he and Swan had worked together on the Gloucester fishing boats for a short time. Swan who was five years older, had been drafted into the army, and came back from Vietnam with a prosthetic leg and a heroin addiction. He was a mess long enough to lose his young wife and their son to divorce before taking a long and painful route to recovery. About six years ago, McKenna had helped Swan secure his manager job at the marina. Swan hid his gratitude under the steadfast pretense that McKenna was a big swell of a boat owner. This, while for years the McKenna family "yacht" had been a diminutive, if sweet sailing, Cape Dory 25 named *Zephyr*.

"Sure. End of the waiting list. You took off, supposedly never to be seen again."

McKenna waited.

"But we'll find someplace for her," Swan said. "Long as you don't mind me shuffling her around."

"I'm going to want to stay on board. Few weeks or so, at least."

Swan nodded. "Yeah, I saw Caroline was back before you. That sucks."

McKenna knew that would be the end of the conversation with Swan about Caroline. He also knew that even if he were still living in the boat next spring, Swan would never say another word about it. He'd hustle the *Wanderer* around to different slips and moorings as long as he could, even if people complained.

"So what's the plan?" Swan asked. He gestured toward the boat. "Gonna put some new plaid cushions in her and start walking people through?"

"Don't know," McKenna said. "Hope it doesn't come to that."

Swan grunted. "You single-hand this back?"

McKenna shook his head. "Picked up a kid in Tortola, let him off in Boston yesterday."

"Work out okay?"

"Yeah," McKenna said. "Worked out just fine."

Later, safe for the night in a dockside berth, McKenna sat below deck. The cabin seemed unnaturally bright, now that he could plug in the yellow umbilical cord for shore power. Fresh water right on the dock. Shower just up the ramp, to the back of the marina main building.

All the comforts of home, including car tires humming over the steel grate of the bridge above, the pervasive smell of diesel fuel, and the sound of an atrocious band massacring an old Van Morrison song coming from the big white restaurant behind the marina.

McKenna thought about how easy it had been to lie to Swan.

How it really didn't hurt. Perhaps simply because, although Swan was a good friend, he wasn't an intimate friend.

Or maybe McKenna was just quickly getting better at lying.

The thought gave him hope.

CHAPTER 20

AROUND NOON THE NEXT DAY, LANGDON CHECKED INTO A MOTEL ROOM on Beacon Street in Brookline. He used the Stephen Cross name. The place was a bit of a dive—Langdon could smell roach spray and see a few of the buggers still skittering off in the corners.

Yet, for his purposes, it would be fine.

He didn't intend to live there, just complete a little work. He was living under another false ID and credit card at the Four Seasons, but he preferred not to stress even that kind of link, in case things had to get ugly. As they so often seemed to do.

No, better to pay cash for a room and a phone.

He swept the small work desk of the skimpy brochures and "Where To Dine In Boston" literature, then he set up his notebook computer.

He pulled out a pad of white lined paper and then waited as the computer warmed up. He was hardly a hacker, but he had learned a few things along the way that saved him a good deal of legwork.

First he tackled the telephone CDs.

Checking for Rob, Robert, or R. McKenna across the top three eastern Massachusetts area codes.

The results didn't surprise him, but didn't please him either. One hundred and twenty-two names. Goddamn mackerel snappers. So many of them in the Boston area. He tried just the 617 area code. Down to thirty. Still too many. Especially since there was every chance that McKenna and his wife may have sold their house because they were on an extended cruise; then there would be no phone number to find them at anyhow. . . .

He checked the yellow-pages listing for marinas and yacht clubs along the Massachusetts coast, and then sighed. It would take him all day to phone all of them. He'd do it if necessary. But it felt too public. Too many people would remember the call, and while he didn't see how they'd be able to trace it back to him, it would mean at least a day of masking his voice. So bloody boring.

He tapped his pencil against the desk.

Langdon remembered something the girl had said: The girl at the store, Laura. About the boat registration being in Boston, instead of Delaware.

Langdon called one of the marinas and played the idiot, telling the gentleman who answered that he was trying to track down a boat for sale he'd seen while on shore and wanted advice on how to find it.

"Was it documented?" the man asked.

Langdon told him simply what he knew. "Just saw the name. The *Wanderer*, out of Boston."

The man grunted. "Then it's most likely documented if it's got the home harbor like that. Call the Coast Guard, tell them you're looking for a certificate of ownership."

Two more phone calls for information, and Langdon reached the vessel documentation automated line at the Coast Guard. He listened carefully, jotted down the numbers, and then set his notebook computer to send a fax. He sent a formal request, including a credit card number for the fee and the motel's fax number for the reply. He used the Steve Cross name for the credit card.

Afterward, he called the front desk and told them to ring him when the fax arrived.

He sat on the bed and watched the soft porn on the television until the phone rang and the manager said the fax was there.

Langdon clicked off the movie. Ho-hum. Mildly arousing, but nothing that he and his sister hadn't done better many times before.

Langdon went to the office and paid cash for the fax, the hotel room, the movie rental, and the telephone charges. The motel manager, a pink-faced bald man with bad breath, glanced at his watch. Only an hour and a half had transpired since Langdon had checked in. Langdon assumed that the bulk of the man's business came from johns and adulterers.

As the man handed Langdon the fax, he winked. "Little business and pleasure, Mr. Cross?"

Langdon made himself redden.

"Come again," the manager said with a smirk.

Bet you say that to all the customers. Langdon thought. But he kept his shoulders stiff, playing the annoyed cheating husband as he walked out to his rental car.

He looked at the certificate of ownership. Mr. and Mrs. Robert McKenna, Seventy-seven River Road, Newburyport, Massachusetts. At least that was their address when the boat was registered, over a year back.

Time for a visit.

First off, Newburyport took longer to reach than Langdon expected.

Then he got turned around a little bit before he found River Road. Stupid, really, because it was right along the Merrimack River.

And then when he did find it, no one was home.

He waited outside the house for two hours, and a young couple with two kids pulled their Honda Accord into the driveway. Nice looking young family. Dark-haired man with a bit of a belly. Pretty wife, late twenties probably. Pudgy little boy, pudgy little girl. Someday maybe they'd look as nice as their mom, Langdon hoped.

He got out of his car and walked across the grass.

The young man said, "Help you?"

He smiled when he said it, but there was a bit of who-is-this-man-walking-on-my-property attitude.

Langdon smiled deprecatingly. "Sorry to intrude." Rather than the private-detective cover, he used the story he'd thought up during the wait. That he had met Rob and Caroline when they were over in London a few years back for a visit, and they'd exchanged cards but had lost touch. Their phone had been disconnected, but now that he was in Boston on business, he had taken a drive up to Newburyport to say hello. Langdon used his most chipper English accent, which he figured would open doors with these two yuppies.

The young man shrugged. "They moved. Sailed away." He grinned. "Open *Cruising World*, maybe you'll see them there." He gestured back at the house, which bore the obvious signs of having been scraped for painting. "Hope I have the same luck, someday."

"Oh, Chris," the wife said, reprovingly. She looked at their two children.

Chris raised his hand as if in apology then let it flop by his side. "Oh, yeah."

"Why, was there a problem?" Langdon asked. He really didn't care, but it was only natural for someone in his supposed position to ask.

Now Chris looked embarrassed. "Ahhh . . . how good a friend did you say you were?"

"I only knew them for a short time, but I'd say we hit it off better than just acquaintances." Langdon gave them his most humble smile. "I showed them around London, and they insisted they'd want to do the same for me in Boston if I ever came to town."

"So you didn't know their daughter?" The wife said.

The way she said it, Langdon knew immediately to look concerned and did. He said, "They talked about her certainly, but I never met her."

The young woman moved closer, separating him from her own children. She looked back at her husband and he said, "Let's go in the house, kids."

The woman told him about the "tragedy." About Sam's death, about her running with that boy R. J. Most of it she knew from the newspapers, because, of course, this wasn't the sort of thing one discussed when buying a house from someone. But she didn't want her children to know that the girl who had lived in the house had died.

"You know how kids are," she said.

"I certainly do," Langdon said as if he'd bounced half a dozen on his knee back home. "My God, I don't want to intrude, but I certainly should find them and at least offer my condolences. Do you know if they're back in town?"

The young woman kept talking. About how sad it was. About the horror of raising your kids only to have something like that happen. About how she wouldn't know what to do with herself if it happened to one of her babies.

Langdon almost hit her. But he kept the polite smile, nodded in the right places, and said, "Of course," and "Absolutely," and "I completely agree."

When he finally got some breathing room, he asked if she knew how to get in touch with either of them.

No, she did not. The realty office which sold the house was Rob's own business, and she knew for a fact he'd closed that when he sailed away.

Nor did she know any of their friends, except for Mariel.

"Mariel?"

"Really, we just bought the house from them," she said. "But you should check with Mariel. She was their neighbor for years, she might know." The woman pointed to the light gray house set back from the river. "I don't expect she's home now, I don't see her car."

"So you have no idea as to how I can find the McKennas?"

"Sorry." The woman shook her head. "Far as I know, they're still out at sea."

"How about where they kept their boat when they were at home? Maybe somebody there would know."

The woman looked thoughtful, then shrugged, and said, "There's a bunch of marinas. Somewhere on the waterfront, I guess."

"Thank you," Langdon said gently and walked away.

Somewhere on the waterfront, I guess. Langdon thanked God silently that he and Ronnie had taken a different path those many years before, fleeing the suburbs.

CHAPTER 21

MCKENNA WAS THINKING HE WOULD GIVE CAROLINE A CALL THAT NIGHT to see if they could get together the next day. *I just want to be friends again and not move too fast.*

Sounded silly, but that's what he wanted.

Get to know her again, he'd say to her. "Rebuild."

Learn how to be a better liar, more like it.

He cracked his first beer of the day and looked out across the river. Swan now had him on the next to last dock. Great view. The sun was low in the sky, warming McKenna and the entire town in light that made anything seem possible.

McKenna almost didn't hear the man coming up the dock, he was so quiet. But, even as relaxed as he was trying to be, McKenna turned immediately at the movement in his peripheral vision.

The man was tallish, simply dressed in khaki pants and a white short-sleeved shirt. Thinning hair and an unremarkable face. But he moved with a kind of contained vigor that made McKenna watch him carefully.

And then he walked around the bow of the *Wanderer* and down the little finger pier to stand in front of McKenna.

The man asked for McKenna by name.

Boston accent. With maybe something else behind it.

A friendly, yet reserved, expression.

"That's me," McKenna said.

"Good." The man smiled. "I've been looking for you."

"About what?"

McKenna's heart began to hammer, but he kept his face calm. At least, he'd like to think he did.

"About Tom Cain."

The man was looking at him closely.

McKenna mentally took a deep breath—but said, easily enough, "Sure. What's up?" His mouth was suddenly dry.

"Do you know where I can find him?"

McKenna shrugged. "Some place in Boston. He got off when we made Rowe's Wharf yesterday."

"Tell you where he was going?"

McKenna shook his head. "I didn't know him that well, even after the time we spent, Mister . . . ?"

"Cross. Stephen Cross." The man put out his hand, and McKenna shook it. The hand was hard and dry, and McKenna sensed a dismaying amount of strength. The man showed McKenna a license identifying him as a private detective with an address on Beacon Street in Boston.

The man searched McKenna's face carefully.

McKenna fought the urge to ignore the man's open curiosity and, instead, do what would appear more natural—ask, with a touch of asperity, "Is there a problem?"

The man stared at him, and then said, "I hope not. Just trying to get in touch with Tom."

"I'm sorry, I don't know what else to tell you. He said he went to school at Harvard and I believe he's from Connecticut originally."

"Did he tell you anything about his family?" Cross asked.

McKenna shook his head. "Nothing other than some comment to the effect that they thought he was a bum for wasting his degree at Harvard by sailing around the world."

"Mmmmm . . ." the man said. "Well, that's partially why I'm looking for him. His father is ill, and they've been estranged over the past few years. His father wanted me to chase him down so they could talk."

"I see." McKenna took a sip of beer to give himself a moment to think. The man was lying. McKenna was fairly certain the name Tom Cain was false. If so, this man had to be lying about the elder, dying father.

McKenna said, "How did you know he sailed over with me?"

The man chuckled. "Took some doing." He told McKenna that he had followed Cain from the U.K. to the Virgin Islands; from there the young woman at the marina store had been kind enough to look through receipts and match Cain with McKenna.

"I'm amazed she remembered us," McKenna said. It scared him to think how easy it had been.

"People often surprise me with how much they notice," Cross said. "That's why it's hard for me to imagine you and Cain sailing all that time on a small boat without at least *some* conversation about what each of you would do once you made land. . . . There's a great deal of money involved, and I understand the father wants to make amends . . ."

The man waited and McKenna lifted his palms up. "Sorry."

Cross took another tack. "Exactly when did you leave him at Rowe's Wharf?"

McKenna had already thought that through, but paused as if considering it for the first time. "I'd say he took off around two o'clock, maybe a little later."

"And what did he do? Grab a taxi?"

McKenna said, "I guess at some point. But he said he wanted to walk over to Faneuil Marketplace and sample something other than canned stew."

"Food got a little old, did it?"

McKenna made a rueful face. "And he said he was a good cook. He lied."

"How about his girlfriend?"

"What's that?"

"He has a girlfriend, I believe."

"Yes, he mentioned something about her," McKenna said. "But I never learned her name."

The man looked impatient. "Nothing? Weeks together on this boat, and you don't even talk about women?"

McKenna lifted his shoulders. "Look, I'm sorry . . . But Cain and I didn't get along all that well. Nothing terrible, but his sailing skills were like his cooking skills—they didn't seem to match the credentials he'd given me. We got through, and it worked out all right—but neither of us was looking to keep in touch."

"Hmmm." Cross looked at him intently. "Did he leave anything on board, by chance?"

McKenna shook his head. "Nothing."

"Mind if I take a look?" Cross gestured to the open cabin.

McKenna raised his eyebrows. "You want to search my boat?"

Cross waved that away. "Just take a look around."

"For what?"

"Anything that will help me find him," Cross said. He grinned. "You've watched television. Postcard, magazine. Old packet of matches."

"Mail delivery is lousy during a voyage," McKenna said. He paused. He wanted this man to be satisfied and move on. Finally, McKenna shrugged. "Suit yourself. But there's nothing of his here."

McKenna stepped back, and Cross swung himself onboard with a lightness that seemed out of keeping with his unprepossessing appearance. The detective stepped down into the cabin. "Where did our friend sleep?" he asked.

McKenna told him to look in the forward cabin.

He felt weak in the knees.

He suddenly felt certain that there would be something incriminating right there. An overlooked bloodstain. A diamond stuck in the cushions, some object of Cain's left in a place where this man not only could find it, but was *expecting* to find it. What if this man had talked with Cain on the radio while McKenna was knocked out? What if he *knew* McKenna was lying?

The detective went up to the bow, and McKenna waited in the cockpit.

After a few minutes, the man said, "Mr. McKenna? Can I ask you what this is?"

McKenna leaned in. "What's that?"

"In here?" the man said. "Can I show you?"

McKenna hesitated.

He didn't want to go down there.

Not into the cabin where he had killed Gleason and Cain. Not when it was all too possible the man simply wanted to extract answers by force.

Luckily for McKenna, Swan came down the finger pier at that moment.

"Gotta move you back to the ghetto, Rob," he said. "The Eastons are coming back and want their slip. You get her lines off, and I'll bring the workboat around, give you a tow."

McKenna turned in Cross's direction and apologized. "You'll have to excuse me. I'm in a gypsy position here, and I have to move the boat now."

Cross came up the stairway, reluctantly. McKenna made a point of introducing Cross to Swan. The two men shook hands. McKenna noticed Swan looking at Cross carefully.

Then Swan went off for the workboat, his prosthetic leg moving stiffly.

McKenna quickly began untying the lines. "I'm going to be a bit busy for a while," he said. "I've told you all I know about Cain anyway."

Cross nodded. "And your wife? Perhaps she can help me?"

"She can't," McKenna said, flatly. "She never met the man. He wouldn't have been on board if she were sailing back with me."

"I see," Cross said. "I'd hate to bother her . . ."

"Then don't," McKenna said. The man looked him, his eyes cold and blue.

Langdon said, "I'd like to come back if I think of any more questions."

"I've told you all I know," McKenna said. He put his hand out to the dock, gesturing politely, but firmly, that it was time for Cross to leave.

Cross simply smiled and stepped off the boat.

McKenna smiled right back. Two, friendly, helpful guys. And then McKenna jumped down on the dock to push the *Wanderer* out of the slip. Once she was moving, he climbed back on board while Swan puttered up in the gray workboat.

He could feel Cross's eyes on him all the way to the next dock. But when at last the boat was tied down in its new berth, McKenna turned to find the man was gone.

CHAPTER 22

CAROLINE CALLED SOPHIA BENCHLEY AROUND TWO THE NEXT AFTER-noon to say she definitely wanted the apartment and, if it was at all possible, could she move in that afternoon?

Sophia sounded surprised, but agreed when Caroline explained that this was her day off from the store. Caroline didn't reveal exactly what was motivating her, but she suspected Sophia would have understood if she had. After her telephone conversation with Rob that morning, Caroline had a sudden but definite need to start her own life.

Luckily, soon after Sophia agreed, Elliott came home for a late lunch. She asked him to drive her over.

"Sure," he said, looking surprised. "Didn't know you'd be moving on so soon."

I need a car, Caroline thought. *This week I'll pick up a car, something cheap, something that will get me around town. No, the hell with that. I'll get something I like. Used Volkswagen convertible, maybe a Saab. Pick up a new apartment, a car this week. Next week, a new life altogether.*

Elliott helped Caroline with her two bags and a small box of books and cookware that she'd bought since returning from the voyage. She looked at her things in the trunk of Elliott's old Volvo and decided that, including the boxes and few pieces of furniture still in storage, she had fewer possessions than when she and Rob were first married.

She and Elliott were quiet on the drive over. Caroline sat in the front seat feeling as if her insides were in danger of shattering like broken glass. Thinking how quickly she had become dependent upon the kindness of strangers. The Blanche Dubois of Newburyport, she told herself.

Or nearly strangers, anyhow. A few weeks ago she hadn't even known Elliott, and now he was transporting her off to her first home alone since . . . ever.

She'd gone from her parent's home to college to marriage.

When they reached Sophia's house, Elliott turned off the car and looked at her directly. "Mariel will be all over me if I don't ask. And I'm naturally nosy anyhow. What's the big rush?"

Elliott's brown eyes were calm and steady. Caroline knew he had been through a divorce himself and had an estranged son someplace on the West Coast. That Mariel and Elliott apparently loved each other, but in their year of being together, marriage was not a consideration.

"I might as well go," Caroline said, lightly. "Talked to my ex this morning and nothing's happening there. Might as well get on with my new life, such as it is."

"He's not really your ex yet, is he?"

"Not technically," she said. After a moment's hesitation, she said, "And I had hoped not at all. But I figure it's time to look out for myself."

"Mmmmm," Elliott said.

She kept on, feeling like she was blathering, but he was a good listener: "Said he needed more time. Wanted to keep his distance for a while."

Elliott made a face. "That kind of talk typical of him?"

"No." Caroline shook her head. "Not at all. But it's what he's saying now. How do I answer that?"

"Hard to know."

"Damn straight," Caroline said.

She'd just been so stunned. Certainly it had been awkward when she'd left Rob at the hotel. But in thinking it over later, she had decided it was more important that he'd wanted to make love to her than that they'd actually had a wonderful, rousing time. That the stress had messed him up, and his wounded pride made him act like an embarrassed teenager. Not that he'd ever behaved that way before, but perhaps that's all it was now. Obviously the affection had been there. The passion.

She wouldn't even let herself think the word *love*, even though she believed it was there, too.

But then, this morning, she had gotten tired of waiting for him to call. At noon, she finally gave in and picked up the phone. Rob's cell phone was apparently turned off, so she called the marina. Swan answered. He seemed shy, but pleased to hear from her. And he was happy to go down and get Rob, had asked Caroline to wait.

She did just that.

But when Rob got on the phone, she knew in an instant it was going to be awful. She could hear the restraint in his voice.

The distance.

"I don't think it's a good idea," he'd said when she offered to get together. "I've got to work out some things."

"Like what?"

"Nothing to discuss," he said. But his voice wasn't just cool. More like tense. More like *guilty*. She thought again about the look on his face when she had asked if he had a girl in another port. Surprised. As if he hadn't even considered it. As if that would've been the least of his problems.

Although Caroline could try to read the tea leaves to figure out what his pauses and inflections might really mean, there was no mistaking his words: *"Caroline, I don't think we should see each other for a while."*

Elliott opened his door and started to get out. Then he looked back at Caroline and said, "You think he's started up with somebody else? I see it all the time. No law says you got to take him back."

"That's what you do?" Caroline said. "Follow people, take pictures?"

Elliott nodded. "It's not pretty. But that's what I do when I can't get something really satisfying, like an insurance contract to catch some guy dancing without his crutches."

Caroline thought about it. Wondered if this was what she was meant to do. Riding in this old Volvo, getting ready to hire a private detective to find out what her ex-husband was up to.

But broken glass inside her or not, she knew better. "No," she said. "Not that way."

Elliott nodded. "Good enough. Help you up the stairs with these boxes?"

CHAPTER 23

LANGDON CAME BACK TO THE MARINA JUST AFTER TWO IN THE MORN-ing. The moon had gone down and the docks were only faintly illu-minated by a few lights.

He parked his car several blocks away, then walked across the shell-covered parking lot as if he had a simple and obvious purpose.

He had stopped in briefly twice before that night, at ten and mid-night. He didn't think there was a night watchman. It appeared as if the one-legged man had a small apartment back near the workshop.

Langdon felt if he couldn't handle a middle-aged man with one leg, he was truly losing his touch.

He was pumped: felt he would make much better progress tonight than he had with Vincent. And even that hadn't turned out so badly. Had gotten him where he was now.

Langdon was fairly certain McKenna was lying. About what, he wasn't sure. It seemed hard to imagine that Tom Cain would share his story willingly. But McKenna knew something more, and Langdon wanted to know what it was.

Mostly it was McKenna's manner. Just a tad too casual. Accepted the dying father bit without any questions even though his eyes were skeptical. Then there was the cracked wooden door. The one heading toward the bow of the boat. Plus the vee berth cushions usually in a boat like this one were gone. Maybe they were out getting washed, but the blue ones in the main cabin were still there. Langdon had covered up more than his share of crime scenes in the past, and he recognized a subtle but identifiable sense of something being cleaned over, something being hidden.

There was also that stock denial that cops the world over had heard, and Langdon had said himself more than once. . . . "I've told you everything I know." That and the flash of genuine fear when Langdon had mentioned visiting the man's wife.

Caroline McKenna.

You're lying, Mr. McKenna, Langdon thought as he stepped onto the dock beside McKenna's boat. He took the gun out and laid it against his leg.

Langdon felt, rather than saw movement behind him. He was halfway onto the boat, one foot on the rail, the other still on the dock.

In other words, in an awkward-as-hell position to deal with the sudden movement behind him. The sudden movement from the cockpit of the sailboat beside the *Wanderer.*

Nevertheless, Langdon almost made it. He shoved himself backward, and was bringing the gun around when something hit his arm. Something black and hard, and then that something whistled and he took a staggering blow to his left temple. Damned if he didn't feel his grip loosen on the gun.

The man drove Langdon against the sailboat and grabbed at the gun. Since Langdon couldn't seem to make himself work properly, he simply dropped the gun behind himself into the water. He shoved off the sailboat once more, but his knees were weak and the man backed away and hit him again and again.

Langdon took in that it was McKenna—the amateur, the sailor, Langdon's next *victim* for Christ's sakes—swinging the big club.

And then McKenna got Langdon on the head one too many times, and he passed out altogether.

* * *

When Langdon awoke, he was inside the sailboat. McKenna was shining a flashlight into Langdon's eyes. Langdon supposed that's what he had been using to hit him, one of those big police flashlights.

McKenna was still breathing heavily. Langdon expected he had just finished slinging him down the stairs.

"Mind if I feel around to see what damage you've done?" Langdon said, mildly.

McKenna waved the flashlight at him. "What're you doing here, Cross? Why'd you come down to my boat with a gun?"

His voice sounded hoarse and shaky.

That made Langdon feel a bit of relief. The man was scared.

Langdon's right wrist felt very sore, but he could move it. He felt his face and there was blood there and a pulpy feel to his left side of his forehead. "Mind if I sit up?"

"You try anything, I'll go to work on you again," McKenna said.

Scared. Definitely scared about what he'd done.

Langdon carefully sat up, thinking that if it was a good thing Ronnie wasn't here to see *this*. He said, "Avon calling."

McKenna drew back on the flashlight, and Langdon raised his hand, "Please. Just a joke."

"What do you want?"

"I think you know."

"Answer my question!"

Langdon didn't bother. He said, "I also want Tom Cain."

"He's gone."

"Gone where?"

McKenna shrugged. "Just gone. Don't waste your time."

"No waste." Langdon looked at him steadily. But now McKenna had closed down, and Langdon could read nothing. Which was something in itself. Clearly, he was hiding something.

"Let me guess," Langdon said. "You ripped him off yourself."

"Don't know what you're talking about," McKenna said. "But I know you'll get hurt if you keep following me around.

"You got very lucky here, my friend."

"Don't come around again."

"I'm afraid it's not that simple. There's property of mine that's missing. And my business with Mister Cain is urgent."

"What property?"

Langdon stared at him. "If you have it, you know."

McKenna said, "But I don't."

Said it a rather too quickly for Langdon's taste.

Langdon made himself relax. Made himself sit back. Telegraphing that there was nothing to fear in him, that all he wanted to do was to talk.

And then he kicked McKenna in the balls.

At least that was the plan. But the man was quicker than Langdon had expected. McKenna turned slightly, took the blow on his thigh.

From there, he wound up quickly with the heavy flashlight, and Langdon barely made it to his feet before the first blow arrived, crashing against the side of his head, right on the same damned spot.

Lucky, Langdon thought, falling to his knees. The flashlight whistled down again.

Thank *God* Ronnie wasn't here to see this.

CHAPTER 24

McKenna loaded Langdon into the back of Swan's pickup truck.

Swan had loaned him the spare set of keys to the marina's pickup truck a few days back and said he was free to use it off hours if anything urgent came up.

McKenna figured three in the morning, as transportation for an unconscious—possibly dying—man qualified.

Cross was still breathing. But when McKenna felt his throat, his pulse was fluttery.

McKenna was shaking. Adrenaline was singing through his veins.

He'd almost killed the man right in the boat. Almost didn't stop himself.

Now, he threw a tarp over Cross's body and got behind the wheel of the old truck. It took a while to crank over, and he said aloud, "Stay in bed, Swan. Just stay there."

Swan's window remained dark.

McKenna took off out of the parking lot and headed toward town, wondering just what the hell he was going to do next.

God Almighty.

What he *should* do was clear.

Not clear the way it had been when he made that first mistake with Cain. Back then, "clear" meant doing the right thing. Call the Coast Guard over, let them haul Cain away. Christ, he still had that kind of choice: the police station was all of about two blocks away from the marina.

But McKenna barely considered that.

"Clear" now meant he should kill the man in the back of the truck. Cross, or whatever his name was. Bludgeon him, or stab him, or cut his throat.

Hide his body.

McKenna stopped the truck at a light in Market Square. Thinking about what killing the man entailed. Had the boat's prop not been damaged the obvious thing to do would have been to motor out to sea and drop the body. Hit him with something, the flashlight, McKenna supposed, until his head was crushed and his heart stopped.

Dump him like his predecessors, Cain and Gleason. Sink him in the black water, and then scrub the boat. Erase him from McKenna's life before he encroached any further. Before he found his way to Caroline.

Now McKenna's choice seemed to be to hide the body on land someplace. Or dump him off a bridge. But all the bridges McKenna knew of in Newburyport were too public. Too easy even at three in the morning for someone see him.

A horn honked behind him, and McKenna realized the light had changed. And that now there was someone who may remember a man woolgathering in an old truck at three in the morning.

McKenna accelerated slowly through the town center.

Civilization, under the shroud of darkness.

Buildings where people worked, lived, made love, and struggled through their days. Perhaps some of them did wrong to each other from time to time, but most of them followed the law, followed the tacit agreement of how people behaved toward one another.

McKenna felt alien from them, from the human race as he knew it.

He told himself the man under the tarp would have almost cer-tainly killed him. Tortured him, perhaps. Even though Cain and Gleason had been fully capable of leaving him to drown—this man would have done worse.

McKenna could feel it.

He arrived at his destination without really thinking about it. Saw what he was going to do, saw that it was a stopgap that he would almost certainly live to regret.

"Ah, damn it," he breathed.

He just couldn't kill the man in cold blood. McKenna simply didn't have it in him.

Instead, he turned off High Street and went to the hospital. When he reached the emergency room parking lot he immediately walked around the truck and dropped the tailgate. The man was still breathing. McKenna hauled Cross off the tailgate, dragged him under the awning, and slung him into a wheelchair. It was as awkward as hell because the chair kept rolling away. McKenna had to bend down to put the man's feet onto the foot plates, and then he spun the chair around and shoved it at the automatic door.

It opened and Cross rolled into the vestibule. By then, McKenna was already in the truck, and from his peripheral vision, he could see through the glass doors that a nurse was running toward the slumped man in the wheelchair.

McKenna took off, certain he had made yet another bad choice.

CHAPTER 25

WHEN LANGDON AWOKE IN THE HOSPITAL ROOM, IT TOOK HIM A GOOD few minutes to know where he was and why. Then he figured it out or at least thought he had. McKenna had brought him in himself. Langdon chuckled ruefully, even though it made his head hurt.

Amateur.

He was dizzy and, when he turned his head even a bit quickly, he would get double vision. Concussion, he realized. He'd had more than one of those in his years, and the news made him tired. He wouldn't be in much shape for anything for at least a few days.

Damn that McKenna. Add it to his bill.

A plainclothes cop walked into the room. Badge attached to the pocket of a too-small sport jacket. Carrying an old brown briefcase. He was a big guy, perhaps a high-school football player going to fat. His collar unbuttoned, his neck thick. He reminded Langdon of Mr. Vincent. Dark thick hair, bristling mustache, burst blood vessels in his face, and a big red honk of a nose. A drinker. Smoker, too. Cigarette burns on his coat and tie.

But his eyes were intelligent looking, red rimmed or not. Langdon told himself to be careful.

The cop introduced himself as Detective Pollock.

Langdon chose his Boston accent and introduced himself as

Stephen Cross. Might as well, seeing as that was the only ID he had on him. Presumably the emergency room staff would have already looked through his pockets.

"How're you feeling, Mister Cross?" Pollock asked.

"Wonderful, thanks."

"You should feel *special*."

Langdon raised his eyebrows.

"Oh, yeah. Very special," the detective said. "Getting mugged in Newburyport. That's what you babbled about when you came to, the doctor said. Said that you were claiming to be mugged. This isn't Boston, we don't have that kind of trouble too often. Bar fights, sure. Domestic abuse, you bet. But not muggings."

Langdon saw where this was heading, so he simply waited.

The cop sat down, leaned forward so his face was inches away from Langdon's, and said, "This mugger was so frigging stupid, he left you with your wallet and cash. Just who the hell are you and what are you doing here?"

Langdon raised his palms. "Bit of recovery, that's all."

The cop said, "One, there is no Stephen Cross registered as a PI in Boston. Two, if you are legit, what're you doing in town without stopping in to clear it with us?"

"I'm not here on business. Just a day trip to see your beautiful town. I can't explain the bookkeeping at the registry."

The cop rolled his eyes. Clearly didn't believe him and clearly didn't much care.

They both looked at each other, and then Langdon smiled. The man had nothing.

Langdon said, "I'll be on my way soon. Thanks for your concern."

The cop sat back. "All part of the service. I like to keep my town as trouble free as I can." Pollock unsnapped his briefcase and took out a small point-and-shoot camera.

"I'd rather not—" Langdon began to say.

But by then the cop had raised the camera to his eye and squeezed off a shot. The flash hurt Langdon's eyes, making his head throb even worse.

"Don't you worry, Mister Cross," the cop said. "We'll make

enough prints so every cop in town can be on the lookout for you. We don't have that much to do around here, so in case you come back, we'll be watching—just to make sure nobody hurts you again." The cop grinned. "How about that?"

"What can I say?" Langdon said.

"How about, 'Good-bye and have a nice life.' " The cop slipped the camera back into his briefcase and walked away.

Langdon touched his head, feeling dizzy again. *Just put it on McKenna's bill.*

The chance to submit that bill came along far sooner than Langdon expected. Around three o'clock that afternoon, McKenna walked into the hospital room. He was carrying a small vase of flowers.

"How's the head, Steve?" His voice was tense, but straining for hearty. Presumably for the benefit of the nurse behind him. He closed the door.

Langdon felt something akin to fear, a quick tripping in his heart. He almost threw himself out of the bed, but he took in McKenna's full hands, his clear-eyed, if nervous, appearance. Langdon decided to just wait.

"You shouldn't have," Langdon gestured to the flowers.

"Gift shop downstairs. Makes it easy for impulsive guys like me."

Langdon waved to the chair. "Guess we got off on the wrong foot last night."

"Your gun threw me."

"Ah, that. Live and learn." Langdon touched his bandaged temple. "It was kind of you to take me here."

The two man stopped talking. Just sat watching each other for a moment.

Finally, McKenna broke the silence.

"All right," he said. "Let's get down to it."

Langdon nodded.

"I want this to be over." McKenna's voice was hoarse. "Tell me what you're looking for—and I'll tell you if I can help."

Langdon wondered if it was a setup. If the man was wearing a wire. But he didn't think so. He thought this lucky bastard knew better than to think he would win another round. Nevertheless, Langdon proceeded cautiously. "Mister Cain took off with some . . . valuable property. I want them back. And I want Cain himself."

"Describe the property."

"I don't think that's necessary."

McKenna shook his head impatiently. "Look, I'm trying to get my life back together, and I don't need your brand of trouble."

Langdon considered McKenna. The man was bristling with repressed energy. Scared, angry, pumped up. Langdon said abruptly "Bright and pretty things. You'll know them when you see them."

McKenna's shoulders seemed to sag. If Langdon could read the man's face correctly, relief was heavily mixed with disappointment.

McKenna reached into his inside coat pocket and withdrew a bulky yellow envelope. He tossed it onto Langdon's bed.

Langdon undid the clasp and looked in.

He smiled. He poured the stones into his cupped hand, made a quick survey, and figured most all of them were there. Probably all of them. He slid them back into the envelope.

What a relief.

Langdon touched the bandage on his head and said, "Looks like I've been approaching things the wrong way all my life. Here I thought it was the victor who won the spoils."

McKenna nodded, looking out the window. Looking pretty glum now. "That's the way I always heard it, too."

"Now then," Langdon said. "This is a wonderful start."

"That's it," McKenna said. "Take them, go away."

Langdon made a face. "Not quite so simple. I need to meet with Mister Cain."

"I can't help you there. He's gone."

"Just forgot these, did he?" Langdon tapped the envelope. "Must've felt like such a fool when he got home." He let his eyes meet McKenna's, let him see the monster behind his well-developed mildness. Softly, he said, "Where is the little shit?"

McKenna's face whitened. But then he shook his head. "Gone. Don't waste your time."

Langdon cocked his head. "Is that right? This is something you know—something you *did*—yourself?"

McKenna made a face, somewhere between a laugh and a grimace. But he wasn't enough of an amateur to actually answer the question.

"I need some proof," Langdon said. "I have an associate who will insist upon proof. And there's a girl. My friend will be very interested in contacting Cain's young woman."

"I don't know anything about her." McKenna gestured to the diamonds. "That's all you need. So stay away from me and my wife." He stood up. "Now we're done here. You go back to doing whatever you do—and I'll do the same."

Relief was now the most evident emotion on McKenna's face. Like he was waking from a nightmare, or, better still, striding away from one under his own power. In control of his destiny.

Langdon smiled genially. *The fool.*

Langdon checked himself out of the hospital around eight that night. The doctor, an intense young Pakistani woman, followed him around talking in severe tones about the effects of his brain colliding against the inside walls of his skull, about swelling, about pressure, about the potential for permanent damage, possible seizures, and death. Langdon finally put his arm around her and said with all sincerity, "Either bugger off, or I'll give you a concussion of your very own."

She shrank away, and he paid the bill with the Stephen Cross credit card. Truly, she might have been right, he thought as he rested against the counter while waiting for the card authorization. He felt nauseous, dizzy, and very, very tired.

But the thought of people working on his head—of him talking while he was under anesthesia—was a bit scarier than death. Langdon had been arrested from time to time, but never done a day of prison time. He had absolutely no plans to spoil that record.

He caught a taxi to the marina and got his car. He had to pull over twice on the way back to the Four Seasons in Boston to wait for his vision to clear. Thank God, there were valets to park the car.

His knees were wobbling as he left the elevator and found his way to his room. All he wanted to do was sleep, although the young doctor had made that point, too: depending on the nature of the injury, he might move from a deep sleep to a coma.

Bugger that, too, he thought. He needed the sleep.

And so he walked into his room, dizzy, disorientated, and far from the top of his game. The light was off. It wasn't until he was almost to the bed that he realized someone was there. Langdon didn't have his gun, and tired as he was, he fell into his stance, legs planted firmly, ready to take on the white shape slipping out of the bathroom.

Dobyns's people, he figured. Maybe McKenna.

Whoever it was gave a small shriek.

And then there was laughter, and he stood grinning, flushed and happy. "Almost knocked your bloody head off," he said.

Ronnie flipped on the light. She was wearing one of his shirts, nothing else. He could see she had been napping in the bed. Flying exhausted her. She looked tousled, her dark hair a tangle, her eyes sleepy. And yet she still took his breath away.

Ronnie's smile faded. She took in the bandage on his head, the way he was weaving. "Oh, sweetie. Who did this?"

She hurried to him and touched him lightly, her hands cool. "My brother doesn't play well with anyone but me," she murmured.

He reached into his coat and handed her the envelope.

"Oh, baby," she breathed, opening the packet of diamonds. A single tear streaked down her cheek. "Baby, baby, you take such good care of me. It's my turn to take care of you now."

He closed his eyes and took it all in. She stroked his face, the line of his jaw. Her touch was light, yet it made him tremble inside. It was as if she owned their very libido. Her sexual force was theirs to share, but hers to control.

She could have others, but he never could.

"Did you find Tommy?" she whispered. "Did you find his pretty little girl?"

"Just the diamonds for today," he said, lightly. "Just five million dollars."

Her hand paused.

He kept his eyes closed, not wanting to see her face harden, watch the cold ice form in her eyes.

He waited.

Twenty-nine years together, and he still couldn't tell if she truly loved him. But he knew she considered him to be hers. Hers to manipulate, hers to rail against, hers to seduce, hers to send forth to commit murder and mayhem.

He, of course, loved her unconditionally.

CHAPTER 26

JIMMY DOBYNS POURED HIMSELF A GLASS OF MILK. IT WAS ALMOST three in the morning, and he couldn't sleep.

Jimmy didn't consider himself a nervous man. But his gut hurt, and his doctor said that he should come in and get it checked out, that it might be an ulcer. Said to stay away from milk, too. But milk was cold and seemed like it should be good for that burning spot in his belly, so fuck the doctor.

Jimmy looked out the kitchen window to the surf crashing up on the beach. He was worried about Gleason.

Not worried like he was pining for the errant son he never had. Not worried like the bird you feed seeds to in the park who hasn't shown up lately; cat must've got him.

No, it was more like where the hell is this guy? What's he doing? What's he *done*?

Gleason had been on Dobyns's payroll for damn near twenty-five years. Recruited him right out of high school. Ugly son-of-a-bitch who was rumored to have rigged a car battery to explode in the face of the football star who liked to rag on him in front of the girls.

Gleason knew too much to be out of sight so long. But Dobyns couldn't really see him sitting down with the FBI and telling tales.

Dobyns would have at least heard *something*. There hadn't been a word, a whisper, that Gleason was even seen with them.

Dobyns brooded on it for a while. Dobyns had trusted Gleason, but he was always willing to change his mind on the subject of trust.

Gleason was a guy who thought for himself, which was handy when you wanted to give him a job and see it done. Good with electronics, explosives, remote hits. But also a guy who could do it the old fashioned way: sawed-off shotgun, baseball bat, or a knife from ear to ear. Dump the body at sea, and then put in two to three hours of fishing on the way back. Said it was good for the alibi to come back with a mess of fish.

Dobyns finished the milk, washed the glass out, and dropped it into the dish rack. He rubbed his side gently as he walked to the living room door off of the kitchen. Buddy was on the sofa reading *Sports Illustrated*.

He looked up. "How're you doing, Mister D.?"

Dobyns said, "You go to Gleason's place?"

"Yeah." Buddy looked worried. Dobyns had questioned him about this several times already.

"His boat there?"

"His boat?" Buddy was confused.

"His boat," Dobyns snapped. "That piece of shit he was always talking about. Was it on the trailer in the parking lot?"

Buddy made a face. "I didn't look. You told me to check out his car, and *it* was gone."

"Well go. Take a look and tell me."

Buddy nodded. "First thing in the morning."

Dobyns snapped his fingers. "First thing right now. Get off your ass and find out."

"Yes, sir." The big man got up and pulled on his leather coat.

Dobyns yawned. "Call me when you get there."

"Sure thing, Mister D."

Dobyns grunted as he rubbed his stomach. He went back into the kitchen and looked out the window onto Boston Harbor. Maybe the doctor knew what he was talking about, after all. Dobyns's stomach was starting to burn. He'd like to think Gleason's disappearance only meant that some big fish had pulled him overboard, eaten him.

Dobyns hoped that's all that had happened.

Because he kept thinking about Captain Barrett, dead in London. Now Gleason was gone. The two of them queer for fishing. Gleason going out on Barrett's boat every chance he got.

Buddies.

Barrett out of sight for over a month before he turned up burned and cut in that motor sailer. Gleason gone for just a few days. So maybe there was no connection.

Dobyns had talked again to Barrett's wife that morning. She didn't know much, sad, dim-witted cow that she was. But she did know that Barrett had chartered that very same motor sailer a few months back, was gone damn near two months, and came back with a case of imported scotch.

Dobyns burped softly. He had an idea forming and he didn't like the taste of it at all.

The more he thought about it, the more the story that Langdon had told about some vase sounded like bullshit.

About thirty minutes passed and the phone rang. Dobyns picked it up and it was Buddy. "Yeah, Jimmy, I guess I should've looked before. But I didn't even think about it, you know?"

"You saying it's gone? The boat?"

"Yeah."

Dobyns slammed the phone down.

He went back into the living room and saw that no one had replaced Buddy on watch. Nitwit Buddy, probably didn't let the next guy know.

Dobyns flicked the intercom to the upstairs bedroom and said, "Hey, who's on up there?"

There was a pause, and then a sleepy voice answered, "Just your token nigga."

Jerome. That's why Buddy hadn't called him. Anything to make Jerome look bad. "Get your ass down here," Dobyns barked.

Dobyns paced, waiting for Jerome to make it down.

On better days, Dobyns found it as funny as hell to say he was an equal opportunity hood. Privately, he thought of himself more as a talent scout. Truth was, these days even in organized crime, there were more people who needed dealing with. Outside organizations. Not just the Italians anymore. *People of color.* Jamaicans, Colum-bians, Mexicans, Japanese, Chinese. Blacks. Dobyns couldn't hire all of them. But he had the Spic kid, Luis, and having Jerome along for the ride made some deals go easier.

One with such an old-timey black name, too. Jer-*rome*.

As good as Jerome was, having him in the group made for prob-lems. Sometimes the other guys made assholes of themselves. Buddy, for sure. And Gleason. Dobyns rubbed his gut. They could all be such girls. But the fact was, Dobyns found it easier to shoot the shit with Jerome than he did with Gleason, even after all those years.

Jerome didn't need to be handled, appeased, screamed at, coached, or otherwise worked. Easy to be around, good sense of humor, and he'd do absolutely whatever you paid him to do.

Jerome came down the stairs. Tall, thick through the chest, long arms, huge hands. Black jeans, running shoes, black leather jacket that creaked when he walked. Not coming out with any of that drawl now, he could see that Dobyns had something on his mind.

Dobyns said, "I want you to get me the Fort Point fag. Art history guy."

"Chapman?"

"Yeah. Get him now. Make sure he's shaved and dressed good, and bring him here. Don't scare him too much. I'll want to take him out to see somebody this morning."

"Uh-huh. Then what?"

"Then get yourself over to the Four Seasons. Follow that Langdon guy. Want to know exactly where he goes, what he does, and I want call-ins at least twice a day. Get Luis to help you out, take the van and his big mother of a camera and lens so you can give me a Kodak moment. Just be careful, I don't want Langdon to know."

Jerome nodded.

Dobyns rubbed his stomach again. Goddamn on *fire*. "And tell Leanne to get up and run an iron over a suit for me. Lay out some breakfast by six—something easy on my stomach. And tell her to get me some Maalox right now."

Jerome nodded. "Some shit happening?"

"Maybe already did," Dobyns said.

He stared at Jerome, thinking, and then made a fast decision. He gestured to the sofa. "Sit down a minute. I gotta bring you up to speed. Some shit from before your time."

"Got something to do with Fatty?"

Jerome's name for Gleason. *Fatty Gleason.* He'd hum *The Honeymooners* tune whenever Gleason walked into the room.

Christ, no wonder Gleason hated him.

Dobyns said. "That's what we're gonna find out."

CHAPTER 27

McKENNA CHECKED HIS WATCH. JUST AFTER NOON ON MONDAY.

Caroline should be off from the store. He climbed the steps to Mariel's house and rang the bell.

After a moment, Mariel herself answered.

A big black man stepped up behind her.

McKenna had the distinct impression he was interrupting something. Mariel was dressed for work, but her face was flushed and the top buttons on her white blouse were open. McKenna and Mariel were old friends, so he just grinned.

"Gee, sorry," he said. "Should I come back in twenty?"

"Oh, shut up and get in here," she said, grinning right back. "About time you came around."

She took him by the hand and pulled him close for a tight hug. The man behind her simply smiled, and McKenna said, "Hey," over Mariel's shoulder.

She stepped back and introduced the two of them: Elliott, this is Rob. Rob, this is Elliot.

Then she turned back to McKenna. "So let me guess—you're so out of touch with your wife you think she still lives here?"

McKenna felt his face blanche.

Mariel caught it and grasped him by the arm. "Easy boy. She just moved into town. She's got her own apartment. Can do just fine without you, if you're not careful."

Elliott said to Mariel that he had to get going. She kissed him, and said that she would see him that night. He and McKenna shook hands and he took off.

Mariel pulled McKenna back into the kitchen. "Coffee?"

"Please." He pulled out a stool from her kitchen island and was swept with a sense of déjà vu. It felt like the life he'd once had, his wife and daughter safe back at the house, when he would take a few minutes on a Saturday morning for a cup of coffee with Mariel.

After her husband Van had left her, Mariel had leaned on McKenna and Caroline as if they were family. For almost two years, McKenna had taken on the tacit role of Mariel's surrogate husband, minus the physical aspect. From the mundane aspects of minor plumbing tasks, to putting on storm windows, to late nights where he would just be there to listen, McKenna and Mariel had their own closeness.

McKenna felt a sting in his eyes, so sudden and real has his past life become for that moment. Trying to shake it away, he said, "Tell me about Elliott."

So she did, telling about how they met (when she hired him) how they started dating (lunches that lasted too long), and finally, "Who knows from here, but I'm in love. . . ."

McKenna listened, happy for her. Mildly disturbed to find that the man was a detective, but he figured it'd be easy enough to keep his distance.

Finally, McKenna said, "So where's Caroline?"

"Don't know that I can tell you," Mariel teased. "You're not one of those abusive types, are you?"

The image of shooting Cain flashed before him, in harsh black and white. But he said, "Not so I've noticed."

She took a pad of paper from one of the island drawers. In her quick, clear handwriting, she wrote out the address and included the phone number for the apartment. And, then, just to make her point, she sketched a little map to show him exactly how to find the apartment.

"Here," she said, pushing the piece of paper over to him. "Go see her. You'll find her under her maiden name—but it doesn't have to remain that way. I know the two of have you have gone through living hell because of Sam. Caroline still loves you, but she can't— and won't—do it on her own."

McKenna toyed with his coffee cup. He felt relief. Maybe this would work out better. He had come to the house looking for Caroline, thinking that he had to try to get her away for a while. Somehow get her to take off for a week or two in case Cross came around again. Even if it meant taking her away himself—somehow finding a way to be with her without telling the truth.

But maybe this would work just as well now that she was living under her maiden name.

McKenna said, "During the whole voyage back, I did a lot of thinking. I need some more time. Maybe a week." He looked up at Mariel. "She's the most important thing in my life, but I can't see her right now."

"I don't get it," Mariel said.

"When I do, I'll let you know."

When Mariel started to argue, he put up his hand. "Please."

"Men, men, men," Mariel said. "Thank God you're such jerks, it pays my mortgage."

McKenna smiled. "Love you, too. Another thing. Tell her there's a guy working on the Four Winds complex who's been trying to track the two of us down."

The lawyer in Mariel moved to alert. "For what?"

McKenna spun a quick tale about a scam artist who had almost certainly faked a fall down the front steps of the Four Winds building, then sent a private detective out to "secure confirmation" that McKenna had warned the new owners that the steps were dangerously slippery in the rain. "The inference is that if we don't cooperate, maybe they'll go after us, too. It's all bull—there's nothing wrong with the steps, and I never suggested there was. He wants to interview Caroline, too. She was down on the lease as well, but she's been far from that end of the business for God knows how long."

"That's ridiculous," Mariel flared. "You've been free of the place for a year and a half!"

"That's what I said. But he's a persistent bugger—the name is Stephen Cross. In any case, if he calls you looking for her, do me a favor and don't pass along Caroline's name or number."

"Not a problem. And if this keeps up, contact your lawyer. You used Ray Cassall on the Four Winds sale, right?"

McKenna nodded.

"Good." She jotted Stephen Cross's name down on her legal pad. "Normally I'd just call this guy for you myself, but . . ." She let the thought trail away, and McKenna could see sad defiance in her eyes when she looked up from the legal pad.

McKenna thought he could read her. She was concerned about the possible conflict of interest—that if it came down to it, she would align herself with Caroline and lead the divorce against him.

"I understand," he said.

CHAPTER 28

JIMMY DOBYNS WAS WATCHING DAVID CHAPMAN EAT WHEN THE PHONE rang. The kid was wolfing down his pancakes. Turning into a pudgy little guy, with a roll of fat pushing down over his collar. Would've been easier if he undid the buttons at his neck, but, hey, where was the style in that? Dobyns took the call, listened, said all right, and put the receiver down.

Chapman, as usual, was wearing entirely black. Only bit of color was on his new cowboy boots—black ones—with turquoise insets and mock silver spurs.

The Sarsaparilla Kid, Dobyns thought.

Chapman had that sneering look on his face, but there wasn't much heat in it. He looked scared in front of Dobyns, which was the way things were supposed to be.

Dobyns had already eaten his breakfast and had told Leanne to wash the dishes and table with lots of hot water and soap after they left. Dobyns was deathly afraid of AIDS and didn't believe shit about it being hard to catch. Not that he had any evidence that Chapman actually had AIDS. It was just that Dobyns was more than a little homophobic.

But as far as Dobyns was concerned, who better for analyzing art?

Like getting a Jew for a lawyer, or a mean nigger like Jerome for sticking people with knives. Go for the best.

By the time Dobyns got to him about five or six years back, Chapman was damn close to becoming a street hustler. His parents pretty much dumped him soon after his fiancée finally smelled the coffee and called them at home to lodge a tearful complaint. Chapman had an impressive, but financially useless, degree in art history, and he was in the middle of an art-conservation program at the Fine Art Institute of Boston that he was desperate to finish.

Dobyns made sure he did. And he made sure Chapman could at least keep up the appearances of wealth—the car, the big loft in Fort Point, all that. Because what Chapman could do for Dobyns was move the stuff that Dobyns had started to dabble in, stolen art collections from out-of-state home break-ins. Chapman could talk the art talk, he already had a reputation as a rich little collector who was constantly buying and selling. Stuff that Dobyns would've had to hustle out of the trunk of the Caddy, Chapman could move with the right crowd and sell for a good price.

Of course, his real value to Dobyns just opened up—hell, skyrocketed—over the Rosalyn thing. Dobyns had been working him about a year when that opportunity came up. And the little shit loved it. Made him think he was the man. Chapman once told Dobyns that his "most cherished secret" was that he had "chosen" the buyer for the Rosalyn Museum heist.

Dobyns, thinking that the boy might work his way up to trying to jack him up for a bigger fee, had put Gleason on him with instructions to hurt him, but not do any permanent damage. "Teach him to keep his secrets to himself," Dobyns said to Gleason. "Like a real man."

Now Chapman looked worried. "You're suspicious of what, exactly?"

"You tell me when we get there," Dobyns said.

"Does Alcott know we're coming?"

Dobyns shook his head.

"What if he's not there?"

Dobyns stood up. "Just shut up and move it."

Chapman immediately put his fork down, picked up his black bag, and followed Dobyns out of the house.

It wasn't until they were in the limo that Dobyns spoke to him again. "That was the call I got earlier. I sent Buddy out this morning with a pair of binoculars. He says he saw Alcott himself."

"What if he won't meet with us? People with his kind of money tend to have every minute planned out."

Dobyns turned his eyes onto Chapman, saw the boy cringe. The little expert on the world of the wealthy.

"I mean, I could call Amanda for you," Chapman said. Amanda was Chapman's link to Alcott. She had been in the art-conservation program with Chapman. One of those gay guy and a girl friendships that Dobyns couldn't understand. Or maybe it was a bisexual thing. Chapman looked dopey whenever he talked about her, like he was sniffing around her, but knew the best shot he had with her was as a "friend." Dobyns knew her pretty well himself—far better than Chapman knew—and Dobyns figured that if anyone could bring a fag back to the way of God meant things to be, it would be her.

She was in her mid-twenties, a drop-dead gorgeous woman with brains, attitude, and talent. So much so, Dobyns actually found her a bit intimidating himself, but he never let that on.

"He'll see us," Dobyns said.

The boy shut up after that, which was good. Dobyns wasn't into mollifying his employees, but he wanted Chapman focused on his work instead of being scared of him.

Time for that later.

The maid brought Dobyns and Chapman into the foyer.

Some maid. She was wearing the typical uniform, short black skirt, but managed to make it look like she was just fooling around. Maybe it was the small diamond stud in her nose or the way she held herself. She called up the stairs, "Company, Greg," before drifting off.

Dobyns sighed. Alcott's millions were wasted on him.

Alcott came downstairs. He was in jeans, barefoot, wearing a U2 tee shirt. He needed a shave. Gregory Alcott was a thirty-eight-year-old teenager. Alcott was a guy who kept track of the trends: his hair was buzzed short and he wore an earring. Four years ago, when Dobyns first met him, he had had a thick beard, ponytail.

"What the hell are you doing here?" Alcott snapped. He looked tired, puffy, and a bit scared.

"You called me," Dobyns said equably.

"That was a hypothetical. I told you I hadn't decided yet. And if and when I do, I don't need a damn house call from you."

Dobyns brushed past him. Beautiful staircase, wide foyer. Big enough to dance in. He had always liked this place. Far too good for the current resident.

"Still seeing that girl?" Dobyns asked.

"Did you hear me?"

Dobyns repeated his question, looking Alcott in the eyes this time.

The man faltered, and then waved his hand toward the stairway. "Amanda's upstairs."

Dobyns said, "I want to say hello to her before I go."

"Why?"

Dobyns ignored the question. "Now, listen. Of course you're gonna sell. For that, you need me."

"What do you know about my finances?"

"What I read in the paper," Dobyns said. "Enough."

Alcott's father had been the founder of a computer-hardware company called GenComm when Greg, in his second year of school at Yale, announced to his family that he wanted to be an artist.

Entirely coincidentally, his mother and father crashed and died in their private Lear jet not long after, leaving Greg with over a hundred and twenty million dollars in stock and a business that appeared to be thriving—but was actually just peaking. Either out of a misguided sense of family duty, or simply because he could, Greg Alcott quit school to run the company, over the strenuous protest of the senior staff. He quickly fired those "dinosaurs" and brought in a new staff of his own.

By the time Dobyns got to Alcott, ten years had passed; his stock had been devalued to about fifty million and was then split again after a disastrous marriage and divorce. The board kicked Alcott out as president, and he cashed out most of his GenComm stock, except a small "secure fund" to start a new company as an Internet search-engine supplier. Like many internet companies, his stock soared. Also like many others, his spiraled and crashed just like his parents' Lear jet. He spent a fortune finding out what everyone at GenComm already knew: brains sometimes skip a generation.

He retired at age thirty-four to return to his "lifelong dream" of being an artist.

Not long after, GenComm announced it was going bankrupt; with it, went Alcott's remaining "secure" money.

Now trying to regain some face, Alcott said to Dobyns, "Yeah, keep pushing for that commission. There's other people I can go through."

"Naw," Dobyns said. "There's not. 'Cause all it'd take would be a phone call from me and you'd have the FBI rooting around your base-ment. You don't need a jail sentence to add to the shittiest year of your life, do you?"

"And what's to keep me from naming you?' " Alcott said, his handsome face getting ugly. "Your people actually did the break-in!"

Dobyns cuffed him lightly. Just the merest tap, practically a sign of affection. "You do that, and I'd have to send somebody to empty a gun in your mouth."

Alcott put his hand to his face, stunned. "You hit me, you son of a bitch!"

Dobyns did it again, backhand this time. "Yes, I did. You paying attention, now? There's a chance somebody may've already put it to you. On the art. You might be a lot poorer than you think."

Alcott's face whitened under the spreading red marks on both cheeks. "Bull. I looked at them this morning.' "

Dobyns nodded toward Chapman. "Let him take a look. We've got to know before we put them up for sale. We screw around on this level, there's enough bullets to take us all out."

"I'd like to see them," Chapman said to Alcott. "Can't wait, in fact."

Alcott rubbed his face where he'd been hit. It really seemed to be sinking in, what Dobyns was saying. "All right," Alcott said. "Yeah, you better."

Dobyns watched Alcott and Chapman go off together. Alcott was frankly scared now, but trying to hide it. Chapman looked eager for the challenge. Ready to open his black bag of tricks and take his tests. Dobyns knew how boring this part could be, in spite its importance.

Worse came to worst, he could have the two boys taken out. Sanitize the situation. He'd been forced to do that before, waste his own personnel, kill partners and witnesses. He hated to do it. He put so much work into pulling together the right people to get things done. Plus, every murder was another opportunity to get caught.

But sometimes erasing the blackboard and starting fresh was the only logical choice.

Dobyns sighed. He saw a bellpull in the foyer and gave it a yank. The maid showed up a moment later. "You rang?"

Saying it with an insolent tone, but keeping her face straight. Pretty little piece with red hair, tight body. Alcott probably picked her up in a bar, figured he'd give her a job. Probably tried to pull her into threesomes with the lovely Amanda.

Unless Dobyns's burning gut was absolutely wrong, he knew Alcott wouldn't be able to afford either of their attentions much longer.

"Can I help you?" The girl was getting impatient now.

Dobyns said, "Tell Amanda to come down. I want to talk with her."

"She just stepped out a few minutes ago."

"Huh." Dobyns gestured to the front door. "I'm surprised I didn't see her."

The girl shook her head. "She went out the side door. Directly to the garage."

Dobyns sighed. Shit.

"Anything else?" the girl asked.

"Yeah," he said. "Get me a glass of milk."

CHAPTER 29

LANGDON AWOKE AS RONNIE WAS COMING BACK FROM HER EXERCISES. She put a cup of coffee on the end table. "Good morning, sweets."

He sat up and sipped the coffee while she stretched. She was wearing leotards and shorts and had worked up a good sweat.

"You go for a run?"

She shook her head. "StairMaster. Nice facility here. Give me a minute."

He lay back, watching her. She could have easily passed for a woman in her late twenties, early thirties. Lucky for both of them that she looked so good. She'd always been a natural athlete. Her skin was still smooth, her cheeks glowing. Taut, flat stomach. Narrow waist and an absolutely lovely back.

She saw him watching and smiled.

Her face didn't have that harsh look that so many woman her age took on when they exercised aggressively.

He wondered how long that would all last. Exactly what the next ten to fifteen years would bring. She already had a brutal fear of aging, and this obsession with Cain's lover—who may've been a fictional device of Cain's for all Langdon knew—only exacerbated the problem. Even with cosmetic surgery, wrinkles and sagging flesh were inevitable. And Ronnie was not big on accepting the inevitable.

He stood up and stretched.

She looked up at him smiling. "He's naked," she said. "How're you feeling?"

"Better. Got a headache still, but I'm only seeing one of you now."

She reached up, holding him. "Ah, you *are* feeling better."

"Much," he said. He touched his sister's hair. Stroking her. Thinking that nothing was for free.

She rolled to her knees and pushed him back on the bed.

An hour later, they walked across Boylston Street to the Boston Garden. They sat on a park bench looking out over the swan boats. The sun was warm on Langdon's face; the park was a rich green in the morning light. Ronnie opened a paper bag and took out two containers of yogurt, bagels, and two cups of coffee. She tucked her legs underneath herself and leaned against Ian companionably. "I'm starving."

He adjusted the money belt slightly and began to eat. Good to have the diamonds on him. He felt famished, too and wasn't sure the healthy breakfast was going to do it for him. Left to his own devices, he would've gone for eggs and bacon, but Ronnie wouldn't hear of it.

"I've been thinking," she said.

I'm sure you have, he thought. He said, "About what?"

"About you. About how you might be thinking we should end it here."

"Uh-huh."

"After all, you might be thinking Amir Abaas agreed to pay us fifteen million. We tell him ten on what we delivered already and call it quits on the two Rembrandts, right? We've got the diamonds, he gives us the balance, we're done. How could he argue? He's got *The Gathering*, for God's sake."

"I could be thinking that," he said. "It's what two sane people would do."

She gently knocked her head against his. With his injuries, that was enough to flood him with nausea.

"Shut up and listen," she said, sweetly.

He set his coffee down on the bench beside him.

She said, "You know that sanity, logic, and theory have got nothing to do with the spot we're in. Abaas *will not* accept partial delivery. I *will not* leave the question of Tom Cain open. And you *will not* let this McKenna do what he did to you and get away with it. For all we know, he's in it with the little chickie of Cain's."

Langdon sighed. Ronnie's desire to turn Cain's pretty young girlfriend into a freak—assuming there really was such a person—was driving Ronnie more than anything else. And what drove Ronnie, drove Ian.

Personally, he could let the thing go with McKenna. The man got lucky; both of them knew it. Langdon had the diamonds and would've been content to fly home. McKenna he could take care of, but the longer they stuck around the more likely that Dobyns might get too curious.

Langdon said, "McKenna just stumbled into the middle and is trying to stumble his way out."

"Stumbled against your head," Ronnie said darkly. "Maybe damaged something for good. You're sounding so forgiving."

"He doesn't mean a thing."

She turned on him. "How do you know? You've got no idea exactly what happened between him and Cain." Ronnie put her hand up against his cheek. Let him feel her warmth. "Please, sweetie. Don't go soft on me now. I've *got* to know what happened. I've got to settle things with this little girl. And even if your sailor boy isn't the key, he might be a nice piece of bait."

Langdon sighed. He knew she was right there. If he could find his way to McKenna, chances are someone else could, too. And if they did, there was a chance they might lead back to the Rembrandts. And the girl, of course.

"We can still have it all," Ronnie said. "You see what I mean, don't you, Ian?"

"Of course," he said. "I always do."

CHAPTER 30

MCKENNA WAS FEELING POOR.

Walking down State Street in Newburyport, looking in the shop-windows, thinking that it was all over. The terrible adventure. But an adventure, nonetheless. The good news was that he wasn't looking over his shoulder as much, and that was very good news indeed.

The bad news was that he had to get a job.

Until he had handed Langdon the diamonds, McKenna hadn't quite realized how much he had accepted the idea that someday—somehow—he would exchange those pretty bits of light for at least several million dollars.

He looked into those store windows, thinking about money. Thinking about how easily cash flowed out, like water, but how hard it was to make it flow in when you didn't have a job.

McKenna stopped outside a real-estate office. Ned Baxter's, a nice guy. Once one of McKenna's competitors.

Can I ever walk back into this life? McKenna was thinking when someone waved to him from the inside.

"Hey, Skipper!"

He smiled.

It was Sheila Payne, one of his former employees. She came to the door, took his hand, and went up on her tiptoes to kiss his cheek.

Sheila was a young grandmother, in her mid-fifties. Hair still bright blond. A bit too much makeup. Big blue eyes. Black jeans and a wine-colored turtleneck. "Come in out of the sun." She tugged his hand and he followed her back to her desk. Sheila had come to work for McKenna shortly after her only daughter had left for college.

"Ned's out with a client. I know he'd like to see you," she said.

McKenna sat down. He blinked. The office felt like a cave after the bright outdoors. He found himself looking around the room with a faint sense of wonder as they chatted—Sheila leading the conversation mostly—about the real-estate market, about her daughter, about McKenna's other former employees.

McKenna couldn't believe he had spent so many years doing this sort of thing. His work was more heavily commercial than Ned's, but nevertheless, the setting hadn't been all that different: an office filled with people talking, selling, moving paper.

With a dawning sense of both relief and dismay, McKenna realized his real estate expertise was now worth nothing. Twenty years' experience, useless.

Because there was no way in hell he was coming back to this.

Just then his eye caught a photo thumbtacked onto the bulletin board beside Sheila. It was a black-and-white photo of a young girl. For an instant, McKenna saw her as Sam, about thirteen years old. He felt a sharp stab in his chest. But when he looked closer, he saw the girl really looked nothing like his daughter, except perhaps in the amused set of her mouth. Too sweet to be haughty, too devilish to be innocent.

This girl had a chain saw that looked at least half her size cocked on her hip. Behind her, there was a small mountain of cut logs, firewood length, ready for splitting. The implication was that she'd cut all the logs herself, but her smile made McKenna wonder.

"What a shot," he said.

Sheila handed him the card wordlessly.

He studied it, impressed at how the photo grabbed his attention. He flipped the card over and gave a short laugh.

"Thought you'd like that," Sheila said.

Melanie Walsh had taken the photo. Melanie of the spilled mayonnaise and mustard, the kiss that almost happened.

The postcard announced a gallery opening in Boston that night featuring her photo essay about the northern Maine loggers and their families.

"You two were always such friends, weren't you?" Sheila said.

"Well," McKenna said, shrugging. Not wanting to go into it.

"I hear Caroline has the top floor of Sophia Benchley's place."

McKenna nodded. Sweet as Sheila was, he remembered her as a gossip. And it troubled him to see how easily Caroline could be given away if Langdon *did* come looking.

He held the postcard out to Sheila. "I've really got to be going."

"Keep it. I haven't seen Melanie since she left."

He slipped the card into his breast pocket.

Sheila looked at him innocently. "But I know Melanie would love to see you." McKenna remembered then that Sheila was not only a bit of a gossip, but a matchmaker. And, at times, a bit of a troublemaker. "I'd never tell," she said.

McKenna laughed shortly and left.

McKenna came to the decision during the walk back to the marina. What would have been a momentous decision before, now appeared to him as self-evident. If his marriage was to have a chance, he needed to clear his mind. And the boat was a daily reminder of the killings. Besides which, they needed the money to start another life.

He had to sell the *Wanderer*.

Maybe someday, there would be another boat.

That decision made, he saw a Ford pickup truck for sale at the gas station down the street from the marina. The truck was battered looking, but there was no evident rust. McKenna opened the door, catching the faint scent of oil and sweat. The odometer showed just over one hundred thousand miles. The gas-station owner came out, a balding, heavyset man named Carl that McKenna had known slightly for years. "Compression's good, big mother V-8. Transmission's fine. Tires are for shit, and she's not exactly pretty no more."

He tossed McKenna the keys.

McKenna drove through town and out onto the highway. Indeed, the truck had plenty of power. He felt that he could see the gas gauge go down when he goosed the accelerator. He brought the truck back, and Carl put it on the lift and pulled the wheels. McKenna went over the Ford carefully. Not much life left on the brake pads and rotors, but adequate for the short term. The exhaust needed work. No obvious oil leaks, and the head gasket was relatively clean. The upshot of it was that McKenna left a deposit against the full asking price with the agreement that Carl would tune the engine, supply four retreaded tires, and replace the muffler.

McKenna then walked back to the *Wanderer*, fully aware that he had just traded his beloved boat for an ugly old truck.

A few hours later, McKenna went through his checklist. The *Wanderer*'s driveshaft was repaired. A new Harken roller-furling system gleamed on the bow. He cast a critical eye on the topdecks and decided he already had it in pretty good shape. He focused belowdecks. He threw away the old covers from the main-cabin settee and picked up his truck to drive back into town to meet an upholsterer. He gave the man instructions and measurements to cut new ones for the forward cabin.

He was ready with a tale about the jagged edge of an anchor ripping the cushions, but the upholsterer simply took down the information and said, "Give me a week."

McKenna was coming to the growing realization that lying was easier than he had thought. One of the first rules was to volunteer as little information as possible, and maybe seven times out of ten, no one demanded more.

McKenna then went back and repaired the forward-cabin door. Around six he considered stopping, but felt restless, so he got down and gave the cabin sole a final light sanding. He was almost finished when the postcard fell out of his pocket.

He picked it up and sat back on his heels, thinking. He quickly did the numbers. The opening would run from eight to ten P.M. There was just enough time for him to shower and change and make it down to Newbury Street before Melanie's reception was over.

McKenna hesitated. He wasn't looking for any complications. But the idea of breaking free of the boat—and from himself—for a night seemed like just what he needed.

At least that's what he told himself.

McKenna was hurrying down Newbury Street to the Conran Gallery when lightning flashed. He turned up the hood on his jacket and rushed along as the thunder followed immediately; then the sky simply opened up. McKenna smiled, watching the busy, beautiful crowd scatter. The wind swept into his face, stinging, and he licked his lips, feeling good—but nervous.

He barely admitted to himself how much he was looking forward to seeing Melanie. He hesitated outside the gallery for just a moment, uncertain. Seeing how crowded the opening still was, people inside talking and laughing.

What am I doing here? he thought.

But he wanted to see her.

He went in.

There were probably two dozen people in the place. A good-looking crowd, most of them five to ten years younger than him.

He didn't see Melanie anywhere, and that made him feel both relieved and disappointed. He accepted a glass of wine from a passing waiter and figured he would take a moment to look at her work and then leave.

Black-and-white shots, all of them. Almost two dozen pieces, ranging from small eight-by-ten prints to a mural-sized shot taken from a wide angle. The latter showed three kids in the bed of a moving pickup truck. Melanie must have been crouched in the bed with them, just behind the driver. The picture was in focus, although extremely grainy. The girl who had been in the earlier shot was sitting cross-legged in the back corner of the truck, her hair whipping back in the wind, a strand of it caught in her mouth. A boy that looked like a younger brother was leaning against the tailgate, his hands clasped behind his head, a cigarette dangling from his mouth. Striving for tough. And what must have been an older brother was sitting on the side edge, facing back. He was balanced precariously, seemingly oblivious to the reaching tree limbs that were but a blur on the exposed film. Instead, he was talking to the two younger kids, his hands up, his mouth slightly twisted in older-brother bravado. Behind them, the forest rose around the winding country road. The effect was to isolate the young girl in the middle of it all. Isolate her and yet show her as a natural and assured participant.

McKenna stared at the shot. This alone was worth the drive.

And then Melanie stepped in front of him and gave him a hug.

He hugged her back and part of him wanted to laugh. To realize his intentions, that he had indeed come here looking for something— to start a new adventure, perhaps.

Instead, he had been given a taste of the single life. Her affection was real and he appreciated it, in fact, reveled in it for a moment before pulling back to smile at her.

Melanie Walsh. Dark hair, smiling black eyes, as warm and beautiful as he had remembered.

But, clearly, she was many months pregnant.

Clearly she was wearing a wedding ring.

And clearly she was happy to see her old friend as just that.

CHAPTER 31

IT HAD BEEN A LONG, PAINFUL DAY.

Jimmy Dobyns was sitting in Alcott's kitchen. Alcott was sitting across from him, his head in his hands.

Alcott had sent all his help away so he could rant and rave in privacy.

"Could be worse," Dobyns said. He was trying to finish a chicken sandwich he'd made for himself, but Alcott was ruining his appetite.

It was at times like this, that Dobyns was truly relieved not to be a legitimate businessman. Because it was clear, at least to him, that his own people had participated in fucking over Alcott, and in the legitimate world, that would mean some liability.

But Alcott couldn't exactly go to the Better Business Bureau on this.

So screw him.

"How?" Alcott said.

"Hmmn?" Dobyns wiped the mayonnaise away from his mouth. Realizing that Alcott was talking to him.

"How could it be worse?"

"Well, shit. You've still got two very valuable pieces," he said.

"You don't know that."

"Chapman's probably right on this."

So far, Chapman had that declared eight of the ten stolen paintings were fakes. Reasonably well-done fakes, artificially aged as well as possible, placed in the original frames. But fakes. All except the two Rembrandts: *Storm on the Ocean* and *Gentleman and a Lady*.

Chapman said possibly the artist who was making the switch was waiting until he was ready to do those. Chapman was delicate saying "he" when even Alcott looked like he had been able to connect the dots.

Most likely, it was a "she."

Amanda hadn't returned and none of Alcott's phone calls to her friends had given them any idea where she'd gone.

"I've lost a fortune," Alcott said.

Dobyns waved that away. "Fortune you were never supposed to have. Besides, you sell those two pieces, you'll be in bacon and beans the rest of your life."

Alcott's face darkened with blood. "Damn easy for you to say. I thought you were going to help with security. How about you refund what I paid you?"

Dobyns snorted and said, "Shut up, Greggie."

Alcott tried to look at him hard, but gave it up after a few seconds.

Dobyns finished his sandwich, washed it down with a glass of water. Forget the damn milk. He said, "C'mon down."

Dobyns led the man through his own house, down to the viewing room in the basement. He stood aside while Alcott punched in the code and opened the door.

Dobyns had arranged for the contractor who made the place, a room for Alcott to admire his art—complete with track lighting, a sofa, stereo, and a small L-shaped wet bar in one corner. The place was climate controlled, with a topflight air-filtration system. On the walls were a display of Alcott's public collection, including a wall devoted to his own pieces. Dobyns didn't see all that much wrong with them; pretty New England scenes for the most part—lobster boats and pots and sailboats. Dobyns would just as soon have those hanging on his own walls as the stuff that was supposed to be good, but he was willing to take Chapman's word that they were crap.

Chapman looked up when they came in. "Good news," he said.

"I'd stake everything these two are legit." He then began to prattle about what had tipped him off on the others. Dobyns let him go on for a while. "Under the black light, new paint shows as dark. And see, the forger's hardest job is making the painting look old enough. See how it looks like a varnish was applied here? And those cracks . . . that one's been cut with a razor, probably. And these . . . they baked the piece in an oven to dry it and crack it. I mean, these aren't bad as forgeries go. Maybe they followed the style a little too slavishly, but if you don't know what to look for, yeah, these would pass. . . ."

He kept on, proud of himself.

Alcott's face was a sick sort of white.

Dobyns looked down at the two Rembrandts. He particularly liked *Storm on the Ocean*. Guy clinging to a mast in a storm. Dobyns felt like that himself, surrounded by all the numbnuts. Wouldn't mind having that up on his wall. Maybe after this was all over, he'd get a ten-dollar print and do just that.

"Hot damn," he said.

He walked around the room looking at the other pieces lined up against the wall. Vermeer's *The Gathering*. A Rembrandt etching, a self-portrait. Govaert Flinck's *Landscape with a Pillar*. Five Degas pieces and a Manet. Normally, they hung on one of the four spring-loaded wall panels that Alcott could lift up into the ceiling after viewing. Dobyns and Gleason had installed those themselves. Gleason had been handy that way; his legit cover was as a carpenter.

The idea was that Alcott could showcase his own legit collection any time he wanted and let the servants in to clean. But, as easily as pulling down a window shade, he could admire his pride, the greatest collection of stolen art in history.

Dobyns said, "Damn, Greg, I wouldn't have known they were fakes either."

Alcott looked too sick to answer.

Dobyns put his hands on his hips. "All right, let's talk about it. I'd say it's clear she's in on it. Probably did the forgeries herself or found someone who could do them. She knew the code to this room, right? She knew all about it, didn't she?"

Alcott's face was frozen. But he nodded.

"I told you—didn't I *tell* you this three years ago? I distinctly remember having you come sit in my car, where I said these words to you: 'Before I send my boys in to take the pieces out of the museum, Mister Alcott, you'll have to be happy keeping them to yourself.' "

Alcott's face was gray. But he nodded wearily.

Smart enough to know he'd screwed up.

Dumb enough not to know he'd been set up.

They'd gotten together almost four years ago. The whole thing had taken Dobyns the better part of a year to set up, but the payoff was well worth it.

It had begun as a fluke.

Dobyns had taken his niece to the Rosalyn Museum as part of a high-school art-history class. Just a favor to his sister, Elaine, for his favorite niece, Rachel.

But Dobyns was always open to opportunity. He found it while walking around the beautiful little museum, listening to his niece talk about the wonderful stuff he was seeing—did he know how many millions of dollars some of them pieces were worth?

He'd been floored by the paltry security system the museum had in place. Just two security guards at night. Barely shaving, either of them. Security system could be disengaged right near the main door by either guard's key and there was probably a panic button behind the desk. Video surveillance, but, shit, Dobyns had managed to walk by the broom closet of a security office when one of the guards was going in, and the tape deck was right there. No individual alarms on any of the pieces that he could see.

Dobyns had put Gleason on planning the robbery itself. Two guys, dressed as Boston policemen banging on the door. Figured the guards would open it.

Worked like a charm, too. Didn't even have to hurt the guards, just tie them up, slap a little duct tape on their faces. All things being equal, Dobyns would rather not kill people. Made for too much intensity from the cops.

While Gleason scoped it all out, Dobyns had taken on finding the buyer. No sense getting the art without that lined up. And that's where his investment in Chapman had come in.

When Dobyns had told him that he was looking for a buyer with megabucks who was absolutely queer for art, Chapman had said he had just the guy.

"Greg Alcott. He's a collector. Christ, he doesn't know shit, but he keeps showing up at openings trying to talk the talk. He even likes to think of *himself* as an artist—he buys gallery space and displays some truly awful pieces."

"He's rich?"

"Oh, huge." Chapman had waved his hand, irritated with the details. "Daddy's money. A wanna-be artist. But who's going to tell him his taste is in his mouth?"

Dobyns had grunted. "Not me."

Chapman had been flabbergasted and more than a bit scared when Dobyns had told him what he had in mind to steal. But he had gotten into it. Taken a turn through the Rosalyn Museum himself to help choose some of the more valuable pieces.

"You want me to approach Alcott myself?" he'd asked.

"Naw." Dobyns had said. "Something this big's gotta be figured just right. And unless this guy is a closet queen, you're not what I need for the job."

"Fine," Chapman had said. By then, Chapman had known enough to keep any hurt feelings to himself.

It had taken Dobyns months to get next to Alcott.

He'd recruited a girl for him. Not just a bimbo, but an up-and-coming artist.

Amanda.

Friend of Chapman's at the Fine Art Institute.

Dobyns had seen her one night when he came by to talk with Chapman.

This astonishing girl. Little thing, not more than five-three. Flawless skin that just glowed. Made you just want to touch her. Blue-gray eyes. Black hair.

Standing there in front of a piece Dobyns hadn't understood, but found hard to look away from.

Chapman had said that people who knew her work expected great things from her. He'd said she was a prodigy.

Chapman also had mentioned that, as talented as she was, she still waited tables for a living. "And it's *killing* her."

Dobyns had waited for her outside her South End studio apartment. He had said he'd seen her work on display down at the corner bookstore, and not only had he bought two paintings, he wanted to talk with her.

She looked wary. This fifty-year-old guy outside her place. She apparently didn't recognize his name, which was just fine.

"Wait here," she said, and he figured she went in to call the bookstore to see if his story was true.

Minutes later, she came out smiling—which alone was a thrill.

He'd walked her to the Institute that day. It had taken several more walks and a few dinners and lunches, too. Dobyns had kept his manner fatherly, although he dearly wanted to put his hands on her himself.

From the beginning he could tell that she was too smart to take his interest at face value. He had fed her a bit at a time. Finally, he'd told Gleason to come with him and they had waited outside her apartment until she came home.

He pointed her out to Gleason: "See her? I'm gonna go up and have a talk with her. It goes well, you'll just take me home. If it doesn't, I'm gonna have you go up, kill her, and then dump her body."

"Who's she?" Gleason had asked, but Dobyns had told him it was none of his damn business.

Luckily, Amanda had taken the news well. She'd smiled, puzzled. "The famous Jimmy Dobyns is a pimp?"

"You know who I am?"

"I didn't recognize the name at first. But I checked you out on the Net. Took me about twenty minutes. I've been waiting to find out why a hood from Southie is such an art lover."

He grinned. "People always typecasting guys like me."

"And why not? You want me to be a whore for this guy. Why would I do that?" She seemed more curious than offended.

He was pleased to see that. The artist in her, looking for experience rather than judging.

"Money," he said.

"But I don't care about money."

"That's awfully stupid talk for such a smart girl," he chided her. "It's the way you're thinking about it. Money is freedom. Money is a chance to focus on your art without hustling beer and wine to asshole drunks and having to smile for tips. Money means your work gets seen . . . people can learn how good you are."

He waited, looking at her.

She smiled. "Okay, maybe I do like money."

"Smart girl. Well, right here, you got a shot at settling your finances for the rest of your life."

"What exactly would I have to do?"

Dobyns told her that he planned to steal art from the Rosalyn Museum. He had been pleased to see that even though she was wary, she seemed interested. Pleased also that he didn't have to call Gleason up the stairs and start the recruiting process all over again.

Dobyns said, "I want you to make Alcott want the art as much as he wants you. I want the two tied together. And for that, you'll win the lottery—from me. The sale goes through, you can count on a million dollars. Five hundred thousand right after the sale. Another five hundred K about three, four years from now. You stay with him until then, and you're free to go afterward."

"Stay with him? You mean *marry* him?"

Dobyns shrugged. "That's up to you. Not a good investment, though. I hear he got burned on an early marriage and now keeps gold diggers away with a nasty prenup. I'd say you'd be better off just living with him."

"So who's to say he'll want me?"

"For starters, you're drop-dead gorgeous, as if you haven't noticed."

She made a face. "He's rich. I'm sure he's got lots of pretty girls chasing him."

Dobyns shook his head. "Not like you. Much money as he's got, he's still looking for the respect of your world. He's got the money to help build you, and you'll help him be legit where he really wants to be legit."

Dobyns saw she was thinking about it. He said quietly, "Afterward, you'll always be free to do your art. Always free to be your own woman . . . by what? Age twenty six, twenty seven?"

She paused. "Why four years?"

"He needs watching. See that he doesn't blab. You keep him happy about his expensive purchase, but discreet. He's gonna die if he can't share it with somebody, I figure. So I want that somebody to be you."

"You're assuming he'll go for it."

"That's up to you. First, show that *you* love the pieces. Make him see that when you're happy, he's happy. You know how to do that."

She smiled faintly. "I guess. But then I'm stuck being his watchdog. Watching him watch the art. Sounds dull."

"Hey, waiting tables looks kinda slow, last I looked. If you're as good as Chapman tells me you are, this is your shot."

"I am that good," she'd said softly.

Dobyns had known enough to keep his mouth shut then. Let her fill in her own heaven. She'd do a better job of convincing herself now that he'd led her there.

Finally, she'd come back into focus. "And what if I say no?" she'd asked. "What if I tell you to walk out of here and leave me alone?"

He let his eyes rest on her. Let her feel the threat. A necessary part of just about every negotiation, he'd found. "Well, Amanda, that'd be a serious mistake on your part. I've been very open with you up to this point . . ."

He let the silence lengthen.

"I didn't ask you to," she snapped.

"That's life," he said.

Again, he waited.

Nobody likes being threatened, and she didn't either. But the way he read her, she had already made her decision.

"So what exactly will I have to do?"

"You let me know if he gets antsy to sell. If he doesn't, I'll tell you when. Either way, you push things along. Tell him you're sick of the risk. That you just want the pieces out of your life."

"And you get your next multimillion dollar commission?"

Dobyns smiled. "And you get your next five hundred thousand dollars. We can funnel it through intermediaries for your paintings. Give you a rep as a big seller, not just an *artiste*. Make a name for you right there. After that you can ride off and paint pretty sunsets."

Amanda nodded, as if to herself. And then said, "I guess I really don't have a choice, considering."

"No, you don't." Dobyns felt flush of pride. With just the right mix of patience, pressure, and incentive, he could land just about anyone.

She smiled slowly.

Dobyns felt himself respond. Not only heady with his own talent, but dazzled by this beautiful girl. Between the two of them, poor Greg Alcott wouldn't have a chance.

"One thing," Amanda said. "I don't do pretty sunsets."

And now, Dobyns figured maybe he was finding that out right along with Alcott.

The guy was on the sofa now, back to holding his head in his hands. Most likely telling himself his lovely Amanda *couldn't* have really left him, *couldn't* have really swapped out his stolen collection of artwork with a series of fakes that he had been too daft to recognize. That surely he'd hear the rumble of her Miata any minute.

Apparently wondering all this and having no clue as to the degree which the man standing over him had not only participated in his undoing, but had been burned right alongside him.

Dobyns gestured to Chapman to join them. Chapman did, looking a bit worried. And why not . . . as far as he knew, *he* was the link to Amanda.

Dobyns pulled out the picture of the man called Tom Cain that Langdon had given him. "Either of you guys recognize him?"

Alcott nodded right away. "That's her cousin. Justus Woodrell. She's had him out here a few times."

Chapman's eyes narrowed. He rubbed his mouth with the back of his hand. Nervous.

"Give," Dobyns said.

"Ah, Justus isn't her cousin," Chapman said. "He's her lover."

Alcott's face darkened. "Since when?"

"Long as I've known her," Chapman said. "Which is longer than you."

"Oh, Christ," Alcott said.

Dobyns felt the same himself. "You think you could've mentioned this to me?"

Chapman looked scared. "You said you didn't want me wasting your time with useless stories. . . ."

Dobyns rubbed his right temple. Headache joining the pain in his gut.

"I don't know where she is," Alcott said. "*Who* she is."

"That makes two of us," Dobyns said.

CHAPTER 32

MELANIE INTRODUCED MCKENNA TO HER NEW HUSBAND, PATRICK.

Nice-looking guy. Tall, rangy, blond wavy hair. He was dressed entirely in black—but he appeared somewhat uncomfortable with the Newbury Street chic. Protective of his wife. He'd come up immediately after Melanie greeted McKenna, and now he had his arm around her.

Patrick's eyes saying to McKenna, *Nice to meet you, now get lost.*

Melanie said she was happy. Her work was getting noticed, she was actually approaching making a living with it, their baby girl was on the way. She whispered that her only real worry in life at the moment was the critic in the corner, Seth Barton.

While keeping her bright smile, she said, "He's over there deciding if he's going to make me or break me. He's a God-awful snob and tends to think photography is 'easy art.' I'm the new kid on the block, and he'll decide if I get to join the gang or stay outside with my nose pressed against the window."

McKenna looked over at the dark-haired man in the corner who was looking at one of her pieces intently and frowning. "Patrick and I could go rough him up, if you think that would help."

"Maybe," she said. "But it might go wrong."

McKenna smiled at her. "Well, he's probably going to love your work. Because it's fantastic."

"Thanks, I—" Melanie eyes widened as she looked over his shoulder.

She said softly, "My, my, my."

McKenna turned. The girl coming through the door was drenched from the rain, but she still knew how to make an entrance. Strikingly beautiful, with big gray-blue eyes, flawless skin.

Smiling in spite of it all. "You," she said, pulling her hands through her thick wet hair and playfully sprinkling Melanie as she hurried over. "What I have to go through for you."

"I'm delighted you made it," Melanie said. "Let me get you a coat to wear."

"Don't bother."

The event photographer quickly joined the two women, and the young woman effortlessly seized the moment. She pulled Melanie in front of her mural and together they cast a quick and charming pose.

Then the girl looked over in the corner and said, "Is that Seth? Get over here, you!"

The critic came over, flushed and happy to receive her attentions. She pulled him between her and Melanie, and he grinned, his glasses winking in the overhead light while the photographer took his picture, too. Minutes later, the small audience gathered around the three to listen respectfully as he praised Melanie's photographs.

"Melanie just got in the club," Patrick said with quiet satisfaction. Now that Melanie had moved away, he seemed more relaxed around McKenna. Patrick looked over, smiling. "And you were here to see it."

"Who's the girl?" McKenna said.

"She's the evidence that Melanie is making it. We sent her an invitation, but we never expected her to come." He gestured with his chin to the critic. "I'm sure he liked Melanie's work before, but this caps it."

"This girl's got that kind of pull?"

Patrick looked at him curiously. "You really don't know who she is?"

McKenna shrugged. "Hey, I've been at sea. And all I really know about the art world is what I like."

"Oh," Patrick said. He smiled, truly relaxed now. Apparently deciding McKenna was no competition at all. "She was a student of Melanie's about four, maybe five years back. Fine-art photography. Mainly, she's an oil painter. Since then, she's come into her own. We haven't seen her for over a year. Not only is she talented, but she's got the connections to get all the applause she deserves. Best of all, her work actually sells for big bucks."

At that point, the critic left the two women. "Day after tomorrow," he said. "You'll want to buy extra copies."

Melanie was beside herself, grinning. "Oh, yes."

The young woman came over to Patrick and called him by name. She stood on tiptoes to give him a kiss.

"We know what you did and thanks," Patrick said. "Really, thanks." He turned to embrace his wife.

The girl shrugged. "Melanie's work deserves it. Enough said."

The girl was actually a young woman, McKenna realized. Most likely early to mid-twenties. She turned her attention to McKenna. Normal good manners, it seemed. Giving the happy couple a bit of privacy. Except those gray-blue eyes held McKenna with such genuine interest.

"I don't think we've met," she said.

Melanie broke away from her husband and introduced them. And told Rob what a wonderful friend the girl had been to come out in this rain and throw her support behind Melanie's career. . . .

McKenna had never heard Melanie so effusive. But he hadn't seen her in years, and he supposed the tenuous aspect of the art world could make anyone behave differently. Or maybe this girl just evoked a certain fervor in others.

It wasn't just her looks. She was pretty, yes. Beautiful even.

But that couldn't quite explain the appeal. He marveled at the effect she had, the quickening of his pulse. In spite of himself, he knew he was smiling fatuously.

She held his hand as they were introduced.

"Aren't you proud of our girl?" she said.

"Very," McKenna answered. His voice sounded hoarse.

She turned to stand beside him, casually linking her arm into his and saying to Melanie, "Go revel in your success, you've earned it. Rob and I are going to take a real look at your work."

Melanie lifted her eyebrows slightly. "Have fun, you two."

McKenna was aware of Caroline being someplace alone. That third floor apartment that he hadn't yet been over to see. The awareness made him feel guilty, but with all the things he'd done in the past few weeks, he asked himself what was a little harmless flirting with a beautiful girl? She held his arm tightly, as if she were cold, which she may well have been given how wet she was. He could feel the swell of her left breast.

She talked easily about each piece.

McKenna thought of himself as reasonably intelligent, but it was apparent just listening to the quickness of her thoughts that she was operating at a higher level. Lots of mental horsepower and charm to boot.

It was flattering to have her play to him. Even if she was a good fifteen years younger. Even if he was bemused with his own reaction. He saw the paint on her hands, fine and beautiful though they were. A blue scrunchy on her wrist, also lightly touched with paint. He could envision her using it to push her hair back quickly when she wanted to work. She seemed genuinely eager as they moved from one of Melanie's prints to another. Finding what was right about each of them and seeming to take a charge, a contact high from Melanie's creativity. A charge she passed along to him.

McKenna felt intoxicated and downright silly to feel so.

It wasn't until they were on the third of Melanie's pieces that McKenna even remembered the girl's name.

Amanda.

CHAPTER 33

LANGDON TOLD HIS SISTER TO WAIT IN THE CAR. IT WAS JUST BEFORE noon the next day. That morning, on St. James Street in Boston, they had stolen a car—a middle-aged Toyota Camry—and driven up to Newburyport. They waited down the street from the house until they saw the woman come home.

"I'm jealous," Ronnie said.

"Yes, I'm sure. You stay here, sweets."

"You never let me have any fun."

"Oh, but you've got an important job," he said. "You're on watch. Anything too strange, you blow the horn and I come running. But I expect nothing but a pleasant conversation with a housefrau."

"Yes, dear." She kissed him lightly on the lips.

He got out and she settled back to watch the house. He walked up the driveway to Mariel's house.

Today he was wearing a disguise. He felt somewhat theatrical in it: the small packing on his gums to make his face a bit round, the grayed hair, wire-rimmed glasses. Simple stuff, but between that and having Ronnie drive him around, he felt he looked different enough not to worry about Detective Pollock's officers who were keeping an eye out for him.

He decided the Stephen Cross I.D. would still hold up. They had bought a laminator and a Polaroid camera, and Ronnie had done a nice job up in the hotel room, cutting and resealing a photo featuring his new look.

Langdon was humming a light tune to himself as he waited for the woman to answer the door. He didn't really like to admit it to himself, but he felt a bit nervous, more than he normally would have in this kind of circumstance.

It was because Ronnie was watching him. She didn't go with him much anymore, but this used to be part of the thrill. All told, he'd just as soon do without it these days.

The woman came to the door.

Pretty thing. Quite a figure in a charcoal business suit. She was about his age, maybe a little younger. Pleasant enough smile on her face, but he could just tell from looking at her that she was a bright woman.

That could be trouble.

"Yes?" she said.

"Maybe you can help me," he said. He went into his little story about searching for Mrs. Caroline McKenna. He was a private detective representing a distant family member who had left her a small inheritance. He had been hired by the estate to find Mrs. McKenna.

Same story with minor differences he'd told McKenna about Tom Cain. Should've worked then, certainly should work now, when all he wanted was a forwarding address from an old neighbor.

"And may I ask your name?" she said.

"Certainly." He pulled out the Stephen Cross I.D. Certain that McKenna wouldn't have told her about him.

But he saw from her eyes that he was wrong.

Wrong about everything.

"Unbelievable," she said, crisply. "As Ms. McKenna's attorney, I suggest you consider the ramifications of this line of . . . bullshit."

"Excuse me, but—"

"No. You're a liar and I don't know what else you're about. But I've got a good mind—" She paused. "No, in fact, I think I *will* call the police. Right now. I don't like the feel of this at all."

She pulled the screen door shut and flipped the lock. She strode back into her house quickly, her high heels clicking.

Langdon closed his eyes. Couldn't believe it. With Ronnie sitting there in the car.

He took a pair of cotton gloves from his coat pocket, put them on, then pulled out his pocket knife and locked the blade open. It was a compact little piece, well made, razor sharp. He jabbed the blade into the screen, made a quick cut, and then reached through the door and flicked open the lock.

Langdon moved swiftly through the house. He could hear the beep-beep-beep of her punching numbers into the phone, and he relaxed just a tad when he heard that she was doing more than three.

More than 911.

She stopped when he strode into the kitchen. He was counting on the element of surprise to freeze her. Give him a little time to make her talk before he did what he had to do.

But the woman surprised him instead.

She froze only for an instant. And then she scooped up a small ceramic vase on the counter and threw it at him. It connected with a dull thud against his shoulder before crashing into shards on the floor.

She scrambled for the back door.

Outside, the horn began to blow.

Damn it! Langdon saw the woman was fumbling for the lock to the back deck, and he figured he had the time to take a quick look. He jumped back into the living room and looked out the front window. A black man was in the driveway getting out of his car. He was looking curiously at Ronnie as she laid her hand down on the horn. He looked back at the house, and then at her.

The woman screamed.

The woman in the kitchen. Langdon ran back, bouncing off the wall as he went. Damn close to out of control, but not quite. He still had time, he figured.

The woman was out of the kitchen and on the deck now.

He followed her out. It was a raised deck, a good fifteen feet off the ground. Stone patio below. She was already on her way down the stairs, and she screamed again, telling him to stay away.

Langdon was vaguely aware that she probably didn't know the black man was there, but it really didn't matter. The nearest neighbors—the well-fed yuppies living in the McKenna's old house—were within easy earshot. If they called the police, Langdon and Ronnie could be in a spot.

He had to make the woman shut up. He started down the stairs after her. He was moving faster, she was still wearing those high heels. She stumbled on the stairway and caught herself.

Langdon was barely aware of movement below him, but he reacted immediately. Turned to see the black man coming around the house. Running now.

"Mariel!" the man called. A big booming voice.

The woman turned on the stairs, relief flooding her face. Seeing her savior, Langdon supposed. Seeing her hero.

Enough of that, Langdon thought, and he jumped.

About half the stairway to go, and he was airborne. Feet first, his left hand just lightly brushing the rail, the knife still clasped in his right. The woman took the brunt of his full one hundred and ninety-five pounds right between her shoulder blades. One moment, she was up, the next her head was snapping back, and she was falling, tumbling down those hard wooden stairs to the flagstones below.

Langdon caught himself on the rail. Took a few splinters through the gloves and almost twisted his ankle regaining his balance on the stairs. But he was standing and feeling pretty much fine. And she was a twisted rag doll below. Right arm splayed out above her in a way nature never intended.

Langdon grunted. Still had what it took. He jumped over the woman and turned with the knife, ready for the man.

Jesus, another surprise.

Langdon was expecting a raging bull.

And certainly the man seemed enraged.

But where Langdon was ready to take the man's momentum and

roll him onto the knife, the man had other plans. He checked his forward charge, made a quick shuffling side step—and kicked Langdon in the chest.

Langdon staggered, but remained upright.

The black man spun and kicked the knife out of Langdon's hand.

And then he came in with another kick to the chest.

This blow knocked Langdon off his feet and he slammed against the house. Dizziness all over again.

Still, his body knew what to do; he rolled immediately to his knees, and was able to get his arms up in a triangle to deflect the man's next kick. The one that was meant to loosen his head from his shoulders. Langdon simply charged upward, butting the man in the gut. That threw the man back a few steps, giving Langdon a chance to get to his feet. He snapped off a quick kick at the groin, but was blocked by the man's sweeping left forearm. Langdon followed that up with a hard chop to the man's neck, but even that was deflected somewhat as the black man bunched his powerful muscles. Still, he gasped in some pain, and Langdon felt a bit encouraged.

He backed off slightly. This competent professionalism wasn't what he expected in the suburbs of Massachusetts. The black man was circling with him now, drawing breath carefully, looking for his opening.

Langdon decided he'd had quite enough of it.

"Sorry, Bruce Lee." Langdon jerked his thumb at the woman. "Nice footwork, but she's already dead."

There.

Pain in the black man's eyes. An inarticulate sound deep inside of him, and he just sort of exploded. Charging forward with a succession of short, hard punches that Langdon took on his arms and shoulders.

Brutal stuff, really.

And perhaps Langdon would've had to acknowledge his taunt as a mistake, a gauntlet he should not have thrown down. But the black man's breathing became ragged.

More important, Ronnie came through.

Langdon heard the roar of the engine and saw his sister slewing the car around the corner of the house. The front wheels spinning and chewing up big black ruts in the grass, until she bumped onto the flagstone patio, and just missed the woman lying broken at the foot of the stairs.

The black man turned to look. Who wouldn't, screaming engine behind him?

He tried to run, but it was really so simple then. Langdon and his sister had been helping each other out of scrapes for so long.

Who could compete?

Langdon shoved the black man in front of the car.

Ronnie screamed for Langdon to get the knife, to do them by the throat.

She was wild inside the car, hitting the horn and yelling at him. Her hair a tangle. "Do it to them!" she screamed. "Do it, do it, do it!"

But, even standing there weaving as he was, he knew better. That woman, the neighbor who lived in McKenna's old house, was standing on the front steps. She was shading her eyes to look at them, a cell phone in the other hand.

Langdon walked around the front of the car and picked up the knife. The black man was slowly rolling to his knees, trying to stand. His face was covered with blood, and he was moving about the speed of a turtle.

"Drive," Langdon said and swung open the passenger side of the Camry. "That nosy neighbor has almost certainly called the police, and if they block off this road, we're screwed. Let's go."

"Then we'll do her," Ronnie said. "Do the nosy bitch, too!"

He shook his head. "Drive, sweets. Right now."

And though she didn't like taking orders, she did what she was told. She put the car back in gear and floored it in the direction of the black man. She almost got him, too, but he just managed to roll behind an old oak tree.

"Later," Langdon said, putting his hand on her shoulder. "It's time to go now."

*　*　*

After about half an hour, she began to settle down. She said, "Well, at least I don't feel so much the clown." Her voice was bright and Langdon supposed she actually meant it. Years since she'd been involved at this level, and it must have felt good to see she still had the talent. And that just as she had been made the fool by Tom Cain, dependable old Ian screwed up sometimes, too.

"Glad it was such a positive experience for you," he said.

She laughed merrily. She had driven them into town and followed her brother's instructions on how to hotwire an old Chevy van they found in a grocery store parking lot. The Camry with the broken headlight was parked head in next to a dumpster.

Now Langdon was laying on a striped mattress in the back, while she drove sedately out of town. The mattress stunk of sweat, beer, and urine. He shuddered to think what crimes they could be accused of if the police caught them in this old shitbox. He said, "That Ford behind you now?"

She looked in the rearview mirror. "No."

She'd thought for a time that a Ford van was following them, but Langdon hadn't seen it himself. Still, she had good instincts about these things; that's why he had insisted they switch cars. Though he was more inclined to think it was Dobyns who had someone on them rather than the police.

Langdon reached under his shirt and ran his fingers over his rib cage. He didn't think anything was broken, but he couldn't be sure. What a kick that black man had.

She said, "You, on the other hand, should feel the complete nincompoop."

"Should I?" He rolled over so he could see her, and she looked back into the rearview mirror.

"Absolutely, sweets. I told you to finish them."

He sighed. He'd be hearing about this for some time to come. "I'm fairly sure the woman is dead," he offered.

Ronnie shrugged. "Maybe. We won't know until we find out if the Stephen Cross I.D. is hidden well enough. Wasn't meant to stand up to this kind of attention."

"I'm sure it will," he said placatingly. "You do wonderful work."

"Only way we'll know for sure is to wait for the bobbies to come pounding on our door. Guess we'll have to give Brazil a try."

Langdon rolled onto his back. Brazil. How often had he heard that? Any time she thought *he* screwed up, that's what she threw at him—that because of him, they'd have to go live in Brazil like Nazi war criminals. Goddamn *forever* he was going to hear about this. He could tell.

"Still . . ." she said.

He rolled back over. "What?"

"What we've done should be enough to cause a reaction, wouldn't you say?"

We.

An improvement.

"From whom?" he said cautiously.

"From our target, dummy. This woman you may or may not have killed—she was a friend of the wife, Caroline, right?"

"It seemed that way. At the very least, the woman was her lawyer."

"Okay, then," Ronnie said. "A good friend gets mauled, maybe killed, that's worth a visit to your old hubby, isn't it? Or a least a phone call insisting he come visit. Right? And we know where he lives. So we watch him, we follow him, we take them together . . . and then we make him talk about little Tommy Cain and our favorite artwork."

"Huh," he said.

"What?" She looked in the mirror sharply. "Why wouldn't it work?"

Why should it? Langdon thought. There were so many variables, not the least of which was maybe the woman's estranged husband was the last person on earth she'd turn to for solace. Yet Langdon had no other plan to offer.

Instead, he said, "I think my visibility in this town's a little too high for me to hang out at the marina just now."

"Poor baby," she said with heavy sarcasm. "You need another rest in a nice hotel to lick your new wounds. You do that and *I'll* keep an eye on our sailor boy." She cast a dark, sulky look back at him. "Find some chambermaid to give you what you want while I do all the work."

Forever, he thought again. Resting his head against that filthy mattress. Goddamn *forever.*

CHAPTER 34

MCKENNA WORKED ON THE BOAT. FILLED THE WATER TANKS. SWEPT and wiped up the sawdust, and put away the tools. Straightened the disarray of the past few weeks of work. Checked his food supply to make sure there was enough for at least a few days. Bent the sails back on.

Kept his hands busy while he tried to figure out just who and *what* he was now.

He had slept with Amanda the night before.

Slept with her, hell.

Hours of talking at Emilio's, just down the street from the gallery. He told her early on that he was still married, but that seemed to matter little to her. Not that it bothered him, particularly, to lie to her. She seemed genuinely curious about his voyage back and asked him about his boat, about sailing. At the time, he felt maybe she was simply appealing to his interests. He couldn't figure out why. He didn't have youth, money, influence, or devastating good looks to offer. But nevertheless, she was with him and he choose not to question it too closely.

She followed him back to his boat in her little Miata. They went into the main cabin. She looked around the cabin, messy from all the work underway, and teased, "Well, at least I don't have to say nice things about your etchings."

First he fumbled, shy and uncertain of himself with a new woman for the first time in over twenty years. Part of him hoping that the problem with Caroline didn't crop up with this young woman, and, in truth, part of him hoping it would. Hoping he might have an excuse to bail out of the guilt that was sure to follow. But she helped him past that. And then her newness, her heat, overtook him.

Now, even as he worked, he tried to add this to the mix of what it all meant for him and Caroline. McKenna had to admit that his night with Amanda was one of the most exciting nights of his life. He felt flushed and shaken by her.

Perhaps it was just the illicitness of it all—being on the boat where he'd made love to Caroline. On the boat where he had killed Tom Cain and that man, Gleason.

Amanda's slim body had been surprisingly voluptuous under her loose clothes. Straddling him, her hands on his chest. Moving with exquisite slowness. All firmness and fine bone, tastes and textures that were so new to him as to be entirely alien.

Now, alone on his boat, McKenna strove for a sense of bemusement. Accept the pleasure for what it had been: something to be forgotten or at least compartmentalized.

But his body was alive in a way he couldn't remember. Hungry. He felt hungry. Could he somehow have them both? Amanda and Caroline.

The idea would have been nonsensical to him in the past. Back when he had Caroline and Sam, McKenna simply knew that such things didn't work. Weren't right and didn't work. The sort of thing his father would have done.

McKenna went up on deck, thinking maybe the stain fumes were getting to him. That it was hard enough to reconcile what had happened on the boat earlier. The death—no, his *killing*—of two men. How could he manage an affair on top of it all?

How could he find his way back to himself?

And, of course, the larger question: was there any good reason to find a way back to himself?

* * *

McKenna noticed the woman on the green sloop was now hosing down the deck of her boat. She'd single-handed her boat in a few hours ago and Swam had put her on one of the inside finger piers off of the same dock as the *Wanderer*. Her boat was a beautiful emerald Hinckley. Thirty-five-feet long, registered out of Salem.

But it wasn't the boat that held his interest. The woman was older than Amanda, most likely in her early to mid-thirties. Stunning woman. He had watched her earlier, had found himself looking out the porthole when he was supposedly working. Looking at her finely muscled legs, her long dark hair. Baseball cap shading lively, and yet classic, features.

As far as he could tell, she never once looked McKenna's way. But nevertheless, he had slowly become more conscious of her throughout the afternoon.

There was something about her that he couldn't define, but felt.

If not her, if not Amanda, he would want someone else. He wanted that experience again.

And it looked as if he would have it. Amanda had asked him to take her sailing. To give her a weekend on the water. She took off in her little car to buy some clothes, saying that she wouldn't bother to drive home to Boston.

McKenna laughed to himself as he peeled away the For Sale sign on the bow and moved it up to the cabin side. A bitter sound. Swan wouldn't say anything, but someone else certainly might. Someone else might tell his wife that he was sailing away with this beautiful young woman. He had given back a fortune in diamonds to keep Caroline safe, but this he couldn't—or wouldn't—deny himself.

Forty-two years old and just discovering how closely tied death and lust could be.

CHAPTER 35

CAROLINE DIDN'T GET THE NEWS ABOUT MARIEL UNTIL ALMOST FIVE o'clock that afternoon. Sophia Benchley called Caroline at the store to tell her she'd heard Mariel had been attacked at her house and that she was in the hospital.

Caroline immediately called the hospital herself and got next to no information when she admitted she wasn't a blood relation.

Within fifteen minutes, Caroline had closed the store down and was striding through the main door of the hospital. She went to the reception desk and found that Mariel was in a private room off the intensive care unit.

A uniformed policeman was outside the room when Caroline got up to the third floor. Caroline knew him slightly—he had been on a beat near Rob's office years back—and he said, "I guess you can go in."

Caroline hesitated just slightly, then stepped into the room. The bandages around Mariel's head were so white as to be almost luminous in the darkened room. There was a brace at her neck and a body cast from her waist down. Her eyes were closed. Her breathing was steady, though.

"Caroline," Elliott said.

She jumped. She hadn't seen him before, tucked back in the dark corner, in an armchair. She had the sense that he was waiting for someone. Elliott was almost as fully bandaged as Mariel. One arm was in a sling and his left knee was tightly wrapped. He said only two ribs had hairline fractures, and the rest were bruised. However, as Caroline's eyes became accustomed to the light, she could see that breathing alone looked like an effort for him. His eyes were glassy, probably from both dope and pain.

"What happened?" Caroline whispered.

Elliott told her what he could. About the woman in the car blowing the horn. Coming around to see the man chasing Mariel down the stairway. About the fight.

"I screwed up," Elliott said.

"No." She squeezed his shoulder.

He shrugged her hand off. Angry with himself, but willing to share it. "Sure I did. Lost control." He took Mariel's hand in his— Caroline noticed distractedly how small Mariel's hand was in comparison. *She* looked smaller, lying there in the hospital bed, and Caroline never thought of Mariel as a diminutive woman.

Caroline said, "Who are they? What did they want?"

"Don't know," he said. "I will, though."

About twenty minutes later the doctor came in. He was a thin middle-aged man, balding, with wire-rimmed glasses. He began to quickly run down Mariel's injuries for them. His tone was regretful, as if he were setting them up to hear to the worst.

Elliot held up his hand. "Take it out in the hallway. Caroline, you can tell me what's up later. I don't want her listening to this," Elliot lifted Mariel's hand.

The doctor said gently, "I don't believe she can hear us."

"I do," Elliott said. "I want everybody to treat her like she can, that clear? She's a smart, tough lady, and you can bet your ass she's working on getting out of this. No sense telling her all the bad news; she knows she's in a spot."

"That's fine," the doctor said. He seemed like he meant it. He took Caroline by the elbow into the hallway.

He said, "Mariel is on the hospital board of directors, so I know her slightly. If anybody could succeed at demanding a recovery, it's her. But there's no getting past it: she's suffered some serious damage. Definite concussion, which is what's induced this coma. Right knee is broken, so is her right arm . . . ball and joint dislocated. But it's the coma that's the real problem."

"How long?"

He sighed. "I've got her lined up for surgery. Tap some of the pressure. Then we'll see."

"So it's a matter of 'if' isn't it?" Caroline said. "We don't know if she's going to come out of it at all, do we?"

"I'm sorry," he said.

"How's Elliott?"

The doctor shook his head, marveling. "Amazing to take what he took and get off with broken ribs and a mild concussion. Plus I understand there was a bit of trouble when the police first arrived . . . black man on the ground covered in blood, white woman close to dead, they jumped to some conclusions until one of the cops in a backup car recognized him."

"Wonderful," Caroline said, bitterly.

The doctor paused until she had regained herself.

Caroline said, "What can I do to help? You've got to understand, Mariel's this person who does everything for everyone else, like everyone's big sister . . ."

A tear streaked down Caroline's face and she wiped it away angrily. Feeling that if their roles were reversed Mariel would have done something—somehow made the situation better.

The doctor said, "You should gather her family."

Caroline shook her head. "She doesn't have one."

He touched her shoulder lightly. "Then gather yours."

Caroline drove from the hospital to the marina in a daze. She was in her new/old car. The Saab convertible that Mariel had told her about. Another one of Mariel's many favors . . . another client upgrading after securing a substantial divorce settlement.

The car growled along easily. Plenty of power even with seventy thousand miles on the odometer. Well maintained, lots of life left in it.

"Perfect car for you," Mariel had said. "You deserve to get what you want."

But what about you? thought Caroline now. *God, what about you?*

She pulled into the marina parking lot, the crushed shells crunching under her wheels. She glanced in the mirror, saw that her eyes were red-rimmed from crying, and took a moment to straighten herself out.

Caroline saw the *Wanderer*'s mast on the third dock and started down the ramp. Being a weekday, there weren't that many people on their boats. She noticed an extraordinarily pretty woman with black hair in the cockpit of a green sloop. The woman looked up from her book and stared at Caroline without smiling, her eyes unknown behind dark sunglasses.

Caroline continued on.

Rob wasn't on deck. She felt a twisting urgency at that; she really wanted him, if only as her friend, to come back and sit with her at the hospital. Caroline was certain he would want to do the same. Mariel was his friend, too.

Caroline noticed that the *Wanderer* was in beautiful shape, better than she'd ever seen it. Brightwork gleaming, the teak recently oiled. As she walked around to the finger pier, she also noticed that all the hatches and portholes were open . . . and she heard Rob's voice. She couldn't make out what he was saying, but a solid measure of relief moved through her. She hurried up the small three-step platform to the cockpit, certain that she was simply going to be interrupting a conversation with Swan or perhaps a mechanic for some job that Rob couldn't—

A woman laughed.

Caroline was already in the cockpit now, had already said, "Rob, it's me," when it happened, that sweet laugh that made Caroline lose her balance.

She actually stumbled. Felt her legs grow weak and fetched a solid and painful blow to her knee. She looked down into the cabin and saw them.

Rob was holding a young woman.

They were dressed, thank God.

At least there's that, a part of Caroline recognized with a dry and intense pain. *At least I don't have to remember stumbling onto them naked.*

The girl saw her first.

Black-haired thing, remarkable blue eyes. Stunning girl, Caroline thought, feeling old, and haggard, and very, very foolish for coming to this man for help.

"Uh-oh," the girl said with an engaging smile. "If you're who I think you are . . ."

Caroline hated her profoundly. Caroline also felt the intruder, her face flushing with hot embarrassment.

Rob pulled away. "Oh, Jesus," he said. The blood left his face.

At least there's that, too, Caroline thought grimly.

Luckily, icy rage came to her rescue before she said something she'd always regret, like, "I'm sorry."

Instead, she said, in a cold, clear voice, "Rob, I need to talk with you. Something's happened."

Caroline got off the boat and walked up the pier to the bow. She was shaking inside, and for a moment, there was a very real possibility she might be sick.

But then Rob was there, and when he touched her shoulder, she had to slap his hand away. That made her feel a little more in control, but did nothing for the awfulness inside.

"Caroline . . ."

She said in the same cold voice as before, "There'll probably be a time when I'll listen to some explanation, but for now please just shut the hell up."

He sighed. "I'm so sorry . . ."

"Mariel's in the hospital," Caroline said flatly. "Someone attacked her and Elliott, tried to kill them both."

If Rob was looking shaky before, this seemed to floor him. He reached out to the *Wanderer*'s bowline and said, "What? Who did this?"

"The police don't know," Caroline said. "A man and a woman. Elliott came in on the middle of it—"

"Well, what's Mariel say?" he asked sharply.

"She can't. She's in a coma."

"Oh God," McKenna said. His hand went to his forehead. "There's nothing? No idea as to who did it?"

Caroline almost put her hand out to him, despite what she'd just run into. He seemed so shocked.

But she couldn't bring herself to help.

Instead, she said, "I'm going back to the hospital. Give me a few hours before you come. I don't want you there at the same time." Caroline gestured at the *Wanderer*, at the beautiful woman somewhere inside the freshly painted hull. Inside Rob's fresh new life. "Looks like you'll be busy for a while anyhow."

She turned and left.

In the parking lot, Ronnie sat in the rental car and dialed the cell phone. Ian sounded sleepy when he finally picked up the phone.

She said, "Get out of bed, sweets."

"How's my sailor girl?" he said. "Got something for me?"

"Oh, I think you'd like her," she teased. "You'd probably would've gone for someone like her if I hadn't led you astray. Looks a little like me, but she's a nicer person, I can tell."

"You know it's Caroline?"

"Definitely. I could tell the way she walked back up the pier after meeting hubby's new girlfriend. Mad as a scalded cat."

"Lots of people get mad."

Ronnie said. "Yes, but this one's sitting in her car crying her eyes out. Trust me, this is our girl."

"Then follow her. I'll pick us up another car and meet you wherever you tell me."

"How about the girlfriend?" Ronnie said. "You think she could be the one we're looking for? She certainly is a gorgeous little thing."

"Follow the wife," Langdon said. "That's who he was protecting before."

"You're sure?"

"I'm sure."

"Love you," Ronnie said, putting the phone down. Feeling so much better as Caroline drove away, and she put the car in gear to follow. Feeling so much more in control.

CHAPTER 36

"Now what?" Dobyns said. They had just pulled off the Southeast Expressway near South Station. He'd left two guys back at Alcott's house with instructions to not let anyone in, and to stay away from the viewing room themselves.

Chapman's face looked green. He was scared, as well he should be. "Head toward Southie."

Chapman had been doing his whine at some length about how he hadn't wanted to bother Dobyns with unnecessary stories after Gleason had beaten him last time. That if he had been told to keep an eye on Amanda, he would've.

Dobyns knew he'd screwed up himself, scaring Chapman so much he'd make such a blunder. Not that he was going to exactly say that to the kid. Dobyns was not big on apologies.

But he had to admit to himself that he might not have done anything with the information if Chapman had given it to him. Dobyns sure as hell never expected Amanda to remain faithful to Alcott. Jesus, an ex-nun would put horns on that guy. From the look at the maid, fidelity probably wasn't a high priority with Alcott either.

But putting horns on Alcott and screwing around with Dobyns's own income were two entirely different things.

Alcott was sitting to Dobyns's right side; Chapman on his left.

Alcott wasn't holding his head in his hands, but looking out the window, brooding.

Wounded.

Jesus.

Dobyns turned back to Chapman, counting mentally to ten. Figured he'd get more using patience at this point.

"David, I understand why you didn't say anything," he said. "Wish you had, but . . ." He made a sweeping gesture as they passed over the bridge on Summer Street. "That's water under the bridge."

The rare use of Chapman's first name seemed to help him relax, which was Dobyns's intention.

Dobyns said, "Just try to point out where you followed her that night." They'd already spent enough time with the phone book to figure that Woodrell didn't have a listed number. But Chapman had remembered a night when he'd dropped Amanda off after dinner, and he thought she was on her way to Woodrell's place.

"I didn't exactly *follow* her," Chapman said.

Dobyns gritted his teeth.

Chapman said, "It's just that she was kind've secretive, not big time, but just 'let me off here, Davy' even though we were still on the bridge."

"Yes."

"So I did. And then it was awkward to just bang a U-turn here. So I went down there, took a right, thinking I could pull a turn there . . . But it wasn't easy, all the traffic. I had to keep following the road all the way down, a right and a left, before I got to a loading dock where I could turn around. And then there was the same traffic *coming back* . . ."

"So?"

"So, it took some time. Maybe five minutes before I could come back, take a left, and go back over the bridge. And while I was just getting ready to take that left, I saw her."

"Saw her *where*?" Christ, there was no quick way to this.

"Right there." Chapman pointed down the street on the right. "See that specialty photo place? Green awning?"

"Uh-huh."

"Door in front of it. Now I've got no idea that's where Woodrell is. I mean, it could be anything. We might go up there and find she's got a new hairdresser, what do I know?"

Dobyns clapped the two of them on the shoulders. "Well, boys . . ."

His two scared boys. Figured he'd keep them moving along if he was easy with them. ". . . since that's all we know, then that's what we'll follow up."

He told Buddy to find a place to park. And to come along with them.

Everything was easier when the landlord recognized Dobyns's face. It was like that in Southie, and this was the edge of Southie. Doors opened when they saw who it was.

The landlord not only opened the front door, he obediently took them up to the third floor and opened Woodrell's door.

Buddy went through first with his gun drawn.

"Nobody home," he said a few minutes later.

Dobyns handed the landlord the picture of Tom Cain, just to be sure.

"Yuh, that's him. Haven't seen him in a coupla months," the landlord said. He was a skinny, gray old thing. Voice quavering, anxious to tell Dobyns anything he could. Kept eyeing the gun until Dobyns jerked his head to Buddy, tell him to put the piece away. The old man said, "Woodrell told me he was gonna be gone. He always traveled a lot, anyhow. Paid his rent in advance. Said that his girlfriend would be using the place from time to time."

"Has she?"

"Uh-huh." The man nodded eagerly. "Not that much, but a good few times I seen her in the past coupla days."

Dobyns took a packet of photos from his inside pocket and showed the old man. He identified Langdon's picture of Tom Cain as Justus Woodrell and quickly identified a publicity shot of Amanda as Woodrell's girlfriend.

Behind them, Alcott groaned. The old man turned, but Dobyns ignored him.

Dobyns walked into the room, Alcott and Chapman trailing behind. It was a big, rambling loft. Little kitchen off to the left. Good-sized windows at one end, laced with chicken wire. Fairly good light at that end; for shit at this end. In the light, he saw several easels in place and lamps stacked on tripods around the easels. There was paint splattered all over the floor.

"Someone's been at work," he said.

He went into the little kitchen. Checked out the refrigerator. A few cartons of yogurt, cereal, a small carton of skim milk, whole wheat bread, lettuce, white wine. The freezer was empty, the rest of the refrigerator was largely cleaned out except for a few condiments on the side. But the perishables were fresh.

"Girl food," Dobyns said. He looked over at Alcott. "This look like her kind of diet?"

He nodded.

Dobyns said to the old man, "How long has Woodrell lived here?"

"Oh, Jesus, I don't know. Coupla years," the old man said.

"Pay his rent on time?"

"Kick him out on his ass if he didn't. But, yeah, he's been no problem."

"What's he do for a living?"

"Dunno. None of my business, I figure. Gone a lot, paints some pictures, I know. But not running drugs outa my place, I woulda known that." Then perhaps thinking that maybe he was insulting his rather dangerous guest, the old man said, "Not that I'd call the cops or nothing. I'm a private man, respect the privacy of others, I always say."

Dobyns smiled. "Good idea. Part of how you got to such a wise old age, I expect."

The old man tried to make a joke out of it, laughing repeatedly, like a horse who couldn't get his whinny straight.

"Shut up," Dobyns said abruptly.

"Sure, sure."

Dobyns walked throughout the studio, noticing the small enclosed room off to the side with the red lightbulb over the door. "What's this?"

"Darkroom," the old man said. "Both him and the girlfriend got cameras." He looked disdainfully at Chapman and lifted his little finger and said, "Artists."

Dobyns went in and flicked on the lights. The room inside was filled with red light, disconcerting at first. But he got used to the light quickly enough. The smell was a different thing, a bright chemical smell in the air. He saw a half-dozen prints hanging from a small clothesline, and he took them back into the light outside.

They were still slightly damp.

He handed them to Chapman. "Tell me what you can."

Chapman felt the edge of each print with his thumb and forefinger. "She must've taken these. Or at least printed them recently. They're still damp. This isn't something he could've done months ago."

Chapman laid the photos out on a table outside the darkroom and turned on the desk lamp.

He frowned. "This is more record-type stuff," he said. "Not art."

"More like surveillance," Dobyns said, looking down on the prints himself. Picture of a boat. Sailboat. He looked at a picture of a middle-aged man climbing onto the deck of his boat. Good-looking guy.

Dobyns stared at the picture. "Do I know you?"

Chapman handed him a loupe, showing it worked as a magnifying glass. Dobyns bent down and studied the man carefully. He had Chapman and Alcott do the same.

Both shook their heads, waiting for him.

After a moment, Dobyns sighed. He didn't know the man but it did look as if Amanda had been watching him carefully.

Dobyns shuffled through the remaining shots and found one toward the end that showed the boat at dock in the marina. Her stern was toward the camera, and he pulled back the loupe again and stared at intently. The name of the boat was the *Wanderer*. And through the magnification of the loupe, Dobyns was able to see the gas dock sign. The sign said Owens Marina and in smaller letters, Newburyport, Massachusetts.

"Okay, then," Dobyns said.

"What?" Alcott said.

Dobyns looked at him askance. Once a president of a major corporation. "Well, genius, as of right now, I figure whoever interests the lovely Amanda, interests me—"

Dobyns's pager buzzed. He pulled it off his belt and used his cell phone to call back.

"It's me," he said. "I'm on a cell. Uh-huh. Uh-huh. Yeah, Newburyport. That's interesting." Dobyns lifted his eyebrows. "Yeah, okay. About an hour."

He hung up. "All right, boys. I'm gonna go my own way. Chapman, you stick by the phone in case I need you. Greggie, I'll let you know how it all turns out. I'll keep my guys sitting at home with you and the Rembrandts."

"That's it? What's happened?"

"Had my boy Jerome on somebody I was worried about. He says this somebody has been making all kinds of trouble up in Newburyport."

"What kind of trouble?" Alcott said.

"You don't get all that specific on a cell phone," Dobyns said sourly. "But if Jerome says trouble, I'd say it was pretty bad."

Both Chapman and Alcott looked quickly at Amanda's pictures of the man on the boat. Alcott bent down over the print, staring closely. Finally, he shrugged. "I've never seen this guy."

"Me either," said Chapman.

Dobyns grunted. The man on the boat wasn't the one in trouble, as far as he could tell from Jerome's carefully nonspecific comments. But Dobyns could state with a fair amount of certainty, that was about to change.

CHAPTER 37

MCKENNA WAS SHIVERING INSIDE.

He walked back along the finger pier, his heart pounding, his breathing constricted. *What have I done,* he thought. *What have I done?*

"Is she gone?" Amanda was standing in the cockpit.

He stared at her, his face blank. Wondering for a brief moment, who Amanda was and what she was doing on his boat.

He climbed up onto the *Wanderer* heavily and sat down in the cockpit. "Jesus Christ," he said, raking his fingers through his hair.

Amanda put her arm around him. "Hey, hey," she whispered in his ear. "I can't pretend to know how awful that must've been. Talk to me. Tell me what you're thinking."

He shook his head. "I can't do this now. I'm sorry."

"C'mon, we've got the weekend for me to make you feel better—"

He laughed.

God knows, he didn't mean to. He surely wasn't feeling that life was particularly funny right then.

But their *weekend*.

Jesus, maybe the attack on Mariel had nothing to do with him; maybe it was some furious husband that she'd taken to the cleaners.

Maybe Caroline could forget what she'd seen.

Maybe McKenna could forget the things he done.

But at the moment, McKenna didn't believe any of it.

He said, "I've got to go to the hospital. A friend's been hurt."

"Who?"

He looked into the girl's eyes. "Look, I was flattered . . ."

"Shush." She put her finger to his lips. "I don't want to hear that particular speech. And I know you could use some good news right about now. Let's go down to the cabin and hold each other. I can make you feel better, I know I can."

McKenna went very still. *Use some good news.*

Cain's phrase. Couples did that all the time, picked up each other's phrases.

She was the right age. He could see them together. The charisma, the looks, the audacity.

And the dismaying thing was, he realized he never had quite believed Amanda's interest in him. He had just gone along because she was such a temptation—an escape—that he wouldn't deny himself.

He said abruptly. "Who are you? What do you want?"

"Excuse me?" She drew back, expressing confusion so nicely. "What do you mean?"

He reached up to hold her by the arm. He didn't hold her hard, no more than his thumb and index finger around her elbow.

"Rob?"

She drew back, but he wouldn't release her. She said, "Let go."

"Why are you with me?"

"I'm beginning to wonder." She tried to tug her arm away.

"Who sent you? Or are you on your own?"

"What are you're ranting about?" she said. "I don't like this—let me go right now!"

"You've been so anxious to get us out sailing. You have someone out there waiting for us? Someone like before?"

"You're crazy," she said. "Hello—you remember we met at our mutual friend's opening? Right? Melanie didn't tell me you were a nut."

McKenna hesitated. Then he saw her handbag on the cockpit cushion, and he grabbed it.

"What are you doing?" she cried. She tried to take it, but he turned his back to her.

The thought passed through him that it was quite possible he was simply making a fool of himself with an innocent woman. If that were the ·case, he figured, that was the least damage he'd done in recent weeks. She'd have no trouble finding someone new, someone less screwed up in the head.

McKenna dumped her purse upside down on the cockpit cushion. Something small and heavy fell out. Blue steel.

She jumped for it, but he deflected her away with his hip and scooped up the little pistol. He looked at it quickly. A .25 automatic. He checked to see the safety was on. The pistol was small enough to hide in his palm. He turned back to her. "Let's try this again. Who the hell are you?"

He saw her trying for exasperation and then suddenly her expression changed.

"Oh, Jesus," she said. "Oh, Jesus." She began to back away. Clearly, she was terrified, and frankly, he couldn't exactly see why.

Did she really think he was going to simply shoot her?

Then he realized she was looking past him. He looked over his shoulder.

He saw a middle-aged white man and a tall black man standing at the head of the ramp down to the dock. They weren't looking at McKenna's boat. Not yet, anyhow. They turned as Swan approached them, presumably asking if he could help them.

Behind McKenna, the girl ducked down. "Hide me," she said. "Please. I'll tell you what's going on. I'll tell you everything. Please just hide me."

McKenna looked back at the two men. The black man was scary at a glance. Stone-hard features. The white man looked like someone's kindly uncle who was a bit irritated about something at the moment.

"Police?" he said.

"God, no." Amanda looked up and down the little dock. The only way off was past the two men.

McKenna stared at her. Remembering the Coast Guard, the people he should've called for help.

But he didn't believe those two men were cops either.

"Hide me." She took his left hand, the one without the gun. "I got into something I should've walked away from, but I didn't . . ."

He could identify with that.

She tried to bolt down into his cabin, but he pushed her away.

"Don't do this, please," she hissed. "They'll kill me."

"Depending upon what you've done," he said, ". . . I might reserve that honor for myself." He reached into her bag, grabbed her wallet, and quickly fished out her driver's license. Amanda Montague with an address in Lincoln. Just what she'd told him. He put the license in his pocket.

"Please!" she whispered fiercely. "They'll kill both of us if they find us together!"

He gestured to the dinghy. "Take that. Go around the front of the dock and hold on to the *Elspeth*." He pointed to the large motor yacht that dominated the outside dock. "Lay up close against her. If you're lucky, they'll never see you."

"What if they do?"

McKenna put the little gun in his pocket. "We'll see."

Amanda moved quickly. She quietly slid off the boat, stepped into the dinghy, and rowed around the stern of the *Elspeth*. She handled the little boat well.

McKenna ducked down into his cabin just as the two men started down the ramp toward his boat. He quickly untucked his shirt, and, after practicing switching the safety on and off quickly, he put the little gun into his belt. The shirt covered it.

McKenna was breathing rapidly now, scared, but the anger was stronger. He'd given the diamonds back, he wanted to be done with this mess.

He was stepping up into the cockpit as the two men started down the little finger pier.

* * *

The older man put his hand out. "Do me a favor and tell me your name."

McKenna told him.

"Okay, Rob McKenna, my name is Jimmy Dobyns. That name mean anything to you?" He looked closely at McKenna.

McKenna said, "If you're the one I've read about in the paper."

"That's me," Dobyns said with a trace of pride.

A few years back, Dobyns had been covered in the news fairly regularly for taking over where Whitey Bulger left off: accusations of corrupting the FBI and the Boston police; of carefully orchestrating and winning a bloody power struggle against other would-be kings; of a Teflonlike ability to get away with it all.

Dobyns climbed up onto the boat without waiting for an invitation. He looked over the *Wanderer* and grunted with satisfaction. "She's a beauty. I've got a boatyard in Southie that I had to take over. Got myself more boats than I can shake a stick at. No time to play with them, though."

He smiled blandly at McKenna. "See you're selling yours. Maybe I can help out."

"What's up?" McKenna said abruptly.

The black guy stood on the dock, his arms crossed across his chest. He made McKenna feel like a featherweight. The tiny gun under McKenna's belt provided little comfort.

Dobyns touched McKenna's elbow and said, "Have a seat, Rob." Dobyns sat down himself.

McKenna resisted the urge to keep standing, to tell the arrogant bastard to get off his boat. But the man was just too good at conveying that he would get what he wanted, one way or another.

McKenna sat.

Dobyns leaned forward, touching McKenna's knee and saying with quiet confidence, "This is the way I see it. You look like a normal enough guy, got this pretty boat, I think you're in the middle of something, you don't know exactly how the hell you got there—but you want your way out. I can help you with that."

McKenna started to say he didn't know what Dobyns was talking about, but the older man interrupted him, saying over his shoulder to the black man, "Jerome, tell the man I'm a great friend to have, but what a mean *motherfucker* of an enemy."

"Mean mothafucka," Jerome drawled. "He put guys like me on your case and say, 'Do what you want.' " The black man winked at McKenna. "You don't want nothin' of what I want, man."

Dobyns chuckled. "When he starts to work, I can't even watch. Makes me squeamish. You're talking broken bones, maybe a gouged eye, knees never working right again. Who needs that? Anyhow, I don't see this should have to happen to you at all, assuming you're straight with me . . . so you got anything you want to tell me?"

McKenna just looked at him.

"Okay, we'll try it this way." Dobyns reached into his coat pocket and pulled out an envelope. He laid three photographs on the cushion next to McKenna. "Tell me who I'm looking at."

One picture was of Tom Cain. He was with a woman in a restaurant, a beautiful dark-haired woman that McKenna didn't know, but she looked familiar. And a picture of Amanda, a black-and-white portrait. And finally, there was a picture of Stephen Cross and a woman sitting on a park bench. McKenna looked closely and realized that the woman on the bench was the same as in the picture with Tom Cain.

And he realized where he'd seen her before.

McKenna turned to look over at the Hinckley sloop. The hatch was closed—the woman was gone.

"Oh Christ," he said. He hadn't seen the woman since Caroline was there.

Caroline.

"Who are they?" McKenna said harshly, putting his finger on the picture of the two at the park bench.

"Maybe you don't get the process here," Dobyns said. "I'm the one asking the questions."

McKenna drew the little gun and jammed it against Dobyns's throat. He thumbed off the safety. "Who are they?" he repeated tightly.

Jerome was already on the boat before Dobyns's words halted him. "Get the *fuck* back! Don't push this guy, you got that?" Then he turned his attention back to McKenna and said quietly, "Hey, asshole. We're in public. You want somebody to call the cops?"

"It's my wife," McKenna said. With his left hand, he picked up the picture of Stephen Cross and the woman and held it up to Dobyns's face. "Them. This woman. I think she followed my wife just now. I think they're the ones who almost killed a friend of ours, probably looking for my wife. My wife knows nothing about this entire goddamn mess, and I'll kill you, Jerome, and anyone else, sooner than letting her get pulled into this. Have you got it?"

"Sure." Dobyns actually managed to smile. "You're the romantic type."

Dobyns looked over at the black man. "Jerome, didn't you say that you followed Langdon—that you witnessed that attack our friend here is talking about?"

Jerome looked at McKenna, his eyes seemingly blank. "House on River Road? Saw 'em cut his way into the house. Heard some screams, then this chick here in the picture took the car around back when a brother like me came runnin' for the white lady in the house. Langdon and the chick took off in their car, and I did, too."

"That chick was Langdon's sister," Dobyns said.

"That's his name?" McKenna said. "Langdon?"

"That's right." Dobyns reached up and gently pushed McKenna's gun away. "See, we can help each other. I'm the practical type. You've got a gun, I've got a mean-ass killer right beside me and another waiting in the car. Let's go look after your wife. And then I expect to have a straight conversation about this 'entire goddamn mess.' Deal?"

McKenna let the automatic rest against his leg. Pointed only generally in Dobyns's direction. McKenna said, "I'm keeping this."

"Sure you are," Dobyns said. "I said you're a romantic, not an idiot."

CHAPTER 38

LANGDON WAS WAITING IN THE HOSPITAL PARKING LOT IN A STOLEN Ford LTD. It could have passed for an undercover cop car: dark blue, wide bench seats, V-8, dual exhaust, big old box of a trunk that he could pop open from a switch inside.

And cleaner than that scabby van.

Langdon saw Ronnie come out of the hospital. She had a paper bag in hand. Coffee, he hoped.

He was bored with waiting and that made him sleepy.

She slipped into the passenger seat. "Here you go, sweets."

He looked in the bag and groaned. There was a small *D* penciled on the top of his cup. "Decaf? I don't drink this for the taste."

"Can't have you getting excited, can we?" She opened a smaller bag. Two large chocolate chip cookies. "And these . . . because you're so good."

"Hmmm. What'd you see?"

"Well, our Caroline's there. In with the woman you hurt. Police-man outside the door."

"Caroline didn't see you?"

"If she did, she didn't seem to recognize me." Ronnie smiled. "Amazing what slipping on one of those hospital coats and putting my hair in a bun will do. Just like in the movies."

"So how *is* my latest victim?"

"Coma. Heard some nurses talking."

"Well, that's not so bad."

Ronnie shrugged. "Not if you like time bombs. She might come out of it."

"And the man?"

"He was there, too. Hovering over her."

"Didn't let *him* see you, did you?"

"Oh, no. You hit somebody with a car, they're likely to remember. Can't believe he's still alive, never mind walking."

"Well, he jumped up. You didn't hit him with the bumper, he rolled over the hood and it was the windshield that caught him." Langdon grinned at his sister. "Out of practice, aren't you?"

"Enough to save your sorry life."

They fell silent. She was doing a good job covering. She had barely slept the night before, still certain that Tom Cain and his girl-friend were somewhere laughing at her.

He sipped his hospital-cafeteria coffee. Bland, watery stuff.

"I'm not sure we did the right thing," Ronnie said. "Maybe it was that girl. Back at the boat. Maybe that's who we should be picking up."

"Possibly," Langdon said. "But it was his wife McKenna was pro-tecting. That's who he seemed concerned about."

"Yes, well . . . you didn't see how pretty this girl was. Confident little bitch, I could see it just in the way she walked. Full of herself." Ronnie sipped her coffee, brooding.

"Well, we're here. Let's just give our plan a chance."

"I suppose," she said.

The plan was simplicity itself. Snatch McKenna's wife in the parking lot when she walked to her Saab. Put her in the trunk. And then go get McKenna and take them to an empty vacation house on the river that he and Ronnie had scouted up earlier. Go to work on the wife until the man spilled everything he knew. Dump their bodies into the river afterward.

Langdon only hoped McKenna would confirm he had somehow killed Tom Cain himself. Langdon couldn't see any other way that McKenna would have had possession of the diamonds.

Actually, Langdon did have some additional hopes. That Ronnie would *believe* the man if he confessed to killing Cain. And that McKenna might be able to give them a lead to the Rembrandts.

Ian knew the whole thing might be a useless exercise. But if snatching and killing the McKennas only brought Ronnie some peace of mind, then it was time well spent.

Very well spent.

Fifteen minutes later, Langdon's eyes were still on the hospital entrance, his mind still on his sister's mood, when a black car pulled in front of them.

And stopped.

Big black limo. Blocking their exit.

A powerful flashlight shown from inside the limo, right into their eyes.

Abruptly the light switched off them, and the front passenger window slid down to reveal a big black man. He had a revolver in his hand, which he used to wave to them in greeting. Not exactly pointing at them, more like putting it on display.

"Ian?" Ronnie said.

By then, Langdon had already twisted the wires back together. The Ford roared to life.

He was ready to drop the car into drive and ram his way out when the rear window slipped down and he saw who was in the back seat.

"I'll be damned," Langdon said.

"What?" Ronnie asked sharply.

He noticed she had grabbed the door handle. *Ready to bolt,* Langdon thought. He said, "It's the local talent I told you about. Mister James Dobyns." Langdon looked closer through the window and frowned. "It gets worse."

"Oh, my," Ronnie said. She could see into the back seat of the limo as well. "So now McKenna's with him?"

"Looks that way," Langdon said. "But Jimmy never holds on to people for too long." He rolled down the window and leaned out. "Jimmy. For what do I owe the honor?"

"You two get out and come talk to me," Dobyns said. "We got some stuff to clear up."

"Certainly. Just a moment please." Langdon sat back and looked at his sister. He gave her the mild little smile that worked the best for them when they needed to keep calm. "Let's think about this."

In front of them, the driver got out and walked around the front of the limo. He was big, blond. Red faced. Buddy, that was his name. The one who'd picked Langdon up at the airport. He was yelling, "Mr. D. said, 'Out,' and that's what he means."

They heard the black man say to Buddy, "Not in between, slick."

Buddy seemed to ignore him.

Ronnie hissed to her brother. "Do you have them on you? The diamonds?"

"Right here." He patted the money belt under his shirt.

"If McKenna tells Dobyns . . ."

"Then he'll take them," Langdon said. "I'm not feeling all that chatty myself, just now. How about you?"

Buddy reached under his coat. "Get your ass outa the car."

Ronnie buckled her seat belt and put her foot up on the dashboard. "Not chatty at all."

Langdon dropped the car into gear and floored it.

CHAPTER 39

McKenna heard Dobyns say, "Buddy, you numbnuts," just as the Ford's engine screamed.

The front end of the car lifted, the headlights silhouetting Buddy as he tried to spin and run.

"Jerome!" Dobyns cried.

The black man reached over with his left hand and slapped the gearshift into drive. He mashed the gas pedal down with his left foot, grabbed the wheel, and was turning back to level the gun when the Ford caught Buddy. The car smashed him against Dobyns's side door. Buddy screamed shrilly, beating his hands against the roof of the limo.

The limo stalled.

"For Christ's sake!" Dobyns cried. Buddy slipped down onto the ground as the Ford screamed in reverse. The Ford hit the parked car behind them, and then came lunging out again. McKenna braced himself, heard someone saying, "No, no, no," before realizing it was himself.

By then, Jerome had the limo started. From his angle, McKenna couldn't see over the door, but the Ford seemed to bump over something, Buddy, probably, before then smashing into the trunk of the limo. McKenna was thrown up against the Plexiglas separating the back from the front. The Ford's tires continued to shriek. Over that, there was the sharp wrenching sound of metal on metal as the Ford shoved past the edge of the limo's bumper.

The Ford lurched free and took off for the exit.

"Go!" Dobyns said to Jerome. "Get us the hell out of here."

"What about Buddy?" Jerome looked in the rearview mirror. "That bastard will talk."

Dobyns looked out the window. "Not without a head, he won't. Let's go."

"Alright," Jerome said minutes later. He was reaching into the open glove compartment while he drove.

"Got something good, hit me with it," Dobyns said. He was fiercely rubbing his face and hands with his handkerchief. Some of Buddy's blood had come through the open window.

Jerome held up a wallet. "Old Buddy's. Didn't like sitting on it, so he left it in the car. It's gonna take them a while to print him and figure out who he is."

"That's good," Dobyns said. "Now shut up and let me think."

They were just about across the town line when Dobyns began to fire off instructions: "Jerome, first you gotta get that blood off the car. I think Buddy keeps a jug of window-washer fluid in the trunk—use that. Call Leanne on the cell phone, have her send somebody up some clothes in the Caddy, meet us at that rest area near Stoneham. We pull up side by side, I slip in. You take care of getting the limo crushed. Tell Leanne to get some people over at the Green Tavern, that's where I'm gonna have been tonight. You get with your chick, go out on the town, let people see you."

"What you want to do with him?" Jerome looked into the mirror at McKenna. His voice was calm and he was keeping the car at a sedate pace.

Dobyns looked at him, his lips pursed. Considering him in a way McKenna didn't care to see.

"Me, you let go," McKenna said. He drew the little gun. He didn't point it at Dobyns, but he let him see it.

Dobyns sighed. "Ah, Christ, I should've had Jerome shove that up your ass the first time."

"Let me out."

Dobyns snapped his fingers and waved to the side of the road. He looked at McKenna. "You want to get out of the car, be my guest. But you're not 'out.' You're in this thing up to your eyeballs."

"What do you want from me? I gave him the diamonds."

Dobyns went very still.

Then he said, "Gave who the diamonds?"

McKenna had a sense of the black man looking back in the mirror. Curious and somewhat amused.

McKenna was confused. "The one in the car, Cross. Or Langdon, you said his name was. Aren't the diamonds what this is all about?"

"Worth how much?"

McKenna told him.

"No shit? Five million." Dobyns made a face in the mirror at Jerome. "Pays to keep your ears clean." Dobyns reached into his coat pocket and pulled out the three photos from before. "Indulge me a minute here." He showed McKenna the shot of Tom Cain with the black-haired woman. "That the guy you're talking about?"

"That's right. Tom Cain."

"Where's he now?"

McKenna hesitated. But he felt nothing in this crazy game would change until he got this out.

"I killed him," McKenna said. His voice was hoarse.

If the news fazed Dobyns, it only seemed to make him look at McKenna with a stirring of respect. He cocked his head. "Yeah?"

"He was going to kill me. He and the other man were going to drown me and sink the *Wanderer*."

"Who was that?"

"Big fat man. Gleason, I think his name was."

"Hey, hey," Jerome said from the front seat with a wide smile. "There you go."

"Uh-huh," Dobyns said. "This all over the diamonds?"

"That's what it seems," McKenna said.

"Uh-huh. Five million." He sighed. "Small-time punks, what they traded it for. Still, those diamonds are mine, wouldn't you say, Jerome?"

"Hell, yes. That art shit just on loan, the way I look at it," Jerome said. "Then your own favorite white boy ripping you off? I'd say them diamonds be yours, yeah I would."

"Unlock the door, Jerome," Dobyns said.

The electric lock snicked open.

McKenna kept the gun on Dobyns as he got out, which only made the older man impatient. "Hurry up. I got a lot to do tonight."

"So I'm out?" McKenna said. "Me and my wife?"

Dobyns found some blood behind his ear. He looked at his hand in disgust, before turning back to McKenna. "Told you already, it doesn't work that way." He reached over and pulled the door shut.

The limo took off, leaving McKenna by the side of the road in the dark.

CHAPTER 40

CAROLINE AND ELLIOTT WALKED OUT THROUGH THE HOSPITAL DOORS. Police-car lights swirled in the parking lot.

"Did you hear what happened here?" Caroline said.

"Some crazy shit," Elliott said. "Guy rammed his way out of here, ran over somebody. Killed him."

"My God. They know who died?"

Elliott shrugged. "Cops don't know jack right now. Hell, in Boston, this kind've thing happens over someone snagging a parking spot somebody else figured was theirs."

"But this isn't the city."

"Tell me. Tell Mariel."

He rubbed his face, and then looked at Caroline. Even in the poor overhead light, she could see his eyes were streaked with red.

"C'mon," she said. "The doctor said, 'Reason for hope.' There is brain activity." The surgeon had come out and talked to them just an hour ago, saying they had successfully tapped the pressure, but now there was nothing to do but wait.

Caroline felt as if pressure were building inside her own skull. She saw her husband with that young woman any moment that she didn't consciously keep the thought away.

She was surprised that Rob never came to the hospital. Could he have just gone back to the arms of the girl after that awful scene? Ignored the spot Mariel was in? Ignored Caroline herself? That didn't gel with anything Caroline had ever known about her husband.

But there it was: he never came.

Caroline said to Elliott briskly. "I'll give you a ride home."

"Yeah, thanks. Let me ask you something," he said. "You know that call I got right before the doctor came out? That was from Pollock."

"The detective?" Caroline had met him briefly in the waiting room.

"Yuh. They're going through Mariel's place, they came upon a name on a notepad . . . I mean, they came upon lots of names, her appointment book, her phone messages, all that. But mostly, I could tell them who it was, how Mariel knew them. But not this name. You know any Stephen Cross?"

She thought about it and then shook her head.

"I've seen it. The name, I mean, and it just came to me when. I've seen it on her notepad, but I didn't think about it one way or another. I mean who does; unless you're a nosy bastard, you don't ask your girlfriend what every name on every piece of paper means."

She smiled at him. "No, you don't." As they reached her car, she unlocked the passenger door and held it open for him. He got in gingerly, "Such a gentleman," he said, his face creased with pain until he sat back against the seat.

When she got behind the wheel, he turned so he could look at her directly. "Thing is, I think I saw Cross's name on the pad *after* your husband came by to talk with her. You know he came by, right?"

She looked at Elliott, not clear where he was going with this. "You think Rob gave her the name?"

"See, I knew the name was familiar when Pollock said it, and then I got to thinking I saw it on Mariel's notepad—the day after Rob came to see her."

"That doesn't mean—"

"No, it doesn't," Elliott said. "Could've been there for a week, and I just didn't see it. Fake name, Pollock's pretty sure. 'Cause Pollock already talked to a Stephen Cross; guy was a patient here at the hospital just a week back. So that's what he's chasing right now."

Caroline turned right onto High Street. "Did you send Pollock to Rob?"

Elliott shook his head. "Like I said, didn't remember where I'd seen the name until about fifteen minutes ago. So I figure I'll just gimp on over tomorrow and talk to your husband myself."

"Why?"

Caroline felt a strange swirl of emotions. Her own anger with her husband was bright, hot and focused. But twenty years of marriage didn't like the sound of her husband being questioned.

Ex-husband to be.

"I can't see how that's necessary," she said.

"May not come to anything, but it's necessary," he said. He lifted his hand and began ticking off points: "One, a guy named Stephen Cross got his ass whupped and someone dumped him off at this hospital about a week ago. Cross said he was a private detective from Boston, but Pollock checked into it and I made some calls myself and nobody's heard of him. Two, his name turns up on a notepad in Mariel's house, and a coupla days later, somebody comes in and tries to kill her. Three, it looks like a scene out of *Death Race 2000* out here in the parking lot of the hospital where Mariel's staying. That's a lot of fast, weird violence around this town."

"And you really think Rob's got something to do with it?" Caroline asked. In spite of her caution, she was beginning to feel a strange kind of elation. As if there were another explanation for it all, another reason for the distance between her and Rob. Immediately, she was ashamed of herself. Ashamed that she was so needy as to hope this death and mayhem somehow might provide an excuse for her lost love.

But, nevertheless, the idea took hold.

"Don't know that Rob's got a thing to do with it," Elliott said, stolidly. "Probably nothing at all. But I figure it's worth a talk."

He looked at her. "Anything going since we last talked?"

She found herself shaking her head. Even though the image of

Rob and that girl pulsed inside her. Even though, at that moment, she trusted and respected Elliott more than her husband

But she wasn't in love with Elliott.

"No," Caroline said. "Nothing."

Elliott shrugged. "So I'll go talk to him tomorrow. See if he can point me in the direction of this Stephen Cross. In the meantime . . . you got a couch?"

"What?"

"In your new place. You got a couch?"

She smiled cautiously. "I've got a couch."

"Do me a favor then. I'll sleep better knowing I'll be around to greet this Stephen Cross if he comes to visit you."

"Why would he visit *me*?"

"Got no idea," Elliott said. "I'd just hate to miss him if he came by. Mariel would kick my ass when she wakes up, she find out I let that happen."

He touched Caroline's shoulder. "I say the couch, I mean the couch."

"I know," she said. "And thanks. Tell me where your place is, we'll stop and get some clothes."

"That'd be good. I'm smelling rank to myself, I gotta be knocking down everybody else." He told her how to find his apartment and then yawned hugely. He shifted in his seat, wincing as he tried to find a position where he didn't hurt.

He closed his eyes and said, "Give me a nudge when we get close."

About a half hour later, McKenna was in his truck diagonally across the street from what he was fairly sure was Caroline's new home. With the flashlight, he was studying the little map Mariel had sketched out seemingly a hundred years ago in her kitchen. He was certain he'd found Sophia Benchley's house, but there was no light on the third floor.

Presumably, Caroline was still at the hospital.

McKenna had walked back to the marina from where Dobyns had dropped him off, gotten the truck, and hurried over to Caroline's place. He supposed the best way to keep track of her would have been to wait outside the hospital. But with all the policemen that must've been crawling all over the place, that didn't seem to be too smart.

He switched off the flashlight when he saw the Saab pull in front of the house. He knew she loved those cars; he wondered if that was now hers. She got out and he smiled. Good for her, got what she wanted. Maybe what he should do is just beg her to trust him one last time, get her to pack her bags, and the two of them could take off in that convertible. Leave this craziness behind.

Figure out something to tell her that he could live with and that she could believe.

Even in the seconds it took to run out this little fantasy, he saw it for just what it was. And just as reality began to intrude, he saw the black man get out of the car.

McKenna leaned forward, more curious than alarmed. He recognized that it was Elliott, Mariel's friend. And that he was going into the house with Caroline, carrying a bag. Staying the night, most likely.

McKenna felt a touch of uneasiness and behind it anger.

Not because he thought the two were sleeping together.

Though he supposed anything was possible, given what Caroline had seen that day; given that she had reason to think he was leaving her behind himself.

But McKenna didn't believe that.

What McKenna believed was that the man was staying to protect her, that Elliott was acting as a friend.

And that was a good thing.

But the anger remained. Blossomed, even.

McKenna was afraid of being found out. Afraid of this detective spending all this time with Caroline. This detective with all the motivation in the world to find out who was causing so much trouble in town.

And while McKenna was surprised to feel the level of anger, he supposed he'd known all along that he was unwilling to pay the price.

He squeezed the steering wheel as the front door closed behind the two of them. The two had been talking as they walked from the car.

They probably would be talking late at night, talking early in the morning, probably spending hours together at the hospital waiting for Mariel to wake up.

How long before Elliott came around asking questions?

"I'm trying to keep you out of it," McKenna said out loud.

But he couldn't escape the fact that people were getting hurt because of his choices. If he had let the Coast Guard take Cain away, Mariel would be fine. If he had killed Langdon instead of taking him to the hospital, Mariel would be fine. McKenna couldn't escape that.

It's just that the idea of going through the courts, of lawyers, of public curiosity and humiliation—of prison—none of it seemed right either.

He wasn't willing to do that. He'd lost his daughter, most likely his wife, and he'd given the damn diamonds back. He wasn't going to let those bastards Dobyns and Langdon just skate away while he acted like a dutiful citizen and turned himself in for the sake of honesty and the pleasure of a prison sentence.

Just keep your mouth shut, he found himself thinking. Raging inside at his wife in a way he never had in nineteen years of marriage. *Just keep your mouth shut and let me take care of this.*

CHAPTER 41

MCKENNA AWOKE ON HIS BOAT JUST AFTER TEN-THIRTY THE NEXT morning. The first thing he saw when he swung his feet onto the cabin sole was the little automatic pistol lying on the rug. It must have fallen out of his hand as he slept.

Lucky me, he thought, imagining the thing firing and taking a chunk out of him while he slept.

For some reason, the image seemed funny, and he spent a few moments sitting on the edge of the bunk, his shoulders moving as silent laughter rippled through him.

McKenna had passed hours watching Caroline's apartment. Anger, fear, and bewilderment had all distilled into a potent drug in his system, leaving him hungover.

He pulled on his clothes from the night before and set the water to boil for coffee. For a few minutes, he sat at the nav station, trying to force some logical thought into his head.

Nothing.

After a while, he climbed up the cabin stairway

The sun was already high. It was still mid-week, so there were only a few people on the dock as far as he could tell. He looked over at the green sloop. It bobbed gently at the dock, hatches closed, no sign of life. He supposed that he should try to get on board. Most likely the boat was chartered, but maybe if he could track down the owner, they might give him a lead to the dark-haired woman and . . . what did Dobyns say the man's name was? Landon? Langdon? That's it. Langdon.

McKenna stood on the stern, breathing the salt air deeply.

And then he realized that the dinghy was back. Bobbing gently behind the *Wanderer*, the painter properly cleated. He hadn't paid any attention to it when he returned from Caroline's apartment, at about three A.M., although he supposed it had been there then.

McKenna's eyes narrowed. The oars weren't in the locks, they were lying the length of the dinghy, held together by something blue. He got down onto the dock and pulled the dinghy close and stepped on. The oars were held together by Amanda's scrunchy. The little cloth-covered elastic hair band she kept on her wrist most of the time.

It held a piece of paper, wrapped around the two oars.

He slid the scrunchy off, turned the white-lined paper over, and read:

My hero! Take a ride with a girl and her brothers. Noon.
                                                        —A.

It took him a minute, but the image was in his head. A girl and her brothers. The girl in the picture. Melanie's picture.

Amanda was saying to meet her back at the gallery at noon.

And she owed him the big picture, at least her version of it.

Remembering, he felt in his pocket and took out the small laminated card: Amanda's license. With an address in Lincoln.

He checked his watch.

About quarter to eleven.

He'd have to fly to make it. First he wanted to stop by a convenience store and buy a street atlas.

McKenna hurried into the cabin, washed hurriedly in the sink, and changed into some clean pants, a cotton shirt, street shoes. He packed a small handheld duffel bag, including the .25 and his little tape recorder. On an impulse, he poured a cup of coffee into the travel mug.

Amazing how you get used to anything, he thought, as he jogged up the dock, careful not to spill his coffee.

He was just swinging into his truck when the black man approached him.

McKenna reached for the gun in the bag and then relaxed.

He'd instinctively reacted as if it were Jerome, back to take care of business. But it was Elliott.

"Hey, got a minute?" Elliott said. He limped forward, clearly in pain. "Don't know if you remember me—"

"Sure I do, Elliott." McKenna reached through the window to offer his hand. "How's Mariel?"

Elliott made a face. "Not good. We're still waiting."

"She's not out of the coma yet?"

Elliott shook his head. His eyes remained on McKenna, watching him carefully.

McKenna glanced at his watch. Five after eleven. "Look, I'm sorry, but I'm running to meet someone . . ."

"This might be nothing, might be important," Elliott said. "I sure would appreciate a few minutes of your time."

"I'm sorry, but—"

"Regarding your friend Stephen Cross."

McKenna was ready. He didn't know who would pose the question, but he figured sooner or later, someone would.

"I'm sorry?" he said. Giving a mildly confused expression, nothing more.

"Stephen Cross," Elliott said. "You gave Mariel that name."

McKenna let his confusion deepen. "*I gave* her that name? What do you mean, I gave her that name?"

Elliott stared at him.

McKenna waited, a perplexed half-smile on his face. "Elliott?"

The detective pulled a photograph from his pocket. It was a poor shot, most likely a copy of a copy. Of Stephen Cross—Langdon—lying in a white hospital gown, a bandage on his head. McKenna barely recognized him in that context, and he doubted anyone else at the marina would be able to place him as the visitor to McKenna's boat. He hoped not, anyhow.

"This him?" McKenna said.

The big man sighed. Gave a short shrug. "Maybe I made a mistake."

"About what? This Stephen Cross have something to do with her getting hurt?"

"We don't know," Elliott said. He told McKenna about the name on the notepad, and the man who had been released from the hospital a week earlier.

McKenna said, "I wish I could help. Mariel's one of my best friends." He looked at his watch. "But I'm really sorry, I've got to rush off . . ."

Elliott backed away. "Yeah." His eyes were still taking McKenna in carefully. "Myself, I've gotten to know Caroline pretty well the past few weeks."

"How is she?"

"Hurting," Elliott said. "Got to say, I don't know who you're running off to see, but whoever it is, you're losing. Letting Caroline go."

"It's not like that."

The black man made an impatient gesture. "It's none of my business. Finding who did this to Mariel, that's my business."

McKenna put the truck in gear. "Well . . ."

"You got nothing to tell me?"

"I'm afraid not." McKenna put his hand out. "Best of luck."

Elliott didn't take his hand. Instead, his eyes searched McKenna's face and apparently found something there he didn't like.

Elliott said, "Looks like I'm going to need it."

McKenna withdrew his hand and drove away.

McKenna kept the truck at a steady eight miles an hour above the limit most of the way to Boston and pulled in front of the gallery on Newbury Street at about ten minutes after noon.

Amanda wasn't there.

"Damn," he muttered. He parked and hurried into the gallery.

A young, balding man looked up from his desk and smiled. "Feel free to look around."

McKenna walked through the exhibit quickly, but she wasn't there.

He walked back out onto the sidewalk, looked up and down, and then heard a horn blow. He looked over at his truck and saw Amanda was sitting in the passenger seat.

Without a word, he walked back and swung in behind the wheel. He started the truck and took a quick look over at her as he pulled into traffic. She was wearing different clothes from the day before and carrying a small leather backpack. Her hair was clean, her eyes clear.

"Tell me something," he said. "How'd you know I was going to be at Melanie's opening? I didn't even know myself until a couple of hours before."

"I didn't," Amanda said. "I was just following you. Had been watching you on and off for a couple of days. Saw you go into Melanie's opening and I knew I had an invitation sitting on my desk at home. Figured what better chance for us to meet?"

"Have you been back to that home lately?"

"Oh, Greg would be glad to see me. But I don't think I'd enjoy the reception, myself. How about you? What happened after Dobyns and Jerome showed up? When I left the message, I didn't know if you'd ever be coming back to find it."

McKenna crossed Massachusetts Avenue and headed west on the turnpike. "Here I am. Looking for what you promised."

"The big picture?" She tucked her leg under herself on the seat, facing him directly. "You just tell me one thing first. Will I ever see . . . you'd know him as Tom Cain. Will I ever see Tom again?"

McKenna looked over at her.

He believed he saw real hope and trepidation in her eyes.

McKenna shook his head.

She turned away.

He couldn't be sure if this was another piece of fakery on her part, but it didn't feel like it.

Finally, she took some tissue from her bag and dabbed at her eyes.

"He was a mean guy," she said finally. Her voice was husky. "Not with me, but to just about anyone else. He'd do whatever it took to get what he wanted. Except with me."

"Not yet, anyhow."

"No. That would've been the easiest thing for him to do, but he didn't." She looked at McKenna. "Did you kill him?"

"No."

"Yeah, you did," she said tiredly. "You must have."

McKenna looked over at her.

"I'm the one he called on the radio first," she said. "I sent Gleason out in his boat to pick him up. They said they were just going to hit you on the head and leave you behind . . . but then neither of them ever came back, and you did. So you must've done it."

McKenna let the silence grow. Finally, he said, "What was his real name?"

"Justus. Justus Woodrell. We'd been together since sophomore year."

McKenna said, "Harvard?"

She gave a short, pained laugh. "That's Justus. But truth was, we were both on scholarship at UCLA. And then I came to Boston for the Fine Arts Institute masters program and he wasn't able to get in. Both of us had the talent, but his career just wasn't going anywhere. Ate him up for a while, and then I think he just figured he'd have it through me. He was going to make us the money; that's when he started couriering jewels. And then I stumbled into this thing."

"Which was?" McKenna said impatiently. He could think back on those little portraits Cain used to draw of him and see the talent. He could also hear Cain planning to leave him behind as a piece of rotten meat.

She paused. "Don't know how I'd paint it. I've thought about it a lot. Keep coming up with things involving hyenas and vultures. Very worn images, but then what we were doing is old and ugly, so I guess that's the way it works. You know about the diamonds, right?"

She said this with seeming indifference, but she was looking at him carefully.

"I know about the diamonds."

"You know where they are?"

He said, "I know about the diamonds. Now keep talking."

"Good for you." She smiled. "How about the art? You know about that?"

He felt blank, so he most likely looked blank.

"See." She touched his shoulder. "You do need me."

As he continued driving west, she told him about it. About the Rosalyn Museum theft, about Dobyns approaching her. About how she first went along with it because she realized that having told her, Dobyns had committed her. "I figured he'd kill me if I refused. I already knew too much for him just to walk away. At least that's what I told myself. But the truth is, I got excited about it, too. You know every artist *says*, 'If I only got the attention, everyone would recognize how good I am.' With me, it actually happened."

"So why weren't you happy with that?"

"Justus wasn't satisfied," she said. "His career was nowhere, and he couldn't even be seen with me. I mean, a few people knew that we were together once, but I had to make it look like a thing of the past once I was with Alcott. I told him Justus was my cousin." She fell silent for a moment and then said, "This feeb, Greg Alcott, becoming a name in the field on my back. And this fat-assed Southie crook whose idea of art is probably dogs playing cards, making millions of dollars."

"So you figured as artists, you were owed that kind of money. . . ."

"Well, think about it," she said. "The value on the collection ranges anywhere from one hundred to three hundred *million dollars*, depending on what you read. *Three hundred million!* Hell, the reward alone is five million. But I couldn't collect that, not without getting myself in trouble. And that's what I mean about Justus . . . he could've turned me in and collected, would've been as easy as could be. But he didn't. The past few years, we thought about it, went round and round on it. . . . Dobyns paid me five hundred thousand, and supposedly I was going to get another five hundred thousand, but what am I going to do if he doesn't pay?

"The way Justus and I saw it, Dobyns might figure he was better off just shooting me rather than paying out. Lot safer for him, once

I'd done everything he wanted. It just ate at Justus, that kind of money. He was tired of taking all the risk, having to hide in the background. He'd been couriering those diamonds for years and said he knew someone in London, this freak Langdon and his sister. Justus said that we could sell the pieces to them, make ourselves about five million. That it would be like cashing in the reward, but we could still be together."

"Didn't it occur to you that Alcott and Dobyns would have something to say about that?"

She made a face. "We figured out how we could get away so that they wouldn't even know . . . And that was the other part of it. The fun part. Here Justus was getting shit recognition as an artist, and yet, between the two of us, we could knock off the masters so well they'd pass for the originals. We swapped out one at a time, over the past two years. Came up with such good forgeries that Greggie sure couldn't tell the difference. Maybe they wouldn't stand up to expert analysis, but we figured for him, God, he could go a lifetime thinking he still owned the world's biggest stolen-art collection."

"Gee, how could anything go wrong with such a flawless plan?"

She smiled at the sarcasm, but answered him anyhow. "Greg Alcott. He let *millions* slide through his fingers. He told me he was planning to sell the paintings. So we figured it was time to hook the Langdons."

Amanda added with no apparent rancor. "Justus was screwing her. Holding his nose, he said. Guess she still looks pretty good, but she's whacked in the head. Plus she must be a good twelve, fifteen years older than him."

McKenna looked over at Amanda. Wondering how she had turned into the person she had become.

"How'd Gleason get into it?"

"Not by invitation, believe me. He followed me one night to Justus's place. Pushed his way in with a gun, saw a couple of the forgeries drying under the lamps. Said he wanted in or else he'd go to Dobyns. He lined up the boat and captain for the deliveries. For Gleason's big help and his silence, he blackmailed me for about everything I had left of the money Dobyns had paid me. Little over three hundred and fifty thousand. And he expected to keep half of the five million we'd bring in from the Langdons. After we'd done two years worth of planning and painting."

"And I take it you and Justus wouldn't put up with that."

"Maybe I would've but Justus wouldn't. Justus said we'd sell the Langdons two of the fake Rembrandts—*Storm on the Ocean* and *Gentleman and a Lady*—along with all the other originals. He said once they had the most valuable piece, *The Gathering*, they wouldn't be so suspicious. That we could pay off Gleason, take our two-and-a-half million and the Rembrandts and take off. That we'd find a new buyer to pay off on those, make us at least another few million. Try to even up at the five million we were owed."

"Owed?"

"That's the way we looked at it by then. All the work we'd done."

McKenna pulled off the exit for Route 128 North.

"Where are you going?" she said, concerned.

"Lincoln," McKenna said. "Woodrell got what he was 'owed' when I dropped his body overboard. Same for Gleason. Now it's time for you to go meet with your clients. Meet with Alcott and Dobyns and beg for their forgiveness."

"Are you crazy? Dobyns will kill me!"

"Probably," McKenna agreed.

"Well, I'm not telling you where Greg lives. What are you going to do, stop by the police station and ask directions?"

McKenna lifted the street atlas onto the seat between them. "Got the address off your license and a street map. Don't think I'll have any trouble finding it."

"You're bluffing," she said.

He turned down Trapelo Road. She kept silent as he drove past the reservoir and wound into the center of Lincoln. She began to fidget. At the library, he hesitated for a moment, consulting the open map before hanging an immediate hard left to head down past the big lawn of the Pierce House.

"Rob," she said. "Please . . . you don't want to do this."

He started noting addresses. He was close.

"Look, I can get a buyer for those diamonds," she said. "What good are the stones to you without that?"

"I don't have the diamonds," he said shortly. "And I don't think you'd understand what I'm trying to do, anyway."

As they came around the next corner, he saw from her face what the address already confirmed. They had arrived.

He swung between the pillars and started up the narrow gravel path.

"No, Rob!" she said, and for the first time, he caught genuine fear in her voice. Apparently she thought he had been bluffing, when, in truth, his plan was decidedly simple: bring together the people responsible for the whole mess and leave them to deal with each other.

Then drive away.

"It's her!" Amanda cried. "You're just doing this for your wife."

McKenna didn't answer.

"It won't be that simple, Rob," the girl said. She clutched his arm. They were just about to go around the next corner. Already he could see the roof of the mansion.

"I won't *let* it be that simple," Amanda said, fiercely. "She has them. That wife of yours, your precious Caroline! She has the diamonds, doesn't she?"

McKenna looked at her. "She doesn't have a clue," he said. "No idea what's going on."

"Bullshit!"

"It's true," he said.

"That won't be the way I'll say it! I'll tell them she's got them. I'll say she's holding them for you!"

McKenna meant to keep on going. Meant to force himself through this, even if it meant hauling Amanda out of the truck kicking and screaming. Even if it meant forcing this Alcott to call Dobyns so he could hand her over to him directly.

"And why should they believe you? I already told Dobyns, I gave them back to Langdon."

That shocked her for a moment, but then she came back fast. "And what'd Langdon do? Came looking for your wife, didn't he? Almost killed that woman instead. You think Dobyns is different?"

In spite of himself, McKenna put his foot on the brake.

She said, "Listen, the truth doesn't matter to these people. If I tell them she's got the diamonds, they're going to check." Amanda made her voice go desperate, as if she were just about to receive a beating, "Please, Jimmy, please! McKenna and his wife were always the backup team! Justus lined them up before he left!"

Amanda said flatly, "They may not even believe me, Rob. But they'll want to be sure. That's the way they think."

McKenna stopped the truck.

He almost hit her.

But he didn't.

She placed her hands on his arm instead. "Listen to me," she said, with quiet intensity. "If you still care about that wife of yours, you've got to look at who can hurt her—Dobyns and Langdon. No threat from me, long as you don't throw me to the wolves. But Dobyns and Langdon, we've got to cancel those two out."

The engine muttered as he looked straight ahead. He wanted to simply take the next corner, haul her out. Be done with them.

She put her arms around him. He pushed her away, but she came back, her touch on his back and arm light, yet insistent.

"Cancel them out and then think real hard about going away," she whispered. "I didn't know you before, but I've got to think you've changed. You killed two men. She's not going to want you back. Let your wife get on with her life. And you and I should think about getting on with ours."

"I don't want you," he said.

She sat back, her hands in her lap. "I don't believe you, but it doesn't matter. You need me. If only to keep her alive."

He turned the truck around.

"You and me," she said as they reached the highway. "It's not as crazy as you think. Maybe I am a selfish little bitch. But you think your wife is going to want you back, the things you've done? You and me, we've crossed lines we shouldn't have crossed. Rob, I'm telling you, there's no going back. I'm saying we find a way to snatch something good out of this whole mess . . . and then we take off. Send your wife some money from time to time, enough to make life easy for her."

"Not interested," he said.

"I didn't get that impression before."

"I know you better now."

She was silent for a few minutes, just looking out the window at the scenery passing by. Then she said, "You'd be surprised. Hell, you must be already, the things you've done. You do something wrong, really wrong, and you think, 'That's it.' And then the next day, you wake up and nothing bad has happened to you. You're still alive, you're still you. Maybe things are even a little better. But there's something else you've got to do to make sure the whole thing doesn't fall apart. And then you find you can do that, too." She looked at him directly. "You know what I'm talking about, don't you?"

She had hit too close for McKenna to deny. Instead, he said nothing.

She continued, her voice low and bitter. "I don't know about you, but I've done some serious damage to myself. My art has just dried up. I can do the forgeries just fine. I can even paint things that the critics like and people buy. But it's 'The Emperor's New Clothes,' and sooner or later people are going to figure it out. I guess all that 'honesty in art' stuff isn't just bullshit. And about all the honesty I've had in the past year or so has been sitting right here and spilling it to you."

"Is this candor supposed to mean something to me?" McKenna snapped.

Amanda paused and then said in a harder voice, "No. All you need to understand is that I don't plan to be looking over my shoulder all my life. And if you want to protect your precious Caroline, you're going to have to help me take care of Dobyns and the Langdons."

"And how do you expect me to do that?"

She hesitated. "Like I said . . . it all sort of snowballs, the things you're willing to do."

He waited and after a moment, she went on, "Gleason had a plan for Greg and Dobyns. It should work for the Langdons, too."

"What plan?"

She paused. "This isn't pretty. But it's a way out for us. And your wife."

"Let me hear it," he said impatiently.

And so she told him.

CHAPTER 42

THEY STOPPED OFF AT A TELECOMMUNICATIONS STORE NEXT TO THE SUB-way tunnel in Kenmore Square so Amanda could buy a cell phone. McKenna gave her the number for his.

She reached out and squeezed his hand quickly. "Let me know how it goes," she said. She tossed her backpack over her shoulder and gave him what he imagined was her most winning smile before hurrying down the stairs into the subway tunnel.

He took a deep breath and got back into the truck.

She had written the address on the back of an envelope, and he had his street directory.

He headed off in the direction of South Boston.

Jerome met him at the door. "Jimmy ain't big on the drop-in."

"I've got to talk to him."

"What you 'got to' do don't mean shit."

Jerome reached out and grasped McKenna's shirt. With seeming ease, he pulled him in and bounced him sideways against the doorjamb, just to loosen him up. McKenna tried to peel the black man's hand away, with absolutely no effect. Jerome pushed him back on his heels across the porch and slammed him against one of the small pillars bracketing the steps. He rested his forearm against McKenna's throat and casually searched his pockets and under his belt. He squeezed McKenna's crotch. "Ain't doin' it for yah-yahs. Where that little popgun?"

"Left it in the truck," McKenna choked out.

"Huh." Jerome spun McKenna around then kicked his heels wide and frisked him all over.

"You check for an ankle holster?" Dobyns said from behind them. McKenna recognized his voice.

"Yuh."

"Take him down in the TV room and have a little fun with him for pointing that peashooter at me. Don't mess the place up, or it'll be your ass. And then bring him up. I gotta talk to him anyway."

Jerome shoved McKenna down into a basement room.

A Hispanic kid was sitting before a computer. He looked over his shoulder and asked, casually, "You need me outa here?"

"Uh-huh."

"Don't mess up my system."

"Naw. I gotta put his head through something, I'll use the TV. Come back in ten, Luis."

The kid faded away.

The place was carpeted, the television and computer over in one corner, a big red-brick fireplace along one wall.

McKenna said, "For Christ's sake, I just wanted to—"

Jerome hit him in the stomach. McKenna doubled over, gasping.

Jerome said, "You in luck. The man say 'little fun' he mean you get to walk and talk after, don't break no bones in the face . . ." He hit McKenna again, two fast hooks just over McKenna's kidneys. "Now you might be peeing red, if I get goin'." McKenna fell to his knees. Jerome cuffed McKenna about the head with open palms that were about as hard as shovel blades.

McKenna saw the fireplace implements. The poker. The sharp edge of the stone fireplace, like the one that killed his Sam.

He told himself to ride with the beating, that it would end soon.

Take it, he told himself.

Then he realized Jerome was humming. Didn't get what the song was, just that the man was truly enjoying himself, and something broke inside McKenna.

He put his head down and drove straight into the black man.

The guy said, "Whoa, whoa," and backpedaled. Half laughing now. Still certain of his control. He got another good blow into McKenna's left side.

And then McKenna reached out with his right leg, hooked his heel behind Jerome's, and shoved with all his strength.

Jerome cursed as he went down. He spun like a cat, trying to catch himself, but he caught his head on the edge of the fireplace, and suddenly blood poured down the side of his head.

"Aw, fuck, man—" He started to get up.

McKenna rolled to the edge of the fireplace and grabbed the poker. His heart was beating wildly; he'd still not regained his breath and felt like he was going to pass out any second. He raised the poker over his head and brought it whistling down.

He almost crushed the man's head. Came that close.

But he saw the instant of fear in the man's eyes, the momentary panic as he covered his head.

McKenna pulled back and struck Jerome in the knee.

It wasn't a crushing blow, but the effect on Jerome was instantaneous. Even as he cried out in pain, he was moving, rolling to his feet. He lunged at McKenna and then stumbled. McKenna backed away, gasped his first breath in, choked, then fought to get another. He felt the blood swell in his face.

Jerome clenched his teeth, his hands on his knee. He said, "You dumb shit!"

The basement door opened and Dobyns stood there, a revolver in hand. "Oh, for Christ's sake," he said, waving McKenna toward the stairs. "Drop that thing and get up here." He looked down at Jerome. "What'd Buddy's spirit get smushed outa him and get into you?"

McKenna sat on the edge of the fireplace and fought to get his breath. He kept his eye on Jerome and didn't let go of the poker.

Jerome was holding his knee tightly, breathing in short gasps. "Son-of-bitch, son-of-*bitch*."

"C'mon," Dobyns said, impatiently. "You girls stop staring at each other. Jerome, go put a bandage on your knee, some ice, whatever you've gotta do. Then get the Caddy warmed up. I'm got something to show our slugger."

"Cops just left an hour ago," Dobyns said as the three of them eased through Southie. Jerome was at the wheel, and his face was beaded with sweat. The bandage on his head was beginning to soak through with blood, and McKenna could see him wince when he had to move his leg for the gas or brake pedals.

He was clearly in a lot of pain.

Dobyns seemed to be entirely unaware.

From time to time, McKenna would see Jerome looking back at him in the rearview mirror.

McKenna's ribs hurt, he felt faintly nauseous from the blows to his stomach, and more than anything, he felt scared. Now that the anger had left him, he could only hope Jerome wasn't offered a second chance.

Dobyns said, "Cops left not a half hour before you showed up. We woulda looked like assholes, a guy from Newburyport standing on my porch, right after we told them we got no idea what Buddy was doing up there."

"I'm not looking to be a repeat visitor," McKenna said. "I'm trying to break free of you people."

"You got some thoughts on how to do that?"

"Yeah, I've got some thoughts. Show me what you've got to show me first."

Dobyns snorted. "You're learning."

They wound through waterfront warehouses, back behind the World Trade Center, and eventually worked their way to a small marina with a grand view of Boston Harbor.

"Stay there and rest that leg," Dobyns said to Jerome.

He gestured to McKenna to follow him, and the two of them walked down to the dock. For such a prime piece of real estate, the marina had a dilapidated feel to it, as if time and construction had grown up around it. Most of the boats on the creaky dock were working boats, with a few older sportfishing boats mixed in. No more than three or four sailboats in the entire place.

"Man, you've got a talent," Dobyns chuckled. "Of all the people to hit with a poker, Jerome ain't the guy. I'll keep him off you for now, but you screw me up in any way, I'll cut him loose. And you won't get so lucky the next time."

"I'll keep that in mind."

Dobyns cocked an eyebrow at him. "You are a lucky guy, though. Amateur like you, still alive. Frigging miracle is what it is, the people you been playing with."

McKenna agreed with him there, but he didn't bother to say it.

Dobyns continued, "I been thinking about you and what you want, and what you're in a position to do. You're sort of in the middle of all this, and I wouldn't be surprised, you start getting some propositions thrown your way." Dobyns looked at McKenna quickly. "From the lovely Amanda? Heard from her yet?"

Again, McKenna didn't answer, and after a moment, Dobyns shrugged. "Okay, then. Langdon was waiting for your wife outside that hospital, he must figure you've got something he wants. You wouldn't be lying to me about those diamonds, now would you?"

The question alarmed McKenna, and he didn't bother to hide it. He stopped and said, "Look, I gave them back. I'm telling you."

Dobyns stared back at him frankly. After a moment, he took McKenna's elbow and continued walking him toward the end of the dock. "Got to ask, but I tend to believe you. Wouldn't have volunteered a word about them before if they were stashed in your sock drawer, I figure." He gestured with his chin to the catamaran at the end of the dock. "You like her?"

McKenna looked closely. She appeared to be a custom job. Powerful rig, hulls about forty feet long. Low for a catamaran. Modern, cold, fast. *Fleetwing*, her name was. She was as different from the *Wanderer* as possible.

"I took her in trade. Guy defaulted on his gambling debts, squared it with this. He stays at home and plays with boats in the tub now, I guess. But I own her, got the papers. She can be yours."

"I've got a boat."

"I had a deal with Amanda," Dobyns continued as if McKenna hadn't spoken. "She reneged on it."

"And what was the deal?"

"You don't need to know that," Dobyns said. "Lot better for you if you don't. All you need to know is I'll take the money I was gonna pay her and send it your way. I'll buy your boat, and sell you this for a song. Say two hundred cash for yours. That's gotta be a good seventy-five grand more than it's worth. And I'll *give* you this cat and write it up as a hundred K sale. Keep your tax low on it. You and your wife either sail away with a clean two hundred K, or as much as four hundred if you just wanna resell the cat. You could really get two hundred K for her easy. Just as long as you do it out of state. I want you two to pretty much disappear after this. Fair enough?"

McKenna paused, looking at the pudgy man with the friendly face and hard eyes. Thinking how dead on he had captured what McKenna wanted.

"And what do I have to do for this?"

"Find a way to put them together for me," Dobyns said. "Amanda and the Langdons. This shit's crazy that's been going on. There's enough money for all of us in this if we work together. But there's no way I'm gonna just let the Langdons fly back to London without me getting a cut, and they gotta know that. Even if they make it back, I'll get a contract out on them, and sooner or later, I'll get them."

"What about Amanda? What would you do to her?"

"You don't have to worry about that," Dobyns said mildly. "Tell me something. If you gave Langdon the diamonds, what was he doing waiting for your wife at the hospital? What do you think he wants, exactly?"

McKenna had been thinking about that a lot. Certainly the man was after the stolen Rembrandts. But as far as Dobyns was concerned McKenna supposedly didn't know about such things. So he told a different version of the truth. One that was more accurate than he could know: "I think he wants to know for sure what happened to Tom Cain."

"You didn't 'fess up to him on the killing like you did to me, huh?" Dobyns grinned. "I'm flattered."

"He mentioned his 'associate.' I guess that'd be the woman in the car? The one who was watching me from the green sloop?"

"Uh-huh. That'd be Ronnie Langdon."

"His wife?"

Dobyns grinned. "You don't know the half of it. That I'll tell you, just so you know what you're dealing with there."

Dobyns told him and then said, "You're safer with me, because with me, it's all business. With them, everything's personal. Far as they're concerned, you had Tom Cain last. And they're not gonna sit still until they found out what you did with him. That, and lead them to his girlfriend, the lovely Amanda."

Dobyns gestured with his chin to the boat. "So go ahead and say yes. You lead them all to me and then I'll let you and your wife sail away. Best offer you're ever gonna get."

"And if I say no?"

Dobyns lifted his shoulder. "I give Jerome your wife as an early Christmas present."

McKenna stepped into Dobyns. "I'm telling you, my wife doesn't know a damn thing about any of this."

The older man didn't back down an inch. "So what?" he said. "You do."

CHAPTER 43

McKenna sat down beside Mariel's bed. Her eyes were still closed, and the doctor said there had been no real sign of her coming out of the coma. "But we're still hopeful."

McKenna made himself look at her closely. Look at the sunken hollows under her cheekbones, the dryness of her lips, the way she seemed to just sink into the bed as if she were part of it now. This lovely, vital woman. His friend. Living encased in her own flesh, because of him.

His choices.

McKenna's anger was cold and gray.

These people. They would do it to Caroline, as well. Any of them. They would do it to him.

And so, McKenna knew what he had to do.

Exactly how was to be determined. Exactly the cost to himself, he could only imagine.

But he knew what he had to do.

He stood up and kissed Mariel on the forehead, then left.

"You want to do what?" Swan said.

McKenna said. "Who can you recommend?"

"Kenny Barber did a real nice job on the Kylers' boat," Swan said. He still looked perplexed. "But the *Wanderer* is a great name."

"The stern and the sides," McKenna said. "Gold lettering. Big. Highly visible. You mind giving me that slip right there for a while?"

McKenna had checked it out from all angles. From the bridge, from land, from the restaurant deck. The boat would be easy to see in the bright sunlight from all those vantage points.

Swan looked over his shoulder. "Yeah, sure. The Potters are out for the week. Make it easy for Kenny to do each side. I'll give him a call for you."

"Thanks. Tell him there's an extra hundred in it for him if he can get started today."

"What's the new name going to be?"

McKenna told him.

Swan brightened. "Not a bad name either." He repeated it to himself: "*Storm on the Ocean*. What's that from? A movie?"

McKenna shook his head. "A painting. Rembrandt."

"Oh, yeah." Swan said, grinning. Final evidence of McKenna's membership in the world of poofy boat owners. "How could I forget?"

CHAPTER 44

"NOTHING." RONNIE SLAMMED THE PHONE DOWN. "WHERE IS THAT damn woman?"

They had tried repeatedly to reach their secretary, Madeline, for the past two days.

"Hmmn," Ian said. Whereas Ronnie was furious, he felt a sense of foreboding. They were not the type of employers that anyone screwed around with. Madeline, plain, mid-forties, and no life at all—she'd never even been late.

"Give me the phone," he said.

"Who're you calling?"

He gestured for the phone impatiently and she handed it to him.

They were in a new hotel room, off Route 128 near Gloucester, and Ronnie had finished her exercises. No repeat of their earlier warmth; she was too angry and tended to blame him for everything. Particularly now that she had firmly decided the young woman on the dock with McKenna was the girl—was almost certainly Cain's woman.

"What's McKenna doing with a girl like her?" Ronnie had said last night as they were settling into bed. She began listing McKenna's flaws: he wasn't rich. He was only passingly handsome. What power could he possess? A former-real estate agent, with an old boat, for God's sake. A girl like that had to be with him for a reason.

"She's it!" Ronnie had hissed. "I *knew* it, and you insisted we pick up the bloody wife. That little bitch is the one!"

Langdon dialed the phone.

Their six days grace from Amir Abaas were two days past at this point. And that's how long it'd been since they'd talked to their secretary.

He got through to the pub across the street, the Stars.

The owner, Benson, knew him. Knew him well enough not to like him, but also well enough to be afraid of him.

"Sorry, Mister Langdon," he said. "Bobbies around. Told them nothing, of course, but it's a mess. Poor Maddy."

"Tell me what happened," Langdon said, evenly.

Ronnie stopped her pacing about. "Who're you talking to?"

There was silence.

"What happened?" Langdon repeated.

"You mean you don't know?"

"Don't make me ask again, Benson."

"I . . . I just didn't know that you hadn't heard. Well, I'm sorry, sir. But Maddy was killed. Right outside your place. Throat cut. Left there on the street. Hands tied with a telephone cord, maybe from her own office."

"They don't know?"

"Huh. How would they? The office, your whole bloody house is gone. Blown up."

"I see," Langdon said, looking at his sister. Watching her impatience grow.

"What?" she said. "Tell me!"

Her pride and joy, that townhouse. Her acquired art, a bittersweet collection though it was. The best of her own pieces. Some of which approached something special, she was sure of it.

"Yes, sir," Benson said. "They say there's no chance it was an accident. They say somebody splashed the place full of petrol and set her. Killed poor Maddy just before. Like I say, the bobbies been looking for you. Should I say I notified you if they come round again?"

"Not if you know what's good for you," Langdon said without heat. "That absolutely clear?"

"Certainly, sir."

Langdon hung up and told his sister what had happened.

She sat down heavily on the bed. Her face went sheet white.

"The townhouse? Everything?"

"Gone," he said airily. "Makes the need to get the Rembrandts more than a choice, but an important imperative, wouldn't you say?"

"Dobyns did this?"

"I wouldn't think so. Possible though, what we did to his man. More likely Abaas. We missed his deadline and—"

"Shut up!"

She screamed it.

Then her mouth began to work, and the tears streaked down her face. As physically powerful as Langdon was himself, he knew to be on guard when she lost it. When she threw herself at him, kicking and scratching. He deflected her and spun her around, pushing her down on the bed. He held on while she raged, making sure she didn't hurt herself or him.

But, as had happened so many times before, her fury, her passion aroused him. And before she would let him do what he needed, before he could appease himself, he needed to make her a promise: "Sssshh. Ssssh, sweets," he whispered harshly in her ear. "I've been keeping track. Keeping record. We'll make them pay. They'll all pay, until the blood pours out of their eyes, they'll all pay."

She shoved back at him.

Bucking against him hard. Almost making him lose it, but then he was back against her harder still. He made his promise again and again, as he ripped at her clothes, and whispered in her ear that he knew who was responsible, and he would make them account for themselves, he surely would.

Hours later, Langdon said, "That's not it."

Ronnie was at the head of the bridge, overlooking McKenna's marina. She was looking through the binoculars.

"It damn well is," she said. "I stared at that boat long enough."

"But the name wasn't on the side—"

She handed him the binoculars, an odd little smile on her face. "Mister McKenna wants to play."

He looked through the glass and broke into a smile himself. The low afternoon sun made the gold lettering on the sides gleam.

"So he does," Langdon murmured. He took the binoculars away from his eyes and put his arm around his stepsister. "It seems it's time to discuss the rules of the game."

CHAPTER 45

McKENNA SAW THEM WALKING DOWN THE DOCK, ARM IN ARM.

The woman waved to him and gave him a dazzling smile. The man looked as if he were bursting with good humor. Friends over for dinner.

They came out onto the finger pier.

"Knock, knock," Langdon said. He offered a bottle of wine.

McKenna just stared at him.

Langdon gave the smallest shrug. He placed the bottle on the cushion inside the cockpit.

"May we?" He gestured to the boat.

McKenna nodded, and the two of them climbed in.

"Lovely boat," the woman said.

"So's yours." McKenna nodded to the green sloop.

"I'm flattered you noticed me."

"And just who are you?" He looked to each of them. "Who are you to do what you've done to Mariel?"

"Terrible people," Langdon said. "Take it at that. We're two rather terrible people you want out of your life." He gestured to the side of the boat, to the new name. "It would seem you weren't exactly truthful yourself."

"I've learned a few things, that's all. I told you what I knew at the time."

"Not everything." Langdon leaned forward, his voice turning confidential. McKenna thought of Dobyns in much the same pose in the cockpit a few days back. These men making their threats and Faustian offers. "My sister and I took a little time before we came down. We know a bit about surveillance, and while we can't be certain, we feel fairly confident we're not being observed just now. As for a wire, you certainly could be wearing something or have something stashed away."

"I could."

Langdon nodded. "But I don't believe you have. You know why, Mister McKenna?"

McKenna didn't answer and Langdon continued. "Because I believe you're a guilty man."

"Is that right?"

"Oh, nothing by our standards." Langdon looked back at his sister, and she laughed as if this truly amused her.

"I'm sure not," she said.

"But here's the thing. If you know something about the . . . art collection . . . and from the name of your boat, it's obvious you do—"

"And information about *him* and the little bitch." The woman interjected. "Tom Cain, you'd know him as."

Langdon looked back at her with what McKenna read as gentle reproof. He then turned back to McKenna and said, "Yes. That information, too."

"Why should I help you?" McKenna said.

Langdon put his hand on his sister's knee before she spoke. He said, "My father used to be in the insurance business, believe it or not. And there's an old joke about a sales contest. 'The winner gets to keep his job.' "

"My job being living?"

"That's right. Yours and your wife's."

"I knew I made a mistake by not dropping your body into the river."

"You certainly did." Langdon smiled. "I'm thankful, but it was a mistake on your part."

"Dobyns is offering me money. What're you offering?"

Langdon made a pushing-away gesture. "How old are you, Mister McKenna? Over forty? You should know better. Whatever Dobyns has offered you, he's also made a threat, correct?"

McKenna gave him that.

"All right," Langdon said. "The threat is all that matters. The best you can hope to make out of this is to keep your skin intact, and sail away with a little travel money. Say fifty thousand from me. If you help us negotiate a settlement."

"That's what you want? A settlement?"

Langdon nodded. "My sister and I are reasonable in our way. We have a buyer for the collection; Dobyns has the final pieces we need. It's time to deal."

"And why should I trust you? All I've seen from you so far is threats."

"Understood," Langdon said crisply. "But through our own sense of self-preservation, we've protected you. You know who Jimmy Dobyns is. You know me only as Mister Cross, which, as I expect you realize, isn't my name. We're not from around here."

"Could've guessed," McKenna said. Thinking that it was pure luck that he hadn't used Langdon's name. Not that he believed a word the man said, anyhow.

Langdon went on. "My point is, you're not the risk to us that you are to Dobyns. And you've operated with me once on good faith already, giving me the jewels back. So I believe you'll operate on good faith again."

Langdon put out his hand to shake. "What I will offer is that if you cooperate with us we'll leave you and your wife alone. If you're the man I think you are, I think you'll take it."

"Provided you tell us right now," the woman interjected. "Tell us right now what happened with Tom Cain. Is he still alive? And what about the girl? How do we get to her?"

Langdon's face showed the slightest impatience. Frustrated with his sister's intrusion just as he was closing the deal.

"What else?" McKenna asked.

"Be our go-between with Mister Dobyns. Lead us to him. As you know, we were rather...abrasive...the last time we were together."

"That'd be when you were waiting outside the hospital to kidnap my wife?"

Langdon gestured to the side of the boat, the new name. "Before we knew how truly cooperative you could be."

He put his hand out.

McKenna looked at the proffered hand. "There's a lot tied into this."

"Including your old life back," Langdon said.

McKenna shook his hand.

He told them about killing Tom Cain.

Unlike when he had told Dobyns, here he had time. And he had a rapt audience. The woman in particular sat forward on the edge of the cushion and listened carefully.

"He died at sea?" she said. "Never even made it to land?"

McKenna nodded.

Her shoulders shook, and she put her hands to her face. Her brother put his arm around her.

"See?" he said.

Tears streaked down her face, suddenly, and though she was crying, she was also laughing. "God," she said, her voice savagely bright. "Bloody God in hell. The son of a bitch never even made it to land! What I've been putting myself through."

"That's right," Langdon said. His own face glowed with ruddy good humor. He raised up the bottle of wine. "May we? Corkscrew and glasses?"

He didn't wait for an answer, just pulled his sister closer and kissed her right temple, hugging her tight. "Silly bastard got his before he could tell any tales. All thanks to our friend, Mister McKenna."

He gestured again to the bottle of wine, and McKenna waved down to the galley. "Top drawer."

Langdon went down, quickly rummaged around, and came back with a corkscrew and three plastic cups.

McKenna thought how he and Cain had sat drinking bourbon as the Coast Guard motored off.

Langdon poured wine for them all and, once again, McKenna found himself drinking with new friends.

CHAPTER 46

CAROLINE AWOKE TO THE SOUND OF THE DOORBELL.

She lay awake for a moment, not sure what had woken her. Thinking maybe it was morning already. But she looked at the clock. A little past two A.M.

The doorbell rang again.

She felt a quick, bright touch of fear and didn't know why.

Elliott wasn't staying with her any longer. Maybe that was it. She was alone again.

She got out of bed and slipped on a bathrobe. She went to the window and looked down.

It was Rob.

He stepped back from the doorway and waved up at her. He did it in a silly, exaggerated way, and she realized he was drunk. Or something.

She hurried down the two flights of stairs. Sophia was waiting near the front door. "Who is it at this hour?"

"My husband. I'm sorry."

"Do I need to call the police?"

"No, there won't be a problem. He's not like that."

Sophia went back to her bedroom, her face carefully neutral.

Caroline opened the door.

Rob was leaning against the porch rail. "Hey. I know it's late."

"You've been drinking," Caroline said. She had only seen him actually drunk a handful of times in all their years together.

"I'm gone," he said. "Gone out of my head. Started drinking with some new friends this afternoon and kept it right up after they left."

"New friends?"

"You'd hate them," he said. "Terrible people."

"Friends of your new girl?"

He looked at her for a moment and then seemed to get it. He gave a short laugh. "Sorry. All you've got to be angry and disappointed with me about, my night with Amanda is just the tip. Tip of a big, ugly iceberg." He leaned on the doorjamb, seeming to think over his own words. "That's the one bothers me the worst, though. Don't seem to know myself anymore."

Amanda. Hearing the girl's name was a new splinter putting a nasty little jab into Caroline's heart.

Caroline began to shut the door. "Look, it's late. Call me when you're not drunk."

He put his hand in front of the door. "Please," he said. "I'm not sure I can do that. I'm not sure of the time I've got."

"What does that mean?"

He stepped back from the doorway. Stumbled, and then recovered himself. "Just want to see your new place. Just want to see you. I know you're angry, know you've got the right. But I just want to talk with you. Even if I can't say anything real. I say anything crazy, you put it to me being drunk, okay?"

"How did you get here?"

"Truck," he said. "Got an ugly truck. Traded in the *Wanderer* for an ugly truck."

She reached out and took him by the arm. "You can't drive in this condition. Come on."

"I'll make some coffee," she said, when they got upstairs.

"Sure." He looked around the apartment, taking it all in slowly. "So this is you by yourself," he said. "What it looks like. It's nice."

"Mostly our stuff out of storage, Rob," she said.

He stood in front of the small hutch, looking at a picture of the three of them: her, him, Sam. Mariel had taken the picture about two years back, a Fourth of July picnic out on the grass in front of their house. Just a quick snapshot, Rob holding his two women.

"Nice of you to keep me in here," he said.

"Believe me, I considered cutting you out the past few weeks."

"Sure." He stared at the photo, and just as she was about to speak, a tear rolled down his cheek. He seemed unaware.

"What's happened, Rob?" she asked quietly.

"Too much to say." He stared at the photo a moment longer, and then said, "She's leaving me."

Anger flashed through Caroline, thinking he was talking about the girl, Amanda. But it faded away just as quickly when she realized who he meant.

She said, "Sam?"

He nodded. "Can't always bring her face up. Right now I can. Right now, she's with me. Maybe because I'm with you. But sometimes she isn't. The way I felt when she was gone, though, that's always with me. How come it's like that? How come that god-awful feeling survives, when she doesn't?"

"I don't know."

He said, "I blamed you."

She nodded.

"R. J. was trouble. I stood there in the headlights, watching him come, and I blamed you for telling me not to worry, to let her make her mistakes."

"I know you did. Do you still?"

He shook his head. "Blame myself. It was me standing in those headlights. Maybe you just couldn't see it. But I knew something bad was coming. And I let it."

"You couldn't have known. You just didn't like him . . . and it was her time. That's all it was, Rob. The sad, hateful truth."

He shook his head. "No. Those headlights are coming again. And I'm not going to just stand there this time."

"What does that mean?"

"Terrible people," he said. "They're all terrible people. And I've learned the way they think."

"Who?"

"All of them," he said. "I've already blown it once, I'm not going to do it again. You're my wife, even if you live here, and I live on that damn boat."

"I know, Rob."

"Tell you that I traded the boat for an ugly truck?"

"You did."

He nodded to himself. "I'm drunk," he said.

She smiled as she handed him a mug. "Come on, the coffee's ready."

He took a sip, looked down into the mug and said, "Another thing."

"What's that."

"Your coffee sucks. Always has."

She pealed with laughter. "I know, honey. I never measure it right." She took his arm, and they went to the kitchen. She pulled out a chair for him, and together they sat at the table. Although the darkened room was different, Caroline felt as if they were slipping into any one of the hundreds of late night conversations around the kitchen table they'd had in their nineteen years together.

She took his hands. "Rob," she said, softly. "Tell me what's been happening. Did you have something to do with the people who hurt Mariel?"

"Don't ask me."

"I am."

"Don't. Don't make me lie to you anymore. All I can tell you is that I'll be taking care of it."

"How?"

He shook his head.

"Rob?"

His voice was thick when he answered. "All I can tell you is that I love you. That I miss you. That I even miss what you and I had after Sam died. I wish I had that back."

"I do too," she said. "We can make it better."

"No."

"What?"

"It's too late," he said. "What I've done, and what I still have to do."

"Why? If you want it and I want it—"

He took her hands in his and lifted them to his face. He kissed each of her palms, and pressed his face against her hands.

"What have you done?" she whispered.

He shook his head. "Can't."

"Rob, talk to me."

He withdrew his face from her hands, and put his arms around her, and pulled her close. He whispered hoarsely, "No matter what you hear, you've got to know that I love you." He kissed her, first on the cheek, and then on her lips when she turned her mouth to meet his. She could feel his urgency, his almost desperate hunger and, rather than backing away, or ascribing his passion to alcohol, she let it spark the same in her.

They left the kitchen table and made their way to the bedroom, something they had also done many times before.

CHAPTER 47

THE DIGITAL CLOCK READ 5:45.

McKenna lay still. Strange feelings; familiar, yet different.

The warmth of Caroline beside him. Her scent.

But the room wasn't familiar.

His head hurt. Mouth tasted awful. He cleared his throat and settled back against her. Not ready to take in reality. Letting himself believe they were in a hotel room someplace or on vacation, perhaps. That Sam was in the other room.

But reality began to tick through his hangover.

He began to remember it all.

The loss of his daughter was hot, and fresh, and made him groan aloud. From there, he quickly came up to speed and remembered what the day ahead might bring.

He padded quietly into the bathroom and closed the door so as not to wake Caroline. He washed his face with cold water, and then cupped his hands and drank until his belly was full. Finally, he got his clothes from the bedroom and put them back on.

McKenna sat on the edge of the bed and watched his wife sleep.

The light of false dawn was revealing her to him. The faint wrinkles about her eyes, the innocent quality of her fist up near her face, clutching the silky edge of the blanket.

He bent down to kiss her, touching her cheek lightly. Not wanting to talk, not wanting to lie.

She shifted, but didn't awake.

"Good-bye, sweetheart," he whispered.

As he was on his way out the door, she rolled over onto her side, and he sensed she was close to waking. He hoped she would just fall back into her slumber.

He kept going.

Back at the marina, he started making phone calls around ten. He got through to Amanda, Dobyns, and the Langdons. Made sure to call the latter by the name Cross.

Dobyns came on the line in a cold fury. "What is this shit with the name of your boat?"

"You expect me to help pull it together; I found out about the paintings," McKenna said quietly. "Besides which, if you had your people watching, why didn't they just follow the Langdons and take care of it directly?"

Dobyns was silent. When he spoke, his voice was calmer. "Guess it makes sense. The guy I had on them is a pretty good snoop, but he wasn't up to taking on those two. Or following them home for that matter. They lost him."

"Good help . . ."

"Frigging bitch to find," Dobyns snapped. "All right, what've you got for me?"

McKenna outlined to Dobyns the truce that Langdon had suggested the previous afternoon on board McKenna's boat. That he and his sister already had a buyer who was willing to pay fifteen million for the total collection. That since most of the pieces were already with this gentleman, it made sense to simply work together, split the income fifty-fifty. Dobyns and Langdon each get seven-point-five million, five of which Langdon acknowledged he had already been paid in the diamonds.

McKenna said, "The way Langdon sees it, you've already made a lot from whoever you sold the pieces to the first time around. This is a second sale on the same work, with Langdon taking the risk."

"That's how he sees it, does he?" Dobyns said.

"What about the guy who bought them from you in the first place?" McKenna asked. "What does he have to say about all this?"

Dobyns laughed. "Don't worry about that. What's more of a problem is Langdon expects me to give him the Rembrandts on consignment. Tell him screw that, he can buy them from me *today* for the five million in diamonds, and then I expect another two-point-five mill after he makes his delivery. He can collect his own seven point five directly from whoever he's selling to. He don't like that, I'll put a contract out on him and sis."

McKenna made another call. Langdon and his sister talked about it in the background, and he came back and said, "Acceptable. As long is the girl is there. We want her."

"So does Dobyns," McKenna said. "But he doesn't have her. He says he wants her just as bad for stealing from him."

Again the long conversation with his sister off the phone. McKenna could hear the heat from Ronnie. But eventually, Langdon got back on the line. "One thing at a time, I suppose. We'll settle with Dobyns on the Rembrandts. We're ready to make the pickup today."

McKenna paused. "I'll talk to Dobyns and get back to you about when and where."

"Do that," Langdon said.

McKenna called Dobyns, who grunted in approval. "Makes sense. You've got a talent for this. Must be all those houses you sold."

"Must be," McKenna said. "And one of the things I'm good at is getting my commission."

"Ah, here we go."

"No. Just what you promised. The cash we talked about and the title to the catamaran. And I'm going to want to leave right after. Sail down the coast, anyway. Can you have the yard fuel up the boat, make sure there's water in the tanks? I'll bring the title of the *Wanderer*, and we'll make the exchange."

"Now I'm a dockboy. Yeah, I can get that all together, but it's gonna take a day. So tell the Langdons we do this tomorrow."

They made plans to meet at the marina.

"How about Langdon?" McKenna said. "I've got to tell him when and where."

"Got that figured out already."

Dobyns told McKenna in specific detail how to get to Alcott's house.

"Seven o'clock tomorrow night," Dobyns said.

McKenna rubbed his forehead. Sickened, and yet elated with how this was falling into place. But he kept all that away from his voice when he said, "They're looking for Amanda, too."

"I bet they are. I kinda like the idea letting them go to work on her, the trouble she's caused me. You get her there, and I'll put a bonus for you in it. Say twenty-five K. Sound like a deal?"

"I'll see what I can do."

Dobyns said casually. "Your wife thank you yet?"

"What?" McKenna became instantly alert.

"Thought maybe you wouldn't have the chance. What with all the calls you had to make this morning."

"What're you talking about?"

"Just a friendly reminder," Dobyns said. "Want you to keep clear what's at stake." He hung up.

McKenna's hand shook as he tapped in the number for Caroline's store. She answered on the third ring. "Hey, you," she said, her voice clearly happy. "Why'd you take off? The coffee's not *that* bad."

"Caroline, has anything happened?" His voice was tense.

"Oh, here's where you act like the whole night was just a drunken blur?" Her voice was light, but he could tell his question worried her.

"Anything? Anyone come by?" he said.

"Well, your flowers, thank you very much. Other than that—"

"What flowers?" he snapped.

"Rob?"

"What flowers?" he said, trying to calm his voice down. "Who brought you flowers?"

"Rob . . ." she gave a small laugh. "*Your* flowers. The roses you had delivered—"

"Who delivered them? Did you see him?"

"Well, sure. I talked to him."

"Who?"

"The delivery guy."

"What'd he look like?"

She was silent for a moment. "Rob, what's going on?"

"Tell me what he looked like!"

"All right, calm down. A big black guy. Scary looking, in some ways, but friendly enough. He had a cane and an acc bandage around his knee. Said they got an early morning call to deliver these to the house."

"He say anything else?"

"Just something about having a hard time finding the place."

"What'd he say exactly?"

"Rob, I—"

"Exactly!" he snapped. Then he took a deep breath. "Please."

"He said he had a hard time finding my house, but now that he knew where it was it would be easy to come back any time. That's all."

McKenna closed his eyes tight. Trying to think. "All right," he said. "Your friend, Elliott. Find him. Get him to stay with you. A couple of days. The entire time."

"What?"

"Do it!" he said.

"Why?"

"Just do it," he said, softly. "But I'll take care of everything."

She hesitated and then said, "Rob, we need the police, don't we?"

"No."

"Elliott knows them. He can help. Tell me what's going on."

"He can help all right. Have him stay with you. Good-bye, sweetheart."

* * *

He hung up and immediately called Dobyns back.

The older man picked up the phone.

"You son of a bitch." McKenna said.

Dobyns said. "Jerome tells me that wife of yours is a peach."

"Keep away from her."

"That's up to you. You play your part clean and simple or I tell Jerome to put on his baseball cap and come out swinging. So keep being a good boy. That's the only message, them flowers. You got it?"

"I've got it," McKenna said tightly.

"Good." Dobyns hung up.

McKenna sat thinking. So Dobyns was having him watched. And once Caroline told Elliott what he had said, McKenna could pretty much assume he and the police would be down to ask more questions. Demand if he knew something about Mariel's attackers.

And the whole thing would fall apart.

McKenna made a decision and began to move about the boat quickly, setting up everything necessary before going on deck. He opened the water-intake valve, switched the electrical system over to the batteries.

Then he stepped on deck, and with as little fanfare as possible, started the engine and walked about the boat dropping the dock lines and the shore-power line. He got behind the wheel and threw the engine into reverse.

He was just clearing the piling when he saw Jerome coming down the ramp. Jerome hustled along the dock, his cane and hurt leg slowing him down. Binoculars around his neck.

McKenna raised his hand and waved.

"Hold up!" Jerome yelled.

"Tomorrow," McKenna said. "Everything's still on. You show up at my wife's, the cops will be waiting. You do nothing, everything works out. Tell your boss."

Jerome stood on the end of the dock, and for a moment, he reached inside his jacket.

McKenna couldn't believe the man would just open fire in the middle of the day, and, indeed, he didn't. Instead, he just backed away and headed back down the dock.

McKenna got on the microphone and called the marina office. Swan answered. "You taking off?" he said.

"Just for a sail," McKenna said. "Been on land too long. I'll be back tomorrow, anyone comes asking."

"Uh-huh."

"Another thing—there's a big black guy coming your way. Might want to rent a boat. The answer's no, all right?"

"You got a police problem?" Swan asked.

"No. Just a privacy problem. Tell him no rentals, all right?"

"You got it," Swan sighed, and then he signed off.

McKenna made one more call.

Amanda picked up. "Talk to me," she said.

"It's all in place," he said. He told her about the negotiations.

"Oh, baby," she breathed. "You're doing great."

He paused, and she filled the silence.

"Rob, it'll take time, but it'll work between us." She laughed, a bitter sound. "It's got to. Who else are we good for?"

"Uh-huh." The sad part was she made some sense. Who indeed?

"You'll be able to handle it," Amanda said. "You can learn to handle anything."

"I've grasped that."

"So you think you'll be able to get them there?"

McKenna said that Dobyns already made the arrangements himself.

"Doesn't mean good news for Greg," she said quietly. "He doesn't deserve that. But even if I called him and told him to run, he wouldn't believe me. There's nothing I can do."

Bet you say that about all the guys, McKenna thought.

*　*　*

Once out of the river, McKenna raised the main and jib and tacked off into a freshening breeze.

The boat handled flawlessly. With all the detail work he had done on her in the past few weeks, she was never more beautiful to him. He set Mortimer, then went below to change into shorts and a tee shirt. The *Wanderer*, or correction, *Storm on the Ocean*, bounded along.

God, she sailed sweetly.

He wondered who would sail her next.

CHAPTER 48

McKenna docked the boat around four in the afternoon the next day, put the little automatic into his kit, and walked up the ramp toward the shower.

Swan was sitting on the rail at the top of the ramp. He was freshly shaved, clear-eyed. Looking better than McKenna, with the weight of his long night on watch and the blinding sunlight during the day.

Swan said. "Nice sail?"

"Beautiful."

"You look like hell. Reminds me of me, back when I rode the horse."

"Yeah?" McKenna cocked his head at Swan. The bright sunlight hurt his eyes. "I look like a drug addict, do I?"

Swan spoke quietly. "You look like a guy in the middle of something. Maybe you got money problems, this thing with Caroline. You try to make some score?"

"What makes you think that?"

"The kind of people who've been coming around. That guy yesterday, I thought he'd kill me when I said I didn't have a boat for him. I know the kind of guy he is, and it scared the freaking life out of me to say no."

"Sorry to put you on the spot."

Swan reached into his front pocket, took out a business card and handed it to McKenna. It was Elliot's.

"He and Caroline came by last night, and then again this morning." Swan said. "She's looking as worried as hell, and this guy's being good to her, but he's got murder in his eye when he talks about you. I get the feeling she's holding him back. He said if you don't talk to him, you'd have to talk to the cops."

"Ah."

Swan stared at him hard. "You helped me get me this job. Helped change my life around. All the shit I give you, I always think of you as a friend."

"I know that."

"If you got yourself in some spot you need help, you tell me. Someone coming at you. But if you got yourself into something with drugs, you gotta count me out. Fact is, I don't even know you if that's what it is."

McKenna smiled crookedly. "No drugs. But hell, I don't even know myself anymore."

Swan nodded. "Been there before."

McKenna told him that there was nothing he could help with, but he'd let Swan know if he could. And McKenna continued on, wondering what his old friend would be thinking of him in a few days.

McKenna shaved and showered, then he got into his truck and headed to the marina in South Boston as the sun began to lower in the sky. Before pulling into the parking lot, he used his binoculars to check out the place. He could see Dobyns leaning against the Cadillac with Jerome behind the wheel. Dobyns seemed to be enjoying the sunlight.

McKenna watched for the next few minutes and finally came to the conclusion that he was simply stalling. He put the binoculars back in a small duffel bag and hid the gun under the seat.

It was time to take his payoff.

* * *

"There you are," Dobyns said as McKenna pulled up. "Just telling our mutual friend here that you'd show. He said you were long gone, but I had faith."

Jerome got out of the car.

Dobyns jerked his thumb at the black man. "He's got to check you out. You throw that toy gun away yet?"

"Said it was in his truck last time," Jerome said.

"Get it."

Jerome looked McKenna in the eye. McKenna could feel his blood pumping in him. This guy showing up at Caroline's doorstep. He waited for Jerome to say something, some taunt.

But the black guy remained expressionless. He simply nodded to the truck and said, "Show me."

McKenna took him back to the truck, and without a word, he reached under the seat and found the little automatic. Jerome pocketed the gun, and then casually patted McKenna down.

"He clean," he announced.

"All right. Stay here, while he and I talk."

Dobyns started down the dock to the catamaran, and McKenna followed. "Don't have the patience for these sailboats, myself. Figure if I want to go, I want to go right then, not wait around for the damn wind to blow."

McKenna didn't bother to answer.

When they got to the boat, McKenna climbed aboard. She was as different from the *Wanderer* as possible while still being a boat. Incredibly wide. Huge cockpit. The hulls, which looked sleek from the side view, seemed to just disappear under the main cabin . . . and the main cabin entrance wasn't a hatchway, but a sliding Plexiglas door.

Inside the cabin, there were two small ladders on each side leading down into the hulls. In the port hull, there was a galley, head, and fore and aft cabins. The starboard side was configured the same way, with storage space instead of the galley.

Dobyns grunted. "Well, what do you think?"

McKenna looked around the boat. It was reasonably clean, though it had the musty smell of a boat closed too long. At a glance, which was all he had time to give it, the boat appeared to be well kept, if sterile.

And *Fleetwing* was a pretty enough name.

He hated her.

"She's fine," McKenna said.

Dobyns took an envelope out of his coat pocket and laid out the bill of sale and the title. Both were signed by a Joseph McNaughton.

Dobyns winked. "Don't worry about it, it's legit. She's yours now."

He handed McKenna a briefcase. McKenna opened it to find it tightly packed with twenty-dollar bills. "That's for the sale of your boat, two hundred grand. Gimme your title."

McKenna gave him that, and Dobyns gave him another name to put on the bill of sale, Bill Sandler. "Okay, remember, you get Amanda there, you're looking at another twenty-five grand."

"No luck, so far."

"How you going about it?"

"She thinks I'm going to rip you off."

This made Dobyns smile. "And how were you going to do that?"

McKenna nodded in the direction of the parking lot. "That little gun came from her."

"Interesting you didn't mention any of this earlier. Or offer us up the gun."

"Oh, yeah. I'm going to walk up to you and Jerome with a gun in my hand."

Dobyns stared at him for a moment and then said, "I can see you don't let yourself get pushed around. And I see you got more on the ball than to expect you'd win some sort of quick draw against Jerome with that peashooter. Now why can't she?"

"She thinks I'm wrapped around her finger."

Dobyns sighed. "Pretty girls. She's as smart as they come, but sometimes a pretty girl gets so used to guys chasing her, she thinks she can lead a guy places that he just can't go. Hell, sometimes the guy ends up believing it himself. That wouldn't be true of you, would it?"

"I can't say how smart I am," McKenna said. "I'm trusting you that I'll walk out of that room, too."

"You will," Dobyns said, looking him right in the eye. "And you can take that directly from a guy who's fat, fifty-three, and balding. Ain't offering you no temptation except the stuff that matters."

He shoved the case of money over to McKenna.

CHAPTER 49

MCKENNA FOLLOWED THE CADILLAC. THEY WENT DIRECTLY TO Alcott's mansion in Lincoln. McKenna noticed a car still behind them as they took the exit for Trapelo Road, a car he realized had been with them since Boston. And possibly before that.

As McKenna pulled into the driveway, the car continued down the road. McKenna looked in the mirror and saw that there was a man driving alone. McKenna was fairly sure it was Langdon, but he couldn't be sure.

So apparently Langdon had followed him to the boat that morning, and he didn't particularly care if anyone knew it.

McKenna parked the truck and walked up to the Cadillac. Dobyns rolled down the window and said. "We wait."

McKenna said, "Who owns this place?"

"Don't worry about it. He couldn't find his ass with both hands, never mind find his way to you."

Dobyns slid the window up, and McKenna went back to his truck. He was too nervous to sit still, so he looked out over the quiet fields that surrounded Alcott's home. He took the time to look over at the four-car garage, the window over the little apartment Amanda said was above there. The place that belonged to Alcott's series of maids; the place she and Justus sometimes snuck off to when her supposed cousin was visiting. The place where she would be supposedly wait-ing with a gun, ready to help McKenna, she said.

There was no one at the window now, which meant exactly nothing.

McKenna dialed his wife's phone number. He didn't know what he was going to say to Caroline; didn't know if he would even speak at all.

He simply wanted to hear his wife's voice.

As it turned out, that was all he got. Her voice. Her answering machine.

McKenna listened quietly, pressing the phone hard against his ear, as she told him that she was sorry to miss his call, but to please leave his number or try again.

He gently put the receiver down when she was done.

Langdon showed up about fifteen minutes later. Indeed, he was driv-ing the car that had been following McKenna.

There was no sign of Ronnie.

Langdon eased the car up alongside McKenna and the power win-dow slid down. Langdon said, "Tell them that half the diamonds are on me, the other half are on Ronnie. She doesn't come until I call her and tell her it's safe."

McKenna nodded, then walked over to Dobyns and relayed the message.

"Ah, shit." Dobyns said. "Can't anybody follow a plan?"

Dobyns and Jerome got out of the limo and walked over to Lang-don's car. "C'mon," Dobyns said. "We got what you want. You got what we want. You can take off with one piece and then come back and buy the second an hour later. No line, no waiting."

"You won't be able to find Ronnie," Langdon said.

"Yeah, that's fine," Dobyns said. "Trying to do business straight here, but I can see you're having trouble with the concept."

Jerome stood before Langdon. "Got to check you out, man."

"Understood," Langdon said. "As long as I get to return the favor."

Jerome gave a lazy grin. "You on."

Langdon raised his arms wide and Jerome patted him down. He found something about Langdon's waist. "What's this?"

Langdon pulled his shirt up to reveal a money belt. "The diamonds."

Dobyns said, "That's why you plowed your way over Buddy, huh?"

"Ronnie and I have always been on the impulsive side." Langdon took his turn. Jerome leaned his cane against the car while Langdon patted him and Dobyns down.

Langdon turned to McKenna.

"Already checked him out," Jerome said.

"All the more reason," Langdon said.

Dobyns grunted in approval. "Go ahead, give him another go-over. Our lovely Amanda tried to send him in with a popgun."

Langdon lifted his eyebrows, and then abruptly shoved McKenna back against the limo. He patted him over roughly, but thoroughly. He said over his shoulder to Dobyns. "This fellow gave me a concussion once. I wouldn't entirely discount him."

McKenna waited patiently until the man was finished, apparently satisfied. "Clean," Langdon said.

"Alright, let's do it," Dobyns said.

Langdon chucked McKenna on the shoulder in a fair imitation of bonhomie. "Shall we?"

McKenna walked behind Jerome and Dobyns through the hallway, down to a basement door. The walls and ceiling along the stairway were mirrored.

Shades of Graceland.

McKenna felt the shake of something like laughter; a bit of hysteria. Finding himself analyzing the home owner's decor, even in this circumstance.

Old habits seem to die hard, he thought

Unfortunately, new ones seemed to come all too easily.

* * *

Amanda's plan was really Gleason's plan, to hear her tell it.

That day in the truck, she'd told McKenna, "Gleason knew about this kind of thing, and he had worked on the room itself. He set it up, and said he'd take care of it. He said that was his primary contribution to the cause, and that was fine with me and Justus. I don't see why it shouldn't work for Langdon, too."

As Jerome and Dobyns rounded the corner to the door of the little room in the basement, McKenna told himself that maybe they truly could play it straight. Maybe it was possible.

But he didn't believe it, because he knew how they thought.

He'd been thinking that way himself.

Dobyns and Jerome turned as McKenna and Langdon walked into the room. Dobyns watched them, Jerome had a little smile on his face.

There was a man sitting at a chair, his arms bound behind him.

A rope was deeply embedded around his neck, and his face was bluish black. His tongue protruded beyond his lips, strangely thick.

Clearly he was dead. His body had been positioned so as to face two paintings on the wall.

McKenna felt his knees buckle, and Langdon caught him from behind and shoved him lightly to the side. "Easy now. Know you're not used to these things."

Langdon said to Dobyns. "I assume this would be the owner of the house?"

"That's right," Dobyns said. "Greg Alcott. Viewing the originals of the *Storm on the Ocean* and *Gentleman and a Lady*. My expert tells me all the rest of these are forgeries, but you'd know all about that, I suppose."

"Not really," Langdon said, cheerfully. "Though I assumed there was some such thing going on. My contact was with a Tom Cain, and I understand he's departed us courtesy of our Mister McKenna."

Dobyns nodded toward McKenna. "Amazing, isn't it? He's done all right."

Langdon nodded. "But . . . overreached his depth. I hope you haven't made the same mistake about me?"

"We'll see," Dobyns said.

There was a creaking sound, and McKenna and Langdon turned to see the Hispanic kid that McKenna had seen at the computer in the basement of Dobyns's home. He was pointing a submachine gun at them.

Dobyns and Jerome moved out of the line of fire.

Langdon said, "I told you, I don't have all the diamonds on me."

Dobyns shrugged. "We'll take what you got. And then you can call Sis, and she can bring the rest, and stay with us while you go complete the deal with your customer and come back with the full slam. Fifteen mill. I'll kick back one million to you in commission, and the two of you get to walk away with your skin. That's the deal."

"That's unacceptable," Langdon said. "I'm not leaving her with you."

"Look, asshole, you horned in on our job," Dobyns snapped. "You got no choice."

Langdon moved around Alcott's body to stand directly in front of the two paintings.

The Hispanic boy raised the gun but Dobyns shouted, "Hold it!"

"That little chattergun will make a bloody mess," Langdon said, jerking his thumb over his shoulder at the paintings. "Not to mention those pesky bullet holes. Sort of thing we in the trade consider as devaluing the merchandise."

"Jerome," Dobyns said.

The black man glanced over at the Hispanic boy and said, "Now you watch. I ain't gonna get in your line, like Buddy did . . . that's just what this boy wants." Jerome stood off to Langdon's side, and then, with a sudden, backhanded swing, smashed Langdon's right knee with his cane.

Langdon cried out and fell to the ground.

Jerome looked over at McKenna and grinned. "My leg's feeling better already, man." He held up the cane. "Put a little lead in the bottom of this baby, gave it some heft."

"Hold on now," Dobyns said. He picked up the two paintings and moved them behind the bar. He leaned against the bar like the proprietor of a pub and said to Jerome. "Treat yourself."

Jerome drew the cane along his belly, made a shuffling sidestep, and feinted at McKenna's face. When McKenna raised his arms to block him, the black man dipped down and shoved the tip into McKenna's solar plexus, lifting him right off the ground.

The effect was instantaneous. McKenna fell to the floor, gasping. White, paralyzing pain. The breath knocked out of him. He jerked spasmodically.

Dobyns chuckled. "Amateur hour."

Jerome kicked him in the side. McKenna tried to get up, tried to crawl behind the bar, to shove his way past Dobyns to the panel Amanda had told him about.

At least this is what he thought he was trying to do. In truth, he probably didn't crawl more than a couple of feet.

"Oh, gosh," Dobyns said with flat amusement. "He's coming. Save me, Jerome, save me."

There was a whistling sound behind McKenna's ear, and that was that.

A man's voice said, "So what you thinking? That all of them?"

"Looks like it to me. Put it this way, if his Sis does have another belt full of them just like this, we're talking more than five mill, we'd be looking at eight, maybe ten. So I bet this is the whole thing. Not bad at all."

Jerome said, "But I do McKenna up there?"

"Yeah. Set it up, him and the wife, her place. Domestic thing that gets ugly. She dies, busted head, broken neck, whatever. He eats the popgun—make sure to wear your gloves."

"Uh-huh."

McKenna thought he was back on the *Wanderer*. Back listening to Cain and Gleason.

But the voices were different, yet entirely familiar.

McKenna flashed back to the car.

To being in the car, the limo. Rushing out of Newburyport. The conversation between two men after Buddy was killed.

This entirely natural conversation between Dobyns and Jerome.

Dobyns said, "You know what to do. Be sure to grab the case in his truck, get my two hundred K back."

"What about Greggie here?"

"Leave him. We're gonna torch this place. We get lucky, they find scraps of the forgeries, declare him the thief, the paintings gone for good. Later on, I'm gonna have you take out that fag, Chapman. Wipe the slate on this whole deal. But listen, get the sister-fucker to his feet, he's faking it now. . . ."

Dobyns raised his voice. "You call Sis in and you do it now. Whaddya need? I gotta a cell phone right here."

McKenna forced himself to contain his breathing so as not to give away that he was conscious. He saw the Hispanic boy leaning against the door. His face looked pale, but he was holding the machine gun carefully.

Langdon was on his feet now. From his angle on the floor, McKenna could only see him from the knees down. Langdon was favoring his right leg.

Jerome spoke, again using the instructional tone he had before, "Now Luis, you lookin' sick but you're doing all right . . ."

McKenna saw something come up behind the boy. The kid stiffened suddenly and the woman, Ronnie, stepped beside him and swept the small machine gun up to the ceiling.

It erupted, spewing orange flame.

McKenna scrambled, trying to get behind the bar. The boy fell to the floor, clawing at his back. The woman had a long handgun in her left hand, and she reached out to take aim at Jerome, but he shoved her brother directly between them.

Jerome then spun into motion with his cane.

McKenna didn't see what happened next. But there was a chuffing sound and a wineglass shattered on the shelf by McKenna's head, so Jerome must've deflected the gun.

Dobyns saw McKenna coming and tried to shove him away.

But McKenna bored his way in, putting his shoulder against Dobyns. The older man fought, but he was off balance, and he tripped over the framed artwork. There was a cracking sound. McKenna shoved harder until he was fully behind the bar.

Langdon and Jerome were fighting. The cane was on the floor. Ronnie was up against the wall, holding her left wrist like it was broken, her face pale.

Langdon and Jerome were fighting their way to the boy's machine gun. Jerome lunged for it, but Langdon shoved him sideways and he caught his foot in Alcott's chair. Jerome fell to the floor and immediately began scrambling over to the dead boy. Langdon dove on top of Jerome and began delivering viciously hard blows to the man's neck and shoulders.

But still Jerome moved forward.

McKenna forced himself to look down.

And count.

Count the drawers along the top counter.

"Third one from the left," Amanda had said. *"Third one from the left is supposedly a false drawer. Just there for decoration in front of the sink."*

She had also told him Gleason had lined the inside of the bar with steel plate, making it a small fortress.

McKenna took a blow from Dobyns. "Get out!" Dobyns screamed in his ear. "Get outa my way!"

One, two, three.

McKenna put his fingers on the two knobs and twisted them counterclockwise.

The little spring-loaded panel opened and McKenna reached in just as Jerome got his fingers on the butt of the little machine gun.

Even then, McKenna had time for a touch of something approaching surprise.

Amanda had told him the truth.

But then he had to set that aside and get started.

Get started doing what it seemed he was meant to do.

McKenna took the big revolver out of its hiding place.

The woman screamed, *"Ian!"*

In all the confusion, all the movement, he saw Langdon respond to her tone and take in the weapon in McKenna's hand.

"Out, Ronnie," Langdon said, and she whirled around the door-jamb, into the hall.

Langdon snatched Jerome by the collar and pulled him in front of himself.

Jerome saw the gun in McKenna's hand then, saw the threat, and even as he was being pulled backward as a shield, he tried to level the machine gun at McKenna.

McKenna squeezed the trigger.

The first shot caught Jerome's arm, throwing off his aim. The second destroyed the man's throat. A gush of blood covered his chest.

Through main force, Langdon lifted and shoved Jerome's body forward, and the black man had enough left in him to stagger forward, the machine gun hammering a short burst into the floor.

McKenna shot him again.

By the time the black man fell to the ground, Langdon and his sister were gone.

McKenna turned to Dobyns.

The man had crammed himself against the wall.

"You don't have to do this," he was saying. "That money, that boat, that's just a start, that's—"

McKenna shot him, too.

CHAPTER 50

McKenna stood in the little room.

The smell of cordite. Blood everywhere. Dobyns had left a fanlike pattern of it on the white wall.

Jerome was flung backward over the Hispanic boy, as if he were sleeping off a drunk.

McKenna supposed he should have been sick.

But then, he hadn't been even back when he killed Tom Cain.

Even when I was just a virgin, McKenna thought.

It hurt when he breathed. That blow to his chest from Jerome's cane. McKenna bent over and picked up the cane. Sure enough, it was heavily weighted at the end.

Then he dropped it. Thinking about fingerprints and DNA—and blood samples. He looked down at himself, saw he was covered with the stuff. Mostly Dobyns's he supposed. Some of it was his own.

He considered taking the little submachine gun, but opted for the handgun with the silencer. Ronnie Langdon's gun. It had a strangely thick grip. He looked at the pistol, saw that it was a Glock. He believed that was a kind that fired a huge number of rounds for a pistol, fifteen or more.

She had come down with a gun loaded with enough bullets to take out a small army. So most likely Ronnie's entrance wasn't just a rescue, it was a double cross. She and her brother were planning to kill them all.

Fair enough, he thought, putting his own revolver in his belt and starting up the stairs with the Glock.

He expected silence.

He expected an ambush.

Instead there were the flat crack of a small-caliber gun and a woman's scream.

Amanda.

McKenna slipped into the room beside the big hallway, a dining room. He could see them hauling Amanda down the steps toward the car. Langdon had a small gun in his hand, and there was blood dripping down his cheek.

She must have shot him. Amanda must have lain in wait inside the house, after Ronnie had gone down.

And now they had her.

"Rob!" Amanda screamed in the direction of the mansion. "Please, Rob!"

"Put her in the car," Ronnie was saying. "Put her in so I can take my time with the little bitch."

McKenna could see Langdon look toward the doorway, but he apparently hadn't seen McKenna at the window.

McKenna stepped back, just out of sight behind the curtain.

He thought about how he had driven Amanda up to this very spot just days ago, with the intent of leaving her for Dobyns. Leaving her to whatever fate she deserved.

He thought about her sending Gleason out to meet the *Wanderer,* to help drown him.

He thought about her as Cain's lover, as the co-conspirator who had gotten this whole mess underway.

Take her, McKenna thought.

But he also saw the tears slipping down her face when he told her

Tom Cain was dead; heard her whisper what he had come to know so well himself: "*You do something wrong, really wrong, and you think, 'That's it . . .' but there's something else you've got to do to make sure the whole thing doesn't fall apart. And then you find you can do that, too.*"

McKenna looked out the window to see the savage triumph on Ronnie's face as she pulled back Amanda's short hair and purposefully raked her across the face with her fingernails.

McKenna stepped through the library windows and out onto to the balcony. "Let her go," he said, taking careful aim at Langdon with the Glock.

By now, McKenna knew how fast Langdon and his sister could move together. So McKenna expected Langdon to react, to possibly cover for his sister, to shove her into the backseat himself. To open fire almost instantly with Amanda's little gun.

And those seemed to have been Langdon's intentions, but Ronnie wouldn't let go of Amanda.

Even as he shoved her toward the open door and sought to protect her with his own body, Ronnie ignored him. He fired the little gun but at that range it was almost impossible to be accurate. The window behind McKenna shattered.

Ronnie pushed Amanda against the car and reached into her jeans pocket for something.

"Let her go!" McKenna yelled again. He jumped off the balcony onto the gravel.

"Get in, get in," Langdon cried. He tried to pull his sister away, but she shook him off. McKenna saw a flash of silver in her hand and realized she had pulled a small knife from her pocket. She swung her arm back and slashed at Amanda. The younger woman got her hands up in time, but she screamed when the knife sliced into her arms.

Ronnie drew the knife back, ready to plunge it into Amanda.

McKenna shifted his aim from Langdon and shot Ronnie in the back.

* * *

Amanda scrambled away on her hands and knees.

Langdon reacted as if he had been shot himself, a keening outraged cry from him as he covered Ronnie with his body. He fired the little gun until it clicked empty.

McKenna took careful aim, knowing he'd made a horrendous mistake before, letting Langdon go, taking him to the hospital. That he couldn't make such a mistake again. He fired.

Langdon's shirt moved just over his arm, and if the round pierced him at all, it only seemed to goad him into movement. He helped Ronnie into the backseat. McKenna could see she was alive, moving under her own power.

The next few rounds from McKenna's gun pocked the car as Langdon vaulted over the hood, and then slid in behind the wheel. McKenna held the gun in front of him, pulling the trigger as fast as he could as Langdon spun the car around in a tight circle.

The car seemed to soak up bullet after bullet; holes appeared in the sheet metal, glass shattered. But the car kept moving.

Sweat was stinging McKenna's eyes and still he fired, a guttural sound coming from his throat, but he just couldn't seem to make it end, he couldn't put the man down.

Langdon looked over at McKenna.

And though the man looked frightened, it didn't look as though he was afraid for himself, afraid for any bullets McKenna might send his way. McKenna saw him reach around and press his sister back as she tried to sit up.

McKenna pulled the trigger again and again. Pulled it too fast, maybe. Jerking the gun. Aiming poorly. Just trying desperately to end this thing.

Trying desperately to make it be over.

He ran beside the car.

Shattering glass, more bullet holes in the driver's side door.

The car still moved.

Finally, the Glock was empty.

McKenna dropped it, then pulled the revolver from his belt and fired the last two rounds.

The car turned out of the driveway and took off, tires screeching.

McKenna found he was breathing as hard as if he had just been running wind sprints. His hands were shaking.

He sank to his knees before he fell over.

CHAPTER 51

McKENNA HELPED AMANDA INTO THE HOUSE. HER ARMS WERE BLEEDing freely, but no artery had been hit. Her face was chalk white, and there were three vivid scratches on her cheek.

He had her lay back on the couch. He gave her a big pillow to put on her belly so she could rest her arms. The blood seeped into the white cloth immediately. She said, "I didn't think you'd come. I didn't think you'd do this for me."

"I didn't either."

She nodded, silent.

After a moment, she said, "So what're we going to do?"

"First I get you bandaged up. There a first-aid kit around here?"

She told him he'd find one in the pantry off the kitchen.

It took him a few minutes to find the kit and a roll of duct tape. He half expected Amanda to be gone when he got back. But she was still there.

"We've got to hurry," she said. "Somebody might've heard something."

"One thing at a time."

He knelt beside her and took gauze out of the kit.

Amanda said, "I was hiding over there. Up in the apartment, watching. She came out of the trunk."

"Langdon's car?"

Amanda nodded. "Nothing fancy, I guess. Followed him in."

"And so you did what? Came down and waited inside? Tried to take whoever came out with the paintings?"

"Not like that," she said. "Just if it was them. Or Dobyns. Not if it was you."

He smiled grimly. "I'm afraid I've grown a little too old in the past few weeks to believe that." He quickly bound a couple of loops of gauze around her arms, and then, moving with unhurried efficiency, bound her hands together with the white bandage tape.

"What're you doing?" she cried.

He pressed her back down to the cushion and covered the white tape with several turns of gray duct tape. She fought him, but she was still weak and dazed.

"Rob, please, don't do this . . ."

"No happy endings here, Amanda. You and Cain. Woodrell, whatever his name was. You had as much to do with all of this as Dobyns. And I'm going to show you what I did to him."

"I don't want to see."

"Too bad." He hauled her to her feet.

"Rob!"

He pulled her down the stairway and down into the little room. She shrunk back, but he forced her in. He gestured with his chin to Alcott. "Far as I can tell, the biggest mistake he made was trying to impress you. And these people . . . maybe they deserved what they got, but then again, so do you. This is what you and Gleason worked up. You like it?" McKenna bent down and picked up the small machine gun.

She pulled back, frightened for herself now.

"I should," he said. "It'd be the easiest plan." He spun her around. "Lucky for you I'm too much of an amateur."

Amanda started to leave the room, but then she stopped. Her eyes widened.

She saw the diamonds. Langdon's money belt was on the floor, the pouch open. Half a dozen stones glittered on the floor not far from Jerome's outstretched palm.

She said, "Rob, it can still work. We take those and the paintings, too. You don't want to be with me, fine, we split up. I can still find a buyer for the paintings. No one needs to know what we've done!"

He shook his head. "You're an awfully slow learner." He took her by the arm, and when she realized he was leaving everything behind, she pleaded, and then she screamed to him the lies—and truths—she was going to tell everyone. "She'll know," Amanda cried. "She'll know what you've done!"

He put her in the passenger seat of the truck, and then got in behind the wheel and laid the gun on the floor.

"Talk with me, Rob," she said. He could see her fighting for a reasonable tone. He could remember Cain doing the same thing with the Coast Guard bearing down on them.

He told her.

She stared at him and then burst out laughing.

Hysteria right there. "Oh, God," she said. "None of this means shit, what we've done. What we've done to ourselves."

"It doesn't. Get used to it."

"I can't have it be that meaningless," she said. "Not like that."

"You deserve worse."

"Deserve," she said wearily. "What's that got to do with anything? What's that mean?"

He called information for the number of the Rosalyn Museum. When he called the number, he was bounced around for a few minutes before he got to the security office. A young-sounding man answered. His manner was quiet, polite.

"I've got some information for you on those stolen paintings," McKenna said.

"I see," the man said. "Just a moment, please."

The call was transferred. Another polite voiced man picked up the phone. McKenna presumed he had just been connected to the FBI.

Amanda tried to take the phone from McKenna, but he shoved her back with his elbow and said, "Sit still or I'll give him your name. You won't even make it out of town."

She shrank back against the car door.

He got back on the phone.

"Hello, hello," the man was saying. He sounded bored.

McKenna smiled tightly. Probably one of hundreds of such confessions they received every year, he expected. How were they to know this one was true?

"What have you got for us, sir?" the man asked.

"Get out a piece of paper, tape record me, whatever you've got to do. Just listen because I'll only say this once." McKenna named the two Rembrandts. "Those two are real. The others are forgeries. You'll also find three dead people in the basement, include Jimmy Dobyns. You know who Jimmy Dobyns is?"

"I do," the man said crisply.

"You writing this down yet?"

"Taping," the polite man said. Now he seemed interested.

"Good." McKenna gave him the address to Alcott's place.

"And your name, sir?"

"You don't need that."

The man explained in a slow, earnest voice that it was imperative that McKenna give his name if he expected to earn the five million-dollar reward. McKenna assumed they were trying to do a trace.

"I'm afraid I'm not eligible," McKenna said and then hung up.

"What'd you just prove?" Amanda said sullenly, as they drove into Boston under a darkening sky. "Some kind of atonement?"

McKenna didn't answer.

"You think she'll take you back?" Amanda said. "Think you can leave that mess back there and say, 'I'm sorry,' and everyone will forgive you?"

He shook his head.

She considered him and then said, "You know, if I put my mind to it, I could lay this all on you. Say that you came in with those guys. Burst in and killed Greg. Home invasion. That I didn't know anything about the stolen art. How could they prove I did?"

"This might help." McKenna reached into the small duffel bag beside them and took out his tape recorder. He pressed the Play button and Amanda's voice said,

We'd swap out one at a time, past two years, we'd work on it. Come up with forgeries that Greggie sure couldn't tell the difference. Maybe they wouldn't stand up to expert analysis, but we figured for him, God, he could go a lifetime thinking he still owned the world's biggest stolen-art collection.

She blanched.

"It's all there," he said. "Our conversation in the truck. Including Gleason's plan; the hidden gun. All of it."

"But you can't play that," she said, trying to regroup. "You're the one who actually did it. You're the one who shot them."

McKenna stopped the truck in front of the bus station. "Oh, I'm in trouble. No doubt about that." He reached into his pocket and took out his pocketknife. "And you're in it right alongside me." He reached over, and she backed away from him as far as she could.

He cut the tape binding her arms.

McKenna took out his wallet and handed her a fifty and five tens. "Get out."

She looked at the money in her hand and at the bus station and said, "Just like that?"

He nodded. "You're free."

She looked relieved until he continued. "So you're free to go work for a living. You're free to live under a new name. You start doing your art again, you better move on if it gets any attention. You can't afford to be visible. You can't afford to be successful. You have to learn to fade into the background."

"I don't want anything to do with that. I can't just disappear."

"Do it out there or do it in prison," McKenna said. "Your choice." He leaned across her and opened her door. "Go on."

"You've got money," she said desperately. She gestured at the case on the floor of the truck. "You've got the boat. Take me with you."

He shook his head.

"Why do we have to do this alone?" She tried to clutch his arm, but he shook her off. "You know how it happened! You do this one thing and everything follows!"

"I know," he said. "But I don't even want to look at you. Now get out and learn to make everyone feel that way about you."

She began to cry. He took her by the arm, pushing her just enough so that she got out. He reached over, slammed the door shut, and took off. He glanced once in the mirror before rounding the corner.

She was already gone.

CHAPTER 52

THE COLOR WAS COMPLETELY GONE FROM THE SKY BY THE TIME McKenna got to the marina in South Boston. He left the truck on the street, away from the parking lot. He checked the machine gun in the dim overhead light, and then he dropped it into the small duffel bag, along with his binoculars.

He put the loop over his shoulder, reached down into the open bag. He could pull it out easily or shoot through the bag.

McKenna had never fired a machine gun before.

He could only imagine the way it would be to pull: the distraction of flame and noise.

The damage it would do to a person.

It would've helped if he were enraged. Would've helped if his hatred for Langdon were such that it could carry him through in the heat of passion.

Because, in truth, he felt cold, jittery, and as scared as hell.

He had shot Ronnie Langdon. The object of Ian Langdon's life, as far as he could see.

From everything McKenna had learned over the past few weeks, he felt certain Langdon's only passion would be to kill him before he escaped to the sea.

* * *

McKenna left the cash in the truck and went down through the grass and weeds to the water's edge. The smell of the bay was rank: it seemed equal parts salt water, diesel fuel, sewage, and rotting shellfish.

He lifted the binoculars to his eyes and searched the marina. Some of the boats were visible under the feeble dock lights, but *Fleetwing* was largely in shadows.

McKenna stared hard and thought he could see something through the long swoop of a Plexiglas porthole. A flashlight beam inside the boat, perhaps. He moved to a rusting drum and knelt to brace the binoculars.

Movement. He saw movement inside the boat.

He held his breath, trying to keep his hands steady.

Someone moved out to the cockpit, looked around briefly, and then turned back to talk to someone in the cabin.

It was a woman.

Ronnie. Ronnie was in the cockpit. She was silhouetted in light.

She was alive and presumably talking with her brother while they waited for McKenna to come down to his boat.

McKenna felt something between relief and despair. Relief that his shot hadn't killed her or apparently wounded her too seriously.

Despair, because now he had to go do the job right.

He found a dinghy on the inner dock that wasn't locked down and stepped in. Water sloshed through his shoes. He began handing the boat past the pilings and the sterns of the boats along the dock to *Fleetwing* at the end. He took his time, keep himself low as he could. The duffel bag slipped on his back, and he had to push it around repeatedly. It was an awkward way to travel, but he didn't see much choice: marginal as the lights were, there would be no place to hide walking straight down the dock.

When McKenna got down to the last three boats before his, he stopped and listened.

If Langdon tried what McKenna had done himself seemingly a million years back, he would've been waiting on one of these boats—waiting for McKenna to trap himself between him and *Fleetwing*.

But after ten minutes of quiet waiting and watching, McKenna saw no movement on any of the other boats. Besides, he had seen Ronnie talking to Langdon in the cabin.

McKenna grasped the nearest piling and stepped from the dinghy onto the finger pier between an old wooden sailboat and a trawler. Keeping hunched over, he moved between them until he was at the junction of the main dock. He looked to the right past the bow of the trawler to *Fleetwing*.

Do it, he told himself. *Go do it.*

Just shoot them.

Finish this.

He told himself that if he could contain it all on his own boat, that conceivably he might be able to dump the bodies. Wash the blood from the boat like he had with the *Wanderer*. Somehow, he might be able to continue off to sea.

But not likely. All he could really count on by doing this was keeping Caroline safe.

Murder.

The word played through his head.

Them or me, he told himself. *Them or Caroline.*

McKenna could see Ronnie now.

She was back in the cockpit. She was talking in a low voice to her brother in the cabin. McKenna couldn't make out what she was saying, but his blood was pounding and he probably wouldn't have made sense of her words if she had been standing next to him.

His breathing began to rush.

Run forward, he told himself. *Run forward and squeeze the trigger in short bursts. First her and then him.*

He took aim, as best he could, and crouched to run.

He told himself that he could do this, kill just two more times. After that, he would be finished.

* * *

And he would have done it, he was sure. In fact, for a few horrified seconds he couldn't be sure if he *had* acted—if what he saw before him was nothing but a desperate mirage, an attempt to bring the bullets back—because just as he was about to charge forward the boat's headstay lights came on.

The lights came on and revealed Caroline, not Ronnie, in the cockpit of his new boat.

CHAPTER 53

ELLIOTT EMERGED FROM THE CABIN, A REVOLVER IN HIS HAND POINTED squarely at McKenna. "Lay it down."

McKenna looked down at the machine gun and then back up at his wife. He felt foolish.

"Rob?" she said.

Guilty and foolish.

"This isn't a problem," he said to Elliott.

"Is to me. Put it on the dock."

McKenna let the gun point down directly, but didn't let it go. "I will," he said. "But not yet."

"Now!"

Caroline said, "Rob, what are you doing? Please, put the gun down."

McKenna looked around again at the boats surrounding them and then back to his wife. "I can't just yet. It's got nothing to do with you. None of this has."

"You made it my business," Elliott said.

McKenna said, "Take her away from here."

"Rob, what've you gotten yourself into?" Caroline said. She stepped off the boat.

"Caroline!" Elliott barked as she stepped between the two of them.

"He won't hurt me," she said.

Elliott moved up to the stern seat behind the port wheel for a better angle.

McKenna reached out with his left hand. She took it without hesitation. She tried to meet his eyes. But he found himself, more than ever, evading hers. He said, "How did you get here? How'd you know?"

She said, "Elliott followed you. Said you'd gotten mixed up with some hood, this Jimmy Dobyns, and that you had a boat down here. That you'd be taking off, leaving me. Is that true?"

He turned her so that his body was between Elliott's and hers, so the black man wouldn't get nervous.

"It's not that simple."

"But it's true, isn't it?" A tear slipped down her cheek.

He wanted to hold her. But he felt dirty, felt the blood on him. Felt that he would infect her.

"Mariel's all right," she said. "You should know she came out of it. Elliott had followed you down here, and then I called him and he came back. She told us that the man who hurt her was this Stephen Cross—and that you were the one who told her to watch out for him."

McKenna felt a spear of happiness. Something he didn't think he would have been capable of feeling.

McKenna looked over at Elliott. The man was still pointing the gun at him, but his arms were more relaxed, his face watchful instead of stone hard. McKenna found himself smiling. Positively grinning. "She's going to be all right?"

Elliott said, "Put the safety on and put the piece down. We can talk about the welcome-home party afterward."

McKenna looked at the machine gun. Ugly thing.

"All right," he said. "At least until we talk."

He set the lock and laid the gun down on the deck. Feeling a monumental relief without the weight of it in his hand. He put his arm around his wife.

Maybe this is it, he thought. Maybe this is all I can hope for.

Because he knew after this came police, questions, a trial.

Prison time.

He looked Caroline in the eye, and found he could do it. "Okay," he said. "We talk."

He told Caroline what he had done.

They sat in the cockpit together. McKenna held both of Caroline's hands in his. He told her about the voyage back. About accepting Tom Cain's bribe. About killing him and Gleason.

She flinched as if struck, but she kept listening. Her eyes on him the entire time.

Elliott sat in the stern, the gun still in his hand, but not pointed at McKenna. Listening quietly.

McKenna told her about Amanda. In some ways, this was the hardest. Seeing the hurt in her eyes regarding his night with the girl. That there was no mitigating answer there. Simple adultery, simple lust on his part.

"And she goes free," Caroline murmured.

"For now," he said.

He told her about Alcott. About the small viewing room.

About shooting Jerome and Dobyns.

At some point, Caroline withdrew her hands from his. She put her arms around herself.

McKenna took it as his due. Even though he knew he had done a lot of it for her, he took it as his due. He said, "I've done a lot of terrible things."

"Yes," Caroline said. Her voice was barely a whisper. "You have."

Elliott said, "Let me get this straight. You turned in the jewels? And the paintings?"

McKenna nodded. "To the FBI, I think."

"Why?"

McKenna lifted his hands. "I told you . . . that's not what I was doing it for."

Elliott laid his handgun on the seat beside him and sighed. "See if a judge looks it that way."

Just as he took his hand away from the gun, a shape came up behind the black man.

Langdon. Coming up the swim ladder, water slicking back his hair. A knife in his hand.

Whether Elliott recognized something in McKenna's face or just felt the movement behind him, he reacted.

Threw himself forward and started to spin.

But the wheel was right in front of him, blocking his way. And Langdon must have anticipated his move anyhow. Langdon plunged the knife into Elliott's right shoulder as Elliott reached for the gun.

Langdon pulled the knife out and slammed the blade into Elliott's upper arm.

McKenna shoved Caroline in the direction of the rail. "Run," he said. "Fast as you can, get out of here." He lunged for the gun on the seat, but Elliott was in the way. Langdon reached past the black man and whipped his blade across McKenna's face in two vicious swipes, leaving gashes on each of McKenna's cheeks. Then Langdon shuffled to the side on the stern seat, and kicked McKenna in the chest, knocking him onto the cockpit floor.

Elliot charged Langdon, using his left arm to pick him up at waist level.

Langdon put his legs behind him like a wrestler and reached around to stab Elliott high in the back, two puncture wounds intended for his lungs.

Elliott cried out and then collapsed.

Langdon shoved him aside and crossed the cockpit to scoop up the gun, just seconds ahead of McKenna.

Langdon shot him in the left shoulder.

McKenna staggered back. At first, there was no immediate sense of pain. Instead, he felt an enormous and focalized pressure. Like someone had wound up with a crowbar and hit him dead on.

And then the pain came on in powerful repeating waves.

McKenna's leg's buckled and he fell to his knees.

Langdon watched him carefully. He folded his knife closed against his leg and slipped it into his pocket. "Don't fade on me yet, you're not hurt that bad."

Langdon stood over him, grabbed him by the collar, and pulled his head up. Showing him that Caroline was on the dock. That she hadn't run away. That she was begging Langdon to let McKenna go.

"Please," she said, her arms outstretched. "Please don't do this."

Langdon bent down to McKenna and said in a clear, harsh voice, "You shot my sister. She bled out in the back seat of the car. She was scared she was going to hell, and she probably is. Twenty-nine years she was mine, and I loved her and took care of her, and you killed her. What do you think I have to do to your woman now?"

McKenna reached down, feeling for something, anything, to fight back with. He touched plastic, then cool metal. The winch handle in its plastic holster against the seat.

McKenna's strength was leaving him though. He could feel it slipping down his left side and pooling onto the floor under his knees.

Langdon reached over McKenna's right shoulder and pointed the gun at Caroline. He jammed his bicep against the side of McKenna's face, in effect making him sight along the barrel at Caroline. "Here," Langdon said. "Why don't you do it? You play with people like me, you might as well shoot her yourself."

McKenna swung the winch handle up as hard as he could. There was a brief click of metal on metal as the handle hit the gun. Instantly, flame spouted out of the gun barrel: whether caused by McKenna's blow or simply by Langdon's reflexes, McKenna didn't know.

But, whatever the reason, Caroline was thrown off her feet onto the dock.

Clearly she had been hit.

Dead or alive, McKenna didn't know.

CHAPTER 54

CAROLINE COULDN'T BREATHE.

Just couldn't get her breath.

She opened her eyes and found she was on her back.

The two of them fighting over there. Rob struggling, a sound coming out of him she'd never heard. He must've thought that she had been hit.

Had she?

Caroline didn't think so. She couldn't be sure, but she didn't think so.

She rolled over and saw the machine gun in front of her.

Instinctually, she knew to move toward it.

Pick it up, even.

And that's what she did. She got to her feet. Saw McKenna and the man were wrestling after the gun in the man's hands, almost like two boys after a football. Neither one willing to just let it go.

She realized then that there was blood all down her blouse, that the left side of her head was hot and wet.

She looked down at the machine gun, and knew she should help Rob, but she didn't have a clue as how to use this thing.

Caroline pointed at the deck and tried to squeeze the trigger, but it didn't give. She felt some relief then and started to walk forward to tell them it was out of her control. But she stumbled and landed on her hands and knees.

That put her only a half dozen feet from her husband, and she saw that he was fighting the man for real. And that he was losing. That the man, this dark stranger whose face was wet and terrifying, whose lips were pulled back from his teeth, was hitting Rob with hard left punches, hitting him right where his shoulder was bloody.

Anger coursed through Caroline, fresh, hot, and clear.

But it wasn't clear what she was to do about it all.

Then the man saw she had the gun, and he hunkered down over Rob, going for the gun with both hands.

"Run, Caroline," McKenna said. "Run!"

Still he was trying to get the gun away, but for some reason he was using one arm against the man's two, and that wasn't going to work.

Caroline lifted the machine gun and pointed it at the man. Tried to say "Get away," and maybe she did, but she figured maybe she was just in shock.

She squeezed the trigger.

It still wouldn't give.

She looked at the gun. She looked at it and remembered feeling relief. Relief when Rob pressed the little switch under the trigger. That Elliott had relaxed his shoulders once Rob pushed that switch and put the gun down on the dock.

Caroline remembered Elliott then and looked up for him. Thinking he'd know what to do. But he was laying over the seats behind Rob and the man. Blood was streaming off Elliott onto the white fiberglass of the cockpit.

Caroline looked back, saw the man was slowly but inexorably, turning the gun to Rob's face.

He was in awful trouble, Rob was.

She pushed the little switch, pointed the machine gun at the man standing over her husband, and pulled the trigger.

CHAPTER 55

ABOVE MCKENNA, LANGDON'S BODY SUDDENLY SHIVERED AND danced back a few feet.

The sound was incredible.

Flames flashed right over McKenna's head, and he saw Caroline lean forward over the rail, the gun kicking and bucking in her hand. Bullets pocked the deck and splintered fiberglass. But mostly she was hitting Langdon. The range was right.

She kept on until the gun stopped abruptly, presumably out of bullets.

He looked over at Langdon.

God, what a mess. McKenna sighed.

More than he could ever hope to clean up.

McKenna was cold.

But of the three of them, Caroline, him, and Elliott, he felt he was the most alert. So he had Caroline come on board. There was blood on the side of her face, but when he had her come to his level, so he could move her hair from the wound, he saw that it was mostly a surface graze.

The shock was setting in with her though. Her eyes were glassy.

"How's he?" McKenna said.

Caroline turned Elliott over. He slumped down onto the cockpit floor, and McKenna could see the blood at his mouth. A least one lung must've been hit.

But he was alive. He looked at Langdon's body, then at McKenna. They could hear sirens coming.

Elliott licked his lips and said, "You're shot. Both of you . . . when they get here . . . you lay down and shut up. Don't talk until we get you a lawyer." He looked at McKenna. "You're gonna do time . . . but you do the next few minutes right, you might get a life."

McKenna started to say something, but Elliott shook his head. "Doing it for her. So shut up."

Elliott winched and closed his eyes. Conserving his strength.

McKenna looked out over the water, saw the police-car lights flashing over the bridge. Just a couple minutes before they arrived.

Machine-gun fire, he guessed. Some people cared about such things and called the police when they heard it.

He looked at Caroline. She was staring at Langdon's body. The wreckage of his body. Most of his face was gone, he was splayed back in a pose that only death seemed to direct.

McKenna could see Caroline was coming out of it enough to realize what she'd done. She was crying.

McKenna felt so cold. Couldn't believe it had come to this. Starting out in all that warmth in the Virgin Islands. So cold now. He put his arm out to her, and she let him pull her close. He said, "It's not your fault. I've got nobody to blame but myself."

He closed his eyes. Minutes, maybe less, until the police arrived.

But he had this. And she was safe.

Afterward, maybe Elliott was right. Maybe there would somehow be a life. But all McKenna knew was that he had her now, had her at this moment.

"I killed him," she said. "I had to do it or he was going to kill you."

"I know," he said. "I've done such terrible things. So I know."

"But look at him," she whispered. Her voice harsh. "Look what I did."

McKenna felt her shivering.

"It's all right," he said. "You'll see."

"What will I see?"

She was crying now. He pulled her face to his good shoulder so that she wouldn't have to look.

He held her even tighter, tried to make her last within him forever. Knowing that once those policeman came down the dock, nothing else was certain.

"What will I see?" she repeated.

He whispered, "You get used to it."

EPILOGUE

Seven Years Later

McKENNA GOT OFF THE BUS IN GLOUCESTER.

His old hometown, where his Uncle Sean had raised him so many years back. It was late April, an unseasonably warm and bright day.

McKenna blinked in the sunlight. Something he still hadn't gotten used to yet, his second day out.

Swan got out of a pickup truck across the street and came on over. His hair was completely white now, his gut a little larger. He carried two Styrofoam cups of coffee, one stacked on the other.

McKenna smiled. His own black hair was shocked with white, too. The result of the past years in the state prison in Walpole. That, and the fact that he was pushing fifty.

The DA had talked of charging McKenna with five counts of homicide.

Artie Sayre, the lawyer Mariel had recommended, said nonsense. That McKenna was a hero who was going to help recover the largest stolen-art collection in the world.

McKenna had argued with Artie privately that he was no hero. His lawyer told him to shut up and let him handle the defense. He saw to it that the transcript of McKenna's call to the FBI was leaked early and often.

Then the FBI captured Amanda in New York City. Under intense questioning, she gave up the forgery scheme and admitted that Gleason and Woodrell had intended to kill McKenna. Artie saw to it that the media focused on the Langdons. The strangeness of their relationship alone made good international copy, especially with her photo. The London tabloids got in on the act and a virtual countdown to the return of the paintings captured the public's imagination. The Boston area media concentrated on Dobyns, playing up his role as a sophisticated and vicious player in the world of international theft.

Within weeks, Interpol found their way to the Langdon's art expert, a Geoffrey Boyle . . . and he helped them find their way to Amir Abaas. Though Abaas never admitted any part in the theft, the paintings themselves were found unharmed in a London warehouse.

In the end, Artie Sayre made a case for self-defense in all of the killings except for that of Dobyns himself. Forensics had shown that McKenna shot Dobyns at point-blank range, and by McKenna's own admission, Dobyns didn't have a weapon.

The DA went after him on that, and McKenna was sentenced to ten to fifteen years in prison. Artie said, "Take it, and we'll get you out sooner."

And here McKenna was, out in seven.

"So how's the violent criminal?" Swan handed McKenna a coffee.

McKenna popped the lid. "Reformed," he said. He took a deep breath of the salt air before taking a sip. Jesus, life's little pleasures. He said, "I appreciate what you're doing."

"Same thing you did for me once."

McKenna raised his eyebrows. "Not exactly."

Swan waved that away. "Ah . . . most people would take a killer over a heroin addict any day. C'mon, let's not keep your new boss waiting."

* * *

Milt Penn looked a lot like his marina: scruffy, disorganized, in need of a lot of work. He had thin white hair, deeply sunburned skin, and a nonfiltered cigarette in the corner of his mouth. It moved up and down as he talked.

"Swan tells me you're smart and know boats; your uncle was once a big man around here. And someday you might even help me manage the rest of the assholes I got working here. That you can do books, and even help figure out how to make a profit around this place. Well I say, I don't know you from jack shit, but I'm taking Swan's word as far as I'm gonna let you cut the weeds in the yard and paint the docks. When you do that good enough, maybe you can take out the workboat and help me drop some moorings. Best you're gonna get from me is that'll I see how it goes."

"Can't ask for more." McKenna held out his hand.

Penn pumped it twice and let go. "All right. I got things to do. Swan, whyn't you show him the room I showed you, and then I'll put him on the clock say in about a half hour. Three o'clock. Whacking weeds around those hulks, clean that out."

Swan grinned as Penn walked away. Swan said quietly. "In case you think there's a heart of gold under that rough exterior, there's not. He acts like such an old salt, but he's only owned this place for six years or so, and before that he owned a gas station. You remember this place from before?"

"Sure. Bailley's. My uncle docked his boat here for a while."

"Yeah, thought so." Penn's marina wasn't too different from Dobyns's marina in South Boston in size, but busier with commercial traffic. The lobster boats were just coming into the harbor, and the seagulls dived and cawed.

Swan said, "C'mon, you can look at your room later, I got something to show you."

Swan led McKenna through the weeds around an enormous rusting trawler. "Look, I know you're not cut out to crawl your way up to being the assistant manager of a shitty little marina. It's just that's all I knew how to scrape up for the parole board. And I figured you didn't want to come back to Newburyport and work as my dockboy in front of all your old buddies."

"No," McKenna said. "No, I didn't."

"But I'm gonna keep my eyes open and see if we can find you something better."

"Don't. This is perfect for now," McKenna said, brushing at the thigh-high weeds. "I've even got experience. Highway cleanup."

Swan looked back at him and laughed, but he seemed nervous. "Well, we'll see . . ."

They rounded the trawler.

McKenna stopped cold.

It was the *Wanderer*. She was a mess. Dismasted. Big worn spot on her starboard side where she clearly had been on her side, grinding into sand or rock.

Swan said, "Believe it or not, I didn't even see her until Penn said he'd take you on and I'd gotten him to put it in writing for the parole board. Insurance write-off. Grounded during Hurricane Lucy couple of years back, and Penn bought her figuring he'd restore her for a profit, but he's never gotten round to it. You're not going to be able to afford it whacking weeds, but you find yourself a real job, I expect you'll be able to buy her for a song."

McKenna touched the side of his old boat. Immediately assessing her condition. There were deep scratches in her gel coat on the port side as well, though not nearly as bad as the starboard. It looked as if her keel had taken a solid blow. Grounded on a rock, perhaps. But there were no cracks around where the keel bolts would be, so it was possible the damage was no more than skin deep. He walked round her stern. Surprised to see a new name on her, *CinSational,* in an sparkling silver typeface.

Swan made a face. "Owner's wife's name was Cindy."

McKenna nodded. The *Wanderer* had been auctioned off by the government years ago, as part of Dobyns's seized holdings.

"Does Caroline know she's here?" McKenna said.

"Yuh. I told her."

"She didn't come to my release."

When McKenna had come out, there was no one waiting but Artie

Sayre and a photographer from *The Boston Globe*. The paintings had been back on the walls of the Rosalyn Museum for more than six years now: McKenna's release was barely news.

Swan made a face. "She tells me you didn't make it easy on her."

About three years back, McKenna had started refusing to see Caroline. He had written to her saying that she needed to get on with her own life. That for all he knew, he could be stuck in there for another decade. That she had to move on.

He offered her a divorce.

From that point on, other than a monthly care package of books and magazines, she never contacted him.

Swan jerked his head at the ladder. "Go check out your boat. You got about twenty minutes before you gotta start in on the weeds."

McKenna started up the ladder.

He dreaded what he would see. And at first glance, she was everything he feared. The stanchions on the starboard side were all bowed in like a line of broken fence posts. The deck was a tangle of moldering lines, dirt, and leaves. The cockpit coaming splintered.

But that's as far as he got.

Because propped up against the washboards was a beautiful wooden box. A case.

McKenna looked down at Swan. "What's this?"

Swan shrugged. "Check it out."

McKenna climbed into the cockpit and opened the box. Inside was a sextant. Well-polished brass, in perfect shape. Better than the one she had given him before. There was an envelope with his name written in Caroline's hand. He took out the note, and read, *Find your way home, sailor.*

He stood alone in his wreck of a boat. The trace of a smile beginning to form. "I can do that," he said. "I can do that."

ABOUT THE AUTHOR

Boston-area resident Bill Eidson is the author of five previous novels: *The Little Brother, Dangerous Waters, The Guardian, Adrenaline*, and *Frames per Second*. He was born in Savannah, Georgia, and grew up in Rhode Island. A graduate of Boston University, Eidson worked in advertising until stepping away from the corporate life to pursue his career as a writer. Eidson was first struck with the idea for *One Bad Thing* one day while motoring through a deep fog off the coast of Rhode Island. Bill is the former New England Chapter President of Mystery Writers of America.

	DATE DUE		